BEST OF THE BEST GAY EROTICA

BEST OF THE BEST
GAY EROTICA

Edited by
Richard Labonté

CLEIS
PRESS

Published in the United States
Cleis Press Inc., P.O. Box 14684, San Francisco, California 94114.
Printed in the United States.
Cover design: Scott Idleman
Text design: Karen Huff
Cleis logo art: Juana Alicia
First Edition.
10 9 8 7 6 5 4 3 2

The following stories are reprinted from *Best Gay Erotica 1996*: "Stroke the Fire" © 1995 by M. Christian. "First Shave" © 1995 by Jameson Currier. "The Yellow" © 1994 by Michael Lassell. "Ganged" © 1994 by Carol Queen is excerpted from *The Leather Daddy and the Femme* (San Francisco: Cleis Press, 1998). "Pleasingly" © 1995 by Matthew Rettenmund. "The Adored One" © 1995 by Michael Rowe. "Aegis" © 1995 by D. Travers Scott. "Hotter Than Hell" © 1995 by Simon Sheppard. The following stories are reprinted from *Best Gay Erotica 1997*: "Tricktych" ©1996 by Pansy Bradshaw. "Steel Gray" ©1996 by Ken Butler. "Cocksucker's Tango" ©1996 by Justin Chin. "The First Branding Journal" © 1996 by Cornelius Conboy. "Heat Wave" © 1996 by Kevin Killian. "Griffith Park Elegy" © 1996 by Al Lujan. "Social Relations" © 1996 by Scott O'Hara, re-printed with permission of Pansy Bradshaw. "Motherfuckers" © 1996 by Emanuel Xavier. The following stories are reprinted from *Best Gay Erotica 1998*: "I Wonder If My Great Great Toltec Grandmother Was Ever a *National Geographic* Centerfold" © 1998 by Jorge Ignacio Cortiñas. "Sexual Harrassment in the Military: 2 Performance Pieces for 4 Actors in 3 Lovely Costumes" © 1998 by Jack Fritscher. "We Own the Night" © 1997 by Paul Reed. "Clothes Do Make the Man" © 1997 by Lawrence Schimel. "Liberty" © 1998 by John Tunui. The following stories are reprinted from *Best Gay Erotica 1999*: "Body Hunger" © 1998 by Grigorakis Daskalogrigorakis. "Six Positions" © 1998 by Andy Quan. "See Dick Decontruct" © 1998 by Ian Philips. "Yellow" © 1998 by Kirk Read. The following stories are reprinted from *Best Gay Erotica 2000*: "Thomas, South Carolina" © 1999 by Dimitri Apessos. "The Nether Eye Opens" © 1999 by Don Shewey.

Forever, again, Asa & Percy

Contents

Introduction

Richard Labonté

Welcome to *Best of the Best Gay Erotica,* drawn from five years' worth of an anthology series which has been both best-selling and genre-defining since its inception in 1996, when it was edited by Michael Thomas Ford and selected and introduced by Scott Heim (*In Awe, Mysterious Skin*).

When I took over editorship in 1997, I found out fast just how much erotic writing/porn authorship there is out there (for the 1999 edition, when I mined the internet for work, I looked at more than a thousand stories). I also discovered how much is good: those are the stories I'd pass along to the judges, between forty and fifty a year, from among which they'd select the twenty to twenty-five winners. I was the funnel; the judges were the fine sieve. The *Best Gay Erotica* anthologies of 1997 to 2000 were the well-refined result of their work: Doug Sadownick (*Sacred Lips of the Bronx, Sex Between Men*) judged 1997; Christopher Bram (*Gossip, Father of Frankenstein, In Memory of Angel Clare, Hold Tight, The Notorious Dr. August*), 1998; Felice Picano (*The Lure, Ambidextrous, Like People in History, Book of Lies,*

New York Stories), 1999; and D. Travers Scott (*Execution, Texas: 1997 Strategic Sex*), 2000. While I worried about the appropriate use of "cum" vs. "come," and helped contributors hone their prose, it was the judges who wrote each year's final table of contents.

What's remarkable to me is how seamless was my weekend of reading through five anthologies, more than a thousand pages and more than a hundred stories: despite their own different styles, ages, interests and output, each judge brought to his book a sharp eye for porn with both a lilt and a purpose, and the constancy among the books is quite simply their quality and diversity. *Best of the Best* is my chance to take the process one step further, by selecting stories which epitomize the perfect blend of the literary and the lusty, by distilling the very best from among the best.

So: many thanks to the four judges with whom I worked, to the writers whose stories are reprinted here, to all the contributors whose erotic fantasies, lurid moments, fevered talents, and literate imaginations have made the *Best Gay Erotica* series possible, and such a success. And: as many thanks to Frédérique Delacoste, Felice Newman and Don Weise of Cleis, a delightful trio to work with, on this book and all others. They're the best, too.

San Francisco
April 2000

The Yellow

Michael Lassell

For John Preston,
who said "Write about what you know,"
and meant it...
and then published it.

It begins, of course, with desire—or, rather, *in* desire—this
time on a Passover Saturday night in New York City, the night
before Easter, too. Where the desire begins is anybody's guess,
perhaps in fever. This time it began in the sky, in a cloud cover
so low—the way it gets in spring—you feel...immersed,
caught in the act, drowning. And the Empire State Building is
lit up a kind of yellow that doesn't exist in nature, not in
healthy nature, but you can't see the top of the building,
anyway, because of the clouds: a translucent mist rendered
opaque by mass, volume, density—the whole thing looking
like special F/X for hell or some urban apocalypse movie.

You know the sort of film. They were popular in the seventies: It's the year two-thousand-something and the Island of
Manhattan is a penal colony, blah-blah-blah...young men

1

encased in tight muscles and leather vests, headbands. Hollywood shit. But not ineffective. The kind of thing that gets under your skin no matter how you resist: hard rival males, little more than school yard Caesars, battling for supremacy and the nubile charms of this year's pouting starlet, a fight to the death that establishes the right of the fittest for supremacy (fitness being measured not only by strength but by cunning and moral rectitude, movies being fiction, after all, and not the glandular dance of the cobra and the mongoose).

Yes, it's on nights like these that the city seems most Darwinian, nights that conjure the Tortugas, amphibians crawling out of the ooze, nights of survival, jazz, and ejaculation.

Soaking into the fog like amyl into cotton, the light looks like an incandescent blotch on heaven—God's urine in stained glass on an awesome scale, a hotly contested work of art, perhaps, by a painter/photographer of Latin-American extraction, or a cathedral, say, in Rome, the flaked and scaling plaster mapped by brackish water and mildew, a cathedral where the Polish pope is no doubt droning Easter mass right now, it being later there than here, so probably tomorrow already. And it's spreading, the yellow fog, like sweat on sheets or hatred. That's what the light of Easter through the unseasonably raw Saturday reminds me of. And of London, Jack the Ripper, fish and chips in yesterday's *Evening Standard*, of unheated bathrooms, longing, and brandy hangovers in an Earl's Court bed-sitter.

I'm watching this sky from the bed of a fourth-floor flat on Ninth Avenue where a somewhat overweight but extremely intense young blonde is finger-fucking me while sucking my dick. No condom. It's still sort of safe now, or it isn't, or it sort of is, or some people think it is, or people are so sick of everybody still being dead they figure, *Who gives a shit?* Resurrections, like the Japanese yen, being in greater demand than supply these days, we pilgrims settle for a naked hard-on incubated for an hour or so in mucous tissue at ninety-eight point six degrees Fahrenheit.

The hair's a dye job, of course, and actually *streaked*...or *tipped*—a subtle distinction, to be sure—but it started out reasonably fair and it's long, the way I like it, and smells sweet—like papaya. There's some kind of scented candle thing going on, too, but they all smell like wax to me. But sweet. All burning things smell sweet. The day after the old ghetto burned the whole neighborhood smelled like marshmallows, but that was long ago and far away—well, about sixty miles on I-95. It smelled like roast fowl, too, but that's because the Mesopotamian next door kept a flock of guard ducks that never got out of their pen.

You just dial, you see, seven little easy-to-remember digits. *Punch in* is, of course, more accurate, since you need a Touchtone phone to proceed. Listen to the "menu," then poke the six to listen to the "*actual voices* of New York's *hottest professionals.*" "Hi, I'm Jim. I'm five-foot-ten, weigh one-fifty. I give a hot-oil full-body Swedish massage with a sensual release, and more." *Oooh, baby.*

Take notes. Choose. Call the number. Leave yours on the machine. Wait. Dial again. Leave your number. And again. Wait. Wonder if any of them will call back. It is, after all, a holiday Saturday night. Desperation rises from the smoldering coals of desire: You will agree to see whoever calls first, no matter how much he charges, no matter where in the city he lives, even if it's the Upper East Side. Desire—sprung from the ether like crocus through the unsuspecting snow.

His name is Chip. Right. He's six-two, one-eighty or ninety, twenty-four, from Massachusetts. Shaved balls for some reason. An angel puppy with a hot mouth—and I've got the bite marks on my unshaved ass to prove it. I did his lover yesterday, who is better looking but less enthusiastic. Neither of them know. It's my little secret (and, by the way, I'd like to have them both together).

A hundred bucks. It doesn't seem like much until after you come. Well, holidays and all...and one from each side of the family tree. Special occasion, that sort of thing. He's Caucasian, not my usual choice. They look better dressed as a rule. Maybe it's the northern light. Too much unrelenting pallor for passion, perhaps, or for honesty, as far as that goes. There's something about white that lies on its face. If you pass white light through a prism it breaks down into its component colors: puritan purple, repression red, entitlement green, conformity yellow.

This white boy is an exception, I think, as I watch the Empire State Building through what looks like the steam that water turns into when hosed onto an inferno. Back in the early eighties, there was a bathhouse in San Francisco that had a steam-room maze. I sucked weenie until I practically passed out from dehydration. I learned about chemistry in bathhouses—not from the red tin box of chemicals I got from my parents the birthday I asked for drums, or from the minister of our church, who did little lab experiments on compulsory Wednesday night services during Lent, turning some clear liquid red, which was supposed to remind us of Our Lord and Savior Jesus Christ's first miracle (turning the water to wedding wine at Cana). I don't imagine that indemnity carriers allow toy companies to market chemistry sets anymore. Although it was all pretty benign. Nothing at home ever turned colors. Just into a sludge, like powdered chocolate that stubbornly refused to dissolve in milk.

In bathhouses, in the pitch dark, you can touch a dozen men and feel nothing but flesh—the same feeling you might get rubbing up against an old woman on the uptown local. And then you touch another man, his arm or chest or waist, and your dick leaps to attention like it's on a spring and you are engulfed by him. That's chemistry, when the elements overcome the prejudices the mind has insulated the senses in.

This Empire State Building yellow is the same yellow they lit it that Friday night after St. Patrick's Day, as I recall, the first time the poor oppressed Irish Catholics who run the city of New York refused to let any queers march in their boozy parade (I keep track of holidays by how much pain they cause—ask me about Fourth of July of '76, or Halloween, 1970). There was, of course, the year the Empire State Building was illuminated especially for the troops in the Persian Gulf. Before it was a footnote—Desert Storm? The war in which American G.I.s were poisoned by chemical weapons invented here and supplied to the enemy by us. It's almost as ironic as the fact that Irish faggots march routinely in St. Pat's parades in, for example, Dublin and Belfast. It's only Fifth Avenue that's too narrow for fairies.

Of course, even piss yellow was better than the red, white, and trite fucking blue they were shoving down our throats before the war was over. Patriotism. Sounds lethal. Like botulism. And it is. You'd think they'd go for something less cadaverous, chromatically speaking, for so prominent and phallic a landmark—a nice white-inspired yellow, like wheat or a Yalie's argyles, suburban kitchens of the 1950s, or sunlight on the arm hairs of a Norwegian sailor, a sapling swabbie on leave abroad and not sure where to berth his buoy, not some revolting color that looks like what's been sitting in a stopped-up toilet at the Eros All-Male Cinema on Eighth Avenue for a week or two underneath that scrawny nude kid who'll take anybody or anything into his mouth or up his ass or all over his body. You've never seen hunger until you've said, "I don't think so," and looked into those eyes while you let loose your stream into a nearby urinal while that scabby desperado nearly weeps to see you waste it. It's nice to be so sure of what you want. I envy that. It's the obsession that frightens me, for obvious reasons.

Here's what makes me puke: that washed-out bow-ribbon yellow florists were doling out to tie around trees in working-class Republican neighborhoods in Brooklyn and Queens during the Desert Storm fiasco, the satin ribbon they paste gold paper letters on to spell out *Congratulations* and *Beloved Uncle Guido* and so forth. Of course, even that isn't as bad as the yellow they aim at the Empire State Building, at enormous cost no doubt, a yellow that has some Gaelic emerald in it left over from the No-Pansies Drunken Mick Pig Parade—or else some khaki in it to remind us how cool America is for having the biggest army in the whole wide Western world.

How long has it been? A year or two, and it's so over it's like it never happened. Except for the dismembered orphans and the troops of veterans who are rotting slowly from the inside, thanks to the American army. All those dead people, and nothing to show for it but an oil slick the size of Nebraska. And don't get me started on Vietnam, where a hundred thousand American boys are buried in rice weed. It's a tourist destination now, and I'd go if I could. Just to be near the place where Ralph died—in the days when boys still died one at a time and not in droves like the firstborn of Egypt. The angel of death doesn't pass over very many any more, ram's blood or no. Maybe blood just isn't as repellent as it used to be now that the national immune system is...compromised.

So the roiling midtown sky is blazing like it's National Water Sports Week instead of Easter. And Passover. Like the skyline is an Andres Serrano "Architectural Icon Suspended in Urine" lithograph. And the country's finances, like those of its citizens, are in the toilet. It was Kenny's humiliation that he could no longer get himself onto a toilet seat that finally did him in. The will just cracks, like the Liberty Bell, like Easter eggs boiled too fast on a gas stove, or a vial of poppers. Twenty years ago, when I was young and Ralph was already dead, on the night of a lonely birthday, I got smashed on beers at a bar uptown and this blazer homo named Wayne took me to his luxury doorman tower to piss in his mouth, which, as I remember it through an amber haze of guilt, memory, and a dozen bottles of brew, kept turning him yellower as I let loose— pulling hard on his scab-crusted nipples all the while—yellower than hepatitis eventually turned my eyeballs: mustard-gas yellow, the spewing sulfurous billow above a chemical plant in Baghdad hit by a U.S. scud, the pus color a kid's legs get when they've been blown off at the knees and there aren't any antibiotics left in the country so the kid will die real slow of infections, of peritonitis, just like Bette Davis in merciful black and white, without brain fever and hallucinations in Arabic. Maybe we didn't really kill tens of thousands of Iraqi civilians, as impartial international observers insist. But, knowing us, we probably did, killing being the thing we do best. I'm so proud to be an American I could just shit shamrocks.

So what do you think, it's a coincidence that the same day Irish queers march for the first time in the St. Paddycake Parade (unauthorized, of course, by the Ancient Order of the Ku Klux Hibernians), two undercover vice goons bust a naked dancer at the Gaiety Burlesk for solicitation? So now there are no more private shows because the Greek broads who run the place are paranoid city, and Joey Stefano says, laconic as August in Ecuador, "Pigs are pigs," and eats a cold McDonald's single burger by the pay phone in the Get Acquainted Lounge, which used to smell of grass, cash, and impending sex, but now only smells of ammonia from where a Lebanese kid mops up the room behind the stage so the dancers won't slip on the generic-brand baby oil they use to get their dicks hard before working the runway for their second of two numbers.

I've spent a lot of time on floors in my day. Wooden floors of back-room bars passed out on coats, linoleum floors of peep show arcades working my jaws over any available hunk of sausage, tile floors of bathrooms in places like the Chelsea Hotel (coming to with dead Danny's dick up my ass), cement floors of various…institutions, let's say. And what I remember most is the smell of Pine-Sol, industrial strength. It's an aphrodisiac to me now, like glue, however toxic when inhaled. Behind the screen at the Gaiety Burlesk, it used to smell like semen and the mellow illusion of possibility, now it just smells like sweat. There'd be a lot less hypocrisy in the world, I always say, if human odors were indelible. Of course, there'd be a lot more flies, too.

I've spent a lot of time at the Gaiety Burlesk, too, and a lot of money in that sleazy little temple of priapus where you tend to run into people like the clerk from the mail room at work and David Hockney. It's a microcosm, you know, although too many of the dancers on any given night are likely to be white. Most of the clients are bigoted old queens who get up and leave the auditorium when the black dancers come on, or the brown ones. Well, one thing about fags, we have not got our race shit together. But there were lessons to be learned at the Gaiety Burlesk, and not all the boys were white.

There were Latin boys of such devastating beauty I could get off just touching their flawless skin. Hairy Italians who all wanted you to think they were tops, and, okay, some of them were. Asians who set off every nerve in my body with their fingertips. And a black man once, a model in need of some emergency cash, who didn't want me even for money I was so fat at the time, but who got so turned on backstage when I went to work on his nipples he came when I did.

And there were special cases, too, boys I'd fall in love with just at the moment I shot a load all over the floor behind the screen wishing I had drenched them in that special way I have of spewing a load so big even the professionals gasp (and I'm not just bragging), and I'd visit them time after time.

Luis, or whatever his name was, a Puerto Rican from New Jersey who was working his way through landscape design courses at Rutgers, I'll never forget. I'll never forget the curving angle of his enormous rock-hard dick as he kneeled over my head at the Paramount Hotel (before the chichi renovation), or watching him shower, or his smile, or seeing him again in L.A. and taking him to dinner, and wanting him so bad through my pants I could feel them dampen. If I still had his phone number, I'd call him right now and dump a load anywhere he'd take it.

And there was Vladimir, of course, who got famous on late-night cable TV, Vladimir who was named after the vampire in a Dracula movie his mother saw once, who came home with me one night-before-Gay-Pride-Parade-Day and waved to his fans along Christopher Street (I was so proud), and then stripped in my bedroom and made leisurely, reasonable love with his bulked up body for an hour or more. And Rocky, who got famous for a minute or two, too, when he teamed up with Madonna for a book and a video, but whose real name he told me when he came to clean my apartment—fully dressed—which was his legit day-job way of making money. Told me once in a hotel room he'd never been fucked (like *that* surprised me) or ever even fucked a man, which did take me aback—I mean, what with his muscles and dick and tattoos and dazzling smile and all, not to mention his profession, I'd have thought there'd be men around with enough cash to cajole him into it. And what was the most amazing thing to me was how he just seemed amazed that gay men could like it, not that he thought it was disgusting or anything, just outside his experience (which extended to war).

There was, of course, Brazilian Julio (in Portuguese, you pronounce the *J*, as in Juliet), who was, as I was, born in July, a real dancer, with career potential. "You are so big," he said to me that first night we met, the night of the hotel that over-looked Lincoln Center's Christmas tree, "You are so big you can do anything to me," he said. So I did. I fucked him—again and again. I fucked him in hotel rooms and I fucked him in my apartment when I finally moved to New York and I even fucked him behind the screen at the Gaiety Burlesk, which ran strictly counter to the dancers' code.

"You are crazy," Julio said once while I was fucking him off the floor by the emergency exit, alternating my dick and half a hand so I wouldn't come too soon. "Do you really think so?" I asked, wondering if it was true. "But it's okay," he smiled, "because I'm crazy too—I love it." And he did, this sweet and generous boy/man who was as beautiful as any many I've ever desired, even in Carmen Miranda drag, which he wore to the Gay Parade for years. He was beautiful beside me at the ballet, too. He was the tiniest man I ever had and I wish I had him again now, to toss in the air and catch on my dick like a game of quoits.

Yes, those were the glory days, when sex was encouraged right smack on the premises, like a cut-rate brothel. But the Gaiety is not the scene it was before the Gulf War (not, strictly speaking, named for the oil company, but obviously fought on its behalf). So...what? You think the bust at the Gaiety was related to the war at all or just a coincidence? Or the parade where you have to be an RC het-breeder to be Irish? Or are the war and the parade somehow linked to this crack-down on grease-smeared ass-cracks just by the general, you know, ethos of the time, the odor of *facismo* on the rise numbing its prey like a giant water beetle?

So, I told myself the first night I turned up at the Gaiety after the "No Sex, Please, We're Busted" message went out, "Well, you might as well tie a yellow ribbon around Rocky's cock since you're not gonna get your lips around it, not tonight." So I stuck my middle finger straight up for those shit-Mick douche bags who booed and spat on the Irish queens in the city's lousy St. Pat-my-ass Parade. I stuck it straight up the fuckhole of a new dancer named Daniel in his room at the Milford Plaza, which cost me a whole lot more than backstage folderol but turned out to be worth it.

Daniel's American-born, but he's one of those border-town Lone Star Latins with hair longer than a girl's and crooked teeth in front. Couldn't be more appealing (as at least one big deal photographer has discovered), though I could do without the safety-pin tattoos. His eyes are swimming in something he uses so his brain won't see things the way his eyes do. He calls me Daddy Bear and has the usual gigantic uncut dick, which is nearly blue it's so dark, but I don't care, even if it does remind me of Roberto, dead and alive. I just want something up his ass. I'd use a shillelagh if I had one. He'll take my dick if I'm willing to re-negotiate, and there is nothing I'd like better than to sink myself up to the ruby pubes in those fleshy buns of his, but I'm not making the bucks I was, so we settle on fingers, which I give him 'til we both come, simultaneously, which I take as an enormous compliment, since even at his age, he can't afford to come with every trick, so most of them don't ever. I've been lucky that way, since I don't find a lot of pleasure in it unless I'm turning on my partner in the process.

"It's a gusher," he drawls in his cutesy way when I geyser all over his too-fleshy middle. He eats a banana, chugs a politically responsible Bud Lite, belches real ladylike, and says, "I 'don't know, I think everybody's queer." It's a hustler's perspective, sure, but you gotta admit there's some truth in it. In the elevator, there's a Chinese escort hostess in silver rhinestone shoes and fake leopard coat who clocks our number before we drop half a floor, and a little blond girl with brand-new breasts who's here on a school trip from Virginia and who hasn't got a clue and never will, unless, of course, she winds up working this same hotel. It can happen. Even in Newport News. She looks like she's dressed for a junior prom sometime before the Beatles' TV debut. It'd be a fun group to get stuck on an elevator with, but of course we don't get stuck (that waits until I'm trapped with a hysterical sumo wrestler who hasn't bathed since Tito died).

We sashay out of the elevator, across the lobby, through the crisscrossed laser glares of the Jamaican security staff, their scrutiny thick as chemical warfare, but nobody says jack shit. That's what business is all about: that smell of printer's ink, of fine engraving and finesse. Which is why it's so funny not long after when this rich Italian entrepreneur gets busted at the Milford Plaza for bringing a far younger and far more African young woman to his room for immoral congress (U.S. legislature take note). Only it turns out—big oops here—the young lady is not exactly working. She is exactly the Italian's *wife*. Red faces everywhere and banner headlines in the *Post*.

Speaking of which, I don't think it's all that much a coincidence that the *Post* does this giant cover story—right after the mayor of New York—the good one, not the one we have now—marches down Fifth Avenue with a clutch of lilting laddies and lasses of the Old Sod and Gomorrah persuasion—with this sensational big mother headline announcing that there are hustlers on Second Avenue at 53rd Street—a fact that every two- or four-legged sodomite has known since Cain set up shop on the northeast corner. Talk about your phenomenal scoop, right? Yeah, scoop of dog shit. Somehow it all comes down to Ireland. I used to like Ireland. Used to think the IRA was a righteous club, a kind of Black Panther Party with red hair and freckles.

In London, once upon a time, before Ralph was dead or I'd ever fucked a man to sleep, I met a drunk in Russell Square, a beggar: Irish, beard/mustache, fingers stained yellow from unfiltered cigarettes, Turkish when he could get them—and I bought him a whole pack near the poetry bookstore and the School of Economics. "Watch out for Ireland," he said, as broad in the blarney, I thought, as he was in the brogue. "Another Vietnam, my son, as sure as I'm standing." And he was, still standing, breathing the most fetid breath I'd ever smelled, being young. I was "Up the Irish" for years after— Yeats, O'Casey, Behan. Now I'm sick of it. Sick of blowing up the English just because they shop in Harrod's. Sick of the prig English, their stiff lips and limp dicks, but mostly sick of every Roman Catholic country on earth.

Fuckin' Ireland. The country's about as big as Staten Island and they can't even figure out how to have two religions without killing each other (a lot like Israel, but don't get me started). No doubt about it, religion has caused more evil in the world than every hooker put together. Religion is the process by which God is eliminated from matters of the spirit and replaced by human will, the empirically fallible will of a self-protective priesthood. Simple as that. And isn't patriotism, like cannibalism, a form of religion, really?

So I just eat an overpriced ham sandwich at Jerry's on Prince and wonder if these really deep, shrewd news hounds at the *Post* know that black men sell dope in Washington Square or that there are rainbow-colored junkies in this city washing windshields for quarters to support minor children. I have a cousin who's missing an eye for refusing one of these over-zealous spot-removers. An oft-wed black sheep (son of an oft-wed black sheep), he was once married to one of the Rockettes, who used to dress up like nuns for the Easter show at Radio City Music Hall and carry white lilies up to this stage-set altar to form a giant cross (for which spectacle we'd wait outside on 50th Street for hours, me mesmerized by the stark naked Art Deco cement men above the entrance to Rockefeller Center, the first men I ever coveted in my heart, and still do).

And I wonder if the *Post* boys know how heroic old Manhattan pissed on the potato-eaters who built the bridges and subways and City Hall, those same County Corkers who lynched escaped slaves from lampposts in the Village during the Civil War riots. Talk about casting a jaundiced eye. I guess that's why they call it "yellow" journalism. Because of the cowardice.

So I go to visit the folks on the Island, during the Gulf War, which turns out to be the usual mistake, and of course, masters of the mundane, they have a yellow ribbon tied around the trunk of a tree I grew up with and got to know fairly well. I even sat in that tree, and here it is hung with this hate-thing. Oh, the next-door neighbors have a bigger one, the Irish neighbors (no one's speaking to the Polish neighbors because the old man, who used to sell Wise Potato Chips, has gone completely dotty), and a flag in the picture window that says *These Colors Never Fade*. Sweet, sweet as new corn. Catholics and politics. So this friend of mine in California, not, to be sure, a bastion of rigid news sourcing, tells me this rumor that's being investigated in Europe that the pope, the Polish one, was in fact a collaborator with the Nazis during World War II, that he actually turned over the names of Jews to save his own skinless kielbasa. I believe it. Popes have been helping Nazis all along—take Pius XII, please! It is said, and by Roman Catholics themselves, mind you, that Pope John Paul I, whose pontificate was shorter than the Gulf War, that Johnny Paul Uno was actually murdered right there in the Vatican by an opposition claque of Machiavellian minions.

Chris (for Christian, not Christopher) says he doesn't believe any of it, but then Chris goes to Georgetown where Jesuits teach Skepticism 101 no matter what the curriculum is called. He admits, though, that the whole clergy is queer, including New York's reigning necrophilic, Cardinal O'Connor (who likes his cock-swallowing acolytes dead, you see), that "We're not in the business of saving lives, but of saving souls" anti-condom pro-lifer, that genocidal bog-hopper with a piss-shooter the size of a leprechaun's. "Why didn't someone try to kill him?" I can remember asking about Hitler, since he was so obviously evil. Same goes for O'Connor. How come he's still alive?

So somebody pistol-whipped a priest in Queens or Brooklyn or someplace to feed a wicked jones with the parish lucre and everybody's all shocked and alarmed. Right. Fucking priests been pistol-whipping faggots for centuries. Kill 'em all, that's what I say. Like cockroaches.

So it's Easter, and Passover, but I don't miss chocolate bunnies under yellow and lilac cellophane. You know what I miss? Rubberless fucking, since fucking with a glove on is no fucking at all, as any man who has ever done both will tell you. Oh, it might be worth giving up "unprotected" sex to save a life, but what's a life that only has protected sex in it? Rhetorical question. It's like a bullfight where the sword stays in its sheath.

Bullfights. They make me weep, they're so inaccessibly beautiful. They are, of course, the ultimate *symbolic* entertainment: Either the matador will fuck the bull (with his sword), or *el toro* will fuck the *toreador* (goring him with one or more horns). It is, Carlos Fuentes assures us, the ritual of man's supremacy over nature. But it's really about fucking, which is to say about man's total abandonment to, and submissiveness in the face of, nature.

The bullfighter is dressed magnificently in second-skin topaz satin, his asscheeks clenched tighter than fetal fists, his bundle of genitalia casting harsh shadows on his hard thighs. The bull comes equipped with a prick the size of the man's arm, two horns, and a lolling tongue that looks like a dick and

15

a tongue combined—one of those giant mollusks on display in Chinatown fish shops. Of course, the bull will die even if he manages to take down his tormentor in the process, immortality, like justice, being a fantasy.

Two men fucking is like a bullfight, too, a ritual of man's confrontation with the nature in himself. No illusions of sanctioned procreation to dilute the event, no easy retreat into the uncomprehending "otherness" of opposites, just man as he is, man doing to himself—and having done to himself—the thing the world has taught him will most surely damn him for all eternity. So, the bull dies, fucker or fuckee. And blood glistens in the parched sand of the arena. A man fucking a woman is beautiful, too, in its way, I suppose. But there is no mortality in it. It is, if ritual at all, an enactment of the myth of life. Queer sex is nature in the service of itself in the present, not the future.

The greatest of all mysteries, *The Mahabarata,* tells us that every man must die, and yet each day lives his life as if he is immortal. In the face of such wisdom, such clarity, it hardly seems to matter if there is an eternity at all.

Once upon a time when Easter and Passover happened on the same day, I was sitting in the administration building of the college I went to by mistake, along with a third of the student body, in protest over fraternity exclusion of Blacks and Jews. I remember a chevron of geese flying overhead and a balmy, spongy-earth day with daffodils blooming wild on green hills, and I remember hope. (That's why preserving the hope of the young is so important, so it can be remembered later in life.)

The upstate May-time sky was clear and blue, like Chip's eyes as he veils his hair now over me and puts his tongue onto my tongue like the Host. The body and blood of Chip. As often as I do this...I remember all kinds of men. Most of them dead. Like the reed-thin corpses of the Holocaust (their exposed genitalia the first human penises I ever saw, enormous-looking, enticing even attached to dead men). Like the saints and disciples. Horrible deaths, most of them. Crucified, stoned, burned, quartered, fed to wild beasts—just the sort of thing the church has been doing to fairies forever.

Now Magic Johnson has AIDS, which is sad I guess, but I can't get all broken up about it. Arthur Ashe has been dropped as a crossword clue in the *New York Times,* so there's some real impact on my life there. "Isn't it awful about Arthur Ashe?" some twinkie in Lycra biker shorts gushed at the gym right after that news became public. To tell the truth, I didn't actually give a shit about Arthur Ashe. Or any other heterosexual. They've had their millennia, and they've blown it (up). The world is better off without them. There are too many people anyway. Too many people who hate. So I guess the world would be better off without me, too, since I have learned to hate so purely. But then, the world won't have long to wait for that. I'll be going one of these days, one of the ways we're dying: bad blood, tainted blood, spilled blood. We're all dying of the yellow anyway, of the Empire State Building piss yellow of religious holidays and patriotism, an oily yellow lost in a mist that looks like it should smell of subways, that bum-urine and burnt electric cordite smell of blue-white sparks on gleaming tracks. Instead it smells sweet. Like the licorice jelly beans my Polish Catholic godmother picked out of the Easter baskets she gave me before she died and went to burn in hell forever for marrying a Lutheran and loving her queer nephew without condition.

So it's late. The car alarm out front finally died after about six hours since the police don't have the authority to do anything but beat up faggots who have the temerity to hail a yellow cab outside the Stage Deli. My fingers still smell like Chip, like the scented massage lotion he rubbed on my body and I rubbed on his, of my own semen and his, of Obsession for Men, and large, luminous eyes, of views of the Empire State Building from the floor-level mattress of a part-time hustler who's moving south at the end of the month to pursue a career in music. It's Easter already by the digital Bulova on my desk. It's raining, which means the smeared diarrhetic dog shit is being washed from the sidewalk out front with the soot from chimneys a century old and more. The acid that turns copper green is washing out of the air onto the cobbled streets of lower Manhattan while a small rat forages under my sink for the poisoned oats an exterminator left there on Good Friday.

The rain falls onto the aluminum hood of the kitchen exhaust fan, reminding me of an intravenous drip and nickels. Some unkillable fungus grows under my toenails (I call it Cardinal O'Connor). But despite it all, despite the pot of coffee and a quart of Diet Pepsi I just ingested in lieu of the blood of Christ, I'll sleep soundly tonight, while junkies curl up in doorways and shoot tepid smack into their veins, grateful not to go to sleep sick. After all, it's a holiday.

I'll take an aspirin against the pains of holidays and age and sleep with memories of Chip in my mouth, of Joey Stefano (higher than a kite, his asshole open to accept the loneliness of the male world). I'll think of lovers who smelled of formaldehyde even before they died and jerk off wondering if Ralph was ever happy. And I'll drift off on clouds of beer-swilling Texican Daniel. He was a rose, all right, a yellow rose that I am dreaming of, of Danny Boy from Dallas, of hate in Irish eyes, and vengeance.

First Shave

Jameson Currier

Barry lies on the bed diagonally and I pull his body closer toward me so that his legs dangle over the edge of the bed. His erection stretches up toward his navel and I grasp his cock and give it a few pumps with my fist. The water is in a large pot on the nightstand beside the bed, and I lean back from where I am standing and dip the tips of my fingers in the pot to wet them, then dip my hand all the way inside, clutching a grip of the warm water in my palm. I lean back toward Barry and drip the water over his waiting balls and cock, his skin soaking in the water as I next run my hand over them, the liquid a slick lubricant as I reach up and play with the shaft of his cock. Barry's eyes are closed, but he smiles as I run my fist back and forth along the head of his dick. I cup his balls with the palm of my other hand, feeling the warmth and wetness of them now, then move my own dick, stiff and needy, to the side of me so that it falls against his balls.

I reach over from where I stand and get the shaving cream from the nightstand, squirt a handful of it into my palm, and rub it on Barry's balls. I let the skin soak this up, and while waiting I use the cream as a lubricant to play some more with his cock. Barry smiles again, wider, 'til his lips stretch almost to his ears, and then he opens his eyes and looks down at my hand, the shank of his neck flushed red from where my movements have excited him. I take my free hand and lightly squeeze his left nipple, and he shoves his head back against the bed, lifting his ass up slightly so that his dick slips in and out of my enclosed fist from the rocking motion he makes himself.

When he relaxes again, I reach for the razor from the nightstand, do a fast check of the shaving cream on his balls, and decide to squirt some more on them. I use one hand to pin his dick against his stomach, then point the razor right beneath the shaft of his cock. I bring the razor down slowly against his skin, feeling the hair on his sack pull a little as I work on him, shaving him in short, firm strokes. Overcome slightly by the reality of my own shyness, I lean back and rinse the razor in the pot of water, even though I could have shaved some more of him. This is my first time shaving Barry, and I feel the tension in the arch of my back. After eight months of irregularly dating one another, Barry finally trusts me enough with a razor at his balls.

Not that he should, of course. We're not lovers, we're not roommates—nor friends, either, really. Merely two men who date one another, something a little more complex than fuck-buddies, however. Barry already *has* a lover. *Isn't that always the story? The way it goes? The good one's always taken? Or at least the sexy one?* Barry's been with Eric for almost twenty years now, and Barry tells me every time I see him that he and Eric haven't had sex in years. Every time he mentions Eric, however, I feel both jealous and envious; Eric has a daily intimacy with Barry I know I will never possess.

Now, using my thumb and fourth finger, I stretch some of the skin of Barry's balls, and with the razor, shave the skin I have pulled taut. Then I push one of the sides of his balls tight against the other, shaving the side of it and slightly under-neath. I do the same with the other side of his sack, dip the razor clean, and then play with his cock to make sure he is enjoying all this attention.

Barry first shaved his balls when he started dating a guy who had shaved *his* balls and ass. Not Eric, of course; Barry has been seeing other guys since his relationship with Eric began, when they were college roommates. They never started out monogamous, Barry told me the night he first slept over at my apartment, but they made a rule, right up front, of never discussing their other lovers, dates, or tricks with one another. How Barry explains his clean shaven balls to Eric now, I have no idea, though I think it might have something to do with the absence of sex between them. But if I try to understand the complexity of *their* relationship, I only become frustrated with the inadequacy of *ours*.

I want more than this, of course; or rather, I want more than what Barry is willing to give me. He likes our arrange-ment the way it is—once or twice a week for a movie, dinner, and, inevitably, sex. When Eric is out of town, one of us sleeps over at the other's apartment.

At first, all Barry wanted us to be was fuck-buddies, an arrangement I was perfectly capable of accepting, though not happily. But Barry wouldn't stop calling me—first for sex, then later, to complain about Eric. He called from the office, from the car, from the lobby of the theater, 'til some-times, we spoke to one another four or five times a day. Then he would disappear for a long stretch of time, only to call repeatedly again. I always expected that Barry would have used me up by now, but instead he arrives with little gifts—toys which we will use later, together, in bed—handcuffs, rings, clamps, dildos, flavored lube. That's how the shaving came about. Barry arrived tonight with a disposable razor and shaving cream.

I continue to talk to Barry's body with my hands. His dick is rock-solid hard, thick and pumped like his morning erections always are, and I sneak a look at the whole package of him, the hefty, well-fed physique of a well-groomed, middle-aged theatrical producer. What is this thing I have for older men, anyway? Barry is effortlessly a man, however, natural and unrattled as a father, with a chest and stomach full of flat, brown hair, the ends of which are tipped in gray, and full round biceps and an ass you would believe belonged to a much younger body. There is a good twenty years difference between us; Barry says, more often than not, that I look like Eric did when they first met. In spite of his comparisons, in spite of knowing I'm being compared, I also find Barry inherently sexy. I play with myself for a moment, stroking my cock as I look him over, then tell him first to turn over on his stomach, then to push himself up, supporting himself on his knees and elbows.

His ass now—the white, creamy complexion of it—is pitched heavenward into the air, and I cup his cheeks with my wet hands, kneading them first and then giving them light slaps. His skin is baby soft but firm beneath the flesh, and I slap and knead, slap and knead, as Barry shifts himself beneath me to accommodate my grips, his ass pushing itself even higher into the air above him, as if trying to drink in the air through his asshole.

Not long after I met Barry, he told me that he liked the slick feel of his cleanly-shaved balls, and that he would go wild when someone just touched him there, cupping them completely into the warm palms of his hands. Now Barry shaves the evening before he sees me, in case he nicks himself, he tells me, in order to give the skin time to heal. I worry a moment about nicking him now, imagine how I would handle the blood if that should happen. But I shake off the thought, mentally chant it out of the room. *That will not happen,* I tell myself over and over, *because he trusts me. No blood. No blood. No blood.*

I run a finger from the base of Barry's spine, down through the crack of his ass, back down to his balls. I cup them with one hand, then take my other hand and rub my fingers against his asshole. The hole is red and almost angry-looking, and I study the hairs along the puckered surface. I reach over to the still-warm water, wet my fingertips, then run them into the crack of his ass, digging a damp finger slightly into his asshole. I play with the water some more against his ass, then squirt shaving cream into my hand and rub it along the crack.

I tell him to spread his knees even further, widening my view of his asshole. I slap the skin some more, then take the razor in one hand and with my other hand spread the skin of his other cheek—first for support, and then, when I am sure of the flesh, to stretch the skin even further apart.

I shave the base of his spine first, then, in short, quick strokes, work my way down the crack to his asshole, watching the warm, creamy liquid drip down onto the sack of his balls. When I reach the more furrowed surface of his asshole, I slow down, almost tapping the razor against his skin. I can tell he is even more aroused now, imagine my quick, light movements must feel as if he is being tickled there, and I smile at the thought of it and continue shaving him.

When I first started dating Barry, I wanted desperately to fall in love with someone, having just emerged from a string of very bad blind and fruitless dates. The moment Barry told me about Eric, I was ready to end it all. Who wants to be the other woman, after all? Had the sex not been so good, so comfortable, so hot and inventive between us, he could never have convinced me to continue.

I rinse the razor and continue shaving his asshole, using the razor a little harder now to get a closer shave. I run a finger along the clean, finished surface of the skin, testing the smoothness. I decide I want it to feel even smoother, and repeat my strokes along his ass. I stop midway, however, reach underneath him, and pump his cock. He groans and shifts his body. I knead his cheeks, then finish with the remainder of his ass.

The shave is done now, but I touch up the underside of his balls to get a closer shave from this new angle. The cream, water, and shave take only a moment, and I use the excess liquid to lube his dick, feeling as I do the damp sensation of his precome wetting his cock. I place the razor back on the nightstand, wet my hand again in the pot, and then begin to finger his asshole. One finger slips easily in, and I wiggle it around inside him, feeling for his prostate. I find it—a hard little nodule beneath the tip of my finger—and massage it. He groans again, and I wedge a second finger into his ass, move it in and out, in and out, listening to his moans to make sure that they emanate more from pleasure than from pain.

Barry said that Eric hadn't fucked him since Eric tested positive, almost five years ago. Barry is negative, and the difference in their serostatuses, Barry said, not only pushed them further apart sexually, but bound them closer together emotionally. How could he walk out on Eric now, Barry once told me, not knowing what the future could mean for either of them? Of course it upset me when I heard it; it still does when I think about it. Eric is asymptomatic, and Barry, I know, does not *want* to leave him. *This is what I have,* I remind myself, and continue fingering Barry's ass. *This is what I get.* If I want more or something else, I know I have to get out and look elsewhere.

From the nightstand, I remove a condom and slip it over my cock. I lean over Barry's ass and push my dick slowly in. Barry takes a deep breath, and I wrap my arms around his waist as I fuck him from behind, my movements slow and thoughtful, in and out, in and out, so that he feels every inch of my dick and balls against his now-hairless ass.

He groans louder as I go in deeper and faster, and my thoughts change from erotic to frustrated. Barry's sexual appetite is insatiable—I'm not his only companion-slash-fuck-buddy. My friend Martin's seen Barry at the bar picking up tricks; my neighbor, Jon, saw him and a date at a premiere at the Ziegfeld. Barry's even taken me to the bar with him a couple of times when he's been in search of fresh meat. Now, instead of pushing myself harder into Barry, I take deep breaths, rapidly and loudly, wanting to believe, as I do, that Barry is not just another jerk fucking me over, using me as a sex toy. Beneath me, beneath Barry's ass, I reach down and pump his cock as I fuck him. Barry suddenly comes into my fist, and I rub his hot cream back up against the shaft of his cock, around the base and onto his slippery balls.

I pull out of him and watch myself come into the tip of the condom, my dick suspended somewhere above Barry's milky-white ass. Barry twists his body beneath me, twirls around so that his ass rests again on the bed. His eyes look up at me, searching for my own. I meet his gaze and watch his lips purse together as if to speak. For a moment, I think he will say something romantic, caring, but I lean down into him, wanting to cut him off, not wanting to hear some sort of half-hearted remark about how nice he thinks I am. Instead, he stops my face right above his own by shoving his hands against the side of my skull. For a moment, the power between us shifts. Barry is twice as big as I am, and he could easily crush my skull in his hands. Instead, he turns my head so that my ear is right above his lips. "Show me you care," he says lightly into my ear. "Come on. I want you to do it again."

Aegis

D. Travers Scott

Soon, Ian thought.

The razor glided across his scalp, leaving a smooth, pink wake in the lather. A chill followed the razor's swath, cold air touching exposed skin. In contrast, a warm razorburn glowed. The hot/cold juxtaposition reminded Ian of raves: flushed Ecstasy-forehead heat against cold menthol jelly on lips and eyelids.

Hot and cold make tornadoes, he thought.

Stevik was steady, careful.

Ian shifted his concentration from top to bottom as the razor made another pass.

Feet flat against the floor-tiles, back braced against the goal posts of Stevik's legs, Ian held himself still as possible. The tattooist's knees jutted out through torn black denim, the cotton fray and kneecap hairs tickled Ian's earlobes. Ian's arms circled back around Stevik's calves, the hard swells from years of bike messengering wedged solid inside Ian's elbows.

Ian focused on the tactile sensations underneath his fingertips and sweaty palms. Stevik had put him on a steady diet of L-arginine, niacin, pantothenic acid and choline to heighten his sense of touch. Boots and jeans flooded his system: Rough canvas cord, cold metal eyelets and supple leather, smooth spots on frayed laces, and rough denim all weave against his armflesh. Stevik's shins ran down his bare back in sharp verticals.

Focusing on these sensations kept Ian motionless. Stevik could work around a nick, but Ian knew he'd prefer perfection from the onset and wanted to give it to him. He opened his eyes. The sun, low on Belmont, shot orange verticals of August evening slicing through the windows of Endless Tattoo. Stevik's boots glowed black-red; the silver ring on Ian's fourth finger gleamed in bright contrast. The oblique light carved deep shadows into the inscription, *BOY*.

Ian fought a shudder. It would take several sessions to do a piece as elaborate as Stevik had promised, as elaborate as the work he'd done on Toad: The outlining, fill, shading, color.

Finally, they were approaching the home stretch.

Once Stevik had marked him, it would happen.

"So," the pierced guy with dreads drawled, "who gave you the ring?"

Ian turned around, surprised.

"No one." Ian's eyes, burning underneath thick, furrowed brows, darted around the club. They lit on the dreaded guy. "Gave it to myself."

The man held his gaze, unblinking. "Self-made *Boy*?"

Ian looked away.

"Someday..." Ian glanced at his half-peeled Calistoga label. His eyes danced briefly onto the pierced guy, gazed past him out into the pit.

"Someday, someone'll give me one to replace it."

The man curled out his lower lip thoughtfully.

Ian scowled into his bottle.

The man with the dreads rose, took one of his two singles from the counter.

"Yeah. Someday," he muttered.

Ian's eyes trailed his dissolution into the crowd.

"There."

Hot/cold prickles ran over Ian's clean scalp, down his neck.

"Okay, Ian. I'm done."

Ian stared at the ring, and his pale fingers gripping Stevik's black laces. He didn't want to let go. He'd waited so long for this—and what would follow—he almost feared its arrival.

"Ian, I gotta get you into the chair to do it."

Ian tilted his freshly-shaved head back against Stevik's lap, looking up into his eyes. Stevik's brown dreads circled down around his face like curtains. His face was a series of long shadows and gleaming sparks from the stainless piercings: Labret below the lips, Niebuhr between the eyes, septum, eyebrow. Ian traced them with his eyes, drinking in the details of the man's face. His black goatee curled down in a point; scars striped his eyebrows. Two dark brown eyes terrified Ian, their enormous potential energy, poised to spring deep into him.

Ian smiled.

Stevik's lips curled into a fond snarl.

He spat.

The hot saliva splattered beneath Ian's right nostril. His tongue stretched to gather it up.

"Fuck," Stevik sighed. "I get so hot thinking about marking you."

Ian nodded. He squeezed Stevik's ankle and laid his face against his thigh. He breathed in sweat, dirt, and crotch-funk through the stiff denim, nuzzled the coarse fabric, sighed.

"I know," Stevik murmured. "Won't be much longer, boy. Not too long. And it'll be worth the wait. You'll have earned it."

Ian exited into the gelid night. LaLuna's neon tinted the wet street hyper-cobalt.

Town always looks like a fucking car commercial, he thought.

Assorted young queers drifted past with affected chattering, unlocking station wagons and Buicks, strapping on bike helmets, revving motorcycles, stretching into raggedy sweaters and backpacks.

Ian kicked around the corner, disgusted. Another wasted night. Tweakers, smoked-out groove-rats, slumming twinks. Even at the freak convention, he felt the freak. The kids, his peers, had all been babbling about the Psychotronic Circus coming down from Seattle, trashing a new all-ages called The Garden, comparing notes on which of the street kids arriving for spring were fags and which ones would fuck around anyway, for money or a dose.

And the older guys: Trolling, married, shut-down, falling asleep...fuckfuckfuck.

What I'd give for one fierce guy.

He cut through the alley, staring at his black Docs scuffing the gravel, listening to the regular jangle of his wallet chain. Chink-chink-chink. Another regular beat, some industrial ambient dub thing. Mix in a little Violet Arcana, maybe, and it could've graced the clove cigarette smoke in the chill room.

Chink-chink-chink-

Juh-jangle.

The dissonant beat startled Ian. He stopped, looked up.

The dreadlocked guy, one hand supporting himself against a dumpster, stood across the alley from Ian. Facing the club's rear, his suede jacket glowed a scabby red in the halogen streetlight.

The man looked over his shoulder. "Oh—you. Hey."

He turned, releasing a splattering piss-stream against the mossy bricks.

Ian stood silent, watching the piss steam slightly, frothy trickles pooling around his boots.

The dreaded man looked back over his shoulder.

Ian didn't move.

The man's boot-heels ground into the muddy gravel. He pivoted to face Ian. His piss-stream, spewing a circular arc like a suburban lawn sprinkler, rained across the alley between them.

Ian met his gaze. The man frowned.

Ian dropped to his knees, immersing himself. The bitter piss ran into his eyes, dripping from his forehead, shoulders and chest; gathering and falling from his face in thick, round drops, splattering on the earth.

The man shook off the final drops, tucked, buttoned. Ian's jaw dropped, the dour drops hitting his tongue. His eyes burned; his T-shirt, soaked and cold.

"Come on," the man whispered.

Ian followed him out of the alley.

"We'll just aim for starting the outline tonight. Just see how far we can go."

"I can take it."

Stevik's hand sifted through Ian's hairy chest, callouses stretching out a nipple like fleshy caramel. "I know you can. I know you can."

He jerked out a couple of hairs from around the aureole. Ian stiffened, inhaled briskly.

"I'll give it to you," Stevik said. "All of it and more. You know I will. But not 'til you're mine."

Ian's hard-on thumped against his belly, disconsolate.

Stevik unlocked the door of the metal Quonset hut. Ian followed him deep into the high-arched space, filled with only a few chairs, a couch, some cinder blocks. Eight-foot sheetrock walls set off a room in the far back corner. In the ceiling's dark recesses, rain splattered against the corrugated metal.

A light clicked on beneath the furthest wall. Ian shut the door behind him and twisted the deadbolt. He felt his way toward the light.

He stood in the doorway, blinking in the light. Stevik sat on the edge of a bed which descended from the ceiling on heavy wooden braces.

Stevik looked up, almost surprised.

"What?" Stevik stopped, holding one boot in his hand. "What do you want?"

"I—ah—" Ian struggled for a response. "Well, why'd you bring me here?"

Stevik rolled his eyes and yanked off the other boot.

"Why'd you follow me here?" he shot back, tossing the boot onto the floor.

Ian shrugged. He took a step toward the bed.

"Look!" Stevik barked, "I don't want to touch you, get it? Little fuck; I don't know shit about you, if you're even worth it. I just…. You can stay here, tonight, if you want."

He jerked his thumb toward a pile of dirty clothes in the corner.

"There. Sleep over there if you want."

Ian stared at him. Stevik rolled away, still in his clothes, and jerked a plaid comforter up over himself. He clapped twice and the lights went out.

Ian found the pile of clothes in the dark. He could smell them.

Ian climbed off the floor into the chair. He stared ahead at the screen Stevik had set between the chair and the store's windows.

"Bet you've dreamed about my dick," Stevik said, rolling open his station's drawer.

Stevik pulled out a rustling sheaf of carbon papers. Ian had seen him working on them. It was the design, the tat for his scalp. Stevik hadn't let him see it finished.

"What it feels like, how it smells. You've only seen it pissing. You don't even know what it looks like hard, how it feels in your hand, all hot and heavy."

At the apex of the Broadway Bridge, Stevik told him to stop.

Ian stared at Stevik, a few feet before him, hands across chest. A curtain of vertical lights rose behind Stevik, a skyscraper-light mirage that made Portland look, at night, like the metropolis it wasn't. The verticals of lights were only expensive houses rising up along the West Hills, but it had fooled Ian that night, years ago, when he'd leapt off the freight train beneath this very bridge.

"Take your clothes off, jack off, and don't look at me."

Stevik sauntered over the walkway's railing and leaned back.

Ian pulled off his T-shirt, unbuckled his belt. He was elated to have run into Stevik again, but wondered where things would go this time. He kicked off his Boks, pulled down his jeans.

Just the boxers left. If someone comes along....

"I said don't look at me, dogshit!" Stevik kicked Ian's shirt out over the bridge's lane gratings.

Ian scuffed off his shorts. He leaned back against the cold metal girder, its single-file row of rivet-heads pressing into his back like a formation of soldier-cocks. He licked his palm and rubbed his shriveled dick, trying to coax a hard-on. He kept his eyes moving to avoid Stevik: The tiny scythe-blades of moonlight on the Willamette River, the splintery wood planks of the walkway, the kitschy yellow lily of the suicide-hotline sign.

A dull roar grew. Cold whiteness rose up his bare side; Ian kept a steady rhythm pulling on his soft dick.

A breeze whipped against him as the truck plowed by; the bridge vibrated against his back and ass and feet. Silence. Ian was raging hard.

Relaxed, he stared up at the stars. Orion guarded him above, bow drawn. Ian stared at his jeweled belt, and came.

"Good," Stevik said. He was standing right at Ian's side, holding Ian's shorts.

"Here."

Ian slipped them on, his jeans, socks, shoes.... He looked over at his tire-tracked shirt stretched across the grating.

Stevik set his jacket on the girder and pulled his own T-shirt off. "Here. Yours is trashed."

Ian swallowed and pulled the shirt over his head, Stevik's smell surrounding him.

"You don't always have to wait to just run into me, you know," Stevik said jovially as they descended the bridge. "You can just come by the shop."

Stevik sprayed disinfectant onto Ian's scalp, minty-cool mist dancing across his raw skin as it evaporated dry.

"I bet you dream about it in your mouth, going down your throat, sucking it dry, swallowing all the cum I can shoot out."

A sticky bar ran across his head, leaving residue. Ian smelled of Mennen Speed Stick, a cloying musk of ineffectual father-macho.

Ian waited across the street at Subway, watching Stevik work. He chewed pepperoncini thoughtfully. Watching Stevik from a distance afforded him moments of striking lucidity, quite distinct from the blind heat saturating his mind in the man's close proximity.

This is so weird, he thought. It was one thing when it was so—casual, but now.... Fuck, Ellen's already rented my room out to that sculptor-guy.

He's never hurt me, though. He's never done anything I haven't loved.

"And your ass just itches, don't it? It hurts—don't it hurt so bad, the way you want it? You think of me up there, my arms crushing your chest, my tongue in your ear and my dick, that dick of mine you dream about just ramming away up inside your ass, plowing into your hot gut. Goin' in and out."

Stevik pressed the carbon against his scalp, the design transferring to the adhesive deodorant.

"Put some music on," Stevik muttered as they entered the loft. He wandered into the kitchen for a beer. Ian flicked on the living-room light and rifled through the CDs.

"Wanna Sheaf?"

"Yeah, that's great." Ian hummed happily. Stev had never asked him to pick out the music before. Some old Front Line Assembly would be fun, he thought. Or maybe more mellow—This Mortal Coil or something. Or Coil—yeah, that'd be the perfect combination.

None to be found: Marc Almond, Everything But the Girl, Annie Lennox, Edith Piaf, Billie Holiday—

God, I've gotta unpack my discs soon.

Stevik walked into the room with the two brown bottles of Australian stout.

"God, Stev," Ian quipped, scowling at the track listing on *Billie's Blues,* "you got anything besides all this diva-queen crap?"

Stevik set the bottles down carefully on the floor. His fist plowed squarely into Ian's gut.

Ian collapsed to the floor, gasping.

34

"Put on the headphones—and listen to that CD," Stevik seethed through grit teeth. "Don't go to bed 'til you get it."

He picked up both bottles and stalked into the bedroom, slamming the door behind him.

Four A.M.

"Stevik."

Stevik rolled over, blinked.

"Can I go to sleep now?"

Ian was crying.

"Yeah."

Ian knelt to spread out his blanket.

"No—"

Stevik pulled off the sheet, stretching out in a black T-shirt and shorts.

"Get in here. You ain't gonna get anything, and don't cling on me all night, but—just go ahead and get up here. You don't have to sleep on the floor anymore."

"You think of me fucking you and you get all weak, doncha? Like your knees giving out."

Stevik peeled off the paper and set it on the counter. Ian stared at the ceiling, feeling the vinyl and chrome of the chair beneath him. Stevik spoke in a steady monotone as he set out his supplies. The ink bottles clinked against the individual glass wells as he dispensed and mixed the colors.

Ian waited on the floor beside the chair.

"So you're Stev's new boy, huh?" The woman looked down at Ian, balancing her water bottle on the shiny black hip of her PVC hot pants.

"He marked you yet?"

Ian smiled, shook his head.

"Oh, so you're still in the—uh, trial run." She laughed. "He let you talk?"

"Yeah."

"But he told you to wait here for him, right?" She smirked. "Been gone a long time, hasn't he? I think he's up on the roof fucking my sister."

Ian bit his lip and tried to sound polite. "He didn't tell me anything," he said, "I just want him to be able to find me whenever he wants. So I'm staying in one spot."

"Not bad," she appraised. She turned around to face the crowd at the far end of the Quonset hut. Stevik broke through, dragging a skinny bald guy under his arm, both howling loudly.

"Well, your wait's over, it looks like. He's bringing over the ex for introductions."

She looked back over her shoulder at Ian, eyebrow arched. "You must rate."

Stevik and the bald guy tossed her happy nods in passing. They planted themselves loudly before Ian.

Stevik slapped the bald guy's chest proudly. His chest, arms, neck and scalp were a myriad of designs. In the dim light, Ian could barely sort out the intertwined images: An octopus sat on his head, tentacles creeping down the neck. Two figures hung down his pecs, crucified at crossed wrists just above each nipple. Geometric spirals rose out from the waistband of his black leather pants.

"This is what real skin looks like, boy, see this? This is real work! This is the kind of work I do when I give a shit about someone."

The bald guy beamed proudly, his blue eyes sparkling brighter than the glinting four-inch steel spike through his septum.

"Don't take all the credit, now!" The bald guy grabbed Stevik's crotch. He crouched down, confidentially, to Ian. "Stevie, now, he didn't do all this, mind you. But, eh, he got it all started."

"Look at this fag's shit!" Stevik yanked Ian's T-shirt, pulling it up over his head.

"See? He's a little lost tribal boy, look at that. My!" He grabbed Ian's arm and stretched it up high. "A chain around his arm! Tough shit! And wait, there's more!"

He reached over and grabbed the back belt loop of Ian's cords.

"Stand up, fuck," he muttered.

He spun Ian around and pulled down the back of his shorts, exposing the dogpatch hair leading down to Ian's ass. Off to the left side, where the hair faded into pale fawn-down, was an ankh.

"Wook! It's a wittle ankhy-wankhy!" Stevik sneered. "Itn't it twoo tweet?"

Stevik howled. His friend belched. Ian stood, patiently waiting.

"Toad," Stevik said to the bald guy, "this little turd wants me to mark him. He wants me to put my art on the same skin with all this other piss-ass shit." He snorted.

Toad smiled. "Now why don't you just, eh, cut out those old ones, eh, Stevie?"

Stevik laughed. "Nah, no scars for him yet. Maybe we get Ben to brand him someday. For now I want his skin clean."

Toad nodded. "Then you'll just have to cover."

They stared up at Ian. He held his head bowed.

"Look at me, fuck."

Ian raised his eyes to the short, dark man.

"You really want to get marked by me? Like Toad here?"

Ian nodded.

"I had to earn this, you see," Toad said with quiet pride.

"I understand."

"It was quite difficult."

Ian nodded.

Stevik and Toad exchanged glances. Stevik shrugged.

"Go let Toad fuck you, asshole. Head's clear."

Stevik jerked his head toward the crowded rear of his space.

"Keep the door open," he called out as they walked away.

Stevik shifted weight in the worn easy chair cushions, his boots propped up on a cinder block. He watched across the space 'til Toad's serpent-entwined arm shoved Ian out through the bathroom door, to the cheers of the crowd. They gathered around Toad, laughing. Ian pegged his shorts back up. He looked around the floor by the chair for his shirt. It was soaked with beer and cigarette ash, marked in the middle with a bootprint where it'd been used to swab the floor.

Ian wiped the wet cum-muck off his face with the back of his arm. Sticky smears clung to his hairy abdomen.

"Sit down," Stevik muttered.

Ian sat, wrapping his bare arms around his chest.

Ian looked at Stevik's boots. He leaned forward.

"Touch me and I'll beat the living shit out of you, right here."

Ian froze.

"Christ, you stink."

"Like you wanna cry. You think about how bad you want me inside you, how you want my dickhead kissing your heart, my cock's shit-smeared blessing. You want it so bad you can't stand it. You think of it and you think you'll just collapse in a big whimpering, slobbering mess, begging for me to do it. Doncha? Doncha?"

He slapped the boy's naked stomach.

Ian nodded, dislodging tears that dripped onto his chest, trickled down the sides of his neck.

Ian heard Stevik tear open the needle package.

"But you haven't, have you?"

Ian shook his head proudly.

"No, you haven't. You're tough. You never even asked me

for it, never went around with your ass in the air like some damn cat in heat."

Stevik ran his gloved hand down the side of Ian's face, wiping away the saltwater, the rubber dragging across Ian's lips. Ian kissed.

Stevik kissed the clean scalp.

"You already got it, man. You already got it. Everything I'm ever gonna give you—you already got it."

Studying the Alliance of Professional Tattooists manual and the Oregon state regs, Ian imagined Stevik marking him. He imagined Stevik fucking him, 'til the two fantasies meshed.

The tat machine and Stevik's all-but-unseen, imagined, longed-for dick merged—the machine's rabbit ear screwed into the base of Stevik's pubis, its mechanism sticking out from the pubic hairs. The armature bar shot upward as the base of his shaft; DC coil, spring contact points and base all curled into an electromagnetic nutsack. The rubber bands were black neosporene cockrings. A dark brown foreskin stretched out over the armature bar and sanitary tube—it skinned back to reveal a five-point grouping of liner needles arranged in an X like five dots on a die, like a man spread-eagled. The red cock-needles shot in and out, woodpeckering Ian's scalp through scaly layer, epidermis, into dermis. Stevik pushed his cock needles further, standing above, Ian bowed at his feet. The needles mixed Stevik's precum-ink with Ian's head-blood, sucking the serum up into the foreskin tube through capillary action, Ian's capillaries got some action, filling with Stevik's Number C Hard Black spunk. Stevik marked deeper, aiming for Ian's fontenels, poking through the skull-joints' cart, past the blood/brain barrier. Ian's whole body spasmed, muscles fibrillating with abandon.

Ian's fantasy lost physical specifics at this point. He couldn't visualize or verbalize, only feel a destruction, absorption, union.

Stevik stuffed cotton wads into Ian's ears.

Ian looked over at the tat machine in his hand.

Time slowed down. Ian watched. Current flowed through the coils and the base of the machine. Electromagnetized, it pulled the bar down, pulling down the needles and opening the silver contact points. Opening the points killed the magnet, and the spring assembly brought the bar back, causing the needles to move up and contact the points, conducting current and repeating the cycle. Again. Again. A cycle of opposite motions and polarities, endlessly repeating.

The first of the needles broke his skin, the ink penetrated his dermis, hundreds of times a second.

We Own the Night

Paul Reed

San Francisco is loved for its spectacular natural setting, its staggering views. But there are other parts that are best described as urban blight. These are the parts we love, especially after dark, in the night, when the fog rolls in and the chilling sea breeze sweeps the streets. The homeless bundle themselves in makeshift tents and cardboard cabins, and the citizens of fogtown burrow into their apartments with drapes closed, blinds shut.

It is a beautiful place then, when we walk these streets, cold and deserted, lit only by the syrupy orange haze of halogen streetlamps. The fog is a blanket, muting sound, chasing even rats indoors. We walk these streets then, for miles, the only sound the scratch of litter chased by nasty westerly winds, the distant moan of foghorns on the bay, and the phantom wail of sirens in some other part of town.

We are a gang of punks. We are petty criminals. We love the dark, with its dreams and its silence, its call to the imagination, its blackness a shroud for our thrilling adventures. We admire ourselves because we adore crime, we relish the utter lawlessness of it, but our moral boundaries prevent us from doing any real harm. Oh, I suppose someone could make a case that we instill fear and terror in the hearts of "innocent" witnesses and unsuspecting victims, and this could be emotionally damaging to some people. And what can we say in our defense?

We have never killed, never maimed, never so much as struck other human beings, other than the freaks and neo-Nazi skinheads who have the unfortunate fate of crossing our paths. Luckily—for them and for us—true skinheads are rare in San Francisco. The city has long been home to so much radicalism and such a hotbed of perversion that truly conservative and the right wing extremists have long since fled to outlying suburbs. And beyond. Since we never venture beyond the city—except in rare circumstances when we go to Berkeley to attend punk concerts—we have few chances of meeting these radical right wing lunatics.

Of course, we ourselves have been called lunatics for years. People see shaved heads and mohawks and colored hair and piercings and tattoos, and all they can think is that we are outlaws, lunatics. To the charge of outlaws, we plead no contest. We are the embodiment of anarchy, the guys our parents might have called hooligans, committing "foolish shenanigans."

But we are not lunatics. If anything, we serve as the saviors of humankind, the preservers of everything that is truly righteous and just. When we deface a public landmark—say, the Henry Moore sculpture in front of the symphony hall—we are making the bold statement that not everyone agrees with everyone else.

We have no use for such things.

We are Randy, Darwin, Cage, Jacky, and Christian. Randy has longish green hair. Darwin always sports a plain black mohawk. Cage's head is shaved. Jacky's is, too. And Christian, he sports a fiercely spiked red and blond mohawk, a sort of retro late-seventies look. We are all average-sized young guys—twenty, twenty-two, nineteen, twenty-four, and twenty-one respectively. That makes Jacky the oldest of the group, but you couldn't tell by looking. We all appear fairly childish, as though we might be only teenagers. This is to our advantage.

We all have very big dicks, too. Randy's is the smallest, an average six-and-a-half inches long (hard, of course) but with a nice girth to it. Darwin is bigger, about seven-and-a-half inches. Cage, at nineteen, has the second biggest dick, a good eight-and-a-half inches, thick and veiny. Jacky's dick is very beautiful, a solid seven-inch column of thick meat that stands arrow-straight and can fuck for hours without losing its erection. And lastly, but certainly not leastly, is Christian's cock, a complete, tape-measure-verified ten inches, with a circumference of seven inches. A monster dick. Beautiful.

Why such detailed comments about cock size? Why not? We enjoy each other's bodies, every night, every day. We are buttfucking, cocksucking queerpunks. We rape each other, whenever we feel like it. One of our most favorite scenes is to hold down little Cage and let Christian ram his monster cock into Cage's very young, very tight asshole. They love it, and when Christian is done, we each take our turns. This is the sex life of our family.

We are not just well hung, we are all well-tattooed. Jacky has prison tattoos, because he spent most of his adolescence in either reform schools or juvenile halls. Crude, single-needle tattoos of lightning bolts and spider webs. Christian, again, has the biggest and the greatest number of tattoos—dragons, tribals, biomechanicals. The rest of us have a sprinkling of tattoos, words like Fuck Society and Biological Hazard tattooed on our forearms, in plain view of anyone who glances our way.

You could say that crime is our foreplay. Most nights we wander the town, starting at our usual meeting place, the whitewashed wall of the cemetery at Mission Dolores. Some nights, we wander the deserted streets south of Market. It is dark and moist, foggy and windy. We stroll the empty streets, listening to the forlorn wail of foghorns in the Bay, the occasional passing car. We look westward, toward Twin Peaks, and see the lonely light of Sutro Tower blinking endlessly. We see an elderly Vietnamese woman shuffling along, en route, probably, to some semi-legal living unit within one of the brick and tin warehouses that fill the streets around Harrison and Bryant, Brannan and Division. She hears us coming up behind her, and we howl like maniacs, surrounding her and joining hands to dance a circle round her. She shrieks into the night, holds out her purse to us, supposing that we mean to rob her, that we want money.

But we want no such thing. We want only to have fun, to see the fear in her eyes, the look of a caged animal. She drops to her knees, sure that we must intend something worse than robbery, but no, we simply break the circle and run away, our retreating forms dissolving into the foggy night.

We feel exhilaration, such a rush. Our adrenaline is alerted, we have attacked but done nothing of any consequence. We wander the streets again, laughing at our memories of her screams, her offering of her handbag. It is quite possible that we are given the biggest jolt of pleasure ourselves by merely confusing our victims, for if we did not touch her, did not steal her money, did not demand any lewd acts or sexual submission, then what did we do?

Absolutely nothing, our point exactly.

We walk closer to the gay bars in the area, the Eagle and the Lone Star. Faggots are easy to frighten. They usually howl like banshees, much more noisily than any woman could ever hope to shriek. We do not understand this prissiness, this extreme sensitivity, because we, too, put cocks, mouths, and asses together for pleasure. We, too, force each other to service our sexual urgings. We, too, slap butts hard, and twist nipples meanly, and tug on ballsacs forcefully enough to take one's breath away. How are we any different from these guys dolled up in leather?

But we are different, somehow. We don't understand it, because, as we have fantasized ourselves, we long for rough treatment. For the choking gag of a long cock shoved down our throats, for the ultimate submission of being raped by throbbing pricks. Why, we wonder, do these men in leather fear us? Why don't they feel stimulated, aroused by the Everyman fantasy of gang rape?

When we reach the Eagle, it is nearly closing time, past last call. Men are leaving the bar and climbing on their motorcycles. One young guy catches our fancy—a dude kind of guy, clean shaven, longish hair, torn jeans, leather jacket, Doc Marten boots. He doesn't get on a motorcycle, he just walks away from the Eagle, along Twelfth Street, towards downtown. We pursue him, quietly, inconspicuously (we think —but then it really isn't possible for us to blend into the woodwork). By the time he reaches the next block, there isn't a soul around, and we step up our pace and come right up behind him.

He looks over his shoulder, and we see the first bit of fear in his eyes. We relish that glimmer of terror, that uncertainty, or perhaps, that certainty that we intend to involve ourselves with him, quite possibly against his will. Before he has a chance to consider his options, we're upon him, tackling him and dragging him into a sheltered alcove, away from sight. He groans a sort of plea not to hurt him, but we don't intend to hurt him, only to make a sex toy of him.

He doesn't understand this and opens his mouth to call for help. Jacky silences him by clamping his hand over the dude's lips. Darwin makes a gag from a couple of bandannas and ties it around his face. Something begins to change in the guy, we're not sure what, but he relaxes, suddenly, as if already giving himself up to us, no fight at all. For a moment we are puzzled, then pleased: he will be easy to use. We grab his wrists and wrench them behind his back. Cage rips the dude's white tank top beneath his leather jacket, while Randy unbuttons the guy's jeans and pushes them down around his ankles.

When his nipples, ass, cock, and balls feel the kiss of the chill night air, his cock stirs, thickening perceptibly, lengthening and plumping. His nipples stand erect, hard buttons on a smooth expanse of a lean, muscled chest. Christian is the first to unbutton his own jeans and let that monster dick swing free, and at the sight of it, the leather guy's dick leaps upward. We take the bandanna gag off his mouth. We force him to his knees and Christian presses his already-hard cock against the guy's lips. He opens his mouth, and, to our surprise and delight, takes the entire length of that thing down his throat. We see the Adam's apple pressed outward from within, no gagging. This disappoints Christian, because he likes to make guys choke.

Next thing, Darwin is on his knees behind the dude, fondling his butt, sticking a finger into his mouth to lubricate it with saliva, and then inserting the finger into the dude's ass. The guy thrusts his butt back towards Darwin, like a monkey in heat, presenting herself to be mounted. This one is easy to gang rape. Something about the easiness takes a little pleasure out of it all, but we press on, taking turns at both of his holes—manpussy, we call the mouth and ass of a guy— depositing loads of squirting jizz into him like he's some kind of disposable bottle.

Soon it gets a little messy, our cum running out his ass and down his legs, dribbling from the corners of his mouth. We decide to quit, buttoning up and racing away into the night. We do not look back. Later, when we talk about it, we laugh at the simplicity of it all, thinking that we are forever to be a fixture in his jackoff fantasies.

We walk home from there, to our flat on Haight and Webster. We strip naked and tumble onto three large futons, a tangle of boys, sheets, blankets, and pillows.

Imagine the sheer thrill of it all—wandering the streets, stirring up fear, arousing suspicion, pure rambunctiousness run amok. We rarely gang rape strangers. We usually save that for ourselves, amongst ourselves. But, as we have just said, occasionally we pick out an attractive rough-loving guy and make him perform for us, service us. We are all so young and energy-ridden that our dicks are half hard all the time, anyway. Satisfying them is as natural a part of the day as eating or pissing.

One night, bored and restless, we concoct a plan to abduct a straight boy from the streets south of Market, some innocent bridge-and-tunnel type, fresh in from Hayward or Concord, thinking he's really something by doing the SOMA club scene, so urban, so chic, so happening. Such boys are everywhere on weekend nights, and we want one that is straight and perhaps even a little bit scared—of the city, of sex, of fags, of leather. And of punks.

We stroll for hours, standing across the street from clubs, examining this and that possibility. Near the Paradise Lounge we spot him, a straight kid, not more than twenty-one or twenty-two years old, dorky haircut (a suburban version of a buzzcut), wearing tight jeans and a white T-shirt, and—this is what we like most—topsiders on his feet. We quickly nod in agreement and follow him. He walks down Eleventh Street, toward Slim's, where he stops and peers in the door. Then he moves on, past the DNA Lounge, and walks into the parking lot beside DNA. We nearly laugh, this is so perfect.

Following him into the lot, we are excited, and he is unaware. We can hear the music coming from the DNA, a mix of Alien Sex Fiend, Reverend Horton Heat, and the Lunachicks—

music from Club Exile. We approach him rapidly from behind, reaching out and grabbing him by both arms, propelling him into the far, very dark corner of the lot, behind parked cars, out of sight of the street. He struggles, we assure him that we intend no harm, just a bit of fun. He relaxes and fails to put up a fight. This is fine. We strip him. He is mystified, his mind clearly puzzled at the reason these punks are stripping him naked. He begins to tremble in fear, and this fills us with delight.

We are already hard. He is completely soft, but Darwin drops to his knees and takes the straight boy's dick into his mouth. The boy gasps—pleasure? fear? sudden recognition that this is not a mugging but a sexual encounter? Whatever, he can't deny the pleasure he feels, or, rather, his body can't deny it, because despite his fear and confusion, his cock instantly swells in Darwin's mouth, and his hips begin an involuntary, natural thrust. Cage drops to his knees behind the boy and applies his tongue to the boy's butt, licking and nibbling. The guy's dick leaps in pleasure.

We hold him tight, as Cage works more magic on the boy's butt, preparing him to take our dicks up his ass. He is lost in a world of pleasure, fear, confusion, anguish, and desperate uncertainty. He has feared sex with boys all his life, but he loves it. He feels he will explode in Darwin's mouth at any moment, and so Darwin, sensing the approaching orgasm, stops sucking and grabs the boy's balls and gives a squeeze. That forestalls the orgasm.

Behind the boy, Cage lubricates his enormous cock and then presses its head against the boy's butthole. The boy tenses but does not resist, not really. He simply yields to this unexpected, unknown sensation, and, judging by the firmness of his erection, he enjoys these attentions. We each take turns at his ass, fucking him deeply and thoroughly until his dick is issuing a steady stream of clear pre-seminal fluid. When the last of us has emptied our seed into him, we spit on his dick and jerk it off. It takes less than fifteen seconds to get him off, and when it is all over, he drops to his knees, spent. He has been transformed, and we swiftly put ourselves together and run away, into the cold wind of night.

Months later, we recount this tale and many more like it to the detectives. It serves to underscore the missionary zeal with which we approach such acts. We are not devoted to lives of real crime—we do not murder, maim, burn, or torture. We enable others to expand their experiences, to see new things, to explore the depths of their terror and maladjustment to this fucked-up world.

None of this makes any sense to the detectives, but what can we expect of such simple-minded folk, who see the world in black and white, who wrap themselves in mantles of forensic science, "criminal psychology," cut-and-dried domestic disputes, drunkenness, and lewd behavior? We do not fit into this traditional world of crime and punishment, of good guys versus bad guys. It makes no sense to us, who see so clearly, who examine the world in terms of experience and feeling— the exquisite world of sensation. We see the world in terms of sex, excitement, or daring and cowardice, hope and despair, and something, of course, between these qualities; that certain gray area.

We are drunk with experience, with sensation. We are the eyes and ears of Mother Earth. It is through our eyes and ears and tongues that the planet sees and hears, breathes and lives. The purpose of life, we believe, is to collect as much experience, as many sensations, as many states of mind as we can.

These detectives think we are nuts, of course. They have arrested all of us on charges of petty theft, bomb scares, rape, defacing public property, and, unfortunately, homicide. They interview us, one by one, to determine "where we are coming from," but they don't understand a word of what we say. They see us as misfits and criminals, nothing more.

But our individual tales, the stories of our lives, are of terrific interest to the court-appointed shrink, who elicits from each of us—one by one, alone—our life histories, you know, where we come from and all that. We have much to tell, the many lives we live and have lived, our vision of America, our hopes for the future. Yes, we have much to tell.

Motherfuckers
Emanuel Xavier

1989

The fiercest, most notorious graffiti artist in New York City: a puerto-rican banjee boy known to everyone as "Supreme."

A legend in the making with his "FUCK-YOU-ALL-while-sucking-on-a-lollipop" attitude: Mikey X.

They first lowered their sunglasses to clock one another while hustling at the West Side Highway piers.

Supreme: limping up and down Christopher Street with his wooden cane, spitting, crotch-grabbing, smoking big, phat blunts to impress potential clients, the whole time cruising Mikey as he sat trying to sell away his bitter youth.

Mikey: feigning boredom with Supreme's played-out machismo and casting him shade, but lighting candles at night and praying to Oshún, santería goddess of love, for just one night with him—fantasizing the touch of Supreme's milky white skin against his own tanned, olive body; secretly worshipping Supreme while having sex with ugly, old fucks.

Mother's Day

After downing two Crazy Horse forties and smoking a joint, Mikey felt more than pretentious enough to step right up, staring deeply into Supreme's blood-shot green eyes, making out with him right there at the piers—the lampposts hovering, casting carnal images over the Hudson River, sounds of lust drowned out by inane laughter and blaring house music in the background. An overly excited faggot beeps his horn as he drives by, hoping to experience a ménage à trois. LUNCH BREAK! LUNCH BREAK! Mikey sings out, making it perfectly clear that tonight they belong only to one another.

Without so much as a gesture, they end up back at Supreme's West Side crib. The loft: small, dark, seedy, the smell of piss and Pine-Sol creeping in from the bum-infested hallway. Mikey: captivated by the graffitied walls revealed by the soft white candles Supreme lights.

I'm gonna rape ya, kid! Supreme gleams, ominously, his first spoken words, half joking. Yeah?...well ya' can't rape da willin'! Mikey smirks, bites his lower lip. Supreme lunges before Mikey says another word, thrusting his wet tongue deep inside Mikey's mouth, Mikey's sweet lollipop aftertaste lingering on his saliva, Supreme pushing his stiff cock into Mikey's growing erection.

Mikey: stunned, yet excited by the violent assault, sucking in his breath as Supreme attacks his neck.

Supreme: tossing him viciously onto a bed Mikey hadn't realized lay just behind him, crushing Mikey with unexpected thrilling strength, grinding on top of Mikey, pinning him to the worn, abused mattress, Mikey letting out angry screams as Supreme chews his neck, longing to produce hickeys Mikey will remember him by for days to come.

Mikey: fighting from underneath, desperately trying to push Supreme off, Supreme's teeth tearing through capillaries and sucking until he has left his tag, pulling away to admire it.

Supreme: watching the growing excitement in Mikey's pearl-black eyes.

You bastard, Mikey curses through clenched teeth, the irony in his fiendish smile making him concubine to the quickly reddening hickey.

Supreme: lifting himself off Mikey, reaches down to pull at his oversized T-shirt, displaying a muscular chest with light, pink nipples.

Mikey: quickly running soft hands down Supreme's definition before peeling off his own tank top, a golden crucifix glistening against his chest.

Supreme: marveling at Mikey's smoothly toned nineteen-year-old body and dark brown nipples, devouring them as if expecting to procure milk, arousing in Mikey a synthesis of pleasure and pain, swelling Mikey's dick.

At that moment Mikey's beeper vibrates with urgent desperation, a trick paging to subdue an insatiable hunger. Supreme snatches it out of Mikey's pocket, tosses it across the room where it smashes against the spray-painted walls.

Supreme: seizing the moment to unzip Mikey's baggy jeans. Underneath, Looney Tunes boxer shorts wrap tightly around Mikey's smooth waist, a thin trail of pubic hair leading seductively from Mikey's belly button towards his bulging crotch, precum stains wet in the image of Marvin the Martian.

Mikey: sighing in ecstasy as Supreme frees his hardening dick from the cotton shorts and feasts on it, closing his eyes to indulge in the warmth of Supreme's mouth engulfing him while gently pulling on his balls, pushing in deeper until Supreme gags, clutching at Supreme's curly brown hair, gently maneuvering himself back towards Supreme's throat and whispering blissful whimpers.

Supreme: caressing the shaft of Mikey's dick with his tongue, pausing to lick his balls, discovering the weak spot between Mikey's legs, resting there, just above Mikey's asshole, then penetrating him with his tongue, saliva streaming down against the hairs surrounding Mikey's entrance, then pulling himself up, edging toward violence, tearing off the rest of Mikey's clothes.

Mikey: lying now completely naked, surrendering on a bed he hasn't yet explored, searching for a pillow while Supreme undresses and introduces his huge uncut dick.

Mikey: tossing the pillow aside, raising himself from the bed and falling to his knees, enchanted by Supreme's altar of a cock.

Now I know why they call ya Supreme! gleams Mikey, gazing up to see his idol smile. It's all yours *papi!* offers Supreme, the words ricocheting in Mikey's mind.

Mikey: skinning back Supreme's foreskin to expose the cock's glistening, purple-red head, licking precum dribbling from the slit, tasting it as it brushes through his lips.

Supreme: beginning to groan, watching as he disappears into Mikey's wet, hungry mouth, his dick getting bigger and fatter, until the foreskin stretches behind the circumference, Mikey relaxing his throat muscles to allow the rock-hard erection in deeper.

Mikey: pushing away to breathe in heavily, fondling his face against Supreme's thick long cock before Supreme digs his fingers into Mikey's hair, pulling Mikey's face back to the awaiting rod, gripping him by the ears, shoving his dick into Mikey's ardent mouth, thrusting until Supreme's cockhead scrapes the back of Mikey's throat, Mikey's crucifix shoved into his mouth along with Supreme's cock.

Yeah, *papi!* That feels good! moans Supreme, while fucking Mikey's face, choking Mikey again and again and again with his shaft, aroused even more by the naked golden Christ ramming in and out of Mikey's throat. Pulling out suddenly, Supreme cries, I don't wanna come yet! picks Mikey off the floor and tongues him down once more, the bitter taste of cock now in their mouths.

Supreme: throwing Mikey back onto the bed, gripping Mikey's arms and pinning him, Mikey struggling underneath him as Supreme spitefully spits into Mikey's open mouth before spreading Mikey's legs apart, ramming his dick against Mikey's butthole, sucking on Mikey's ears, his tongue penetrating deep, as Supreme imagines his cock would, then jumping off the bed and ransacking his drawers for a condom, rolling it down his extended rod, lubricating Mikey's ass, locking eyes with him before jamming deep into Mikey's asshole, feeling the tight bud of skin give way as Mikey shouts in pain, struggling helplessly to pull away from him.

Excited by Mikey's fight, Supreme grabs him by the shoulders, forcing him back down. He is halfway inside before Mikey, using the bedpost, hauls himself away, flipping over. Supreme, lunging on top of him and crushing Mikey with all his weight, mutters Come on *papi!*...ya know ya want me to...ya know ya want me ta fuck you! Sucking Mikey's ear to keep him distracted while he maneuvers his way inside, gradually forcing the resisting muscles to open, Mikey mouthing a silent scream before Supreme inserts his thumb into his mouth.

Mikey: biting the thumb without hesitation as Supreme thrusts harder, pounding in and out, his hollering muffled by Supreme's thumb as Supreme curses under his breath.

Yeah *papi,* yeah, that's it, Supreme screams, that's it. Just bite me harder...yeah...that shit feels good! Thrusting deeper, Supreme feels...hears...Mikey's guts enrapturing him, watches muscled ass cheeks palpitate under his heaving chest. Supreme disappears, re-appears repeatedly, in and out of Mikey, searing the sensitive inner linings of Mikey's ass, hints of blood staining the bedsheets, Mikey's asshole burning like crimson as Supreme pierces roughly, the magic pain intensifying, Supreme pounding, lacerating whatever internal walls Mikey's body may have supported, Mikey reaching down to grab his own dick and jerk off, distracting himself from the mounting pain, the bed, knocking knocking knocking against the hollow wall as Supreme shoves his cock in farther and farther, tearing into the core of Mikey's being, his face one endless contortion after another.

Yeah baby!...I want ta see ya come! Supreme pleads, feeling Mikey jerking off beneath him, Mikey beating himself faster, in tune with Supreme's pumping, the stridency of Supreme's thighs slapping against his ass, escalating with the fierce rhythm of their distorted grunts, Supreme plunging further into him, his cum boiling up. Oh yeah *papi!*...you're gonna make me come!...you're gonna make me come! Mikey yells. Yeah baby yeah yeah yeah, Supreme hollers as Mikey convulses beneath him, Mikey's milky white scum shooting out over the bed. Supreme roars, pulls out of Mikey, snatches off the rubber and jerks himself, shooting his own hot, sticky load across and onto Mikey's back, his cum splattering as he screams and screams before toppling on top of Mikey like a corpse.

Both of them, exhausted, struggle for air until the room stops spinning; lying barely conscious, Mikey dimly aware that the golden Jesus crucifix no longer dangles from his neck.

Consciousness returns, and with it a wicked idea to Mikey's mind, causing him to laugh spontaneously. Supreme, turning him over and staring with abandon into Mikey's decadent glistening eyes, plants a kiss on Mikey's lips, falls victim to his contagious laughter.

Mikey pulls himself up off the bed, sits on top of Supreme, and glowers devilishly. A sudden trickle of golden piss floods Supreme's sweaty chest, Supreme's face contracts into bewilderment. Happy Mother's Day, motherfucker! Mikey smiles, ever so wryly.

The Adored One
Michael Rowe

Today the ground is warm, grass brown like dry death, waiting for the yellow kiss of full spring. Lucas Sebastian watches from the sidelines, eyes squinting in the flat midwestern sunlight. He leans back against the whitewashed boards of the Williams Academy chapel and watches the others play soccer. His Nikon is loaded, and he takes the odd snapshot on the field. His team keeps him off the field this way, telling the coach that he's more useful to the school if can get some good shots of the action for the yearbook.

The truth is, he can't play soccer. He can't kick straight, he throws like my sister, *play him! play him!* the other team laughs, petitioning the coach to send Sebastian out to his death on the field. His team does their best to keep him out of harm's way. *Their* harm, not his. If he was injured on the field, it would solve a lot of problems.

He was the last picked, because nobody wanted a faggot on their team. Just hadda listen to him *talk* for chrissake. If he wasn't a fruit, he could play properly, like a regular guy. The final proof was always in the playing. So the young gods have spoken, and he is banished from the field. So he watches. And there is beauty in watching, just watching.

Muscles strain. Exertion makes taut young chests pink, shirts discarded in the unseasonable heat. Eager sweat cleaves strong pectorals. Hardening muscles flex artlessly beneath the smooth, untanned skin of the half-naked soccer players.

Sebastian sighs to himself, and scans the battle-scarred turf, shielding his eyes from the furious sunlight, and the vision of Trask. He feels his heart quicken, feels the color come hot to his cheeks.

Trask had a first name, but he was held in such awe that his last name, simple, monosyllabic, omnipotent, was all that was ever needed. Calling him anything else would be like giving God a nickname. Trask was the captain of the other team, and it gave Sebastian a private pleasure to silently cheer him on, to wish him well, to hope he caught the ball and bounced it off his forehead into Sebastian's own team's goal net, the way regular guys did.

Sebastian rarely had a need to utter Trask's name out loud. They moved in different stratospheres. But he always whispered it before he fell asleep in his dorm at night. He whispered it quietly, his face in the pillow, like a prayer, too low for his roommates to hear. Sebastian lived in terror of talking in his sleep, of revealing his secret love, his secret sin, the most fierce and private part of him. He nurtured it like a sweet cancer. He knew it was wrong. The headmaster, the Reverend Doctor Power, had told the students that God had reserved a special burning seat in hell for homosexuals. The Headmaster always said *homosexual*, never *gay* or *fag* which were the words the other guys used. To him, these words meant nothing. They could wound, and frequently did, but they bore no resemblance to anything he could feel. He loved Trask. But that was another thing altogether. Dr. Power's word sounded worse to Sebastian, like a sentence from God: sonorous, permanent, and utterly damnable.

But the Headmaster was inside, in his office, surrounded by hockey trophies and lithographs of the Risen Christ, not out here on the field in the searing sunlight watching soccer. Sebastian was as alone as he could be under the circumstances, and he watched.

Sebastian adjusted the focus on his camera, panning it across the field, following the action through the comforting detachment of the lens. He sought out Trask, pulling him into sharp relief, blurring the background. Trask effortlessly bounced the soccer ball off his forehead, neatly passing it to his co-captain. Sebastian fired the motor-drive, stopping the action. Good, good. He spun the zoom dial, trapping Trask's face inside the rectangle of the viewfinder. He wondered what it would be like to feel hands, rough from football and farm work, against his chest. Warm lips, chapped and bruising. The unfamiliar scrape of stubble against his soft cheek. Trask was slickered with sweat, and the rivulets that ran down his chest soaked the front of his white Umbro soccer shorts, grass and dirt-stained at the seat. His skin was winter-white, and his hair was the color of pale dandelions. Soaking tufts of the same gold peeked from beneath the heavily-muscled arms.

As though reading Sebastian's mind, Trask paused in mid-turn and looked directly at Sebastian. His eyes were in shadow, and Sebastian could not read their expression. He fired again, the whir of the motor-drive sounding as loud to him as a rifle shot.

Sebastian lowered the camera and stared at the ground. He felt a sudden horrible stirring below the waist as he hardened inside his track pants. He shifted his position, turning on his side, away from Trask. Terrified, Sebastian thought of girls, pretty and fresh, in order to make the hard-on go away before anyone saw him. Before Trask saw him and realized he was just a little fag after all, for real, and beneath all contempt. He rolled over on the grass. The contact between his erection and the hard ground went through him like a flashfire. He shifted again, waiting until the desire to grind his pelvis against the ground passed, praying that he wouldn't be called, made to stand up, with his stiff sex making a tent in his pants.

But he wasn't called to play. He was ignored, as usual. There would be no Sebastian side-show for his peers that afternoon: No missed goals by Sebastian the retard, no soccer balls to the face, no exclusion from the gladiatorial fraternity of the jocks. No abject, ignominious humiliations in front of Trask.

And the soccer game, of course, finally did end. Sebastian had discovered that one way of dealing with these daily rituals of degradation on the sports field was to imagine them as finite blocks of time, with beginnings and ends. Once he adapted to this thought process, he realized that although it seemed like a game would go on for all eternity when he accidentally scored on his own team, or when the ball knocked the glasses off his face, it *would* end. Eventually. Between four and five P.M., he lived his life in four blocks of fifteen minutes each. Half-time was a promise that there were only two blocks left.

At six forty-five P.M. dinner was served in the large dining hall. Sebastian sat with his group of cronies who had also managed, from their very first day at the school, to find themselves with some sort of immutable label which shrouded them like a miasma and kept them just outside the periphery of the group known as the crowd.

The crowd consisted, for the most part, of the most ordinary boys imaginable. Not bright, not stupid, not particularly accomplished athletically, but who knew all the rules to all the games and never found themselves on the soccer field in basketball shoes and brown denim pants, getting their glasses knocked off by a wayward soccer ball they were supposed to be bouncing off their heads, like regular guys.

In short, they fit. They would grow up and graduate into lives and careers of stultifying normalcy, but at least here, at the school, life left them in some sort of bovine peace. If any of them were sensitive, they hid it with stunning alacrity.

At the far end of the dining hall sat the rulers of the school. From Sebastian's perspective, watching them eat their dinner, all he could see was brawny backs, mostly clad in well-worn button down shirts, or Williams Academy athletic T-shirts exposing biceps corded with thick ropes of hard sinew. The students were allowed to wear jeans after classes, and if there was ever an outward manifestation of the school's hierarchy, it was here.

His group, the outsiders, wore jeans that never seemed to lose their dark blue color, no matter how many times they were washed. The second group, the crowd, wore jeans that faded normally, as jeans tended to do.

The third group, Trask's group, were the denizens of the far table. They wore jeans that were faded to the glorious sky-blue of truly ancient denim. The seats and crotches were bleached almost white with constant wear, and they looked like they would remain that way forever. "Mount Olympus North," as the school's fatboy, Olivier, dubbed it one night in his unfortunately shrill voice. No one liked Olivier. He was, if possible, more of an outsider than Sebastian. But Olivier was unrepentant in his criticism of the demigods of the far table. He hated them all. Sebastian, on the other hand, worshipped them, however silently.

When he thought of Trask, sauntering through the hallways with textbooks held against one lean hip, he always thought of his blue jeans, gripping the round, muscular buttocks and full crotch perfectly, not too tightly, loose in all the right places, as though they had been designed by Sebastian himself during one of his fevered dreams, the dreams he was always afraid would cause him to cry out loud in his sleep.

Once, after a soccer game in the first week of school, Sebastian had caught his first glimpse of God. He'd gone into the shower room after he thought everyone was finished. Through the billowing clouds of steam, he'd heard the subterranean polyphony of water exploding on tile. The shower room was lit with two overhead lights and they were both densely shrouded by coronas of soap-scented fog.

Through the gloom, he'd been able to make out a naked giant at the far end of the shower room, powerful arms crossed, eyes closed beneath the pounding spray. Sun-streaked blond hair soaking, hanging to his thick shoulders like a truncated lion's mane, wet skin burnished with a summer's-end lifeguard tan, it had been the first time Sebastian had seen Trask naked.

Sebastian had stood rooted in his spot near the first shower feeling thin and naked and cold. When he accidentally turned on the hot water full blast and scalded himself, jumping away from the jet and yelping, Trask had looked up and gave him a derisive smirk before turning away again and looking down, leaving Sebastian wishing the tiled floor would swallow him whole. When he'd adjusted the shower temperature, Sebastian stood awkwardly beneath the spray. And lovingly, secretly, he began to explore Trask's nude body.

When Trask briefly turned away from him to reach for the shampoo, Sebastian saw the white ghost of racing trunks against Trask's tanned back and rear. His ass was hard-muscled and marble-white, a man's ass, not a boy's, with sharp indentations delineating each cheek. Sebastian had heard one of Trask's soccer team-mates bragging that Trask had spent the summer at a football camp known for its harsh training regimen. *Linebacker*, thought Sebastian crazily, singing the exotic mantra in his mind. *Halfback, fullback, quarterback, gridiron, pigskin, touchdown, hut! hut! hut!* He imagined Trask straining out endless pushups beneath the blazing summer sun: A helmeted, padded, jock-strapped warrior.

So male. So...*other.* The vision made him reel.

Sebastian's eyes adored the soft hollow at the base of Trask's throat. They reverenced the raw strength of his chest muscles, the athlete's flatness and ridges of his abdominal muscles.

Scarcely breathing, Sebastian had dared to look further.

Between the powerful thighs, Trask's heavy cock was half-hard. Feeling the beginning of an answering response in himself, Sebastian looked away. But as he did, he caught Trask's eye.

Trask stared back, a half-smile touching his lips. He reached down with his hand and lightly caressed his half-erect penis. The gesture was at once defiant and curiously intimate. Sebastian had stared, slack jawed. Then, Trask reached up and turned off the shower. He reached for his towel and secured it around his waist as he swaggered out of the shower room without looking back. Sebastian had felt the moist air move against his bare legs as Trask swept past him.

He'd dreamed of the naked giant that night, unformed, submissive dreams of self-abasement and receptive lust, heat and wetness. He'd dreamed of Trask's hardness, his otherness. But there had been nothing further between Trask and Sebastian, which was right and proper given their relative positions in the school's constellation. Trask never looked at Sebastian again, and never spoke to him.

But today, oh today, he'd looked.

After dinner, there were chores at Williams. The Reverend Dr. Power was a firm believer in the leveling power of manual labor. At the beginning of every school year, each boy was assigned to a duty detail which, among several crews of ten boys each, was responsible for the maintenance of the school property, inside and out. Each crew was supervised by a senior. Sebastian was on the clean-up crew, supervised by Halliday. His job was mopping the front hallway.

Lost in his thoughts of Trask, dreamily mopping the floor, Sebastian missed Halliday's approach. He felt a slap to the back of his head sharp enough to bring tears to his eyes.

"Wake up, asshole!" Halliday snarled in passing. "Quit slacking! I don't want to see any streaks on the floor, Sebastian. If there are, you can expect double-duty next week. With me. And we're doing outside crew. You don't wanna do outside crew with me, Sebastian. You'll wish your mother had never had you."

Squeezing his eyes tightly, Sebastian mopped the hallway with renewed vigor, re-mopping when boys, deliberately or not, tracked mud across the wet surface. He passed the hour this way as the pain in his head subsided into a dull throbbing. There would be a bump there tomorrow. Halliday didn't put in another appearance, which Sebastian appreciated too much to find odd.

Towards the end of the hour, he heard the sound of workboots approaching behind him. He sighed, thinking only of mud on the clean floor, and wondered whether or not he was going to pass Halliday's inspection before the bell rang for study hall.

The footsteps stopped. His stomach clenched, his hands gripped the handle of the mop. Turning, he saw that it was Trask, not Halliday, who stood before him, thumbs hooked in the pockets of his jeans. Instead of relief, he felt the supplicant dread of a pilgrim on the holiest soil.

"Sebastian," said Trask warmly and softly, as though jocularity were the usual currency of their relationship. "How's it going?"

"Fine…" Sebastian stammered. The sound of Trask's voice speaking his name as though he knew who Sebastian actually was made him dizzy. He still couldn't bring himself to pronounce Trask's name.

The older boy suddenly grinned at him, and Sebastian's world went white at the edges. Trask reached out his arm and touched Sebastian lightly on the shoulder. The pain of Halliday's slap vanished from memory. He felt the heat on his shoulder even after Trask moved his hand away.

"I've got a problem I think you might be able to help me with," Trask purred.

Anything! Anything! Aloud, he said, "Okay."

"I saw you on the field this afternoon." Trask's smile widened, and Sebastian felt he might fall into it. "Get some interesting shots?"

"Yeah...I mean, yes I did," Sebastian squealed.

"Get any good ones of me?" Trask smiled languidly.

Sebastian gaped, and said, "Yeah! I mean..."

"I know," Trask said, smiling broadly. "What you meant to say was, 'Yes, Trask, I did. You're my hero.' Right? Am I right?"

This time Trask laughed, full and warm and golden.

Sebastian felt a horrible little giggle welling up in his chest, but before it could erupt and humiliate him one last, terrible time, Trask cut him off.

"I heard you were handy with cameras and photography and stuff," Trask continued. "I'm editing the yearbook this year, and I need someone to help in the darkroom. You up to it, buddy?"

Buddy.

If Trask had mistaken him for someone else, Sebastian was not going to give himself away. At the very least, his doubts about the existence of God had, by now, completely disappeared.

"Yes sir!" squeaked Sebastian. Trask laughed softly.

"*Good man*! And by the way, Sebastian? Call me Trask, not 'Sir'. Better yet," he said with a lazy smile, "call me Joe. But only when we're alone. You know how it is."

Sebastian felt an odd pressure in his chest, not comfortable but not unpleasant. He knew how it was all right, but for the first time, it didn't matter. If this miracle friendship was to be kept a secret to protect Trask's white light from being sullied, he would keep the secret. He would do anything.

"Okay...Joe," Sebastian breathed.

"Darkroom? After study hall tonight? I'll get you a pass from the Duty Master."

Trask smiled again, and turned on his heel. Sebastian watched him walk away down the hall. Trask never looked back.

Sebastian wasn't aware of Olivier coming up behind him until the mop was snatched from his hand.

"Olivier, for Christ's sake," Sebastian snapped. The last thing he wanted was the intruding presence of the school's fatboy. Olivier placed one hand on his hip, and banged the mop handle against the wall with his other hand. He was furious.

"It's my night off!" hissed Olivier, face the color of summer tomatoes. "I've been told to finish your job for you. I have to mop the fucking floor. Your job Sebastian, you fucking slacker!"

"What?"

"Halliday, dickhead," Olivier whined. "I don't know whose butt you've been kissing, but it worked. Way to treat a friend, like I don't have anything to do myself?"

We're not friends, Olivier. We're just two misfits stuck in the same place. If one of us was cool, he wouldn't piss on the other if he was on fire. You know it, I know it. And I don't need any "friends" like you. Not anymore.

But Sebastian didn't say any of this out loud.

Study hall was endless. Each tick of the wall clock was like a drop of water on his forehead. He tried to read his Dickens, but the text kept dissolving, replaced by a pastiche of images:

Trask, running. Trask, laughing, his arm flung around Sebastian's shoulders, both of them suntanned and equal. Trask, scoring a goal in soccer, saluting him like a knight to his lady.

Miracles, he thought, and sighed louder than he intended, attracting the disapproving frown of Mr. Gladd, the mathematics teacher, who had pulled study hall duty.

"For God's sake, Sebastian," he shrilled. "Stop daydreaming and get to work. Your grades in my class, for one, are appalling. Study hall is not for sighing like some lovestruck Victorian heroine."

Sebastian reddened and opened his math text. The study hall tittered. Mr. Gladd smiled primly, knowing that he had picked on a favorite school target and had therefore curried temporary favor for himself with the others. There would be no further trouble from anyone tonight. He sipped his weak tea and smoothed a hand over his sparse gray hair, content that discipline reigned.

But for Sebastian, the study hall creaked interminably forward, and when his enemy the clock finally granted him clemency from his sentence, his excitement was fever-pitched.

As the boys gathered up their books, Mr. Gladd pounded his desk with the wooden paddle he kept with him always.

"Boys!" he shrieked. "Silence! I have two announcements." The noise died to whispers.

"Schimkus and Doolan, you are to report to Dr. Power's office immediately after study hall, to deal with incomplete homework assignments and disciplinary action.

"Mr. Sebastian," he continued crisply, turning his haddock's eyes on Sebastian, "is to report to the darkroom." He clapped his hands irritably. "Please pick up your hall passes immediately."

He could barely suppress a smile at Mr. Gladd's prissy, congealed grimace when he handed him the pass, co-signed by

J. Trask, Jr. Sebastian thought he saw something glitter in Mr. Gladd's eyes as he took the pass, but he would not realize until later that it had been jealously.

The darkroom was dimly lit, the red lamp in the corner casting the unfamiliar bottles and canisters into a weird twilight of garnet-red and blue shadows. Sebastian inhaled the pungent chemical smell as he surveyed the walls. They were papered with photographs taken by the photo club, some even taken by Sebastian himself, mostly of boys playing sports. Here and there were images of churches, the school's sled dogs, boys studying. Photographs littered the floor, some of them cut off at the neck, faces among the debris, smiling tightly.

Sebastian turned when the door opened slowly behind him. Trask's face was wreathed in shadows, his powerful body backlit by the naked bulb in the hallway. *Gods don't need faces*, Sebastian thought giddily as he steadied himself against a table. He could fill in the face from memory.

The door closed. Sebastian felt a rush of heat rise to his cheeks, and he was grateful for the soothing red darkness. Trask's voice was low, and there was an unfamiliar tightness to it.

"Hey," he muttered. "Sebastian..."

Sebastian's heart began to pound, and he heard the answering blood thunder in his ears. He looked towards the door and realized that Trask had locked it. Trask saw him look, and smiled.

"You can ruin film if someone opens the door when you're developing," Trask said reasonably, advancing a step towards Sebastian. The locked door was like a caress to Sebastian, secure and comforting. He felt his erection growing in his dark blue jeans, pressing against the rough fabric of the denim. Each breath seemed individually negotiated. The pungent, chemical-laced air pressed against his hot face, thick and heavy.

"So," Sebastian stuttered. "What are…"

Trask placed both hands on the boy's shoulders. *Oh yes,* thought Sebastian, *hands rough from football, from farm work.*

"I saw you watching me, Sebastian," whispered Trask. "I know what you are. I know what you want. But you have to say it to me. Say it."

How can I say it? I don't know what to say!

"Say it, Sebastian, right now. Say it, or I'll leave!"

"I don't know what I am!" cried Sebastian. "What do you mean? What do you want me to say?"

"Fuck you, Sebastian," Trask said. He removed his hands from the boy's shoulders, and Sebastian felt cold air rush to the spot where Trask's hands had been. "Go to bed."

"Please," Sebastian whispered, reaching out. "I…want you."

Sebastian saw Trask smile then, saw all of his beautiful teeth at once. Trask reached over with his jock's ease, and flicked the light off, plunging the room into complete darkness except for the red safe-light.

He heard the rustle of cloth on skin. His wrist was grasped tightly and guided below Trask's waist. Trask's cock was hot and hard and smooth. Sebastian felt Trask's fingers wrap themselves tightly in his hair, forcing him to his knees among the snippets of discarded photographs, imprisoned memories of afternoons he could no longer see in the red darkness.

He cried for two hours, tears of shame, anger, and violation. Afterwards, he had lain in bed, unable to sleep. The night's images replayed in his brain like a flickering horror film. The pain had been excruciating, and any pleasure that had been taken had been taken by Trask. More bewildering still were the words Trask whispered hoarsely in his ear: awful, foul words, the words he had heard flung at him since he arrived at Williams. But, confused as they were in his mind with the desire which scalded him with its ferocity, the words took on a cunning new meaning.

"Is that what I am?" he whispered into his pillow. "Is it?"

When Trask had climaxed, he shoved Sebastian away from him and began to sob harshly, muffling the sound with his hands. Sebastian, sprawled on the floor, his pants around his ankles, reached out for Trask.

In spite of the burning pain that seemed, when he moved, to cut him in half, the thought of Trask suffering was more than he could stand.

On his knees, still supplicant, he murmured the only words that came to mind.

"It's okay. It's okay." He spoke the way he would have spoken to a frightened dog, or a child who had lost his mother. Mutely, he held out his hands, reaching.

And then Trask hit him in the face.

"Don't you fucking tell me that it's okay, you little faggot!" Trask sobbed furiously. His eyes, swollen and streaming, flickered to the locked door. "Who the fuck do you think you are? *You're* gonna tell *me* that it's okay? You? You're fucking *nothing! Do you know who I am?*"

"Trask..." whispered Sebastian. He felt the fire of each finger across his cheek. He felt the imprint of Trask's heavy football ring above his jawline. Tears stung his in his eyes, and he tasted copper in his mouth.

"Fucking right! *I'm Joe Trask!* Fucking *right!* You made me do this, you little cocksucker! Fucking little asshole. Loser! You're nothing! I hate you! *I hate you for making me do this!*" He grabbed the front of Sebastian's shirt and slammed him against the counter. "Get the fuck out of here you little faggot," Trask rasped. "And if you tell anybody about this, so help me Christ, I'll kill you!"

His fury seemed barely under control, and for the first time ever, Sebastian feared for his life.

Breathing in shallow hitches, he pulled up his dark blue jeans and fled the room, fled the sight of his brilliant golden soccer-god, huddled in a corner, the handsome and perfect tear-streaked face puffy and red, like a baby monster freshly born and covered with slime.

The next day, there was a little more green on the ground, and a warm wind blew white clouds from the west. The students at Williams Academy spent as much time as possible outdoors, and there was a barely-contained euphoria in the classroom. Mr. Gladd lost control of his grade eleven calculus class, paddling Schimkus and Doolan afterwards for what he called disruption. He could have paddled the sunlight instead, or looked for a culprit in the crystal blue of the sky, or the white of the clouds.

After classes, there were the compulsory sports until dinner. Sebastian had gone to the nurse, who was also the Headmaster's wife, and asked for a note to be excused from soccer. He wasn't feeling well, he said. He felt woozy.

She assessed him coldly, her lemon-sucking mouth puckering with distaste.

These nancy-boys were an embarrassment to Williams, always trying to get out of the character-building athletics her husband's school strove so hard to provide. She, for one, saw no reason to make it easier for them to shirk.

"I think you're fine, Sebastian," she snapped. "What you need is a little fresh air and sunlight."

Sebastian changed into his soccer gear and trudged out to Oxford Field. Walking was painful. The blood had stopped, but it still hurt. He didn't tell Mrs. Power. His camera dangled from its vinyl strap, banging painfully against his thigh.

Sebastian heard the pounding of cleats as Trask and Halliday came running up behind him. He flinched as Trask snaked out an arm. But Trask didn't hit him. He slowed to a jog, and clapped his arm around Sebastian's shoulders. Halliday looked, first at Sebastian, then at Trask, horrified.

"*Trask!* Are you fucking *nuts?* What are you *doing?*"

"Relax, Red," he said, punching Halliday manfully in the arm. "This is my man Sebastian."

"Your *what?*"

They were rounding the quad, and Oxford Field rolled open before them like the battlefields of Troy. Trask smiled down at Sebastian, his eyes shining like sapphires in the rosy bronze of his warrior-prince's face.

Trask tightened his grip on Sebastian, beaming heartily. No one saw the fingers dig brutally into Sebastian's arm, squeeze once, painfully, then release.

Trask jogged onto the field to a raucous cheer from his team. Sebastian rubbed his arm to take the sting away, and went to his accustomed spot by the chapel to wait. He wouldn't be called to play today, he knew it. Things would change for him at Williams. The snickering would stop, at least to his face. The catcalls would be for others now, not for Trask's anointed. No one would risk the divine wrath of the far table, and Sebastian was safe now in its shadow. He felt a flicker of pity for Olivier, the fatboy. And he felt envy.

A bargain had been struck. The protection of Trask in exchange for his silence. It would be honored by both of them, he knew.

Reflexively, he reached for his Nikon, but instead of raising it to his eye, he aimed it at Trask as though it were a gun. The motor-drive sang its sharp report. A few heads turned, but not Trask's. He watched Trask rocket across the field in a blaze of alabaster and dandelion, sweat flying like a sun shower. Dazzle, dazzle.

Sebastian shivered in the dying dirty-gold light of the afternoon and thought about the death of gods. Felt a cold like dark winter. Prayed he would be warm before summer.

Pleasingly
Matthew Rettenmund

I never let myself go, I just *went*.

Actually, if you ask *me*, I didn't really go very far, just spread out a little. I'm not "obese" or "fat" or anything, just soft around the middle, blurred around the edges. I'm... *Rubenesque*.

You learn a lot when you gain weight. Like how big a turn-off spare pounds are to your gay brethren. One week, you're right in the thick of things, cruising and flirting up a storm; the next, you don't get noticed unless you make a funny sound or ask an untoward question...like, "How's it goin'?"

Being chubby in a skinny fag's world leaves you with lots of time to look around unnoticed, to see things. Important things like what's passing for glamorous these days, what makes all the guys' heads turn. When a musclebound, shaven-headed, earringed, *faux* macho-man struts past, the other guys are so busy craning their necks for a second look that they don't even realize *you're* checking *them* out, puzzling over how something so homogenous could elicit such ravenous interest.

I may be chubby, but I haven't lost interest in sex. I've never been much of a slut, always the big talker and seldom-doer. Until last weekend, I'd only ever slept with three guys: two steady boyfriends I ended up seeing for almost two years apiece, and one one-week stand in-between them, with a snarky undergrad when I was a graduating senior and old enough to know better. The latter left me with genital warts, quite a feat considering we both wore condoms at all times. Did the fucker have them on his *tongue* or something? Sheesh.

Don't listen to anyone when they try to get you to, "*Relax*...we're having *safer* sex." Safer than what? Not having sex at all? Yeah, but still not safe, not ever one hundred percent safe. Sex is always dangerous. One way or another.

I was probably thinking about sex when I first bumped into Christopher. I *always* think about sex; I'm thinking about it right now, even as I'm trying to describe all the things that led up to the most incredible sex of my life, with Christopher, last weekend.

I had been on my building's elevator for so long I was almost convinced it was stuck. Visions of Keanu Reeves appearing at the vent overhead, pulling me to safety, evaporated when the ancient door slid open: Ground floor. Hooray.

I stepped out and made a beeline for my mailbox, hoping desperately that I'd received my copy of *Entertainment Weekly*. The weekend just isn't the weekend if I haven't devoured everything that just happened the week before. Besides, I'd heard that there was a Barbra Streisand cover story, and though I *hate* that woman (I'm sorry, but where's the *pizazz?*), there was a fifty-fifty chance for a photo of her luscious son by Elliott Gould (go figure).

Standing at my box was this guy, this big, chunky guy, trying in vain to force open my mailbox with his key. The nerve! I couldn't believe it was happening; I started to pipe up just before he glanced over at me and flashed me the pearliest grin I think I've ever seen.

"Hiya," he chirped, as nonchalantly as a person not trying to steal my mail, "How're you?"

"Okay."

He'd straightened and was facing me now, allowing the full effect to sink in. I'm not one for physical attraction; I mean, I get turned on by just about any guy, whether he's classically studly or charmingly nerdy, just so long as he's "cute." But this guy—*whoa!*—this guy was unwittingly pushing every button on my panel without even lifting a finger.

He was my height, five foot nine, give or take, and roughly my build, except maybe even a bit chubbier. That would make him about, what? two twenty? Shut up, already—we've both got broad shoulders and big bones; two twenty isn't the end of the world, even if it *is* nearing the end of the scale. He had short, dirty blond hair, a slight scruff on his round cheeks, and a Kirk Douglas puncture wound (read: dimple) in the middle of his chin. His eyes were sort of hazel, and they were looking at me with keen interest. It was like when you catch the attention of a cat—you get the feeling that no matter how hard you try, they're not gonna stop staring at you until they're good and ready.

"I'm having a hard time with my mailbox," he shrugged, "I'm new."

"You might have an easier time if you stuck the key in the right box," I said playfully, pointing first to the *6-E* on my mailbox, and then to the *6-E* printed on my key. He did a double-take, checked his key, then flushed scarlet and stammered an apology.

"It's no problem," I laughed, enjoying his cute discomfort, "Any time."

When he retrieved his mail—success!—it turned out he lived in 7-E, just a few feet above my head.

"I'm dying of embarrassment," he said, squinching up his face like a nine year old might. A great big, cuddly nine year old in a twenty-nine-year-old body.

"Really," I replied, "it could've been worse—you could've been trying to get into my apartment." We both laughed and then I took off to the store with my mail peeking out of my backpack. As I walked away from him, I had that familiar desire to be able to suck it in—not my tummy, but my love handles—for his benefit. I miss the days of feeling like I was doing someone a favor simply by turning around and walking away, gifting them with a pleasant view. But as I left the building, I turned slightly and saw that he was standing in the same place, watching me leave. Not so shabby after all, I guess, or was I just imagining things?

Later that evening, I found out.

I shopped, came home, put stuff away, and dropped. I'd been working thirteen-hour days trying to finish a mailing list at work, and now that it was over, I felt every lost hour of sleep and relaxation coming back with a vengeance. I thought I could sleep for days lying there on my folded-up futon mattress. I didn't even bother spreading it out, or changing into more appropriate clothes, I just...

...woke up with the shock of submersion. I was dripping wet, suddenly awake, and too annoyed to do more than exclaim. It was pitch black outside; I'd been asleep for hours and had only woken up because a light but persistent stream of water was drizzling on my face from the ceiling, where it was condensing in a two-foot patch.

Oh, shit. All I could think of was that the new (cute) neighbor had left his tub running and taken off for the evening. I was going to have to call the super and get him out of bed to come over, get into the apartment, and wade across the upstairs neighbor's living room to incapacitate the tub.

I dashed out of my room, out of my apartment, and up the two small flights of stairs to seven, pounding on the door to 7-E.

"Anyone there? C'mon, open up!"

To my surprise, someone did. It was the new guy, and he was wearing an enormous white robe, just like Madonna in *Truth Or Dare.*

"What's up?" he asked, warming to the intrusion.

"Water. Is. Pouring. Out. Of. My. Ceiling," I seethed, "What's the problem?"

"It is? I mean, I don't know, I have no idea..." He stepped back inside his apartment and I followed him to the bathroom, but there was nothing overflowing anywhere. It could only be a burst pipe, and that would be a major pain in the ass to fix.

"Call Juan," he said, handing me his phone, "He'll have to come right over."

Juan did, and was taking his sweet-assed time digging around in the tub and under the sink while Christopher— we'd finally exchanged names—and I sat around watching *E!* and criticizing Bianca Ferrere and Steve Kmetko. We really hit it off like that, just joking around with each other like old pals, no awkwardness at all. The whole time, Christopher was still in his diva robe, affording me a look at his hairy chest and even hairier legs. He smelled fucking terrific, too, like he'd used some amazing bath gel in the shower, or maybe it was just a killer shampoo. With his hair dripping in his eyes, he looked like young Marlon Brando, except doughier, blonder, and more approachable.

"It's fixed," Juan barked on his way out, "Don't be so rough on the pipes."

"Oh, okay," I called after him, "Next time we take a shower, we'll do it real gentle-like."

Now came the weirdness. Up until that point, Juan's presence made the evening harmless. Now, I was alone in the room with a sexy guy who was wearing only a robe and a sheepish grin. He was sitting on the couch, and I was sitting on the couch's arm, feeling like Tweetie Bird balancing on the swing in his gilded cage.

"I better go, eh?" I chattered, getting up to leave.

"No," Christopher said, taking my arm, "Stay."

I'm not lying when I tell you that this kind of shit *never happens to me,* but the next step was complete facial gridlock. He pulled me over onto his lap, holding my jaw and kissing my face like a lonely dog. When he got me on the lips, he had his tongue in my mouth before I was aware my mouth was even *open.* Just the way he pulled me over onto him made me weak with wanting it—he was so aggressive.

I ground my ass into his crotch, my knees at my chest, his arms around my torso and pulling me closer. He kissed my cheeks, licked my neck, nibbled the skin at my shoulder blades—in no time flat, I became shirtless without a care in the world that my belly would be exposed. When he reached up and manipulated one of my nipples, kissed it and flickered his tongue over the tip, I nearly lost it—not only did it make me instantly unafraid that my fleshy body wouldn't be appealing to him, it just so happens that with me, it's *all* in the nipples.

"Oh, yeah, I *love* that," I muttered, forgetting that dirty talk usually does nothing for me. This time, it wasn't contrived dirty talk; it was stuff I was saying because I couldn't *help* myself.

"Suck my tits, lick my tits." I bounced in his lap, luxuriating in the attention he paid to the most sensitive part of my body.

Christopher swirled his tongue around my nipples, ran it from tit to tit and back again, chewed them until they were so raw every touch felt like ten. He was really hard under me—I could feel his prick beating against the underside of my thigh.

I was reluctant to give up the nipple work, but there was more to be had. I stood up and unbelted my jeans, pulled them down and off. (Mental note: Use more bleach on underwear.)

Christopher sat still, expectant, smiling, and winked at me while I got completely naked. I wouldn't learn until the next day that he secretly loves to leave the underwear on, to work around it.

My next move was to open his robe. I don't know why gay guys are so afraid of a little meat on a man's bones, but if anyone could persuade them to change their ways, it's Christopher. He is a hunky, meaty man with a large gut and rounded pecs and just about the most beautiful cock I've ever seen. It wasn't porno-huge—they never are, are they?—but just perfectly fat and artistically veiny, and it was leaking pre-cum like my ceiling leaks pipewater.

Condoms.

He had some, thank God, because who knows what I'd have done without them. Sandwich bags? Or just asking lots of sexual history questions and taking the gamble? I pulled a tight one on him and another on myself. He was admiring my dick, too, stroking it so firmly I had to ask him to lay off— seeing his sexy body all naked and glistening, not to mention the most loving pec job of all time, had me ready to squint and spritz.

I went down on him in one big gulp, wishing that instead of mint, they made condoms taste like dick, with a hint of pre-cum. But rubbing my lips over the shape of his dick was exciting enough for now, at least until we could make a trip to get tested. And the feeling was mutual: Christopher just lay there in awe, mouth agape, eyes closed.

I got a major rise out of him when I licked and suckled his nuts—the most sensitive part of *his* body—and a loud roar when I nipped my way from the tip of his cock to the underside of his scrotum. When I lifted one of his legs, he almost stopped me, thinking I'd suck his asshole. Now would I do that? In a flash, actually, but under the circumstances, I was going to settle for faking it.

I buried my face in his ass, licking his crack and teasing his perineum with my tongue. He smelled great, very musky despite the scent of Ivory soap everywhere. I love the smell of a man's ass, and under safer circumstances, I love, love, *love* to tongue a big man's asshole, make him cry like a baby with so much nasty pleasure. I rolled my face in the crack of his ass, hoping to absorb that scent on my cheeks to smell later, when the lovemaking inevitably had ended.

He pulled me back up to kiss me, dropping his hands to my ass, which he squeezed mercilessly. He bunched my cheeks up in his fists and worked them back and forth, with and against each other, my asshole burning from the friction. I hadn't been fucked in a year, and hadn't ever wanted to get fucked as badly as I wanted it right then. He worked his forefingers toward one another until they massaged my butthole from opposite angles and slipped into me up to the first knuckles.

"Aw, *fuck,*" I gasped, wiggling on his fingertips. "I gotta get fucked, man, I have to have it tonight...."

He shushed me, "I know, I know...I'll do it, I'll do it to you good and hard like this asshole," (rubbing the rim of my hole furiously) "needs to be fucked." I hadn't showered, wasn't clean like Christopher—I could smell my sweaty butt and balls, getting all riled up with his touching.

I rubbed his condomed cock with ForPlay, unable to resist jerking it tightly enough to constitute the beginnings of a handjob. He looked like he would've settled for that quick relief, but I couldn't let that happen so I stopped, applied more lube to my butt, and positioned myself over his erection, squatting over it there on the couch. I was preparing to lower myself onto him, but he beat me to the punch. He'd loosened me enough that when he shoved his fat cock upwards at my asshole, it sank halfway in, no problem at all.

"Oh, mother*fuck!*" I called out, seeing stars and losing control. He started pumping up and into me while I held onto the back of the sofa, just squatted there and let him nail me from below. He held my love handles, pinching them hard enough to burn, while he thrust his hips up, fucking me frantically. Toward the end, he was leaping almost off the cushions to get me as deep as he could, and I felt it, baby, I *felt* it.

"I'm gonna..." I stood up on the couch, his prick slipping out of my ass and into his immediately jerking fist. I shot cum onto the bricks of the wall, working my meat with my left hand until I didn't think I would ever come again. By the time I'd collapsed into his lap, he'd spilled all over the coffee table (here's hoping he'd already read that poor issue of *Out*) and was losing his boner, half asleep and satisfied.

"That was so great," I murmured. He agreed, hugging me gently and whispering things I couldn't make out. I looked him in the eye and he looked back, rubbing my belly with one hand, holding me in place—close to him—with the other. I knew then—and I'll let you know if I'm right when the time comes—that I was gonna be with Christopher for a long time. I think he could tell I was thinking that, because he smacked my butt affectionately and kissed my nose.

"Chubby," he whispered to me sweetly.

And then we split a pizza.

Clothes Do Make the Man
Lawrence Schimel

George's apartment was a nightmare scene of half-dressed fags. George designed porn CD-ROMs for a living, but this wasn't a shoot for his latest title. In one of the previous jobs on his long and checkered résumé he'd been a mannequin designer. When the mannequin company had folded, George had been left with more than a hundred wigs in his possession, and while he'd lost or given away many of them over the years, he still had more than sixty left. Every year, a gaggle of fags would show up on his doorstep on Wigstock morning begging to borrow a wig and be made up. Now, ten gay boys had descended upon his apartment like a plague of locusts before the harvest.

I've always found partially-clothed men to be extremely sexy. A man in a vest with no shirt on underneath will inadvertently give you a flash of nipple every now and then, and soon you find yourself waiting for it, watching for it, because it's so unexpected when the drape of fabric suddenly falls back to reveal that pert brown circle. Or your lover will walk unabashedly about your apartment in silk boxers, and your eyes fall to his fly as it gapes and yawns and flashes the dark hair beneath and (what you're really hungering for) a glimpse of cock, momentary, like a flashbulb on a camera. And like that brilliant light, it lingers on your vision even after it's faded away.

And there's something about men who are partially dressed in women's clothing (especially butch men like the Chelsea gym queens now before me) that's even more attractive, because it accentuates their masculinity. For instance, Bernie (short for Bernardo) was one of those deceptive Italian studs: all muscle and meat on the outside, but such a soft and nelly voice, seemingly so out of character with the rest of him. But right now he had his mouth closed as he puckered his lip-sticked lips and, shirtless, postured in front of the full-body mirror on the closet door in a pair of silver elbow-length gloves. He put his hands on his hips and pouted into the mirror, trying on different expressions.

I marveled at the intense musculature of his back, the way his shoulders and biceps faded into those slender-seeming gloves, the way his top-heavy torso faded into his Calvin Klein boxer-briefs, which poked out from beneath his practically non-existent cut-offs. He had a firm, round ass, and his legs were undeniably male: thick columns of muscle. I imagined them wrapping around me and squeezing me tightly, until I was unable to move, pinned by their strength and bulk.

Bernie caught my eye in the mirror and said, "Honey, you're going to need to tuck that thing." He stepped aside and I got a look at myself in the mirror and blushed. I was wearing an orange and yellow dress that looked like it had once been the wallpaper on Continental Airlines back in the seventies, and I had an erection tenting it out in front of me.

I strutted forward, wobbling a bit in my heels (in part for effect and in part because I didn't really know how to walk properly yet), until I stood right behind him. I rubbed my crotch against his ass. "You want me to tuck it in here, did you say?"

I got whistles and hoots of laughter from the other boys, who'd paused in their own preparations to pay attention to this latest mini-drama. Or maybe they'd all stopped to check out my basket. I stepped beside Bernie and stared at myself next to him. How could I properly cruise any of these boys when they couldn't see what my body really looked like? My best friend (who was to be called Royal Flush today) and I had arrived at George's before any of them, and my make-up had been well under way by the time anyone else had arrived. I was done up to look like Agnes Moorhead as Endora from Bewitched, with bright orange lipstick and thickly-applied blue and purple eyeshadow. George had done wonders, but that was always the case. He had a sense of style that could create art—or camp—out of anything or anyone.

I wore chunky plastic rings in various loud colors that matched or accentuated the dress, and plastic yellow bangles. I wrapped a string of yellow pearls around my neck like a choker. My wig was sitting on a mannequin head atop the television: Elizabeth Taylor big hair, same color as my own so I didn't need to worry about the back of my own hair showing through at the bottom of the wig in a little dovetail. All I had left to do were my nails, in a garish orange glitter I'd found for a buck fifty that morning at the corner drug store.

George's latest CD-ROM was playing on the computer behind me, and everyone was ragging him because of the dialogue and the script and the performers he'd cast. Eric sat at the keyboard, controlling the action. "This one's balls look deformed, George, couldn't you have found someone who looks more normal?"

"His cock is big and that's all that matters in these things."

"That's right, it's only when you've got a little dick that you need to have a perfect body and face."

I couldn't keep track of who was talking, but it didn't really matter, the overall effect was more important. George and I were friends, but I had just met the rest of the boys, except of course for Royal Flush, who'd talked me into going in drag, and also Jordan, who was the boyfriend of one of George's friends and had been the boyfriend of someone I'd known at college. There were a few boys I'd been able to pin names to, but I had quickly forgotten most of them as soon as I was introduced. Half of them seemed to know each other already, although I couldn't tell if they were friends or just remembered each other from George's apartment last Wigstock. I saw at least two of them exchange phone numbers, and there was a fair amount of cruising going on, especially as guys took off certain articles of clothing to struggle into dresses.

I had my eye set on a boy named Nathan since the moment he walked in. Right now, he was just sitting on the couch, watching it all happen around him, and there was something about the demure way he sat that really turned me on. That semi-overwhelmed look made him seem so wholesome, like a Midwestern tourist on his first visit to New York, and in some way it made him seem young, even though he was probably three or four years older than I was, maybe twenty-eight, twenty-nine. Which was a bit young for how I usually liked my men, when I wanted a relationship, but just fine for some hot and sweaty guiltless sex.

Nathan was wearing a very slutty clubbing shirt, very East Village, an all-white sequin crop-top with a wide collar and a zipper down to his navel, but all very much a boy's cut. He wasn't planning on wearing a dress today, just a wig. Half the boys, it turned out, were just doing demi-drag, although they were having fun trying on various dresses while they were getting ready, and using it as an excuse to strut their stuff for each other. Nathan had found a little blond bob, like Marilyn Monroe in Some Like It Hot, which suited him quite well.

I didn't know him, and I didn't know the couple he'd come with, but as an excuse to start talking with him I took the bottle of orange nail polish that worked so fabulously with my equally-garish dress, sat down next to him on the couch and stared into his eyes while I asked him, fluttering my mascaraed eyelashes and trying to sound forced-innocent as I held the bottle out to him, if he would do me.

He gave me the once over, unmistakably undressing me in his mind, having caught the obvious double-entendre. I felt even more turned on than I usually did when I was being checked out, because I knew he was able to see the male me beneath the dress. And also because I knew my body was different because of the drag: I'd shaved. Chest, legs, armpits, all smooth flesh. Soon I'd have stubble all over my body, coarse and prickly, rubbing against the inside of my clothes, rubbing against other flesh. I tried to imagine how it would feel to run a tongue across my stubbly chest and nipples. This decision I'd made—to do drag for Wigstock with my friend—was going to be with me for many weeks.

My friend Miss Flush was a swimmer, and had even taken a medal at the Gay Games. I remembered the stories she'd told me (her makeup was done and she had her wig on, so her gender had changed when we talked about her, mine too, since I was also done except for the nails and wig) about shaving down before the meets, how everyone was checking each other out, how it was all intensely erotic, male flesh everywhere bulging out of tiny Speedos. The scene here was like that, with everything serving to remind you that underneath the makeup and the wigs, underneath the shaved chests and armpits and legs, these bodies were still male .

I'd never done drag before, except once during my freshman year in high school when I'd had to play Juliet in a skit we performed at a pep rally. As the youngest member of the track team, I was given the most humiliating part, and because I had that lanky young boy runner's frame I looked much more femme than any of the women, who were all rather square-shouldered and thick-calved from running with the team and working out for years.

"Sure," Nathan said, and took the bottle of polish from me.

The phone rang. George picked it up and said, "Salon."

I looked over my shoulder to watch the computer screen for a moment. They were picking strippers, and a not-especially attractive skinhead with a big dick was beating himself off on the black leather couch that Nathan and I were sitting on. I tried to imagine this apartment as the set of a porn shoot. One way to cut costs.

"Look at this," Eric was saying, "the leather guy just said he was twenty-five in the sound byte, but his statistics say he's twenty-nine."

"Can't we watch the guppie sequence again?" Bernie begged.

"Look at how long his nails are," Peter exclaimed, as the action moved in for a close-up of him fisting his meat just before the cum shot.

I looked down at my own nails. Nathan was working on my third one, painting with even strokes from the moons towards the tips. I couldn't help glancing down past our cluster of fingers into his crotch, so near at hand, as it were, and looking oh-so-inviting.

"Flo has such lovely long fingers," Nathan said, lifting my hand for a moment to show everyone his handiwork, then replacing my hand on his knee. "I bet they'd feel great wrapped around a cock."

He didn't look up as he said this, but continued to paint the next nail. It was the same sort of machismo semi-porn talk everyone had been making all afternoon, so I didn't really think he meant for me to act on it. It was all bravado. But I wanted to take him up on it so badly, and I wondered what he'd do if I called his bluff. He was flirting with me, I knew, which felt great since I was not sure how I looked right then. I'm not usually much of an exhibitionist, but then, I wasn't usually wearing a dress; maybe there was something about already being so far out there, in terms of my appearance, that made me bolder than I normally would be.

"That can be easily arranged," I said, and with my free hand I unzipped his jeans. My fingers snaked into his fly and worked their way across his underwear, groping along his cock and balls. I could feel him begin to stiffen through the fabric under my touch. He was wearing some sort of white briefs, and I tugged at the elastic waistband to free his cock. I pulled it through the fly of his jeans, as it continued to swell within my hand, and began working my way up and down the shaft.

Around us, everyone was going about their business as usual. The phone rang and George answered it. "Futura Bold."

Simon declared, "Looks like we've lost two queens before we've even started." But once they'd gotten a look at Nathan's prick they went back to their own preparations.

Except for Bernie.

Bernie was digging about in the cardboard box of wigs and a moment later came striding over to us with a long blond braid that was meant as an extension. "I always knew you were a bottle job," Bernie told Nathan, as he wrapped the extension around Nathan's cock and balls, tying it off with a flourish and a bow. "There, now," he said, "crotch wig slash cock ring," and turned on his heels away from us.

I was still pumping up and down on Nathan's cock as he painted a second coat on the nails of my left hand. His strokes were no longer even, but he was trying.

"So, how do they feel?" I asked him, squeezing as I brought my hand down toward his balls.

"Good," he said, his voice cracking a little, unexpectedly, as his breath caught.

I smiled. "Good. Now, blow on these until they dry," I said, holding my hand in front of his face as if I wanted him to kiss it, "while I blow on this."

I slid off the couch and with my free hand pulled my dress under me as I crouched between his knees. He gripped my left wrist with both his hands, and his stiff cock jerked in anticipation. I wanted it down my throat, but I was going to tease him until his balls ached. I leaned forward and kissed the head, all lip, leaving an orange lipstick crown.

The phone rang and George answered it. "Helvetica Black." At the same time, the doorbell rang.

My heart began to pound as I realized I was having sex in front of mostly total strangers. With a total stranger, for that matter, although that didn't bother me. Not knowing the onlookers, however, especially not knowing who had just come in or how they would react, did disturb me. Sure, most of the guys weren't watching us all the time, and they weren't watching us with the intention of getting off from watching us, but they certainly looked over at us from time to time, curious, if nothing else. I wondered what they were thinking. They hadn't exactly voiced their acceptance of our sex, but they hadn't withheld their consent either. The newcomers hadn't had a chance to withhold their consent. As my face hovered in front of Nathan's eagerly twitching cock, I wondered what to do, how they would respond. A zillion other hangups and concerns held me frozen with indecision.

Then I remembered that I was a bitchy, irreverent drag queen. None of these queens would recognize me out of drag, anyway. I opened my mouth. My tongue met the warm, dry flesh of Nathan's cock and eagerly began bathing it in saliva, wetting it down for my now-orange lips to glide smoothly along the shaft. With my right hand, I grabbed the base of his cock and pulled it toward me, positioning it. My lips sunk lower, toward the blond braid that Bernie had tied on. I rocked back and forth on my high heels, his cock sliding into and out of my mouth with the motion.

My own cock throbbed insistently beneath my dress. With my right hand (I was afraid the nails of my left weren't dry) I reached beneath the folds of fabric to grab hold of it, poking out from my loose boxer shorts. I began to jerk off, thrusting into my palm each time I rocked forward onto Nathan's cock.

My knees began to ache, and I stood up. They felt like I'd been doing squats at the gym for two solid hours. "Now, don't you move," I told Nathan. He twitched his cock. "Well, you can move that," I conceded.

I reached beside him on the couch for my clutch purse and opened it. I pulled out a condom. "A girl's got to be pre-pared," I said, and tore it open with my teeth.

Before I had a chance to roll it over Nathan's cock, how-ever, Nathan had lifted up the skirt of my dress and tugged down my boxer shorts. He pulled me toward him, and his mouth closed around my dick as he eagerly shoved himself onto me.

"I told you not to move," I complained, although I didn't mean a word of it: I wanted him to move and keep moving, his mouth sliding up and down along my dick. His pointed tongue probed into the loose folds of my ballsac. My entire shaft was in his mouth. His tongue swirled around the crown when he'd pulled back.

The couple who had come in when the doorbell rang—a towheaded blond and his dark-skinned Brazilian-looking lover—were staring at us, curious and unbelieving and semi-uncomfortable at such blatant sexuality. They looked away when they noticed I'd seen them watching. I didn't care, let them watch. Not that they could see anything, anyway. My skirt had dropped over Nathan's head, so all they could see was the bobbing orange fabric. All I could see was bobbing orange fabric, too, but damned if it didn't feel fine.

Nathan pulled off my cock for air, and lay back against the couch as he caught his breath. One hand still held his own cock, which he'd been tugging on as he sucked me off. His dick was bright red, swollen from his desire and the crotch wig slash cock ring. I delicately stepped out of my boxer shorts, which I realized were foolish things to be wearing when I knew I'd have to be in drag and would need to "tuck." The unrolled condom in my hand had begun to go dry, but I had a small bottle of lube in my clutch purse. "A girl's got to be prepared," I said again, as I knelt down in front of Nathan with the lube in one hand and the condom in the other.

I greased his dick and rolled the condom onto it. "Hold this," I said, and lifted my skirt. Nathan held the edge of the fabric for me, and I lubed my ass quickly, slicking my hole down for easy, painless access. I squirted some more lube onto his condomed cock for good measure, and then straddled him. He was still holding my skirt up, as if he were a voyeur peeking at my genitals. That turned me on. Slowly, I lowered myself onto him, positioning his cock with my hands.

It is always a curious feeling, I think, to have a man's cock inside your body. No matter how much I want it, my body still resists, at least a little bit, something to overcome. I wrestled with myself—I wanted this cock inside me now—and tried to relax. He was in, but something still was not right. I shifted, I adjusted, I breathed deeply. His cock felt good in there, I felt good. I flexed my legs, lifting myself off him slightly, and then slid back down. I was in control. Nathan lay on the couch as I fucked myself on his cock, holding my skirt up so he could watch what was happening, the inches of his cock disappearing up my ass.

I felt I was getting near to coming so I settled onto him and stopped for a moment, resting, delaying the moment of orgasm to draw out this delicious feeling of sex for as long as possible. We didn't move, but we changed roles. He took charge. I unzipped his sequined crop-top. His stomach beneath was pale, with a small thatch of hair on his chest. The sides of the shirt fell back as his body shifted on the couch, thrusting his cock up into me. I tweaked his now-exposed nipples, but soon abandoned them to lift my dress. Again, I felt a delicious exhibitionistic thrill as I held the skirt of my dress aloft. It felt so dirty, like I was flashing him, and I think that feeling turned me on even more than the mere fact of our flesh sliding together.

I was bouncing up and down on his cock, holding the dress away from my cock, which flopped rhythmically against his abs. And then my cock spasmed and I was coming, orgasm rolling through my entire body in quick shudders. Four of them, then a long sigh.

My cum shined on Nathan's chest like melted white sequins. His cock was still inside me, and once I caught my breath he continued to thrust up into me. I leaned forward and rolled his nipples between my fingers again, urging him on toward climax. Suddenly I tugged on them, hard. Nathan cried out and began to come. I clenched my ass, holding tightly onto him as his cock squirmed within me, shooting his cum into the condom's reservoir tip.

When he lay still, pleasantly spent from his orgasm, I grabbed my purse, which lay beside him on the couch. His cock was still comfortably inside me, and began to go soft. I took out my lipstick and, using the mirror in my compact, began to touch up my make up. When I was satisfied, I leaned forward and left a perfect lipstick mark above his right nipple.

Nathan smiled dreamily, and started to sit up, to disentangle his body from mine, where we were still joined together under my skirt. I pushed him back down on the couch. "Where do you think you're going?" I asked him, and handed him the bottle of orange glitter polish. "You've still got to take care of my other hand."

Social Relations
Scott O'Hara

Fuck. Pull out. Beat it to get it hard again. Re-insert. Fuck. This time, after a minute or two, it slips out on its own. Beat it. Re-insert. Fuck. This time the director calls a halt. "Let's do some dialogue and reaction shots," he says, wearily. "Then we can get back to this after you've had a rest."

Believe me, the process of shooting a pornflick is nothing like the product.

Tommy and I were actually hitting it off rather well: he was an enthusiastic bottom, and I was in a relatively toppish mood, so my dick had twice managed to achieve that upcurved-banana look that is so riveting to viewers. Nice. Fact is, I think they'd already gotten plenty of useable footage, but directors always want extra to play with. My first director told me they liked to work with a three-to-one ratio—three minutes shot for every one used in the video. Mind you, I've seen some of his subsequent videos that looked like they were one-to-one, but I understand about ideals not always being the same as results. And hey, I'm a performer. ("Talent," they try to call us, a term that makes me shudder.) I know how difficult it can be to get useable footage.

So Tommy and I got to relax awhile; when we spontaneously started playing with each other's tits, the director knew it was time to get back to shooting. And this time, for some reason, I was really into it, I guess, because it felt like we'd initiated the sex ourselves instead of being directed; and my dick got really super-hard, and I managed to plow him from every angle for about twenty minutes before the director finally asked his cameraman, "How much tape do we have left?" A good director always asks that before he tells the performers to give him a cumshot. And there was plenty of tape, so he nodded to us, and we both started working up to shoot our loads. Tommy, as I said, was enthusiastic: he was one of the few bottoms I know who really stayed rockhard during the whole fuck. Didn't have to beat off or anything. Fact is, he should've been a top. So I rolled him over on his back, bent over and went down on him: directors always like that number, and it turns me on, too. And he went wild and started bucking up and down, fucking himself on my dick and fucking my mouth, and within about thirty seconds he started moaning that he was gonna shoot, and at the appropriate moment I pulled off and let him spray all over his stomach, while I was ramming against his prostate. And then a few seconds later I pulled out and mixed my load with his. Perfect double-cumshot.

And then, while we were still in position, it was time for reaction shots—all those "oh, fuck, yeahs" and "aw, shit, I'm gonna come's!" and grunts and groans and moans and facial contortions, while I'm pretending that my dick is still hard and that I'm still fucking him. And then finally, five minutes later, we could move. I just slumped down on top of Tommy and kissed him, real deep. He didn't seem to mind in the least. Far too many of my co-stars, once the work is over, just want to get into the shower and get outta there. Tommy seemed to share my love of the work. I think he was really just doing it because it ensured a steady supply of big dicks up his ass. I can understand the feeling, even though I don't share his obsession with size.

So we lay there smooching, and got comfortable on the dingy old ripped mattress (we were supposed to be in a back alley somewhere, and there were trash cans on both sides of us), while the techies took down the lights and reflectors and other equipment, moving it all into the next room for another set-up; and we talked. He asked me, curiously enough, about my family.

"They're Mormons. Nothing much more to say about them. Haven't seen them in years. Lots of brothers and sisters, teeming hordes of nephews and nieces. When I told them I was doing porn, Mom told me I was going to hell. And yours?"

"Oh, about as opposite as you can get. My mom collects all my videos. Dad died when I was a kid, Mom got a great life-insurance settlement and decided to spend the rest of her life having fun. I swear, every time I go home, she's got a new young stud hanging around the house. Nowadays, some of them are younger than me. She writes, too. Romance novels."

This rang a bell, somehow. "Where did you grow up?" He looked at me funny.

"Southern Illinois. Why?"

"Like, in Cairo, by any chance?" And I pronounced it right: Kay-ro.

"Yeah…"

"I think you lived just a couple blocks from me. You were two years younger, we never saw each other at school, but I remember my mother spewing fire and brimstone about that terrible loose woman down the street, how she ought to have her child taken away from her, all that noise. I guess she never succeeded."

The light was dawning in his face. "I remember you now! And I remember one summer at the city pool, when you and I were the last ones out of the shower, and you..."

I'd been hoping he'd forgotten that particular episode; I found it a little embarrassing, in retrospect. But he obviously didn't; he described it in excruciating, and lascivious, detail. Hey, we were—what, maybe nine and eleven? I'd just shot my first load of cum a few months before, and I was eager to show my new-found talent to anyone who I was sure wouldn't tell my parents. And Tommy (I don't think I even knew his name, but I'd seen him around, knew where he lived), given his background, seemed like a good candidate. To my surprise, however, he proved to be way ahead of me. "I always wondered why you never wanted to play with me again, after that." There was a slightly vulnerable, childlike look on his face, now; I guess I'd penetrated one of his earliest insecurities.

"And I, well, I guess I felt guilty about 'seducing' a kid as young as you. I thought about you a lot. But then, you know, we moved West the next summer."

"Yeah, I know." Tommy was looking at me with a semi-worshipful gaze, which then turned thoughtful. "Did you ever do anything with Buddy?" Buddy was my younger brother, Tommy's age in fact, and when I was growing up he was just a pest to me; I never much thought about him even having a cock and balls until suddenly, on one of my visits home during my college years, I saw him come out of the shower—I shared his bedroom on these visits. And he was...well, stunning. I didn't put the make on him or anything, I didn't have that sort of self-confidence, and he was a butch bruiser who could easily have decked me by that time, but I did spend the rest of the visit watching him pretty closely. And that was the visit, right at the end, when I came out to my family. They weren't thrilled. They didn't quite kick me out of the house, but that night they suggested that Buddy go sleep over with one of his friends, and he seemed quite eager to leave. I left early the next morning, and haven't been back since. I'd like to see what Buddy's developed into—he's the only one of my siblings still unmarried, so he probably hasn't developed a potbelly yet— but I don't feel like braving the fires of hell just to find out. I assume he's away at college somewhere—he was always an intellectual sort—but I don't know where.

I told all this to Tommy. A smile hit his lips. "You know, I played with him. The same summer you and I met in the showers. We used to meet out behind those sheds, down by the river, and beat off together. And he's the one who taught me how to suck cock." Now he was grinning broadly, perhaps at the open look of shock on my face. "Of course, I don't know if he turned out queer, but he sure liked playing with my dick."

Suddenly I realized that I was humping my quickly stiffening dick against Tommy's thigh. A wave of lust surged through me. I kissed him, hard, sucking his tongue into my mouth, and he responded with a moan deep in his throat. I pulled back. "So, get down there and suck his big brother's dick, cocksucker," I growled in his face, and pushed his head down.

Tommy was, without a doubt, the most eager cocksucker I'd ever met. He didn't poke around, licking and kissing and teasing. He dove for the whole banana, taking it right down his throat. Even when, as was the case right now, the dick was too hard to bend down his throat, he still forced it right down there. I suspected he might have sprained it, but at the moment I didn't care. I just started fucking his throat, holding onto the back of his head and slamming it home. Suddenly I wasn't exhausted any more. You'd never think that I'd shot a load just half an hour previously. Imagining him down on his knees, doing this to Buddy—when he and Buddy were just nine years old, yet!—had really awakened something in me that I'd effectively suppressed for years, and suddenly I wanted to plant a load where my younger brother's had gone. (Had he been able to shoot yet, I wondered?)

Tommy forestalled me. After a couple of minutes of serious cock-diving, when he was wheezing and gasping and his eyes were running with tears, he pulled off and looked up at me with a half-wild, half-mean expression on his face. Guess I'd aroused something in him, too. "You know, I didn't just suck Buddy off," he said, in a knowing way, his voice suddenly huskier, deeper. (Was it so obvious what I was fantasizing? I guess it was.) "I fucked him, too. We had a blanket that we'd spread out on the riverbank, and he'd lie down on his stomach and stick his ass up in the air," and Tommy was stroking my upstanding dick while he was relating this, and with his other hand he was rubbing my asshole, which suddenly, unexplainably, felt empty, "and I'd lick his asshole until he begged me to put my dick inside him. I bet I shot about fifty loads of cum up his ass that summer. Sometimes I'd shoot twice without stopping."

I moaned. Yes, he'd hit a mental spot as sensitive as any prostate. Almost without thinking about it, almost without volition, my body heaved itself over, and I was on my stomach; and quick as a flash, Tommy was behind me, with his tongue slathering spit all over my butthole.

Now, being rimmed has never been one of my biggest turn-ons. It's enjoyable, but it doesn't send me into the stratosphere, the way it does with some people. But I wasn't myself any longer: I was my little brother Buddy, that hunky teenager I'd watched for a week as he changed and took showers, until I almost couldn't stand it any longer. I was that boy, and I'd never felt anything so incredible as this tongue squirming its way up my ass.

In what seemed like no time at all, my asshole was spasming and opening so that Tommy's tongue was going in with virtually no resistance; that was when he scooted forward and slipped his dick in. And there wasn't any pain, just the sensation of a space having been finally filled, the other half of the puzzle supplied, the whole joined. The smooth slide of one slippery, spit-covered mucous membrane against another. I swear, I could feel his dick against my heart. And he didn't fuck, right away: he just lay there, moving in and out a little bit, holding me while I shook with sudden, wracking sobs.

After a few minutes of that, my ass started reacting of its own volition. It began humping up against Tommy, trying to take every millimeter of him, right down to the pubic bone. That's when his sadistic streak started coming out. He pulled out to the point where just the head was inside my ass, and kept it there. No matter how frantically I pushed back, I couldn't get any more of him inside. Then, about every ten seconds, when I was clawing the mattress and crying in frustration, he'd slam it balls-deep and grind it for a few moments, flattening me to the mattress, and then pull out again. God, he knew how to make me crazy. And then, while he had me pinned to the mattress, he leaned down next to my ear and whispered, throatily, "This is the way I used to make Buddy crazy," and slammed it in with that extra-hard hip-twist that rocketed my prostate right into heaven and made my cum start spilling out all over the mattress, even though my dick wasn't even all the way hard. "And this"—shove —"is the way"—shove—"I shot my cum up Buddy's butt"—and I could feel his cum-tube pulsing, and he grabbed me in a ferocious bear hug, and for once in my life I was very glad there wasn't a director leaning over us telling us where to shoot our loads, because from a cinematic viewpoint, we'd clearly fucked up big-time. No cumloads visible. But oh, I liked where we'd left them. I swear I could feel his load swirling around in my guts, practically percolating: all those spermatozoa beating frantically against the walls of my asshole, trying to find someplace fertile.

And we lay there contentedly for another ten minutes (we could still hear the sounds of the next scene being shot in the next room over), kissing and stroking each other and breathing hard; as our heart rates slowly returned to normal, Tommy eventually rolled off me, and I scooted down so I could suckle on his dick. There's nothing like, for me, the act of sucking on a dick that's just come out of my ass: sucking the remnants of a cumload out of it, cleaning my own shit off it (What does my shit actually taste like? Although I've sucked dozens of dicks after they've come out of my ass, I still couldn't say), letting him know that I really worship his dick, that I appreciate the pleasure it's just given me. And Tommy was looking down at me with a curious mixture of pride and wonder; and I guess I could have predicted what he said next. "You know, that's exactly what Buddy used to do after I'd shot a load up his butt. Do you suppose these things run in families?"

"No, not really," I mumbled around my mouthful of dick. "I just think I know my brother well enough that I knew, subconsciously, just what he'd like. That's what relations are. People you know better than you want to."

Griffith Park Elegy
Al Lujan

If this story were a pile of bones, I would fracture them, pulverize them and scatter them across beautiful landscapes like the ashes of so many beautiful lovers. So intense and horrific was that afternoon that all I could really do is romanticize it, when all I should really do is let it go and not repeat what took place. Or what I believe took place. It disorients me.

I was in Griffith Park, in the heart of the City of Angels. Hanging out in a section referred to as the "meat market" where men young and old, rich and poor, gay and not gay, follow their instincts and their hard dicks like divining rods, through a series of dirt paths that wind, in and out, through the heavy brush. Most paths twist back onto each other or branch out into small clearings where men pose, pout and hold up the trees till coaxed into the moaning bushes. They circle through the maze in search of the Minotaur, sometimes finding him in the rustling plants. Other times what they find instead is an undercover cop busting them for obviousness.

That afternoon I marched to the topmost clearing with intent. Without distraction. It's the second highest lookout in the park. It faces west across a field of dense, brown haze that blankets the basin, except for the shaggy heads of the sixty-foot palm trees that poke through here and there. That area ain't too popular with the guys, although the bushes to the left and the bushes to the right are particularly squirrely. Wide open areas make these guys uncomfortable. Some would probably go into an agoraphobic coma were they caught without a bush to scurry about in.

The vista is accessible by a dirt road that connects from the east side. Park police off-road vehicles frequently tour the area, shooting pebbles into the foliage with those knobby tires they use to hug the hillsides. Scares the hell out of those bush queens with sex-offender histories. But not enough for them to actually leave. The vista is visible from the observatory on an adjacent peak. If you put a quarter into the binoculars and aim in the right direction...welcome to Los Angeles.

Me? Well, I'm an exhibitionist. I love the great wide, white sky, the fires of dusk and the risk of getting caught, as much as I love my fond memories of blood, mean teachers and the fist fights I've won.

I planted myself on one of the C-curved benches put here some forty or fifty years ago when this area was some hetero lover's lane or tourist lookout before the observatory was built. Benches of wood and concrete, unpainted since the seventies, carved with symbols and initials. (T.D.+S.G.'63, EL HUERO CON LA PEE WEE CON SAFOS Y QUE, and I SUCK DICK 4 P.M. to 6 P.M. M thru F).

I sat at the foremost bench facing out. A bench where winos died drunk and lovers fell together entangled in arms, scarves and hair. A bench with a personality like mine. Quiet. Private. With a secret history in this part of town. There I sat with my legs spread and a look that said, "I've got less important things to do, only the serious need apply."

My olive and black Pendleton was folded across the knee of my pants, pressed with origami-tight creases. Just like my T-shirt. Just like my boxers. I resisted dressing this way growing up in East L.A. Dressing like my brother, Flaco, and his *pachuco* homeboys from our block. They hung out in our garage since I can remember. Pants slung low, lowrider posters, *Calle Diesiocho* along with every members' *placa* on the walls. A weight bench, beer cans and KRLA on a radio connected to a car battery. The smell of weed, sweat and anarchy in the barrio.

Now, my *cholo*-without-a-gang look worked me an angle on that hill. Unapproachable, rough trade, mean-dicked, risky challenge. The bold motherfuckers who cruised me knew they'd either be getting to blow a sadistic, gang-bangin', drive-by Richard Ramirez *maniaco* or just be getting punked. Only the biggest freaks would conjure the nerve. The kind I could do anything to and who'd do anything I said. Like a Dockers-wearing CPA type who gave my shoes a real spit shine. A nervous, fey princess with fluffy hair whose hairbrush I broke smacking it across his bare butt. Or a tweak freak who tells me that I don't need to use a rubber with him. Yeah, right.

Every once in a while I hook up with a man who turns the tables. But that Sunday afternoon was particularly quiet. I could hear birds and winged bugs nearby. The sounds of slurping and grunting, down the hill, were more than audible, they seemed amplified and exaggerated, like porno. I felt horny and impatient. I'd been up there for over two hours and no one made it up. Not even an obscured "pssssst" beckoned me for a blowjob in the bushes.

The sun was sinking into the grimy distance and I felt February on my face and hands. The salmon-colored streetlights that pacify the barrios and the ghettos were coming on in sheets across the horizon. I hit my flask to pacify the chills that were making my body jerk. I reconciled a fruitless afternoon of meditation. I stood and put my Pendleton on. Buttoned only the top button like a true *vato loco*. I turned to the path behind me to head for home. Home to call fuck buddies who would come to me, although that was not exactly what I was in the mood for when I planned that afternoon.

I looked back once more. Goose bumps covered my arms. The blood in my body felt cold and thin. A man was seated at the opposite end of the bench I'd just left. My heart was racing, for a couple of reasons. I thought about my options and said, "What the fuck?" I sat back down. The warmth that my body had left on the bench had dissipated. It was cold on the backs of my legs. In fact, the temperature had fallen considerably in the last couple of minutes.

We sat under the elongated shadow of an olive tree some twenty-five feet away. The fronds of the palm trees, just ahead, swayed and rustled in gusts of wind that I could not feel. The winds picked up clouds of dust from the paths leading down, obscuring them.

The impending dusk gave the stranger a dark, menacing feel. He sat quietly, staring ahead at the swirling, cherry-vanilla clouds that were changing shapes as fast as they were changing color. His profile was still and sharp like stone carving. His dark hair was pulled back into a tight braid down his back. He wore charcoal-colored Dickies with knife-like creases and a white T-shirt that was luminescent against his brown Aztec skin. A stray *cholo* on the hill. My lucky day.

He sat next to me, staring ahead; I dared him with my eyes. He had tattoos on his forearms, hands and neck. Blue-black letters and symbols. A portrait of some ruca and a spider web on his left elbow that, in prison, signifies that he killed a man while doing time. At the edge of his eye, a black indelible teardrop. This man was trouble and he was unraveling my upholstery. He was the number thirteen, black cats, burning crosses, bad luck personified. He had the quiet disposition of a seductive cult leader. He oozed: run and don't look back. But I couldn't. I wanted him.

My mother would sometimes tell me, "*Mijo,* el diablo is exactly who you want him to be. If you recognize him you must be in trouble with *Diosito.*" Then and there I finally understood what she was talking about. That evil ain't just some white dude with a goatee and a tail. One could see that and run. Evil is in every nationality, in every religion, and every sexuality.

It was too late. This seduced fair Catholic wanted to capture that tattooed dirt-under-the-nails hard-drinking boyfriend-smacking welfare-check-stealing lying cheating *demonio.* I pressed my thigh against his. He didn't move his away. Well, that's all the encouragement I needed. His smell drove my hand. I reached over to feel his thigh. Without turning, he intercepted it and held it in his fist. I tried to pull back but he held tight. For the first time he turned to look at me and that's when I freaked out. His eyes were black and shiny. I don't just mean that he had dark eyes, I mean they were solid black and cold. His face showed no emotion. He was silent. My heart was absent in my chest. He pulled at my hand still in his grip. I resisted and then yielded. He leaned into me, I imagined, to tell me never to go where I'm not invited. He led my hand to his face and released it onto his smooth cheek. He pressed his hand onto mine and guided it across his cold lips. Now, I've made some fucked-up choices in my life. Gone against my better judgment plenty of times. But the fact that I resisted withdrawing my hand scared the hell out of me. He led my trembling hand to the back of his neck. With his free hand he did the same to me and pulled me into him as if to kiss me. That surprised me because prison trade never, never kiss on the mouth.

I tried to look away from those crazy eyes, at the darkening sky, but his strength had us face to face. He held my head and put his mouth on mine. His, our mouths suddenly warmed to fire-like temperatures. I was drunk with lust and horror. Euphoria tinged with a residue of uneasiness. The kind of uneasiness that makes most men impotent.

My ears were suddenly filled with high-volume moaning, sighing and gulps for air. The sounds our bodies make when excesses of pleasure and pain push language past mere words. Terrible, beautiful, animalistic music.

That's what my ears heard. Within his violent kisses I felt his voice. Smooth and deep like silk boxers that give me erections as I walk. And that's exactly what his voice was doing to me. He wasn't necessarily saying anything. I can't recall specific words. But events in my life were being narrated by our twisting tongues. He knew things about me. Things I've never told anyone.

He knew that I sat at my father's bedside for three days as he rotted with cancer, and that just before he started that gasp for air that signaled the end, my father's last words to me were: "You disappointed me."

He knew that it was me who burned a swastika on the side of an old dead tree by my house with a butane torch I stole from school when I was ten. (I wasn't being anti-Semitic. I didn't understand what it meant. I had a crush on the only white guy at my school, and he had it on his pee chee folder. I wanted him to notice me.)

He knew the terror I felt later that night as the sky exploded in amber when the tree that smoldered quietly all day ignited.

He knew the shame I felt as a child when we would have to sleep on the floor during certain holidays so we wouldn't be struck by random bullets coming from intoxicated, hot guns and how I prayed for God to make me an angel before dawn so that I could fly myself out of that barrio for good.

He knew that I reached around and felt my sharp shoulder blades protruding and that that's all that they were. That I was simply a child testing the existence of God.

He knew that my lover, reeling with AIDS dementia, forgot that he was gay, that I was his lover, or even who I was, which allowed his family, with their high-priced lawyers, to lock me out of our home. And that after a while I just couldn't fight them anymore. He died without me.

He knew these things about me. These profane ordeals in my life. And I still wanted him. My shirt was drenched with sweat that turned icy in that night that turned black while my eyes were closed. I pulled away unable to catch my breath. I tried to stand, to flee. I felt light-headed. The blood that supplies my brain with oxygen was pulsing in my lips and groin. He steadied me and pulled me back onto his lap. Before I could scream, I heard the ripping of the seam of my pants. He impaled me onto what felt like a knife, cold and hard like his lips started out, but soon it seared me inside. He sat there, motionless, with me on top kicking and flailing. No thrusting, no sounds, no more words.

With his mouth he punctured and gnawed on the back of my neck. I felt my spinal cord being sucked out of my neck and out of my ass. I prayed that the wetness that soaked my pants was my piss and not my blood mixed with his cum. He squeezed my torso to the point where things went black. Then a bright electric jolt shot through me with such force that my fingernails and nose shot blood into the dirt.

"Goddamn...that felt good." Did I say that or did he?

I awoke sitting erect on that bench, my head thrown skyward. The sounds of sirens all around me. Intense hot breath enveloped my aching body. The violent suns that illuminated the black fog were in reality a series of palm trees engulfed in balls of flames. They surrounded me on all sides. Black ash snowed upon me and all I could do was sit there and cry.

All that I have left are burn scars, bad dreams and three cranberry-colored, crescent-shaped hickeys on the back of my neck that won't go away no matter how hard I scrub. If you'd like me to show them to you, put on your hiking boots, bring your faith, and meet me at the park some sacred Sunday afternoon.

Six Positions

Andy Quan

I'm making love to the oldest man I've ever been with. His hair is white as Egyptian silk, his skin is translucent, blue and pink. I can see his heart beating from excitement. I am drawing an arrow down with my tongue, shoulder to opposite hip, a ribbon of saliva like a banner from a beauty pageant. This one says, "This man has tasted and been tasted by men for decades." Blood ricochets around his body and builds at his surprising erection. The wrinkles on his face, arms, hands, so loose, a multitude of scrotums all over his body, which I take into my mouth like dinosaur eggs, rare plums, a tulip's head unopened. With veneration, I lift, squeeze softly, hear a gasp like an ocean caught in shells. It is the last ocean. It is wet. The tide recedes like sadness.

I'm making love to the fattest man I've ever been with. His anus cannot be found amidst the mounds of flesh, but his mouth, pink, red, puckering, surrounded by two round cheeks, has a passing resemblance. He laughs a great thrusting belly laugh for the whole time we grapple, him turning and flopping, me dodging the weight whirling all around for my own safety. Every part of my body is a phallus, my fingers, hands, arms, legs, head. I press these into skin that says, yes! and takes me in, out, in, out, sweating, sliding, surrounded by warmth, by darkness. Somewhere in this maze I find a cock that is fat and round like a root vegetable. I punch at it, grasp it with my hungry hands, hear a voice as if outside of a room or all around, of god, of a pregnant mother, *huh huh huh*. The sticky fat flood smells of appetite.

I'm making love to the most exotic man I've ever been with. He has eyes like jungle animals. Tigers, wildebeests, possums, crocodiles, sloths, night owls. His skin turns color depending on the angle of light: dark as petroleum, as the center of your skull, then yellow as the eyes of those jungle animals. As slight as a bamboo reed, then a tight round muscularity on fire with bound-up strength. Then two-breasted and big-cocked and more pictures, pretty pictures, so many I'm almost blind and I fuck him I fuck him I fuck him until I am covered in the fluids of my own exertion, thigh muscles, stomach, arms, still tensed, energy hanging on me still. Shivering, and when the thought returns to my head, I understand him not a bit more.

I'm making love to the thinnest man I've ever been with. He is so thin and long that he is sharp. I bleed with pleasure. He presses his fingers down on me and leaves a lovely symmetrical arc, five small half-moon-shaped pricks. The air on my skin, and my cuts, feels spiny like a cactus, a tall spindly one with a downy white veil of spikes. Like pins and needles, when a part of your body has fallen asleep, and you have to shake and shake to get the blood back in. I am in a desert of sensation, so quiet that every grain of sand is noticeable. But I do not notice as he clothes himself head to foot in rubber and enters me from behind. I don't know if it's his penis, his arm, his leg, his whole body. I just remember he's thin. It's suddenly an Arizona night and the stars are twinkling in time with an orgasm soon to arrive. Sensation pours through the star-holes, the rest is black. Each time I exhale, one of the stars goes out.

I'm making love to the smallest man I've ever been with. Small is beautiful. He has attached his mouth to my cock, his legs dangling down. I feel *enormous*, I am enormous in comparison. He leaps and lands on my tit, and bounces on my nipple as if it were a trampoline, does cartwheels and somersaults up my stomach, around my neck. My touch on him is crude but large; he rubs into it like a cat, then returns to my crotch where he gives special attention to each square millimeter. When he finishes the last, I explode. I worry I've drowned him, but he shakes himself off in a triumphant dance, slides down my leg and disappears.

I'm making love to myself. Really. With elasticity and extra parts, I am seeing what all the others have seen before me, I am tasting my nipples, which come alive and harden, punctuation marks in the air all around me. My voice, *oh oh oh*—periods. *Uh uh uh*—commas. *Awuhaaahh*—question mark. Gasping hyphens, sighing slants, I grunt out underlines. I am writing myself onto my page as my cock extends long, so long, I'm entered. I'm thrusting into myself. I have ten hands. I have eight tongues. A line between my balls and thigh. The slit in my throbbing head. A dimple where chest meets abdominals. All fingered. All stroked. All tongued. The skin of the page curves into its wet stain. Words run into each other.

Tricktych
Pansy Bradshaw

1.
"what i really want..."

out cruising...i meet up with this man...he is...maybe...
fifteen or twenty years my senior...well past six feet...military
coif...shaved on the sides...short on top...salt and pepper...
his rugged face bears a five o'clock shadow at two a.m....
there's a paratrooper's tattoo on his left biceps...a pack of
smokes rolled up in the sleeve of his t-shirt...narrow at the
hips...broad at the shoulders...he looks like an illustration by
blade...he's a major buck...i've seen him around...

he releases smoke from his lungs and suggests his
place...cool i say...we walk silently the approximate ten
blocks down market...then into the tenderloin...four flights
up sour dimly lit stairs...along a dingy corridor...he shoves
me against the wall...his tongue probes my mouth...i
recognize the flavor...cigarettes and too much beer...

he lights a smoke...flicking the still-lit match to the floor...i want to yell fire...and run screaming from the building...but i do not...he blows smoke into my face...through the haze i see my father...staring back...as an afterthought he turns and unlocks a door...

as i follow...a line from an old song wafts...through my mind...where you lead i will follow anywhere that you tell me to...

a freakshow light cast by a street lamp outside the only window...fills the room...the space is small...chaotic...with a mattress on the floor...filthy sheets thrown everywhere...there's a dresser...drawers partly open...with clothing appearing to explode from within...a single open door reveals the toilet...i think he smells like his room...he sprawls...fully clothed...on the mattress...

take yer clothes off he says...his voice is loud...though he is not shouting...what i really want is to suck his dick okay...but he has other plans...obviously...

i pull off my boots...taking time with the complicated laces...setting them aside...i unbuckle my belt...unzip my jeans...standing first on one foot...then the other...i remove my pants along with my shorts...stop he says...he stands...towering over me...i feel...on display...lift yer arms he grunts...i do this...even while wondering...might he have some ill...purpose...in mind...for me...

he's got another cigarette...dangling...dangerously...from the corner of his mouth...will he burn me...will my friends and co-workers read about me in the papers...how my badly decomposed body was discovered...in an abandoned tender-loin rat-trap...will my brother be able to...identify...my mutilated remains...

he blows smoke on me...and then with surprising gentle-ness...lifts my t-shirt off me...i lower my arms...but he takes my wrists in each of his hands and raises them again...placing his mouth first against one armpit...then the other...he kisses and tongues them...he is making sounds which i can only...imagine...as animal-like...i respond with my best... guttural vocals...

his lips are on mine now...we kiss each other hard...i bite his upper lip...he stands back from me...takes a deep drag off his smoke...flicks the butt out the window...as he exhales...he punches me in the gut...

i drop to my knees...i cannot breathe...fuck you he grunts...he slaps my head with the back of his hand...i'm trying to breathe...he kneels in front of me...grabs my face with both hands...puts his mouth on mine...blows air in...and releases...i exhale violently...still trying hard to breathe on my own...he lets go of me...calmly lighting another smoke...inhaling deeply...he grabs my face again...he exhales smoke into my mouth...forcing it into my lungs...i black out...

when i come to...he is lying next to me...naked...i wonder if i have been...used...while unconscious...but i sense no...violation...back there...you okay he asks...gazing at me with something bordering on...indifference...i manage a meek...yeah...my stomach is sore...roll over he tells me... when i do...he straddles me...and begins to stroke my back...his hands are large and rough...they move over my flesh with a familiar deftness...i know him somehow...yet...i do not...every so often...he slaps me...hard...deliberately...and it burns...

he climbs off me...and the mattress...and walks into the toilet...i can see his backside...i see his balls hanging through his legs...will he let me at them...or what...he's pissing up a storm...i am jealous of the porcelain bowl...he strolls back to the mattress...kneels at my head...look at this he says...his cock and balls are in my face...the odor of smoke and shit...emanates from his crotch...i breathe in this divine essence...the skin over his dickhead is pulled back...just enough...to see the slit...glistening...in the room's bizarre light...open up he orders...i do...and he places his cock in my mouth...

he tastes like piss...cheese...and someone else's ass...he pushes it in more...he slides the foreskin back...and i gather the full benefit...of his natural treasures...i close my eyes and suck...he fucks my mouth steadily...taking his time...every so often pulling out completely...he whispers...come on boy...clean daddy's cock...or...lick me faggot...i wonder to myself...can it get any better than this...

he pulls back from me...and crawls around between my legs...his hands are on my ass now...each hand envelopes one cheek...he spreads me apart...slowly...thoughtfully...i can feel the rush of his breath against my butthole...then his tongue...causing me to shudder...i want to ask him if he can touch his nose...with his tongue...but i do not...it's rough...wet...he continues to probe my hole...he shoves his face in for more...i push back so he can...have at it...

he stops now...to readjust...he spreads my legs further apart...grabs my hips...and with one swift motion...lifts me...into a kneeling position...with my face still...prostrate... in his filthy mattress...i wonder...am i facing mecca...he speaks softly now...almost a whisper...tell me what you want...tell daddy what you really want...

2.
"afternoon on the hill..."

all in all...it had been a dull morning...so up the hill i went...with a full load in my pocket...sunny...with a cool breeze...it's so different in daylight...first of all...you can see...and what i was seeing...wasn't pretty...i must admit to a little apprehension...as a frequent visitor to the hill...at night...i mean...like...what kind of...holes...was i sticking my dick in...when i couldn't see nearly so well...as in broad daylight...oh what a dude will do to get his nut...

just shy of the peak...there is this shelter...of low-hanging trees...with horizontal trunks...and a sandy floor...covered with the remnants...of past tawdry moments...i parked my ass against a tree...and whipped out my...thang...when it's soft it doesn't look like much...and it takes me some time to...get it up...it amuses me to pull on it...i just love to...spit and pull...until it gets wicked hard...right there in broad daylight...with the air...and sun...touching me...it's hard to keep from...blasting off...if you know what i mean...

i noticed some guy...crouching...in the bushes...just past the entrance to my...special...place...he was wearing glamour sunglasses...for fashion's sake...reminding me...a bit...of jackie onassis...i was not in the mood for calling up the...

memory of any of the...dead kennedys...of course if it had been...john john...that would be different...i decided to ignore him...he split...only to be...replaced immediately...by another man...

this one was like...a construction worker...he crouched...just like jackie o...an impersonator i thought... even though he looked...the type...work boots...jeans and t-shirt...with a black baseball cap...for effect...all of him seemed...respectfully...dirty...the visor of the cap...pulled down so low...i could hardly see his eyes...

i shook my piece pretty hard...causing my precum to...whip through the air...like a serpent about to strike...its heavy liquid...leaving an...s...shape...in the sand at my feet...

well...he got down and...crawled...through the brush... towards me...up close...he smelled of funk and dirt...my favorite cologne...his eyes...blue...his skin...deeply tanned... from working outdoors i guess...though it might have been...salon induced...goddamn that's a big fuckin' piece of meat you got there...he says grinning...i just stare at him...i let go of my cock...just so he could...catch a look...at the big picture...he grabbed it...giving me a couple of good pulls...then...unbuckling his belt...and unbuttoning his jeans...he unleashed...a fucking whopper...i mean...fuck... okay...i had not expected that...and all the while...he kept talking to me...about my own...big manmeat...and shit like that...but my eyes had seen the glory...so i leaned toward him...so close...my lips...could feel the heat off his body...and i whispered in his ear...can i suck your dick man...he looked at me kind of surprised...then he said...yeah buddy...go for it.

so i pushed my pants down...around my ankles...and knelt...as shakespeare said...before the god of my idolatry...i yanked his pants down too...i opened my mouth wide...and swallowed hard...i gave him deepthroat but good...burying my face in his sweaty pubes...pulling my mouth off of him... to lick his balls...he tasted just like sex...

he slapped me with it...smearing...that juice...all over my face...its force of impact made me whirl...using his thumbs... he opened my mouth...further...his cock...flapping about... as if it had a life all its own...he pushed the fingers...of one hand...into my mouth saying...suck 'em...and believe me...i sucked...while he slapped me...with his free hand...tears streamed down my face...i was sure i would gag...but he knew this...warning...don't you dare fucker...withdrawing his fingers...and sliding that...mean ol' pecker of his...down the...abyss of my throat...

i swallowed...as fast as he would feed me...looking up into his eyes...i could see...he knew...exactly...what i needed...so he gave it to me...he spit right in my face...i went down more...willingly...after that...his cock swelled up...he grabbed my ears and...fucked my mouth...the way his pelvis pounded my face was...like a punch...i was beginning to feel dazed...when he suddenly pulled out and shouted...fuck fuckfuckfuckfuck...aiming that nasty...thing...at me...and shooting sperm...all over me...

i was still...pulling on my own...piece...while he was beginning to relax...after being wracked by orgasm...i felt like saint theresa...treated to a...vision...of almighty ecstasy...while the urge welled up in my balls...he let go a stream of hot piss all over me...and that did it...i tried to...catch...as much as i could...while it splashed on my face...poured down my neck chest and stomach...drenching me...i blew my wad in the crotch of his jeans...

later...walking down haight street...even the street punks say...i smell like piss...when i catch...my reflection...in a shop window...i see...i look like shit too...

3.
"chainsaw fuck..."

recently...i took a big risk...i let a stud from hell...fuck me gently...with a chainsaw...and no condom...you can imagine my thrill...feeling the icy hot metal...rip into my... flesh...blood and feces flying in every direction...my last words to my trick...before he set the saw in motion...fuck the lube...i want to feel this sucker inside me...at first i thought the risk was mine alone...but as i watched an arc of blood...from a badly severed artery...squirt him in the eye...too bad he didn't have goggles on...well...it was then i wished i had a safety monitor to tap one of us on the shoulder and say...excuse me...but i really care about you...and i think you're taking too great a risk here...the thought was rather touching...as last thoughts often are...it was at that point...the saw made contact with bone...causing the chain to slip off track...backfiring...is that the right word for what those chains do...when they whip off...and slice up the dude holding onto the handle for dear life...whatever...i thought... as he bled to death before my eyes...too bad i won't find another guy like this one...

I Wonder if My Great Great Toltec Grandmother Was Ever a *National Geographic* Centerfold

Jorge Ignacio Cortiñas

Most days I sell weed in the park and from the spot I claim right by the footbridge I see them before they see me, walking up the grassy hill and staring at their feet. They won't look up till I mutter, Mota. Then I wait and see how they act.

They do shit that lets me know. They try and look under the bill of my cap, they smile when I hand them the weed, they say Adios or some shit like that and then stick around, like it takes 'em longer to walk away. If they want to give me stuff right away, a ride or a bag of speed, then I know for sure. That's the type of white man who will pay if I let him put his mouth on me. If there's nobody right by me and if I feel like it, I say, Aiight, or Sounds good, and the guy will drive me someplace, someplace of his.

He'll kneel before me. He'll open his mouth to me, close his eyes and bathe my scrotum with his tongue. This is what he pays me for. He'll take me into his mouth, he'll swallow me whole, he'll drink my sperm and believe that he knows me, believe that he can taste soil on the tip of my penis. When I come, his eyes well up with sorrow, his hungry mouth like a little baby when they got no teeth. I stare down at the bald spot on his head, at his big eye expression. Afterward, my body feels spent and raw, his tasteless saliva shrinking as it dries on my skin.

Taking money from these men is easy. They all hold it out in the beginning, hoping I'll put it away real quick in my back pocket, three twenty-dollar bills, all facing the same way. Like all three Andrew Jacksons agree. I never say thank you. That's for them to say into the silence of my poker face, a face I make look like I'm thinking of something else. They always say something. They want to. Some of them say Thank you, softly. Some of them say it loudly, like they're trying to convince you of something. Either way it's the same. When I leave their house I walk out the door and don't look back. I don't say nothing. My backside is taunt enough.

I always bathe afterwards, and change my socks and underwear, even if it's only eleven A.M., the day is just starting and I got no place to be. I never return their phone calls. Sometimes I listen to them, but I don't say I have. Then I call them out of the blue, tell them to be ready in fifteen minutes, have a bottle of Añejo and the money ready, cash, up front.

It's harder to get them to buy me things. That takes time. Maybe I drop a hint. Most times they'll ask if they can help, like, Is there something they can get me, something I need. I'm careful not to smile when I think about the full-length Fila bubble jacket stuffed with goose down that is way above the counter at FootLocker, behind two employees dressed like referees and under the watchful eye of the security guard, where brown and black hands cannot reach it.

Like I tell this man to drive me out of my neighborhood, past my corner, where I might run into one of my crew. Keep driving, into the next neighborhood, where I just barely know people's names, but know enough to keep a low profile and not fly my colors. Drive, past mom and pop stores that sell canvas Carthartt jackets and polyester Ben Davis, to the FootLocker, all windows and polished metal. When he gets me there I make a beeline for the jacket, wait for the man to catch up to me, and then point with my chin and say only my size. Large.

He doesn't know I was there two days before. Considering my options. Trying the jackets on.Asking if they thought the inventory would hold out till first thing Sunday, when I can come back with this man and his stack of credit cards that he holds out like shiny glass beads.

I walk him back to his car but don't get in. On the sidewalk mothers with small children push past. He looks up with eyes that say he was expecting to at least suck me off. I tell him I have to get to work. I lie because it's best to leave them dangling with their desire pent up and twisting, so that they begin calling over and over, ready to spend. I lie because I will always put myself in charge, show him and myself that it's me calling the shots, not him, the green he's got, or his appetite for men with a full head of hair. I lie because I know the kind of man he wants me to be, like men at home in a language he does not speak, men who care enough to shave, brown men who might cry when they're drunk and might even let you touch them while they close their eyes and think of someone else, in another country. I walk home, thinking I'm leaving this white man only the view of the black Fila jacket he paid for, but through the heavy polyester and the pressed cotton shirt underneath, I feel the stare of his mouth slide up and down my spine.

I wonder how far I can drag his gaze with me, when I come up to this Norteño on the corner who also stares at me, hard. In another neighborhood, at another hour, the stare of this rival guëy might mean something else, the way he locks onto my pupils, doesn't let go, holds me up to the streetlight and shakes out my pockets to see if I'm afraid. But high noon on

Sunday, flanked by his homies, his eyes are a dare, mad-dogging me, asking why my jacket even looks blue, on his corner, and do I wanna start something.

The Norteño stands his ground, makes me take a step around him and when he exhales a slow, 'Sup, I look straight ahead, and nod. As I pass him, my eyes rotate to the side and I just barely catch sight of his features, my height and looking like some kind of king in his red forty-niners jacket, round Olmec face set in gangsta stone. I want to brush up against him. I want to think of something to whisper in his ear. But I only pick up my pace, because in the sunlight our eyes never meet.

Cocksucker's Tango
Justin Chin

1. Queen

The Cock of Last Resort. I am in an alleyway, a basement let-in, the leather blindfold firmly in place, gripping my eyes until I can feel the moist condensation of sweat between the fragrant leather and my short-sighted eyes. The puffy eye pads press into my eyeballs so tightly that I see green and purple spots as if I were on acid watching a Grateful Dead lightshow, but there are no unwashed hippies here, no skanky flower-children that never grew up nor teenage converts to the nostalgia trip, just the sound of shoes and boots scuffling around me, flies unzipping, the smack of cocks in hand, the ale smell of crotches and unwashed pubes, the occasional grunt and cough, the sticky smack of semi-dried lubricated cocks against flesh.

The Cock of No Contest. There are those who will grab your head and there are those who will grab your ears like a teapot handle. There are those who will hold your shoulders and those who will try to reach down and pinch your nipples. There are those who you will feel nothing but their cocks in you as they are busy pinching their own nipples as hard as they can. Then there are those who have absolutely no idea what to do with their hands.

The Cock of Dreams. Cocks fill my mouth, caress my tongue, poke blindly at my lips, slap against my cheeks, one by one they drip their load into my face, in my hair, dribbling down my chin, down my throat, on my lips, on my tongue and I take it in like so many deep breaths, the last gasp of a drowning dog. The very first time I had a cock in my mouth, I gagged so hard, I vomited so much I scared myself. The man I was sucking fled the toilet stall. At that moment I decided that I would never gag again, no matter how large or mean or deep the next cock got. I practiced with fat marker-pens, broom handles, shampoo bottles, beer bottles, carrots, cucumbers. I practiced on the dog to make sure that I could tolerate even the most disgusting cock. I practiced hard and, like musicians training for the symphony, I got good.

The Cock of Wine & Roses. Once I was falling so fast that I woke up in a pool of piss. Once I was falling and when I woke I was falling and when I got up, I was still falling. There is a Chinese boy who I meet with sometimes, our relationship is wholly undefined, he is not a hustler, at least not in my eyes, but someone I pay. But that is a different story altogether. We agree on a number and it is his job to get me that number of loads. We use dice for this, sometimes one die, sometimes two. He blindfolds me and puts my wrists and ankles in shackles and ties me to my bed, he puts a gag in my mouth, he saves his load for the last one of the session. In the meantime, he gets on the phone and calls phone-sex lines and party-room conferences, he gets on the computer bulletin boards and invites anyone to come and feed me. He takes pictures of the men who come through to feed me. I know, I can hear the click and whirls of the Polaroid camera, I can see the flash through the edges of the blindfold. After the session, after he empties his cock into my mouth, he unshackles me and holds me while I cry like a whipped child. He whispers into my ear, describing the men who I have eaten from. He never shows me the pictures, though, in my imagination, I like to think that he masturbates to them in private, maybe he sells them to other people, saying, look, here's a picture of a pig, a real pig, (oink oink) do what you want to do to him, here's his address.

The Cock of Understanding. When did you learn how to suck cock? The artist Louise Nevelson was once asked how she created her art, and she replied in her croaky Bette Davis voice, "Honey, how do you eat a peach?" Sucking cock is nothing like eating peaches. It is nothing like sucking, even as the prominent verb/continuous tense of its namesake suggests. Suck: to draw into the mouth by inhaling; to draw from in this manner; to draw in by or as if by suction; to suckle. In my youth, terrified by the crudeness and suggestiveness of language, we called it "eating ice cream." But it is nothing like eating ice cream at all. It is nothing like breathing, it is nothing like art. It is its own act, its own tense, transitive verb, noun, dangling pronoun. It is its own universe, not made of atoms but of stories, so many stories you wish you were deaf.

The Cock of Love. Once, I considered pulling all my teeth out. I had met a man who promised me nothing but load after load of jism from his beautiful cock and I had partook of it enough to believe him, it was his suggestion. The gumjob, the selling point of men who have gotten so decrepit that that's the best they can offer on phone-sex lines, sight unseen, all that's known is a mouth, void of teeth, just a fleshy wet slobber to face-fuck and a voice that cries, *Please.* I chickened out at the last minute. More likely, I couldn't make the sacrifice of having a wound in my face, unable to suck cock for weeks while I healed. Sucking cock has nothing to do with monogamy, I recalled telling myself and I got on my knees in the backroom of another bar and I never ever saw that man again. It is no loss. Not yet.

The Cock of First Offense. There are two kinds of hell. One is an icy world where sinners are lodged in a lake of ice, their heads two-thirds popped out of the lustrous sheet, mouths trapped beneath the frozen solidity, the air is dry as meat lockers. In the other, the more common version, hell is the fire-and-brimstone land that children are told they will be sent to if they misbehave, don't obey or tell family secrets. Here, demons rip out the glutton's bowels and drape their intestines on pine trees that are on fire. Liars are fed hot coals. Idolaters have their eyes poked out with blunt pencils. Those who love gossip have their eardrums perforated with biting insects. We're told that it is the hottest place that anyone will ever experience. The hell you want to go to, though, is that place somewhere between the two hells. Here, there is no sand, as all the sand has melted into glass. But, unlike the fiery hell where melted sand remains in liquid-glass puddles collected on the floor like clogged storm drains in New York City, rank and foul-smelling, floating with the flotsam of discarded memories, the melted sand in this place, by virtue of the clashing temperatures, condenses into a sparkling expanse of glass that you may walk on. It is like walking on an eternal sheet of shattered windscreens, cracked, shattered as an exquisite spider web but still holding to each chip, smooth as the underbellies of lizards, the size of a desert. The fierce light from the Fiery Hell and the coldest intense light from the Ice Hell light this place and the waves of light sneak through the cracks in the glass and make it radiate into a quintillion spray of light. It is a hell worth going to.

The Cock of Heaven & Earth. Someone's beeper goes off, someone is chatting to another in the background, someone is preparing for another shot, someone pops open a canned drink, someone can't get hard, someone has the cold flaccidity of a tweaker, someone I recognize, someone has brought a friend, someone is being re-acquainted, someone has a new piercing, someone has a fever, someone has strange bumps on his cockhead, someone is severely deformed. This is democracy in action. I take it all. I accept it all. I accept them all. Like a mother of a nation, I hold them all dear to me. Here on my knees, in this alley this basement let-in with this blindfold in place, here at the wee hours of a new dawn, week after week, I am queen, and I will rule here forever and ever. Watch my coronation, watch me ascend the throne.

2. Pisser

You tell me that this kiss means I'm your boy and that your lover doesn't understand your craving for young smooth boys to play dead for you, the bear of a man that he is and how you now cannot bear the sight of his face nor his body nor his cock, you need a boy to lie across your lap *tell me a secret* you whisper in my ear *tell your daddy your secrets* and I spit my spirit of transaction into your ear. This is such a fucked-up way to score but—shit—what's a person to do when your dealer changes his phone number and doesn't give it to you— you either take it personally, take it as a sign from the almighty to get clean or you improvise, easy choice when the only voice on the other end of the line plies your ear with sweet promises in some adult bookstore, yeah desperation and dependency can make me fake it good, yeah, I can fake that virgin-shit, that innocent-fuck-shit, that I-haven't-had-good-sex-until-you shit, being a bespectacled chink helps and he wants to know a secret so I tell him about how my uncle buttfucked me when I was ten which explains my daddy-fetish and *oh daddy daddy, feed me your cum daddy.*

I lie like mad, and he laps it up like a stray mongrel licking Sizzler throw-outs *feed your boy your cum, daddy* I whisper and he feeds me with semen, sweet greens, money, gifts, promises. Oh he feeds me good and he feeds me like I was some starving Third World child touched by the blessed golden hand of Sally Struthers and the Christian Children's Fund and he feeds me and oh, I eat, I eat and I eat like I was that starving Third World child wide-eyed visited with the blessing of All-You-Can-Eat, every meal was like the last meal on death row, belly full, and I shat the whole day to keep up with my feeding schedule and I ate till I puked until I kissed sweet sleep.

But like the well-fed, contented with my buddha-belly filled with yummy treats, hips swelling fat, I learned to give it away for free, I thought I found my twenty-four-hour open-all-night 7-11 of satiation, yeah, I gave it away, I thought I found the high road to all that I couldn't bear, every wisp of grief that I couldn't bear, my heart, my lungs, my liver, my guts, my eyes, my ears, my heart.

I give it away all the time and I also take too much, but the buffet table doesn't go on forever, nothing ever does, and he moves on to some little Latino kid who satisfies him better than I could.

I see you through the glory hole at the adult bookstore, you have him in the black sheer crotchless panties that you once offered to put me in. He is sitting on your lap, you are masturbating with one hand, one hand free to feed the tokens, he is curled on your lap, your head is buried in his skinny chest, he is curled silent as an aborted foetus and you are stroking him and cooing like a pigeon on speed. I do not notice that I am kneeling in a pool of someone else's cum. After you leave, I sit on the small stool and bring my knee up to my mouth and suck at the fluid in the fabric, sucking out someone else's cum that I say is yours, that you put your dick through the hole and left your cum just for me and now I am feeding on it like a hungry mosquito, like a baby hungry for a spurt of teat milk.

But nothing goes on forever, not that craving for some consecrated high in slosh and grind, not for anonymous cum, nothing goes on forever but this bursting in my chest, this new addiction that I hold in my ribs, this bursting this little pisser desire, this queer desire, I take a swig of my heart and baby, lean in, let me tell you one last secret, if I were to leave my body and never come back to it, if I were to leave my blood and never again taste the metal of it, if I were to leave my semen in some stranger's rectum, leave my brain in some discarded pool of my past, I will know that in the crux of any reckoning, this queer desire defines a locus wider, more than where my dick has been and who it has regretted.

Liberty
John Tunui

My adopted parents treated me to a vacation in New York. We had been friends for three years, and one day at my Fourth of July party, I introduced them, in front of all my gay friends, as "my new adopted parents, whether they like it or not."

"Honey, you look just like your mother," one of my 'sisters' said. Both my adopted parents are white.

It was my first time in New York, a most magical city, and I absolutely fell in love with it. I'd bought myself a poster of the Statue of Liberty and was taking a break from sightseeing in Washington Square when I spied a guy looking me up and down. I had seen him on the subway, and also on Christopher Street, and now he was sitting on the bench across from me...wow, I thought, I could get to appreciate this fair city even more.

The guy was bold, and his confidence caught me off balance. As for myself, I couldn't believe I was suddenly overcome with shyness and starting to blush. He noticed, came up to me and asked if I needed directions or something.

Damn, I thought: he stole my line. The park was crowded and I wanted to try to make it look as if the guy was really giving me directions, so I unfolded a map. He pointed to it and said, "My place is not far from here."

He spoke with an accent. At first I couldn't place it. His eyes, deep blue, bored through me: I could not believe his speed. I thought I was quick, being a former Polk Street hustler, but this guy had me beat, and he wasn't charging. He introduced himself as Gaël, from Paris, and said he'd been living in New York for a year.

We wandered to a nearby café to get better acquainted, and he said he thought I'd been following him, and I said I thought he'd been following me, and one thing led to another, and finally he led me to his apartment—this absolutely gorgeous twenty-two-year-old French boy, with shoulder-length blond hair, electric eyes, and a killer smile, and it seemed he was not a whore like me. (There's only one thing worse than sleeping with a cheap john, and that's sleeping with a fellow whore.) Anyway, Gaël's interest surprised me. I had been so busy cruising everyone in New York that I hadn't noticed someone had noticed me.

He was a student in English, living the poor-student life, and his small studio didn't have much furniture. His bed was just a mattress tossed on the hardwood floor.

We hit that bed, kissing quickly and passionately, undressing each other with practiced speed. He had a lean, smooth body and an uncircumcised penis. I assumed the bottom position while Gaël donned a condom and stroked on some lube.

"Take it easy, honey, I haven't had it in a while," I whispered through the curtain of his blond hair dangling in my face. My legs were already wrapped around his neck.

"How long has it been?" he asked in his sexy and somewhat formal French accent.

"Oh, not since San Francisco," I replied.

"San Francisco is not as far as Paris."

"Oh, yeah? New Zealand is as far as one can get," I said. "Aaahhh, take it slow, once you get it in, keep it there for a while, okay? Please?"

Gaël silenced me by kissing me hard on the mouth while he penetrated me.

"You have many sheep in New Zealand, no?"

"Oh, too many, too many sheep," I moaned.

"New Zealand sheep like to get it up the ass, no?"

"I don't know, aaahhh, slowly, honey, slowly."

"This sheep is tight, no?"

"Just shut up and do me, honey."

"You sing me a New Zealand song while I make love to you, please."

"What? I don't know any New Zealand song. Just shove that thing into me."

"Please?"

"Okay, but I have to warn you I'm not a good singer. Bah bah black sheep... owww, no no, take it easy, have you any wool ahhh, no, no, please, no, ohhh yes yes yes sir, yes sir, three bags full give me three bags full sir, please sir, give it to me, one for the master, one for the dame, and one for the little girl who lives down the lane, honey."

"You are a very bad sheep, no?"

"Bah, bah, yes sir."

"The master will have to punish the black sheep, no?"

"Bah, bah, yes sir, I've been a bad black sheep."

"Master must fuck black sheep up the ass, no?"

"Bah, bah, yes sir."

Our sweaty bodies climaxed simultaneously; I returned from cleaning up in the bathroom to find Gaël's beautiful lanky body at rest, a Gauloise jutting from his mouth at a jaunty angle. It was like a French film. I knelt to kiss him, and

I was in awe that this sweet and beautiful angelic being had just fucked me like a beast.

I unrolled my poster of the Statue of Liberty and held it in front of me. I turned to face Gaël: "Liberty," I proclaimed.

"Liberté," he answered, with another cute smile.

"Liberty is a white French bitch standing in the water."

"Oh, you are from San Francisco and you are crazy," he said, and pushed his lovely white body off the bed and walked into the bathroom for a shower. I stuck the poster to the wall with a thumbtack from his cluttered study desk, then dropped back onto the bed with the TV remote, channel-surfing to the news. The headline was "Trouble in Paradise," about the Tahitian people protesting the French government's decision to test another series of nuclear bombs in the South Pacific. The footage showed native people attacking French functionaries in Tahiti.

I heard Gaël whistling in the shower, while on TV I watched police arrest a number of the protesters, one of them my Uncle Oscar, who was handcuffed and hurled into a police car. I was horrified. My uncle's face was pained, his kind and gentle eyes were now dark and sad and angry, a window into his anguish and suffering. Back in the bathroom Gaël was still showering.

As the images flickered, I wondered what would happen to Uncle Oscar and the rest of my people being arrested. I recalled how the French government had annihilated the native Kanaks of New Caledonia, its other South Pacific colony, some decades ago, and I remembered the dark cloud which showered dust on Aitutaki when I was just a kid, and I recalled the native Tahitians who came to New Zealand frantic for cancer treatment, cancer the French denied had anything to do with their bomb tests. And I remembered more recent history, the attack on the Rainbow Warrior Greenpeace vessel in Auckland, New Zealand by the French secret services, killing or injuring the defenseless crew. The newscast showed file footage of a bomb exploding. A tall, white figure rose from the water. I gazed at the tall white figure of Liberty on the wall, looked back at the figure on the TV screen. "that white French bitch in the water," I whispered to myself.

Gaël turned off the shower, and I turned off the TV as he stepped into the studio, drying himself with a towel.

"Baby, please get me some wine from the refrigerator," he asked as he dried his body, his hair falling over his face as he bent to dry his toes, before raising one leg and towelling his testicles.

"Are you okay, my baby?"

"Yeah, yeah, I'm fine." I opened the fridge, brought out a bottle of wine, poured him a glass.

"Pour yourself one."

"No, thanks. I don't drink this," I said. He sipped at the glass, smiled that sassy French smile, reached out with his hands and pulled our bodies back together. We kissed, quickly.

"Baby." He grinned. "You're not smiling." He grinned again, a sweet and innocent and beautiful smile, the sort that is so rare.

"Oh," I said, "I'm just letting you soak in, that's all. You were wonderful, and you're still wonderful."

I welcomed his comforting kiss, took his wine glass away, laid him down on the bed. We made love again but this time I wore the condom and he wheeled and squealed while I penetrated him. He moaned and wept and tried to push me away. He swore in French and struggled to escape me, but I was too big and too strong and too upset with what was happening in Tahiti, and soon I ejaculated inside his white butt and he ejaculated into my hands. I rolled off his beautiful body and he went back to the bathroom.

"Baby, that hurt me real bad," he said when he came back, and then he beamed another of his sexy smiles. "But I liked it."

He walked over to the kitchenette, poured more wine and stood in front of the TV, next to the poster of the Statue of Liberty, the wet cotton towel draped over his shoulder, a cigarette suddenly lit in his raised right hand, the glass of wine at his side.

Liberty had never looked sexier.

And then he said to me: "That's why I prefer making love to a black man. You are best when you are angry."

Body Hunger
Grigoris Daskalogrigorakis

I wake up grudgingly a split second before the chirping cricket of my digital time ball, and, by the lack of sound anywhere else, am the first consciousness to rouse in my building. I'm up until dawn the night before waiting for my heart to stop pounding. When I go home late at night and there's no one else around, I try to lie down and nod off, but after a while I start to get the shakes. It's no use. I just can't sleep.

But by daybreak I've usually fallen off. I'm lying in a puddle of my own sweat. This morning, the bedroom is redolent with the smell of rotting gardenias swept into the room by a morning breeze. It's already blistering outside and the sun's begun to singe them. Through the filter of the beginnings of a roaring migraine, the sharp perfume stings my nostrils and excites me at the same time.

It is so difficult to dredge myself out of the torpor of deep sleep and the first crackling pangs of a headache that, half awake, I know I have to resort to the usual solution and I start to pull myself off, languidly at first, the sensation almost too abstract to instigate true arousal, then my heart becomes alert and beats faster, my mind pools and the first identifiable image in it is an oval, blotted in emollient, rubbing against the plate of my mid-brain until it soft-focuses into a face, the lambent face of Terence Stamp, the way it looked in the movie Billy Budd.

That visage fades too soon into a profusion of nameless mugs attached to disembodied mouths, loins, napes, cocks, and asses, so dissociated, in fact, that they become mere landscapes of flesh anchored in smell, in spit, in mucous, in the metallic stench of harsh pheromones, all those forbidden particularities and associations I only manage to cut loose from their straitjackets after teen age. Out of that private, heavily-guarded sanitarium, they've turned into detailed, inflammatory things I've made friends of, that I can touch, that wake me up—sort of—during that perfunctory release, squeezing out a few drops of seminal fluid, the sobering up, the "little death" that almost always pulls me out of the "big death" every morning and leaves me distracted now, worrying, still half asleep, wondering for a moment why I'm estranged from women, how repelled I am by the thought that I bear any resemblance to the father I loathe as I look at myself in the bathroom mirror.

But this anxiety rapidly dissolves down the drain. I splash rusty water from the faucet into my eyes, then pull myself back to sitting on the edge of the bed and turn on the TV while I stretch on my socks. There is a local news brief on about summer recreational facilities on the Castaic Reservoir about forty miles northeast of where I am now. But the sight of the gleaming, waterskiing bodies only serves to remind me of the time I am stuck on the nearby "grapevine" on Interstate 5 with a hopelessly debilitated car for eleven hours.

I am driving to San Francisco with three acquaintances. We've just filled up the gas tank, spirits are high, and escape is in the air, when suddenly trucks are playing chicken with my stalled car and passengers on a steep incline as I watch them helplessly in the rear view mirror from the middle lane. Against my pleas, the others vote to stay put until the highway patrol can come to our rescue, but from my privileged position I am seized with such terror watching the transports barely missing us that I can hardly breathe from shaking so violently. Seeing my panic, the others are finally convinced that we're sitting ducks unless we get out. Even having made this decision, it takes fifteen minutes for the convoy of night freight to die down enough for the four of us to sprint to the road shoulder, then clamber up the steep walls of the canyon rising up from the sides of the freeway. Just in time it seems, too, when a passing motorist stops and gives us flares to alert the trucks because the car's hazard lights are too dim to see in the one A.M. dark. They are all annoyed. I just feel humiliated and disappointed. Two of the other three hitchhike back to the city and take buses to the North.

I am left alone with Billy. We both want to get away this weekend from an emotional parasite that's broken into both our lives and attempted to ransack our souls. The two of us spend the night alone by the roadside rehashing every sequence of events that has led to this crisis of being stranded, every forewarning we've ignored that there was something desperately wrong all along.

It is one hundred and four degrees within a few hours after the sun comes up. Two weeks later my car ends up being abandoned at the turnoff to Magic Mountain amusement park not far from Castaic. Even now, despite the foiled escape and automotive disaster, I can recall with some fondness the mechanic at the auto repair—Jim, a crude, attractive blond man with a moustache, in his early forties, an ex-sailor gone to seed with an anchor tattoo on one arm and a not unattractive beer gut. The mechanic tells me jokingly that my car has had an "aneurysm" as he holds out the small, obscene, thick section of rubber hosing that has burst in the effort to get the old '72 Dodge Dart Swinger up the steep grade. And then I wait here for what seems like hours, days, eras until someone comes to drag me back to L.A. But for the time being I'm stuck in this auto dump with its proprietor, chatting, being attentive to and verbally rough-housing with big Jim, who occasionally calls orders out to his teenage son, learning his daddy's trade at his daddy's knee. Later on I think that it is almost worth having paid two hundred sixty-nine dollars and having to abandon the car after all, five miles away, when it overheats again, just to have inhaled that aura, a mixture of axle grease and a day's worth of sweat squeezed out by dry Saugus heat.

For an instant the sight of all the unbridled swimmers and waterskiers on the Castaic reservoir carries me back to the old Athletic Model Guild studios where my best buddy Jack and I went one Saturday night to see a presentation of a friend's male nude photographs for a slick local magazine. He is showing the slides of his shoot because he recruited his models through Physique Pictorial's cornerstone and founder. His series of photos turns out to be part of a monumental slide show that lasts three and a half hours in a makeshift auditorium in the middle of what is an indoor studio with a backdrop against which many of the young male models, who are part of the show, have been captured. The unwitting celebrities of the evening, in fact, can be seen loitering around outside by the pool area in the dark, simultaneously trying to look available and at the same time embarrassed at the impending, shameless display and exhibition of their raw-muscled bodies about to go on inside. I remember the period from the '50s to the mid-'60s when I go to magazine stands and sneak looks in physique magazines, older versions of these bodies, never having either the nerve or the money to buy one.

The evening commences inexplicably with an episode from the TV western "The Rifleman," and a short documentary on FDR. Then the actual slide show begins. The avalanche of images quickly casts an infectious spell of something akin to sexual nausea, but continues relentlessly, lengthens, elongates, extends moistly, a garrulous caterpillar covered with prickles, a clenched forearm alarmed with hair, a profusion of naked men, strays, servicemen, hustlers bent into impossible shapes and positions to facilitate the revelation of their softest and most secret parts to the invading eye of the camera, facing appendages made vulnerable by exposure, lost boys reduced to their uncertain sphincters and fleshy apertures, placed on artificial landscapes as alien as the set of a '50s science fiction film. Sandwiched at random in the midst of this prodigious display of young male animals are occasional summer vacation shots of people recreationally playing in and around the Castaic dam.

The water on the dam swirls into the water in the bathroom sink where I'm poised to piss. In the mildewed room, still dazed, I pull out my dick, stroke it roughly to take the last vestiges of erection out of it so I can piss through it and in the process regard the scar around the glans. For a moment I am assailed by the recollection of my own circumcision with a local anesthetic at the age of ten. My mother takes me and my eight-year-old brother for a routine physical and, at the family doctor's insistence, our genitals are both butchered the following weekend.

Since I am the first, I notice one attending young physician is really cute, an overgrown boy, who winks at me and musses my hair in a gesture designed to put me at ease. This makes me feel especially vulnerable, laid out before him on the operating table, a green cloth draped over my midsection and legs with a hole where my groin is, leaving my generative organs looking wilted and exposed in repose, a wrinkled rubber bath toy awaiting execution. This unfamiliarity with my own body vanishes sharply during the administration of the local anesthetic, six shots of Novocain they inject around my scrotum and the base of my penis. The operation quickly swirls out of control when the surgeon starts to use the scalpel before the anesthetic takes affect. Queasy, yet still alarmed, I lift my head up in time to see blood spurting from the crown of my little prick. For ten days afterward we take stinging pisses through bandages and suffer the humiliation of our mother pulling down our pajamas to show any interested neighbor lady. Perhaps what she is really trying to show them is to what lengths she is willing to go to make her family fit into its adopted culture. I look at this indelible mark of Cain and Abraham and recognize the trace of its scar as the same one I have seen stamped on hundreds of fellows fallen beside me, especially when I can feel the pulsations of their heads and hearts throb within my clenched fist and swollen lips.

Disoriented and dizzy, I stumble and stagger into the kitchen and realize that I probably won't successfully shake the fog out of my head until I'm in the street and on my way to work. Just out of my sight, on the periphery of my vision at the edge of the kitchen table under a pile of newspapers, I spot an SX-70 of what looks like a mound of meat. I vaguely remember a night when I suggest to a friend that we finish a pack of film taking portraits of each other, then tease and torture the pigment into distorted phantasms of ourselves that reduce us to caricatures out of *Gargantua* and *Pantagruel*, beings escaped out of a Rabelaisian universe, refugees from the grotesque, reproductive body of the mother.

I casually rifle through the small pile of picture cards and discover it's a close-up I took of my lost friend Scott who was visiting Los Angeles for a week at New Year's three years ago. The color is bad, all monochromatic and red, making Scott's head look like a fruit and his complexion ruddy. In real life he has coal-black hair and green eyes and skin as translucent as egg shells. I have known Scott now for twelve years.

After the summer I first meet him I don't see Scott again for nine years. Scott joins the Air Force. I get one or two letters a year, even for the five years Scott is stationed in Germany. When he comes back to the United States to the Army/Navy language school in Monterey, Scott contacts me and we renew our acquaintance. Scott is a tall, lanky, sensitive man, obsessed with playing the piano and with the possibility (but not the actuality) of having a fulfilling relationship with a woman. Except for Scott's obsession with the piano, this makes him different from me only in the gender designation of the peculiar form of his desire. Years later, right before he vanishes from sight, Scott miraculously meets, has an affair with, and marries a schizophrenic woman, the perfect recipient for Scott's vast, untapped resource of love.

One night the two of us take a number of SX-70s of each other, squeezing the color in some of them afterwards until the light streams from the beacons of our head holes and orifices, two subjects made out of vibrating shafts of light, although one I take of Scott has the clarity of one of Caravaggio's boys. "We should exhibit these in the Louvre," Scott suggests, laughingly. A Pre-Raphaelite Saint Sebastian, I think, as I gaze at the Polaroid of Scott—an etiolated martyr carved in marble.

It's been two years, almost three, since I lost track of Scott. I even try the Air Force Locator but am given the whereabouts of another airman with Scott's name instead. I never follow it up. After Scott comes and visits me from the Air Force base in Monterey that time, he calls me up long distance afterward and tells me he would have liked to have had an affair with me but is too afraid to because of his position in military intelligence. This information comes out of the clear blue sky and knocks me absolutely speechless. It turns into fantasy stuff for me in the following years, especially once, in the steam room of a bath house in Toronto, surrounded by young men of British ancestry, where I fancy that the towels must really be Irish linen and that Scott's peeking at me through every cloud of steam, or from just behind every booth door in the toilet.

There is a lesson in futility to be learned here but I adamantly refuse to learn it. The day before Scott returns to Monterey, I take him to the barber to have his already short hair made even shorter to conform with regulation length. The whole time I just sit in a chair leafing through a stack *of Field & Streams* and *True Detectives*, half turned on by the smell of Scott's dirty socks a few feet away, which lingers acridly on the periphery of my attention. How much nicer, I think, it would be to be sitting in one of those ubiquitous Charles Eames chairs in an airport on the way to Germany with Scott rather than on this torn vinyl bench at the barber's. At the bus depot Scott asks me to button the hard-to-reach button behind the collar of his white Brooks Brothers shirt. Task accomplished, I slip my hand momentarily around Scott's neck in a caress. Right before Scott boards the bus I embrace him impulsively. There has been no physical precedent for this. Scott is caught off guard and his eyes tear in response. He doesn't even attempt to hide it, I notice, surprised, as he disappears into the bus. Scott is the kind of guy, possessed of such profound empathy, that later he seduces and has an affair with a friend of his who has grown suddenly suicidal, to keep him from killing himself, and it works.

The sequence of thought that's led to Scott weighs heavily on me. What might have been, if only—you could waste your whole life in such idle conjecture, such vain contemplation. I flop back onto the bed. "Oh hell, work can wait another hour," I mutter to myself. Thoroughly distracted now, I idly pick up a *Time* magazine to the right of the mattress. In an article about the Vatican Exhibit at the Metropolitan Museum in New York I am reminded of the vandalism of the Pieta years ago and of the effigy of the boy and his mother, that limp masochist across the nurse's lap. The only way I am going to get Scott out of my system, I realize now, is to masturbate again, and it doesn't take long to pull a few pertinent figments out of that visual generic pool of melted lubricant and congealed hearts and sketch them with something resembling desire.

This is how it goes: Me, I am clad in a pair of shredded BVDs (the twentieth century loincloth), a torn T-shirt and black Banlon socks that have seen better days, propped up on a rough-hewn throne of marble. Scott, barely conscious, is draped over my lap and in my arms in nothing but his Jockey shorts, dying, ostensibly. Although it's a daunting task, I gratefully attempt to soothe him as best I can with my hands, eventually annihilating my mouth somewhere in the vicinity of the elastic selvage of Scott's underwear, the upsurge at at the apex of my thighs pushing up into Scott's back—one martyr dying, lying on another martyr's lap—a latter day Pieta for a new age and another picture for me to file away in my image repertoire. The formality of this eroticized psychodrama rapidly deteriorates into something less solemn and more frantic. For a fleeting moment, and only ephemerally, I am disturbed by the possibility that none of this fantasy is particularly correct politically, but I quickly dismiss that thought with a stroke of my hand. A few dry spasms are summarily achieved and my brain is flooded with beta-endorphin-induced nothingness, relief and remorse. I file away this series of icons lovingly for later, instant replay.

Unable to procrastinate any longer I pull myself out of my overwhelming inertia and get dressed. As I put on my coffee-stained work pants and green and pink flower shirt, I play my current favorite song on my pre-hi tech record player. I've been playing it to death lately, trying to suck as much pleasure out of it as possible—a dirge in which the vocalist's plaintive wailing insists that "...you don't give me love, you give me pale shelter." If the truth were told, I realize, I have hardly ever been in the position to voice such a complaint legitimately except in theory because there's never been a willing, appropriate "you." But somehow it manages to strike a sympathetic chord nonetheless. On the way to work the radio in my car plays another song by the same group. "This is going to be some day," I mumble to myself, my headache radiating into clusters of stabbing pain behind my right eye. I decide that it's not just "body hunger," as my ex-friend Pam calls it, that gives me the shakes at night, but an ache that's deeper and more difficult to define or relieve. I pat my groin and realize that the soreness I feel there is due to too much agitation so early in the day. But I can be sure that by dawn of the next morning there will no longer even be a vestige of this present ache.

The Nether Eye Opens
Don Shewey

When Jerry called, I knew from his name and his tense, timid voice that I'd given him a massage once before. I found him in my client log, but the entry didn't churn up any detailed memories. The creature who arrived at my door might as well have been a total stranger. He was short and nearly bald on top, an out-of-shape blob of a middle-aged man with reptilian slits for eyes. My notes reminded me that he was "overweight and ashamed of it."

He didn't seem to recognize me or remember that he'd seen me in the past. So I pretended I didn't know him, either. He went to the bathroom and came back wearing only his white button-down shirt. He slipped off the shirt and wanted to hop right onto the table. I said, "I'd like to have you do some stretching before we put you on the table, to loosen you up." He looked at me like I was crazy.

Reluctantly, he took a step away from the table. As I directed him to close his eyes, take some breaths, and become aware of his body, he followed my instructions, but he acted like a little kid annoyed at having an adult make him do stupid things, like walk downstairs one step at a time.

When I had him stretch him arms up to the ceiling, I noticed he was holding something in his right hand.

"What's that in your hand, Jerry?"

He showed me the white plastic inhaler.

"No," I said, feeling shaky. "I don't use poppers."

He said, "You don't have to."

I said, "I don't mix poppers with massage."

He said, "They help me relax."

I said, "I'm really a good masseur. You'll be plenty relaxed."

He dutifully deposited the tiny bottle on top of his clothes, which he'd left on the chair next to the massage table. As he lay on his back and I stretched out his arms and legs more, I tried to lighten the atmosphere with some chitchat. He didn't respond. He kept his lips pressed together tightly. He seemed to be pouting about having his poppers confiscated. It made me nervous. I felt guilty for shaming him about using poppers.

He resisted a lot of the massage. He seemed restless and impatient with my slow tempo, scratching himself and coughing. He never sighed and sank into the pleasure of being touched. I got the picture that he's someone who's used to going to masseurs for a half-assed backrub and a hand job, no questions asked. Perhaps at the beginning I could have broached the subject of his real desire and made some accommodation. Often I do say something like, "What's the experience you'd like to have today?" Not that anyone ever says, "A half-assed backrub and a hand job, please."

Guys like Jerry who crawl around in a snail shell of sex-shame rarely have much experience at asking for what they want. They either expect you to read their minds, or they're masochistically resigned to whatever you want to dish out. In my desire to be conscious about sexual touch, you'd think I'd have developed a smooth routine by now of letting shy, sexually undernourished guys like this know what they're in for with me. For instance, I could say, "I'll get around to focusing on your erotic body, but first I'm going to spend about forty minutes massaging the muscle tension out of your back and your legs and your feet." I refrain from being that direct because I want to avoid sounding too much like one of those wholesome Danish sex-education films. Rather than tease clients up to my level, I suppose I tend to sink down to their level of inarticulateness.

In any case, now I was launched into my usual massage routine, and there was no way of stopping it gracefully. I knew giving him a thorough massage had value. I also suspected that he couldn't give a shit.

Everything changed when I got around to his butt. My notes told me I had done butt work on him before, so I felt confident in moving in for close butt touch. When I spread his cheeks and lightly brushed the coarse black hairs and the shiny pink skin around his stretched-out butthole, he twitched as if shocked by an electric current. When I rested the palm of my hand against his pelvic floor and rocked him back and forth, his erection swelled out from under his ballbag, the snail poking its head out of its shell, antennae first. Even if I'm pretty sure that someone wants butt massage, I like to check. Sometimes people have hemorrhoids or loose bowels or some other condition they'd prefer to conceal. I leaned in close to his ear and said, "If you like, Jerry, I could put on gloves and do some more massage around your butt."

"Okay," he said.

I stepped over to my supply cabinet and grabbed a pair of gloves and a tube of K-Y. When I turned around, he was reaching for the inhaler he'd left on top of his shirt.

I was on him in a flash. "If you insist on using poppers, Jerry, I can't continue with the massage."

"What?" he said. I couldn't tell if he was hard of hearing or just selectively so.

I retreated from my ultimatum. "I'd rather you not use poppers during the massage."

"Okay," he said again. He returned his head to the face plate like a child scolded.

"I want to invite you to keep breathing and taking in all the sensations you're feeling, Jerry. Does that sound okay to you?"

He shook his head yes, face down, buried in his shame.

I climbed up on the table and knelt between his spread legs. The sight in front of me—the hairy back and flabby butt of a middle-aged man—wasn't the most appetizing I'd ever encountered. I wasn't turned on but I wasn't turned off either. Some people can't imagine touching let alone giving an erotic massage to somebody they're not attracted to. For a lot of young gay men, the idea of having anything to do with a guy like Jerry would be absolutely unthinkable. I don't mind. In fact, I like it. I like the feeling of control, of being entrusted with another human being's vulnerability. I have a hard time only when clients assume that, because I'm touching them erotically, that we've suddenly moved into some kind of recip-rocal sex mode and they're free to grope me.

I guess that sounds awful. Like, "Don't kid yourself. I'm the attractive one around here. I'm the one who gets to touch and have power." Well, it's true. I want it to be clear that I'm in control. I want them to behave. There's definitely arrogance on my part. But no contempt. Anyone who presents his tender butt for loving touch gets a big gold star in my book. He can rest assured I'm going to take good care of him.

With Jerry, I felt like a spelunker ready to hunt for trea-sures in the secret cave. I pulled on first one white vinyl glove, then the other. The latest box of surgical gloves I bought were the smallest size, and they're skin tight on my hands. They make me look like Mickey Mouse in evening wear.

In contrast to his lassitude during the back massage, the man on the table now began to respond to my every move—

the cool breath on his tight butthole, the firm pressure of three fingers over the opening, the cool slipperiness of lubricant being rubbed rhythmically over the folds of skin covering his sphincter. He jerked and twitched whenever I hit an especially sensitive spot. I knew I wasn't hurting him. I knew he was flinching because he wasn't breathing smoothly enough to distribute the intense sensations. So I coached him to breathe all the way down to his toes.

I went into him easily, one finger then two. I brought him up onto his knees with his head resting on the table, his butt in the air. He wrapped his feet around my calves. When I slid the length of my middle finger across his swollen prostate, he groaned with pleasure. "Deeper," he requested. I adjusted my posture so I was a little higher and slid a third finger into his ass all the way up to the last knuckle, held it there, and vibrated it. With the other hand (whose glove I'd peeled off), I stroked his inner thighs, circled his balls, and tugged on his hard cock. Then I reached around and put my left hand on his lower belly just above his pubic bone and pressed inward, so his prostate received pressure from both sides.

To be this deep inside a man is about as physically intimate as you can get. The quality is so different from fucking, in some ways much more intense. Articulate, multijointed fingers can reach places inside the body that a hard cock cannot. They can increase or modify pressure on the sphincter or the prostate at will. And while someone who's fucking often has to keep sliding in and out to receive pleasure and to stay hard enough, a hand can stay put when it hits a spot that produces moans. I know when I'm fucking, I can get very mental about the state of my erection, wanting to please my partner and prolong my own pleasure at the risk of losing it altogether. Doing butt massage, I'm liberated from that anxiety.

Touching Jerry, fiddling with his erotic knobs like an engineer tuning up a delicate machine, I felt detached, distant, powerfully in control. Like the most beneficent of gods, at once servant and master, giving exquisite pleasure and requiring nothing in return.

Once he was accustomed to being penetrated, I picked up the pace. Now I was fucking him—with my hand, anyway—in and out, pumping his butt. Wordless murmurs issued from his throat. He raised his butt higher. With my free hand I slapped his big rump hard, first one cheek then the other, again and again. He jerked and cried out with each slap. His cry did not say "Stop." The sound of bare hand against bare butt excited me. I escalated the strength of my slaps. Then I paused and ran my fingertips lightly over the reddening skin. I reached down and wrapped my fist around the base of his bulging cock and balls and pulled them toward me.

"Do you have your whole fist in me?" he suddenly asked.

"No, not quite," I said. "Three fingers."

"Can you fist me?" His voice was quiet, not timid but hopeful.

"Have you ever been fisted?"

"No. But I'd like to try."

"Let's see how it goes," I said. I put some more lube on my hand and slid all four fingers inside him. He groaned with satisfaction. I could feel his belly, his bowels, his rectum, his insides breathing with me, letting go. When I slid my hand back, a few bubbles of air pressed their way out, relieving the interior pressure. Without clenching or clamping, his ass wrapped itself around my hand, like a starfish on a rock.

I got off the table and stood next to him. I ran my free hand up his back and stroked his shoulders, his neck, the scaly top of his bald head. I leaned into his butt, which opened slightly wider. He sighed. Now I slid my thumb into him, so my hand formed a wedge that pushed all the way in until my knuckles rested against his sitz bones.

I noticed that he was no longer hard. It occurred to me that he might be hurting. He might have had enough. But the gurgles he released whenever I bore down on his prostate told me he had entered a deeper zone, that altered state of erotic experience that is beyond erection and ejaculation. It's a mystical place, akin to dreaming or nearly dying, where the membrane that separates matter from spirit becomes very thin. Memories and emotions slither up from the murky depths. The nether eye opens to what's usually hidden. The roof of the planetarium slides open, and the infinite beckons. I knew he was travelling through space, like those scenes in *2001: A Space Odyssey* where suddenly the spaceship would be hurtling through a blur of stars. Only this was inner space, a tunnel of quiet dark. Vaulted ceilings. Echoey stairwell. A horse's eye. I hung out there with him.

Almost an hour and a half had passed since he got on the table. "I'm going to slow down now and start coming out of you, Jerry," I told him. One finger at a time, I brought my hand out, cupping my palm over his hole before releasing it entirely. Then I laid him flat on the table again, cleaned his butt with a Baby Wipe, and toweled off his back before turning him over.

"How are you doing?" I asked him.

He looked up through his slit eyes and said, "Good."

I knelt at the end of the table looking at his face upside down. I saw his stubbly chin, his thin lips (relaxed now), his fleshy ears.

"You've been on a little trip I think."

"Uh, huh," he said.

"Uh, huh," I confirmed. I rested my hands on his shoulders and looked down into his steely green eyeballs. They were the eyes of someone on a trip, who has seen something from the other world and not averted his gaze. He didn't seem confused or shy or embarrassed.

"Did any images or memories occur to you during this session?" I asked.

"Yes," he said immediately. I was surprised. I like asking the question but usually people don't relate to it.

"Tell me," I said.

"I remembered that my father used to take me over his knee," he said slowly. "He would pull down my pants...and pull down my underwear...and spank me."

"And that was exciting to you?"

He nodded.

"Did your father know it excited you?"

"No."

"Did you get a hard-on?"

"No, not at the time."

"But later when you thought about it...?"

"Uh, huh."

I let that memory sink in. Inside me something large and dangerous moved, like a giant octopus tentacle flopping across the room. When I started slapping his big hairy butt, little did I know that I was stirring up his oldest erotic fantasies. Or mine: the forbidden daddy-love-touch.

"There's something about an older man, your father, taking an interest in your naked butt that's very exciting and forbidden, isn't there?"

"More forbidden," he said.

"Ah," I said. "Many things that are forbidden are exciting."

He was quiet for a minute.

"Anything else?" I inquired.

"Yes," he said.

I was overjoyed. More!

"I was in Morocco once," he began. "Have you ever been to Morocco?"

"No," I said. "I'd like to go."

"This was many years ago," he said. He spoke slowly, as if in a trance. "I was there with some other people on business... and we were all taken to this bathhouse....There were men and women there....I got separated from the people I was with....I saw some stairs....I went up there....It was a little room....I met a Moroccan guy....He was big...well, not big. Stocky."

He paused.

"Then what happened?" I said, barely controlling my impatience to hear the whole story.

"There was a bench there....He pulled it over to the middle of the room....He had me get up on it...the same way you had me do...with my butt up."

Aha.

"And then he...you know, he fucked me....And there were two other guys...Moroccans...Three of them all together."

"They all three fucked you?"

"Uh, huh."

"One right after the other?"

"Uh, huh."

"That sounds hot," I said. My dick grew in my pants. To tell the truth, I was jealous.

"It was," he said immediately. "The other guys were walking around the place....I didn't know where they were....Men and women...."

"Oh," I said, "it was a place where everybody was there having sex, men and women?"

"Yes," he said.

"But they could have walked in at any time and seen you?"

"Yes."

We both quietly took in the thrill of that scenario.

This guy had more going on inside him than I ever would have suspected by looking at him. I got up and sat on the table next to him. I picked up his arm and let it rest against my chest as we continued talking.

He wanted to know more about fisting. "Do you think you could get your whole hand inside me next time?"

"I don't know," I said. "For fisting it's a lot easier if you're in a sling, because your whole body is able to relax. When you're on a table, your muscles unavoidably maintain a certain tension."

"Do you have a sling?" he asked eagerly.

"No," I said. "Some people have them in their private playrooms, and some sex clubs have them."

"I couldn't see myself doing it in a sex club with just anybody," he said. "But I could do it with you. What if I lay on my back?"

"That might be easier," I conceded. I started feeling slightly apprehensive. I've never fisted anybody. This session was as far as I'd ever gone in that direction. I didn't want to set myself up as an expert. But his eagerness to explore touched me. He didn't seem like a numbed-out thrill seeker. From the stories he told, I understood that intense body play connected him to his deepest erotic fantasies and memories. What else can you call these things but experiences of God, memories of heaven? In those moments, brief and eternal, you feel most alive in your body and most spiritually connected to the tempestuous energy of the universe, that mystery at once so physical and so invisible. How many saints and monks, meditating days at a time on their dusty mats, have dwelt on just this, remembered or wished-for episodes of ecstatic buttfucking?

"We need to stop for today, Jerry," I said.

"Can you help me get off?" he asked.

"You want to squirt?" I asked, a little dubiously. I thought he'd gone way beyond it. I thought he'd had a sacred-sex breakthrough and realized that you don't always have to ejaculate to have a powerful erotic experience.

"Sure," he said. I looked at his dick, which he'd been idly toying with during our conversation, and I saw that it was stiff and dark pink. I oiled him up and stroked him. He had a medium-sized dick, maybe five inches long erect, circumcised, with a big split down the middle, a thick frenum. Pressed flat against his belly, his cock looked like an arrowhead—or a devil's tail. As I worked on his cock, he started running his hands over my body. I found myself tensing up, afraid that he was going to start invading me and grabbing my cock. I didn't invite him to touch me, and I wasn't at all turned on at the moment. I wanted to finish up the session and get rid of him. Sacred sex is sacred sex, but after an hour and a half your time is up.

I pumped his cock with one hand and reached my other arm under his neck and around his shoulders. He lifted his arm to pull me down to his face. I resisted, but eventually I allowed him to press some stubbly kisses against my face.

As I pressed my hairy chest against his, his thin lips smacking against mine, I became for a moment that angry daddy pulling down his underpants, that stocky Moroccan towering over him and swallowing him up, the horned god appearing by magic in the forest clearing where the chubby boy lay on mossy grass pleasuring himself. The world turned upside down with a lurching sound like a train pulling out of the station. Blossoming flowers erupted from the earth. Waves of air pressed into his lungs until he burst.

How do I want you to touch me, Daddy? I like having power over you. I want to be somewhere you can't hurt me. I like it when I can see you and you can't see me. I can see every part of your fat hairy body. I see your scar under your shoulder blade. I see the razor line of your barbershop haircut. I see the curled callous on the edge of your big toe. I see your pink balls peeping out from under your thighs. You're face down, so I can spread your cheeks and look right into your wrinkled butthole.

I can see where your sallow skin turns rosier, the color of the inside of a velvet cape lined in silk. Whorehouse pink—not garish but muted. I could write on your butthole with a Magic Marker. Little hieroglyphics. Sportina Cheese. Marco Wuz

Here. Close Cover before Striking. Bad Advice. Liar. I could slide the Magic Marker in and out of you, like Midwestern boys caught fucking themselves with pencils. I've turned the tables on you, Daddy. I'm fucking you.

I don't want you to notice or say anything. Not right now anyway. Later I want you to tell me I'm wonderful and give me some money. Right now I want to squeeze a pile of slippery goo onto my rubbery fingers and slide them into your butt, so you feel me fucking you, you feel me towering over you, planting a seed, mowing your lawn, making you pregnant, making you moan. You reach out and grab my leg. Suddenly I feel like Don Giovanni in danger of being dragged to hell. What do you want? Let me go. Let me go! You want something from me, something more, and I don't want to give anything more. I want to say no without saying no. I turn you over, and you look at me with your slanted reptile eyes, dark green, from just under the surface of the water, you alligator with the crooked smile (no lips) and hairy belly. You reach up to touch my cheek. I lean in to your ear; you turn your head to kiss me. I open my mouth, and our tongues press together like cheese and burger. We fry. I'm kissing you, Daddy. I always wanted this.

We're both hard. I'm running my hands through your hair. Now I've given up shame. I have no restraint. I strip down to my jockstrap and take that off too. I wrap it around your neck. I climb on top and slide into you without stopping. I pump into you and pull the jockstrap tighter around your neck. Your eyes bulge. Your dick swells. It's unbelievably huge. It's like a big balloon. It's a baby lying between us. It's a baby boy growing out of your crotch, and the longer I fuck you, the bigger he grows. Now he's sucking on your tit, and I'm fucking you, and your face is getting redder, like fire around your watery eyes, and I flood you, I flood you, your banks overflow, blood trickles from the corner of your mouth.

I take the baby and wrap it in your T-shirt and run. I run through the snow looking for a taxi. There's no one on the street but me. We get to the airport in no time. I don't have any luggage. They let me walk on board with the baby, both of us naked and crusty. I sit in first class, order a beer, and toast you, Daddy, love of my life.

Ganged

Carol Queen

A Tribute to John Preston

We join our protagonist Miranda, a bisexual cross-dressing femme switch with a taste for leather daddies, not long after her meeting with Jack Prosper—the only gay man she's ever picked up who didn't throw her out when he figured out she was really a woman—even after she changed into femme drag.

Jack and I had been running together for several weeks. He knew which bar I hung out in; a couple of times he had sauntered in and found me there. He didn't stay to meet my friends; he'd haul me out and back to his place. We usually only got as far as the alley before his dick was out.

He had been to my apartment only once. It was more comfortable at his place; he didn't have any housemates, whereas I could never predict when mine, Ariel, would come home, half the time dragging a john. So mostly our relationship developed within the charmed and secret space of his rooms.

The one time he was at my place, though, I found him nosing around my room when I came in from the kitchen where I'd gone to get us something to drink. At the bedside table, he picked up a book—a very battered copy of *Mr. Benson*. He grinned, and slung himself on my bed as though he habitually lounged there to read. He held the book in his left hand and of course it fell right open—to the part where Mr. Benson takes his new boy to meet all his friends.

"Stroke book, eh?" Jack was, I could tell, amused.

I just said, "You've read it, I suppose."

"Read it? Honey, I'm sure you were still in junior high. For a while there, this character was everybody's role model—or dream daddy." Jack was fingering the teeth marks where one time I had bitten the book during an especially big come.

I blushed. "Well, that historical moment may be over for you, but the dykes have gotten hold of him now."

"I'm not even sure I can picture that," Jack said. He stroked his mustache absently. "You know, I have a few buddies of my own. But god knows, Randy, you'd embarrass me. You look like *baby* chicken when you're in drag."

I'd all but forgotten about that when I got a call from Jack on my voicemail. "Okay, Randy, I want you over here tonight at eight o'clock. Punctually. Butched up as much as your fey little ass can get. You won't need your girl drag, but bring your make-up."

I showed up at five minutes 'til eight and sat on the steps 'til it was time to ring the bell. I had on my engineer's boots and Levi's, and in a jockstrap, I was packing a small one. My breasts were bound down and I had a worn black T-shirt under my leather jacket.

Jack answered the door. "Randy, for christ's sake, you look like a dyke."

"Jack, there's hardly any difference in this town!"

"Oh yes there is. Get in here, kid. You need a little more work."

Jack put me into a black leather bar vest that just fit me. He didn't tell me where it came from, but it was much too small for him. He asked me for my make-up. With the dark pencils and mascara brushes he found in the kit he darkened my eyebrows a little and stroked the fuzz on my upper lip with color until I had a mustache. "This stuff better be water-proof," he muttered. Finally he stood back and looked at me. "Where in god's name do you get boots that tiny? If only you were a few inches shorter. I could just tell them you're a dwarf."

"Jack, you're a total bitch. Who's 'them'?"

"Never mind, son. You'll see soon enough. Now drop to your knees, boy."

Happy to be back on familiar ground, I knelt with my cheek resting on Jack's thigh, filling with whatever the emotion was that his Daddyness brought up in me. An instant later, I felt a chill coil of chain wrapping my throat and I started; Jack had never collared me before. At the click of the lock, my cunt spasmed as if he'd flicked his tongue over my clit.

"You're *my* boy tonight, got it? You're going to keep your mouth shut and your jockstrap on. I'm upping the ante on our little social experiment, boy, and you're in it 'til it's over. No safe words, no femme drag, nothing but what I tell you. I'm taking you to a little party. You *might* just be the guest of honor." His eyes narrowed—I could see he was dead serious. "But if you don't keep up your end, you'll never be invited back—and I probably won't either. Don't fuck it up."

I stared up at him, welling up with the weirdest mixture of pride and stricken fear. I had only about a shred of an idea where we were going, but it was pretty clear Jack wanted me to pass on whomever we met. I had no idea how I was going to pull that off. I don't think I'd ever passed on anyone for more than about a half an hour in my life.

He put a blindfold on me before he handed me a helmet and straddled his Harley. I was left to grope my way on, and I held him tightly as the bike's acceleration threatened to knock me off balance. I tried, blind as I was, to follow the turns he took, but I was lost within a couple of blocks, and all I knew was that soon we were speeding up even more, crossing a bridge—I guessed the Bay Bridge, for in the middle the sound changed as we whipped through a tunnel. I clasped him, feeling the dildo I wore nudge his butt-cheeks while his big bike throbbed under us like a very butch sex toy.

He didn't take the blindfold off until we'd entered a house, which might have been in the Berkeley Hills, or Oakland, or who knows where. It was a large house, obviously, and Jack had let himself in without ringing. We left our helmets on a shelf in the foyer. We weren't the only ones here, I noted: some helmets were there already, a briefcase or two, and a profusion of coats. Most, but not all, were leather. Jack instructed me to hang my own jacket on a hook—he always said it was too fucking ratty to be seen in—and kept his on. He led me down a long hall.

The room we entered at the end made me gasp. It was clearly a dungeon, though it was not the low-end made-over-basement I was used to from the city. Somebody well-to-do lived here, and he had obviously put all the care into constructing his playroom that some other gay man might spend collecting art or learning to be a four-star chef just to impress his friends.

At one end, it didn't look like a dungeon, but a really classy den, a library without the bookshelves. It had several wing-back chairs arranged around a low table and facing a fireplace, where a small blaze flickered and cast shadows. A sideboard held a silver coffee service—a nice antique one, I noted—and several plates with sandwiches and other easy-to-eat food. A bottle of champagne lay icing in a silver bucket, but the cork hadn't been popped—no one seemed to be drinking. Three of the chairs were occupied by men in leathers, men who would look just as sexy and appropriate wearing very fine suits as they did in this Gentleman's Club atmosphere.

The other end of the room was, like the part that looked like a den, wood-paneled. It might have been in a restored Victorian, except the rest of the house looked newer. Setting off the dark wood was wrought iron fashioned into cages and suspension bars. A wooden St. Andrew's cross, leather-upholstered horses, and other dungeon implements furnished the place. I had been inside a few dungeons before, but they'd all looked tacked together compared to this.

As Jack stepped into the room, one of the seated men got up and extended his hand. Jack clasped it. "Sir Sebastian," he said, with affection as well as great respect in his voice, "how good to see you again. Thank you, as always, for your hospitality." Sir Sebastian, like Jack, had an impeccably trimmed beard, but it was mostly white, and he had white at his temples, too. I put him at fifty, perhaps. He was distinguished, calm, had seen everything. His grey eyes shone with warmth at the moment, but I could imagine them glittering menacingly; power was all over him. If Jack was my daddy, Sir Sebastian could be his.

"Jack, my darling man. You're welcome here at any time." He had looked me over once, the moment we entered the room, and now he continued, "And what have you brought for us tonight? It's fortunate this isn't a public place, my dear. No wonder I haven't seen you in the bars with this lad."

Jack only smiled. "Sir Sebastian, his name is Randy. In my experience, the name suits him very well, and he is not entirely new to all this. Tonight, of course, will be a test for him." As Jack said my name, I sank to my knees and bowed my head. He hadn't told me what the rules were, except "don't fuck up"; I figured at the minimum I ought to put on good dungeon manners and hope I didn't miss any cues.

"Randy is forbidden to speak tonight," Jack said, "and I do hope none of you gentlemen will take offense when he does not verbally answer you. Also, his cock belongs to me, and neither he nor anyone else may touch it." I had a wild image of popping the little Realistic out of my jockstrap and handing it over to Jack for safe-keeping. "He is bandaged from a cutting, a rather extensive one, so I'd like you to leave his shirt on. Beyond that, however, he will be at your disposal."

At that, my heart jumped wildly. Somehow I'd expected Jack to test my passing skills in a dark leather bar, not in a playroom full of masters. Why couldn't he have just snuck me into Blow Buddies? More was at stake tonight than whether I could keep the dildo on straight. I'm not a heavy sensation bottom, and while this place was beautiful, it could've hosted meetings of the Inquisition. I prayed I wouldn't break.

Jack ruffled my hair for the tiniest instant, then left me kneeling and turned to the other men. I stole glances up at them as best I could. One man was enormous and muscular, his head shaved, his tits pierced. I couldn't tell his age—somewhere around Jack's, perhaps. Jack called him Stone when he greeted him. He addressed another man, a lithe young blonde with icy blue eyes, as Marc. Marc seemed a good deal younger than the others, maybe even younger than me. But he wore authority like so many men in the bars wore leathers with the squeak and smell of Mr. S still on them.

Two more men came in. One was substantially older than the others, his hair quite white, and when he spoke I heard the tones of well-bred Oxford English. He, unlike the other men, did not wear leather; he was dressed in a suit that doubtless came from Savile Row. Jesus, Jack ran with some power daddies! "Ah, St. James, sir," Jack said when he saw the man, reaching to grasp his hand and, I noticed, inclining his head respectfully.

St. James' companion stepped forward to greet Jack, and at the sight of him, I almost forgot to keep my head bowed. Tall, black, with sculptured muscles, he was one of the most beautiful men I'd ever seen. He had a similarly galvanizing effect on Jack. "Demetrius! How long have *you* been back?" he cried, and to my surprise threw his arms around the man. Demetrius laughed and hugged Jack, and even when the embrace was over they stood close, with their hands on each others' arms. I realized I was looking at someone who meant a lot to Jack—a lover, probably—and from my post on the floor, I studied him as carefully as I could. He wore a white silk shirt which draped over his muscular arms and tucked into black leather pants almost as tight as his own skin. His boots were fine leather, unadorned, and polished to a high black gloss. His voice was deep and smooth.

Sir Sebastian had stepped to the sideboard and rung a small bell. A very pretty young man entered the room. He was dressed like a formal waiter, except he didn't have on any pants—only a leather jockstrap. His sandy hair curled around his face—he'd do flawless drag, I thought, then reminded myself that I probably wouldn't be let loose to play Barbie with Sir Sebastian's staff. Maybe Jack could get the loan of him sometime and we could play lesbians. He couldn't possibly have his obvious need to cross-dress indulged hanging around with these leathermen.

The waiter-boy bore a tray with several champagne glasses. He set it on the sideboard and opened the champagne, not getting at all ostentatious with the cork, I noticed approvingly. It exited the bottle silently. He filled the glasses, presented one first to Sir Sebastian, then to St. James, and then to everyone else. He looked at me kneeling, poured a glass for me, and left it on the sideboard. "Anything further, Sir Sebastian?" he asked, and left silently when the man shook his head.

"Well, this is quite a lot to celebrate," Sir Sebastian said smoothly. "Jack has brought his new boy to meet us. And Demetrius has come back from his wanderings. Shall we toast?"

Jack picked up the glass from the sideboard and sat it on the floor in front of me, returning to lift his own glass. "New acquaintances and old friends," said St. James, and as the men all toasted, I bent down and lapped from my glass like a rich old lady's over-indulged puppy. So far, this party was a piece of cake, but that couldn't last. I repeated Sir Sebastian's statement "Jack has brought *his* new boy"—in my head. Well, that was worth several hours of conversation about commitment and relationship status, eh? Jack's collar lay heavy on my neck, comforting as the touch of his palm on my nape. I stole another glance up through my lashes—he had his hand on Demetrius' strong, silk-clad shoulder, but I noted that he was reiterating to him and St. James the rules regarding my conduct. No speech—thank goodness; no removing my shirt, no touching my dick. Jack had done everything he could to set it up so I could pass.

Minutes later, Jack was at my side, giving a lift to my collar. I scrambled to my feet, and at his gestured instruction, placed my hands behind my back at waist level. He beckoned and I followed—to the cage.

Inside the cage, a set of leather cuffs dangled from chains. Jack adjusted them to my height, then held one open. Meekly, I lay my wrist onto the fleece padding, and he buckled first that wrist in and then the other. The cage was tall enough for a full-sized man, but fairly narrow. Even with my wrists restrained, I could move right up to the bars on all four sides.

Jack took my chin, lifted my face up so I could gaze into his eyes. He was not quite expressionless—I thought I saw a hint of a smile. I figured that if we really pulled this off, Jack would feel like the cat that got the canary, and I—well, let's just say like the cat that ate the cream.

Then he released my chin and unbuckled my Levi's—the jeans fell down around my ankles. Jack slapped my ass once and grinned, then the cage door clanged shut; the lock snapped into place. He crossed the room and rejoined his friends.

"The devil never does get enough cock," Jack was saying. "He's a little pig, really. I think I've satiated the little bastard and ten minutes later, he's pulling on my balls again. He's tiresome! I finally decided the only thing to do was bring him here." The assembled daddies murmured sympathetically.

"I'm sure we can help," Demetrius said.

"Oh, I know *you* can," Jack rejoined. "A cock like yours is really the only possible answer."

I listened to Jack with amazement. He was going to get me ganged! I rubbed my dick against the cage bars, felt my cunt simmer.

Sure enough, he returned accompanied by Marc. Each was unzipping his leather pants.

"Now, boy, I know I don't need to tell you to be good to my friends. You're here for our use. Take this."

Jack thrust his cock near enough to the cage bars that I could just get to the pisshole with my tongue. I looked at him imploringly, the look that would have been accompanied by a "Please, Daddy!" if I'd been able to speak. Jack laughed and stepped closer, grasped the bars so he could press his pelvis right up against the cage, and his big cock came in for me to work on. I couldn't get hold of it with my hands—the restraints gave me some movement, but not enough—and so the only part of me that touched him was my mouth. I tongued him all over, the taste of him getting my saliva running, 'til his cock was wet and I could slurp him in. Marc stood just to one side of Jack, stroking his own cock—it had a downward curve, it would slide right down my throat.

"Look at this fucking cocksucker, Jack—where'd you find him? Look at this fucking kid." I knew how Jack liked it by now—he made a low little noise each time his cockhead slipped past my throat muscles, and when he pulled it out, I laved my tongue all around the corona. Once in a while I let it slip out of my mouth so I could scramble for his balls—this part was harder with no hands, but Jack stayed close, his cock bobbing up to slap his belly with a soft thwack whenever its head escaped my lips. I could only get one of his nuts in my mouth at a time, here without the use of my hands—when my hands were free, I knew, if I opened really wide I could just get both of them in, and then I could suckle them. Now, though, I returned to his cock after a little attention to his balls, sucked him rhythmically, my tongue alert as it stroked along his shaft for the first pulsing signs of his load coming.

He didn't give it to me this time, though—gasping and swearing, he pulled out before I could finish him. Marc was in his place almost before I knew there was no cock in my mouth. His dick was a little longer than Jack's, maybe not quite as thick, but substantial, and with that downturn. "Little sucker," Marc growled, "you can have my load, punk, if you can work it out of me," and I went for him.

Demetrius and Stone stood a few feet back now, watching too. As I breathed deeply, opened my throat, and started wiggling Marc's long curved one down as far as I could get it, Demetrius moved behind Jack and grasped his still-high cock in his big hand. Jack moaned, thrust into the fist like it was my cunt, started working it. When Marc's cock was all the way down my throat, I started a fast gulping kind of suck. It flirted with my gag reflex, but I didn't care—that cock fit so perfectly in my throat, I didn't want to pull off it at all.

I was just about to drool from the saliva I wasn't bothering to stop and swallow when Marc started thrusting faster. This added movement pulled the long cock up and out, slid it back down and in, fast, hard, repeatedly, as the blond man built up quickly towards his come. Jack was right on the edge of it too, but he wasn't missing a thing. "C'mon," he growled, "use that pig! Fill him up! Spray it right down his throat, man, that's what he's for!"

Marc bucked, knuckles white on the bars of my cage, and the next thrust, I felt the first hot pulse of his jizz hit the back of my throat. Jack's dirty talk had the same effect on me it always did—added to the sensation of come spurting into me, filling my mouth up with bitter, creamy spunk, waves of come took *me* over, too. I could just reach the bars and I held on so I could keep on Marc's cock even as my come threatened to tumble me off my feet.

Stone had inched closer to the cage. Now the huge man snapped the codpiece off his chaps as he stepped up to take the place Marc vacated. Not only his head was smooth— Stone's cock and balls were shaved too, and a sizeable Prince Albert matched the rings that stretched out his nipples.

"Lick it up, little boy. Get it hard." Sucking in Stone's soft cock with the metal ring felt wild, and I suckled on it the way I liked to suckle Jack's balls. As it started to fill up, he took it out of my mouth and, holding it, nuzzled it around my face, sometimes past my lips, sometimes under my chin. My whole face got slick from the sliding cock, and I hoped the fucking make-up on my upper lip was *more* than waterproof—I didn't think they behaved anything like this in the Max Factor test labs.

"Jack, I'm gonna fuck your kid, okay?" Stone slapped his almost-fully-engorged cock against my cheek. "Sure, just get a rubber," said Jack.

Not an instant later, the beautiful waiter-boy was at Stone's side, bearing a tray. Now where the fuck had he come from? I remembered that I'd heard Sir Sebastian's bell ringing a few minutes before. The boy must have come in then.

I could see his long pretty-boy meat outlined hard in his leather jock. I wondered if the help got to get laid around here, or what.

Stone picked a rubber off the tray, pulled it out of its wrapper, and worked it over his dick. The ring through his cockhead made the rubber fit a little funny, but I figured it'd probably work. Then he took a second one and repeated the process. While he suited up, Demetrius reached over Jack's shoulder and took a condom too.

I heard the sound of a zipper. Whose was that? Stone and Jack already had their cocks out. Then I heard Demetrius say, "Peaches, my pants, please," and the waiter knelt in front of him to help work the leather pants over his shiny boots. Peaches folded the pants carefully while Demetrius shucked the white silk shirt, then took them away. Over at the other end of the room, disguised by the woodwork, I saw a door swing open, and Demetrius' clothes went inside.

Stone, clad in rubber now, moved to the back of the cage. "Get your ass up here," he rasped. He reached through the bars to position me—there was just enough room for me to press my ass against the back bars and still be able to reach a cock fed to me at the front. Peaches reappeared silently, lube on his tray. Stone slathered up his cock, worked a finger into my ass. I shook with wanting this pierced-dicked giant to shove it in.

He didn't shove it, he worked it, and it felt so fucking good I could have screamed. I just grunted, low as I could pitch, and wiggled up onto him. "Jack, you're right, he's a fucking little pig," said Stone, "and I'm gonna fuck him just like one, ready, you little fuck, ready to get it jammed up your fucking pig butt?"

He had only arched into two or three hard thrusts when I felt my mouth opening again for cock—Jack's. I could have died of happiness. I sucked him down, *you want pig, Daddy,*

I'll show you what a pig you have—and it was a minute before I noticed that Jack had shed his pants, too. Peaches stood near, still holding the tray which held the lube.

Then Demetrius, rubber on, started working his cock into Jack's asshole. Jack responded with a long groan, and I remembered that he'd been right up under an orgasm ever since I sucked him the first time. I backed off a little to give him time to get used to all the stimulation.

Pretty soon, all four of us turned into a fucking machine, Stone and Demetrius pumping into Jack's and my butts simultaneously, me swallowing Jack's cock each time they did. We were all growling and all three of them were muttering, "Yeah. *Fuck! Fuck* your fuckin' ass, *fuck!*"

Thank god Jack's cock was too far down my throat when he started shooting to allow me any air to scream with—I was feeling like squealing, like the pig that I was—but his spasming cock kept me quiet. The minute he slid out of my mouth, all cummed out, he bent forward and sucked his jism out of my mouth. The kiss shut me up again when I was about to howl. The minute his mouth left me, there was Demetrius' cock, out of Jack's ass, rubber shed, at my lips.

His dick must have been as big around as my wrist—at least. It had the most prominent head on it I'd ever seen—though of course, I couldn't *see* it right that minute. As it popped past the muscle at the top of my throat, it burned, and I tried to shake my head, afraid I'd choke, afraid I couldn't. Stone, behind me and still riding me hard, saw. "*Take* that cock," he bellowed, giving my ass a stinging slap. "Take it, you fucking little punk!" I took it, seeing stars, stretching wider than I ever thought I could, oh fuck, I thought, I'm playing with the big boys *now.*

Jack was back in commission. He was kneeling next to the cage, his face right next to mine, watching me growl and stretch to accommodate the thick meat. "Good boy," Jack murmured, "you're making me so proud, *little* man. Sucking that big hunk of cock. You can suck him, boy, you can get fucked by him, I know you want that, baby, don't you, can't get enough meat, hot little man."

That was it, wasn't it? I was where I'd always wanted to be, and I turned into a little demon, throwing my ass back on Stone's hard-pounding cock, suddenly finding room in my throat I didn't know I had. My hands clutched the bars for support and I worked both men for all I was worth.

"*Chew on it.*" Jack was still right at my ear. "Chew that dick, boy. Don't worry about biting him, he likes it." I growled like a junkyard dog around Demetrius's substantial cock, chewing it like Jack told me to. Freed from cocksucking's one overriding rule—*don't bite!*—I lost myself completely in the sensation of being filled up as full as I'd ever been. Thank god all the head I'd given already had filled my throat with that thick cocksucking slime—it lubricated even Demetrius's thickness. Stone pounded away behind me, and I had a feeling I knew how he'd earned his name.

But at last even Stone, who had been rhythmically fucking my ass for what seemed like an hour, started fucking even harder and faster. "Take it, you pig!" he grunted, really close to shooting, I could tell by his voice, and I felt Demetrius speed up too, both of them about to hose me, mouth and asshole, full of hot cream. "Comin'!" cried Demetrius. "Comin' right now!" And naturally, I was shooting up the ramp right along with them, I'd be a fine pig if I couldn't come right along with my tops, *right Daddy*? I opened my eyes to look at Jack, wanting to know he was seeing this, pumped full of his friends' jizz. I couldn't suck any more—my mouth was open as far as the muscles would stretch it, in a silent orgasmic yell—but that was okay, because the big black man in front of me was fucking my face now with pounding thrusts.

I remember the first half of the orgasm, but not the second.

I blacked out. I lost it, don't know exactly how it happened but it must have had something to do with my engorgable throat-flesh forming a seal with Demetrius' expanding, coming cock. I couldn't get enough air, I guess.

When I came to, I had no idea where I was.

I felt damp clothes, chill air and motion, saw nothing but darkness, smelled the reek of not-quite-fresh piss. Where the fuck was I? A vehicle—a *trunk*? I felt around me in the utter black and yes, I was lying in a capacious car trunk, not bound, my leather jacket thrown over me, some kind of scratchy car blanket under my head, what felt like trash bags underneath my body. If I hadn't had such an extraordinary night, I'd have been terrified—but I was pretty sure this was part of Jack's buddies' idea of a good time.

The vehicle slowed, turned, turned again, and after a short distance stopped. I heard almost immediately the familiar sound of Jack's bike. Next, a car door slamming, then another. Two people? Then the trunk lid lifted.

It took a second for my eyes to adjust even to the dim alley light. We were outside Jack's place, back in the city. Jack and Demetrius stood there with a man I didn't know. He had on a driver's uniform, so I guessed that Sir Stephen had lent the use of his car to get me out of there. What would a distinguished man like him do with a pissy piece of fucked-out chicken? After all. But had I pissed myself? It wouldn't have surprised me.

Demetrius reached into the trunk and lifted me like I was an unwieldy but not-very-heavy teddy bear. Jack had his keys out. The driver stood silently by. Sir Stephen's help weren't a very talkative lot, were they? But at last, as Jack stepped up to the door, the driver said, "Shall I wait, Sir?"

"Yes, do," said Demetrius, and he had me up the stairs and into the foyer.

"Here, let's clean the pig up," said Jack, gesturing Demetrius through his room and into his bath. He had the water running in the shower by the time we got there. Demetrius supported me while Jack stripped off my jacket, the bar vest, which I noted with chagrin was pissy too, and my boots and pants. He was about to thrust me under the hot spray with my shirt and jockstrap still on when Demetrius spoke up. "Go ahead, strip the girl down."

Jack and I both looked at him, eyes wide. I was stricken. I had been so exultant about passing! What gave me away?

Demetrius started to laugh, a low swell of a laugh that turned into a roar when he looked at me and saw my face. "Randy girl, you did good. I don't know what the fuck that was all about, but you pulled it off. No one else noticed a thing. I'm the one who carried you into the car, darling, and I took the liberty of feeling you up. Yes, I know your Daddy made a rule, but I've broken plenty of his rules before." At this, Jack started laughing too. "Well, it's not like my meat hadn't just been all the way down your little throat. I felt further familiarities wouldn't be inappropriate. And your sweet little dick just seemed to come off in my hand. I tucked it back in, of course."

Jack was howling.

"I trust you have a bigger one than that, since you appear to be keeping Jack interested. I liked ganging Jack with you very much, dear, and I'd be glad to do that again any time you two want to give me a call. Jack, I'm back at my former number. *Do* phone me when you get time. I see we have more catching up to do than I thought. Randy—it's been a pleasure." With that, he gravely extended his hand, and as I took it I started laughing too.

Jack still laughed as Demetrius engulfed him in a bear hug—god, he was larger than Jack by almost as much as Jack outsized me—and I went ahead and shed the damp T-shirt and jockstrap and unwound the binding. As I stepped into the shower, Demetrius took a look at me and said, "Sure enough, she's a girl, all right. Jack, you sick fuck! If St. James ever gets wind of this, he'll have his traditionalist boys come and turn your dick inside out. You and Little Bit here can go down to City Hall and register as domestic partners, and then you can spend your afternoons drinking coffee at the Whiptail Lizard Womyn's Lounge. You fucking wild man!"

Jack kissed Demetrius goodnight as I scrubbed the piss off. He ducked his head in the shower and kissed me too, and then he was gone.

Still grinning, Jack dried me off, capturing me for a minute in the big white fluffy towel. "Want some ice cream?" he said. "Good boys get ice cream."

"God, yes, I'm starving, Jack. I passed out before Peaches could come by with the sandwich tray."

Jack installed me in the flannel-sheeted bed, disappeared down the hall, and came back with two bowls. Before he started on his, he stripped down, took a fast shower, and then joined me in bed. "Kid, you're more fun than a barrel of novices. You were terrific. I'm very proud."

I glowed as much from this as from the still very-memorable fuck I still hadn't come all the way down from. The cold ice cream felt so intense on my throat that I almost squeaked. It was pretty sore from all that action. "Jack, I got piss on your bar vest. I'm so sorry. I don't know how it happened."

"No, *I* got piss on your bar vest. Leathers have to be broken in, child. We all doused you after you went out."

"*What?*"

"Sometimes it wakes people up," he said innocently. "Don't worry about going out, by the way. I think the first time I got down on that man's cock I passed out too. I was younger then, of course."

Then he told me what happened after I blacked out. I'd have fallen over but the men's cocks kept me suspended—Jack saw it as soon as it happened, though he let the guys finish coming. At first, Stone and then Demetrius pulled their softening meat out of me, Jack reached into the cage to hold me up, and before he could even call for him, Peaches was there with the key, unlocking the cage door so Jack could undo my restraints.

"Jack, who were all those guys? Why didn't Sir Sebastian and St. James play? Didn't they like me?"

"Don't worry, honey. St. James loves this group of men, but he almost never plays. He's an old-timer. A traditionalist. He doesn't approve of the free-form way so many of us play now. I think he has a group of men he plays with back in London. He wouldn't be caught dead playing in a room with people who switch. Talk to him if you ever get a chance. Not many like him anymore. Sir Sebastian would have joined us if St. James hadn't been there, but he's too flawless a host to let a guest sit unentertained. As to who they are, I'll tell you the whole story of how I fell in with them, but how about over breakfast?"

Jack snuggled me under his arm, the scent of which almost got me going again—but I was just too exhausted. I started to nod off to the sound of his murmurings, mostly of the "good little cocksucking pig" variety.

Right before I slipped under I whispered, "Thank you, Daddy"—and then, "Daddy, can we borrow Peaches?"

Sexual Harrassment in the Military: 2 Performance Pieces for 4 Actors in 3 Lovely Costumes

Jack Fritscher

ACT 1. USMC SLAP CAPTAIN

QUANTICO, INTERROGATION ROOM. 3 AM. USMC Slap captain: Fleet champion kickboxer, clad in fatigue pants, military-issue T-shirt, heavy combat boots. Rubbing his hands, callused from extreme-fighting martial arts: numchuks, pugil sticks, boduka. High on his left biceps, a tattoo: red cobra, fanged, coiled, ready to strike, in colorful relief against his dark hairy skin. His head shaved short in a white-sidewall military burr. His neck: thick, powerful, cruelly muscled. Long athletic arms: strong, hairy, muscular, threaded with veins. His shoulders: solid as a baseball slugger. His hard-palmed hands: meaty, thick, brutal as a boxer's.

"Shoulders back!" he barks at the young Lance Corporal. "Stomach in. Eyes straight ahead. Don't look at me, boy, unless you're gonna ask me for a date. Get your back straight. Head back." He slams his right fist into his open left palm. "Take your eyes off me, mister. Maybe you're thinkin' you want to get in my pants?"

"No, sir!"

A .22 pistol jammed in the waistband of the Slap Captain's fatigues. Convincing. His breath, moving close in: thick spit-spray, sweet from his nightly Tampa Nugget cigar. "You want the back of my hand, boy!"

"No, sir!"

"Then sit your ass down, punk!"

The Lance Corporal sits on the heavy wooden chair bolted to the concrete floor. Padded asylum restraints snap around his ankles. Handcuffs lock his wrists together behind his back. Behind the chair. His head swerves to resist the black cloth blindfold.

The Slap Captain's hard palm open-hands the Lance Corporal up against the side of his head. He feels the hot burning imprint of the slap across his face. Then the blindfold is knotted, secured. He can see out from underneath: thick fingers make metal-toothed electrical clamps chow down on his nipples. He moans at the sharp pain. The Slap Captain open-hands him again. Slaps his face. Hard. Right. Then left. Then right again. Harder. His ears ring.

The Slap Captain chains the clamps together. His finger crooks and catches the dangling chain at its center, raising the clamps horizontally, pulling them outward.

"You wanna kiss me, boy? Hey, boy, kiss me. Kiss me, boy." It's an order, but the Slap Captain's voice is reassuring. The Lance Corporal tilts his cropped blond head up in the direction of the Slap Captain's dark voice. He is not certain how he is supposed to kiss a man, even for the Corps; not certain how he can kiss a man he cannot see.

He leans his whole torso forward, pulled by his tits, raising his blindfolded face up to this man, offering his lips.

But it's not a kiss the Slap Captain wants.

A fast slapshot.

The Lance Corporal's face rebounds ninety degrees to the right. Then is back-handed to the left. His cheeks burn. Redden.

The intense ringing in his head clouds out the Slap Captain's voice. His head turns tentatively, as ordered, back to the front.

Under his blindfold he sees the Slap Captain's thick gorilla fingers unbutton the green fatigue fly. His calloused palm lifts out an extra-large USMC jockstrap pouching his big hairy balls, overlaid with thick long uncut cock. The Slap Captain gropes his sweat-stained jock-cup with his left hand. His thick-muscled right arm swings out from his massive shoulder. The Lance Corporal, nose and mouth upraised, sniffs the wet drip of the Slap Captain's hairy pits.

A pause. Shorter than his breath. Then starts the cadenced tattoo of open-handed slaps: left, right, left, right. Ten. His head slap-lashed, hard. Twenty. Back and forth. Thirty. His face: a boxer's fastbag. Forty. Saliva in his mouth turning to blood. Fifty. Through the ringing in his ears, words, alternating with the stinging slaps, come through. Sixty. What is the Captain saying? Seventy.

Again. Another volley of open-handed slugs. The big uncut dick swinging free and mean and hard. The hot spit from the Slap Captain's mustached mouth wetting his cheeks, escalating the stinging of the hard slaps.

He wants the Captain's dick. He wants the Captain's mustache, lips and mouth and tongue. He wants to swallow his heavy spit. He leans forward. Again, the unseen hand slaps his face. Hard. Left to right. Again, the ringing over rides the voice he can hear but cannot distinguish.

His blindfolded head flushes warm up from his neck, to his cheeks to his temples. He sucks and swallows the warm salt-blood taste in his mouth. The slaps bruise his inner cheeks against his gritted teeth.

He cocks his head. Hardened for the Corps. Angles his face toward the heat and the dripping sweat off the Slap Captain's wet fatigues. Anticipating. Unquestioning. Waiting. Wanting. He sees the thick dick and balls drop out of the piss-wet jock.

The balls hang low. The dick, uncut, blind, hard, rampant shows its rosy pisshole.

He leans forward.

The Slap Captain's piss sprays in a direct shot into his mouth. He gulps, swallows, thirsty for the hot bubbling thick Marine piss that streams faster than he can drink.

Piss: spilling down on his chest, running down his belly, soaking his dick and balls, dripping down the inside of his naked thighs, pooling up under the wet pucker of his asshole bound into the worn seat of the wooden chair.

Again, he leans forward.

The Slap Captain's tough hands box his face back and forth. His teeth clench. His eyes squeeze closed under his blindfold. His mouth tastes metallic. He smells the crusty cheese of the Marine dick swinging free near his bleeding nose. Both nostrils trickle blood down his upper lip. The hard slaps whip the trickles to blood-spray. He holds his head steady against the rhythms of the Slap Captain's hand. The slaps slow. The palms grow sticky with the Corporal's blood. Somehow the slaps increase his hunger for the Slap Captain's dirty cock.

The Slap Captain plants his hand on the back of the Corporal's neck. "I want me a bloodfuck USMC pussy-mouth!" He holds the burr-cut head in his hard-knuckled grip. "Now come on, boy!" The Slap Captain pressures the back of the Lance Corporal's neck, pivoting the shaved head, with the bloody blindfolded face in his hand, positioning the mouth like a bulls-eye for his crusty cock.

"I figure I got me one of two things. I either got me an ambitious young Lance Corporal. Or I got me a .22 pistol to give a tight-lipped gyrene a new asshole."

Still cupping and guiding the Lance Corporal's head, pressing it down with all the power in his warrior-hand, the Slap Captain nuzzles the bloody nose and swollen lips against his big-veined cock. "Clean it up, boy!"

The Lance Corporal sticks his tongue through his bruised lips, and works his tongue tip in, under, and around the inner lip of the thick foreskin, sucking out the clots of cheese, old cum, sweat, piss, and gun-grease. Not needing an order, he pulls back from the hard cock, with the cheesy smegma melting on his tongue, and swallows.

"That's my boy. That's my good boy." But the level, low voice is cut off by another slap that starts the ear echo-ringing. Behind the blindfold, the lights in his head are dazzling. He is being beaten, slapped silly. He is obedient. The Corps is all. In a moment, less than an instant really, he turns his head round again, straightforward, offering his face.

He is ready. Even for the heavy-handed wallop of this palm-and-backhand slap, stinging his cheeks, purpling his temples, blackening his eyes. The Slap Captain's hands reshaping his boy's face into the tough, hardened, experienced face of a Marine.

The Slap Captain giving him a Marine's face.

He feels his nose ready to give way, to break, but the Slap Captain pulls back; pulls his slap-punches; takes instead his big hand, gripping his hard dick like a brutal nightstick. He beats the bruised, tenderized face with his huge dick, wet with blood and cheese and piss.

The handcuffs cut into his wrists. Sweat and blood pour from his face, down his chest, over his clamped and torn tits. The Lance Corporal's mind goes blank behind his battered face: Halls of... Slap!... zuma... Shores... Slap!... Punch... Shores of Trip...Slap...Punch...Punch! The rhythms of the Slap Captain's fist and dick beating his face. The ringing in his ears. His chin held tight by the Slap Captain's hand.

"Kiss it. Kiss it real soft, baby."

He opens his mouth. He's learned what kiss means.

"Kiss it." The commanding voice becomes almost soft. "Kiss it...sweetly."

As his bruised lips touch the swollen cockhead, its shaft, backed by the Slap Captain's fullback butt and thighs, rams the rod through his lips, past his bloody teeth, across his tongue, and fucks long and hard deep down his gagging throat, until choking on the spit and blood and pumping cum, he feels the huge cock pulled like a deep root from his throat, still shooting white clots of cum on his face, feeling the large boxer's hands rough-massage the slick seed into his bruises, slapping him lightly, always slapping him, across the cheeks with his angry red cock, pulling on the chains tearing at his tits, feeling the thick bristle of the Captain's mustache and the Captain's hard lips and the Captain's mouth pressing hard in lust and discipline against his own lips, feeling the pressure of the Captain's tongue sucking the bloody saliva from his beaten mouth, feeling the Captain's fingers squeezing his cheeks, feeling the mix of the Captain's spit, and his own blood, cum-honkered forcibly back down his throat, swallowing, writhing, tit-ripped, restrained, bound.

His man's face, his Marine face, blindfold ripped away, seeing the spit-wet uniform of the sweaty, dark, handsome Slap Captain pulling his tits, making his sweat run, his moans deep.

He looks up at the smiling cruel face, the disciplined face taking him deep now into the Corps, initiated now into the inner rank of the Corps. His hard-muscled body, understanding, thrashes up, bound to the ungiving wooden chair, into a painful arch of ecstatic handless coming. The Slap Captain pins, with one solid punch, a pair of squadron wings into the Lance Corporal's chest, metal into flesh. Fist into blood.

"That's my boy." The hands hold him very tight. The handsome mouth, mustache, and lips, press sweet, hard agony against his own. "That's my man."

ACT 2. CIGAR SARGE

SARGE IS HOT. REALLY GOOD-LOOKING. You offer him
a cigar. He takes the box slowly. He pulls the cigar out slowly.
Long. Fat. Brown. Wrapper crinkles. Cigar is soft inside cellophane. Sarge tears wrapper deliberately with his strong teeth.
Feels cigar. Smells good. Aroma. Wets lips. Inserts first one
end of cigar. Then other. Licks it smooth and wet. Taste feels
sharp on his tongue.

You kneel between his spread thighs. Look up to watch
him reach into his fatigue pocket for a match. Cigar locks in
his teeth. Poised. Wet. You wait for the moment. Incredible
moment. When a man strikes fire. Lifts it to his face. Match in
one hand. Cigar in other. You watch his face. You know the
taste of a cigar lingering in a thick mustache.

Sarge rubs his hand across his crotch. Your mouth burrows
down into his fatigues. Your eyes look up into his face.
Instead of lighting the cigar, he holds the match. He stares
straight into your eyes. The butt-end of stogie juts square
from his mouth. Surrounded by moist lips. Locked tight in his
teeth. The match burns. Sarge gives the cigar another slow,
long lick. He clenches it hard. Your hand moves faster in
anticipation of the moment the match will touch the tip.
When deep blue smoke will rise from the hot, red coal.

Sarge touches the match to the cigar. Burn point. Smoke
curls. Fills his mouth. Rises in a rich blue halo around his face
and close-cropped hair. He pulls on it. Easy. Smooth. The tip
glows hot. Red. A burning coal. A weapon.

You kneel adoringly between his legs. Worshipping cock.
Worshipping his face. The cigar smoke is his incense. Is your
incense. The cigar is a thick cock. Wet. Hot. Burning.
Commanding in his face. He exhales the smoke down on you.
Spews smoke down on you. The smoke has volume. The
smoke is thicker than poppers. The taste in your mouth is

better than you imagined. The smoke lifts you higher. He puffs. He puffs, and between his thighs, you sniff the smoke he exhales. You snort the aroma.

You go down on him. Your eyes never leave his mouth. His cock is in your mouth. You pull your lips out. To the head of the dick. It's your trick. You know it. He knows it. It's your signal. You want him to hit his cigar and hold its heat. Hot against the back of your punk-ass neck. To keep his dick buried root-deep in your mouth. The back of your neck carries faint erotic marks of past cigar-sucks. You want his heat. You want his fire. You want his cum. You want the wet splash and the hot burn. You want the smell of cigar in his hair and mustache. You want the smell of his sweat. You worship his mouth. His prick.

You strip off your shirt. You drop your jeans. You hold your mouth open wide, coming up off his cock. Your wide wet oval of mouth goes down on his cigar butt smoking in his mouth. He puffs it heavy and hard. You wrap your mouth wide around the burning cigar. You inhale the smoke billowing from his mouth, curling up and out of his hard-bitten teeth. Again in perfect balance. Sarge on the cigar's wet end. You on the hot. Cigar-locked together like two men fucking. One up the ass of the other: the fucker orders the fucked not to move, not to dare even flex his ass, or the cock buried hilt deep will shoot despite the fucker's warning. Two men on one cigar. Smoke shared. His eyes roll back in his head. Close to your face. Down the length of hot cigar. You see all.

You feel him piss. Warm. Wet. All over your belly. You worship his face. His mouth. His cigar. His cock. His body. His energy sears you more than a match to a rich dark Havana.

Your eyes beg him. Your empty mouth pulling back from his cigar-mouth begs him. Your hands frame a small area on your belly, above your cock.

He looks at the space like a firebomber over target.

You need him. For once, finally, you need him to do it. Your eyes say he must. Please. Your face shows your need. Please. Your hard cock shows your commitment. Please. His own meat hardens. More. With three last stoking puffs on the butt in his mouth. You need it. He wants it. Again a balance. Control between you both. Consent. Mutual understanding. You need what he can give. He likes what you can offer.

Sarge pulls his cigar stub from his mouth. Your hands milk his cock. Pull his meat. His hand lowers the glowing tip to your groin. Your eyes lock together. Your eyes beg him. Your dick moves fast in your one hand. His cock moves fast in your other. His thick arm, cigar butt curled into the palm of his hand, moves down between your moving arms. The glowing tip is inches away from your belly. Three inches. Two. You can feel the heat from the tip moving warm toward your skin.

The energy locks totally between the two of you. Perfect partners. His eyes search your eyes one last time. Never has any man so totally offered what you so totally need.

A shadow falls heavy across his eyes. It says NOW.

His fist with the burning cigar butt moves in for that last body-inch and holds. The pleasure. The pain. His heat pours into your belly. Contact: the briefest second. A tick of pain. Seared. You come. Now. You come. His face moves in to yours. An inch away. You rock, jerk your cock. Worship him. Think of him. Together, you separate: his hand moves away from your belly. Your belly moves away from his hand. He keeps his eyes locked into yours. Balance.

Sarge tucks his dick toward your groin. He licks his hand. He shoves his cigar back between his teeth. Locks it down. He pumps his hard greasy cock over your red-spotted belly. He pumps his dick hard. Until the smoke filling his mouth, his nose, his chest fills your mouth, your nose, your chest. Until in the blue haze around the pair of your faces, his cock comes wet and hotter than any cigar, shooting healing seed, salving juice over the loving brand that will all too soon fade to a lover's scar. Made by him. Made by this man. Made by this toker. This taker. To carry hidden and secret for the rest of your life.

Somewhere out there, Sarge waits for you.

Because you know what Sarge has and Sarge knows what you need.

Thomas, South Carolina

Dimitri Apessos

> *Thy neck is as a tower of ivory; thine eyes like the*
> *fishpools in Heshbon, by the gate of Bathrabbim; thy*
> *nose is as the tower of Lebanon which looketh toward*
> *Damascus.*   SONG OF SOLOMON 7:4

Right on the northern tip of South Carolina we stop in a town
called Thomas, mostly as a joke, as that is my ex-boyfriend's
name. "You've got issues," Geof quips as we park outside the
biggest building in town: a Masonic temple. Right away, it's
clear that something is wrong with the town of Thomas.

There are only two things I hate about being on the road. One
is that my eyebrow ring often becomes inflamed when I go too
long without showering. The other is the trucks. I have nothing against truck drivers and have often considered trucking
as a future profession that would allow me to drive and smoke
simultaneously. But I have never managed to get over the story
of how Thomas lost his virginity, as he told it to me once in
Barracuda in New York, on a humid afternoon in July.

Turns out that Lexington, Kentucky, where Thomas grew up, had a bar which, although not gay per se, had drag shows and hence attracted a mixed crowd. Unable to get in anywhere else, Thomas would go with a friend who claimed to be bisexual but who had never tested his hypothesis of sexual fluidity.

When he was a senior in high school, Thomas met a big, muscular truck driver there who took an interest in him and bought him a couple of drinks. Cheered on by his eunuch friend, Thomas went back to the man's truck and gave him the most valuable thing a closeted seventeen-year-old boy in the South has to give.

The back of a truck, Thomas?

"He had it made up really nice, back there. He had this carpet and lights. It was nicer than most houses."

A truck driver, Thomas?

"He was buff. He was hot. He was really built."

Perhaps. Still, I cannot see a truck without conjuring a vision of the young Thomas, not then knowing that the gay metropolis lay in his future, frightened, silent, following this man to the far end of the parking lot. Parting his immature legs, facing the truck's inner wall, his arms lifted in painful ecstasy, a large, unkempt man of the road behind him, thrusting and pushing into him the frustration of life on the highway, further excited by the disbelieving relief of having found a boy for the night. In how many towns was he this lucky? One out of three? One out of six?

Biting his lip, Thomas tried not to cry. In the back of this majestic sixteen-wheeler something was starting—a life of clubs and bathrooms and missed connections, casual sex and failed relationships, trying to return to that spot, trying to get back to that place that hurts so sweetly and feels so good, because it allowed a seventeen-year-old boy to be held by someone so much larger, so much stronger than himself, that he couldn't help thinking it may just be okay after all.

Not a single person is walking in the streets of Thomas, South Carolina, and the only shops are of a religious bent. People are staring at us from behind dirty store windows and dusty windshields. The population appears to be predominantly black and exclusively Methodist. Maybe a freed slave colony?

A pair of young black men roll down their car window and, without slowing down, throw an exaggeratedly queeny catcall in our direction.

"Hey boys!"

Are they really gay? Do they think we are? We decide to get the hell out of Thomas, South Carolina, without finding out.

My fondest memory of Thomas is not of the Sex Scandals through History Halloween party we went to dressed as Socrates and Plato. Nor is it of the Valentine's Day weekend we spent at my schoolmate Valerie's in Vermont, back when I was still in the closet and we pretended to be just friends, frightened that she would figure us out and overjoyed when she told us the only space to sleep was her roommate's double bed. No, the fondest memory I have of Thomas has no specific date attached to it. It is of a random sunny midsummer morning in my frat house in New York.

I don't know if it was a weekend, or if I just had woken up with enough time to waste before we both had to go to work. What I remember is sensing the luxury of time, with the early morning sun searing in through my window and the faint humming sounds of the city's construction workers and garbage trucks providing a permeable screen to reality.

Thomas was always a heavy sleeper, and this morning was no exception. The smell of him in my bedroom, excitingly alien yet comfortably at home, and the sight of his lean, boyish body on my mattress, sparked a flashback of all the affection and tenderness I had ever felt towards him. Usually he was the forward one and I was the one who let it happen;

he was the aggressive initiator of intimacy while I went along for the ride. But not this morning. Waking up next to him, seeing him lying there on my bed half naked, gave me a devoted urge I had never thought I would experience. I wanted to serve and service him, please him while receiving no pleasure other than that of knowing I had pleased him. I wanted him to lie back, half-asleep, and to be reeled slowly into the reality of the day by my lips and my fingers.

Running my fingers along his naked torso, smoothing his skin, caressing his form, sliding my hand down to his waist, then lower, reaching the daily morning anchor between the sleep and the body, I was turned on as never before. Energized, I sat on his legs, placing one hip on either side of him, and started kissing his neck. Taking in the smell of his body—a blend of sleep and sweat and morning dust—I worked my way down, kissing his bony collar, his lean chest, his hollow stomach.

At his waist, I paused to honor his strong morning hardness. I licked the bulge in his briefs, still taking in every smell as he slept. His cock twitched, moving purely because of the friction between my tongue and his skin, like a flower turns to the sun without the earth's awareness.

Excited beyond the point of control, I pulled down his underwear and leaned back to admire the full hard size of his thick and long morning glory. I kissed the tip with tenderness, as if I were meeting his mouth or exciting his ear, and then parted my lips to go down on it as far as I could. His sleepy moan startled me; I had been viewing him as a painting or a photograph. I had objectified the picture of him glowing under the sunlight on my bed, knowing already that the image would stay with me—a memory fueling nights of longing and nostalgia long after he and I went our separate ways.

Loving his half-asleep, half-awake excitement, I took his erect cock deeper into my mouth, faster, faster again, with confident rhythm—a circular motion from the neck, as he had taught me. When he put his semiconscious hand on the back of my head, I lost it. Moaning now with each circling of my neck, as his hand guided me, I stayed on him for what seemed like hours; in reality it was probably forty-five minutes. (Thomas always took a long time—especially in the morning—but this particular day I did not mind.)

When his own moans intensified and his neck arched, pushing his head back as he propelled his pelvis upward, I knew what I had to do. For the first time ever, I swallowed his morning juice, completing the connection, directly from his insides to my insides, through his cock and down my throat.

When it was over, I couldn't bring myself to move off him, so strong was my affection for the form of his body. I stretched out my legs and lay my head on his chest, falling back into sleep with him, the sunlight illuminating the dust as it descended on us and around us, filling my bed and the room with particles of the morning, of New York City, of the Upper West Side, on a lazy summer day.

Before leaving Thomas, South Carolina, we get a double cheeseburger with fries at Hardee's and buy a Jerry's Kids muscular dystrophy shamrock. I sign it *George Rupp* and the lady behind the counter puts it up on the wall next to the cash register using messy Scotch tape.

Walking back to our parking spot, we see a woman in her fifties leaving her car, without locking the door, and walking towards a gloomy shop offering "What Would Jesus Do?" paraphernalia. It appears that in South Carolina the law requires only one valid license plate, because her car's front is adorned with an impostor. It says "I" followed by a heart and ending with an empty, complex circular shape. I love clouds? I love smog? I love the sound of one hand clapping?

Geof asks her.

"Cotton," she answers, without a hint of humor.

Just the other night, Thomas slept over again. We broke up almost a year ago, and in the meantime we have traveled many times back and forth on the road between civility and talking shit behind each other's back. But college was only a couple of weeks from being over, and I wasn't even sure where he would go or what he would do. I had been thinking about him but had too much pride to call and talk to him.

Tony and I had been downtown, hitting the bars, and I didn't get back to the neighborhood until three in the morning. I needed one more beer before going to sleep, but I was completely broke. Maybe my friend Sheila would be bartending at Saints and maybe she would treat me. It was worth a try.

Of course, when I walked into Saints, Sheila wasn't there. But Thomas was, sitting at the bar with two of his fraternity brothers, drunk off their asses while he was sober. I sat with him, and we talked until the bar closed. He told me about the job he would soon be starting, the studio in Brooklyn he was moving into, what he had been up to, and he promised to call me when he had his new number. Almost an hour later, mutually shocked at what seemed like an indication that he and I could be friends after all, he walked me home.

On my stoop, we hugged. I took in his smell—and all the old memories flooded back. We stood hugging on the corner of 113th Street for fifteen minutes, maybe more, as I breathed him in and relived the greatest moments of the most romantic year of my life.

On his neck I smelled all the overly long lunch breaks we had taken from our summer jobs together at the Manhattan Mall; how sexy he had looked crying on the night I told him I needed to be alone; how good it felt to be held by him when I broke down in his arms after I came out to my parents. Most of all, however, I smelled on his neck that summer morning in my bedroom, and at that moment we both knew what had to happen, even if it was just once for old times' sake.

We kissed. I asked him to come upstairs. He asked if we were crazy. I didn't answer. That night I relived the full year I spent with him, the year that I discovered the male body, the looks you get when you walk down the street holding a guy's hand, the innocence and relief that is only associated with coming out with a loving, experienced, totally devoted boyfriend. The knowledge was in there—in the bed with us all night—that this could not be a return to what we had once shared. Too much time had passed, and we had hurt each other too much. But for one night it felt great to pretend that we were still together. that nothing bad had happened, and that I was still with my first boyfriend, thinking that what we had may just last forever and unsure of what I would do if it didn't.

The lady outside the WWJDshop points at my Che Guevara T-shirt and asks me if that is a picture of John the Baptist. I tell her that it is, then Geof and I climb into our car. Driving off, we pass by what seems to be the only theater in town. It's playing *Arsenic and Old Lace*—an extremely old movie about two nice elderly ladies who kill their dinner guests. I recall Peter Lorre being in it.

"At least now we can both say we've been in Thomas," I joke as we rejoin I-95 North.

Geof groans. After a week in New Orleans, a night in Savannah, and that gay bar in Mobile, I think he's getting sick of my faggot shit. (I appease him by promising to take him to lesbian night at Life when we get back to New York.)

Steel Gray
Ken Butler

The bar was dark, and I searched for a seat as my eyes adjusted to the light spilling over from the dance floor. I found an empty stool at the bar and slid onto it. The guy on my left was lucky that the bartender hadn't carded him—if he was twenty-one, I was a straight arrow. Since I'm attracted only to older men, I ignored him. After an initial gawk and hesitation, he actually had the guts to cruise me with his eyes, but one hard stare from me and he quickly turned away. I ordered a beer and took a look around.

The guy on my right seemed much more interesting, even though I couldn't see his face. He was in a fairly intense conversation with the man to his right, and all I could see was the great shock of silver-gray hair covering his head. But his shoulders were wide and his waistline was just perfect as far as I was concerned—not fat and not fit. A small paunch had begun to creep over his belt and the butt on the stool had begun a little spread of its own. Just my type.

I didn't have a chance. In a few minutes, he stood and left with his companion after calling a good-bye to the bartender.

The voice was a relaxed baritone that sent a wave from my gut down to my cock. I cursed my luck as I watched his back leave the bar. Damn, not even a glimpse of his face, I thought, as I signaled for a beer.

The bartender, who couldn't have been farther from my type but assumed that I must be attracted to him simply because he was good looking, sauntered over with a longneck for me. Tony was taut, muscular like me, and wore only a worn pair of chaps behind the bar, his sizable meat swinging freely between tree-trunk thighs.

"Who was that, Tony?"

"Don't know. Haven't seen him before. Good tipper, though, especially for a Friday." He sauntered away, sure he had broken my heart once again.

The next week, I was at the bar a half-hour earlier in the evening, but that shock of silver-gray was nowhere to be seen. The same the next week, and the next. I decided I'd give him one more week. Hell, maybe he was a travelling salesman with a month-long route. I couldn't believe how obsessed I was becoming with a man whose face I'd never seen, but that wasn't going to stop me from sitting on that bar stool for at least one more Friday.

I had to work late that Friday, so I didn't have time to change clothes, but drove straight to the bar, still in my suit and tie. The shoulders I'd memorized were not in evidence, though, so I found a stool and didn't even look up to acknowledge Tony when a beer appeared.

"Thanks," I mumbled.

"What's with you?"

"Nothing, I guess."

"Yeah, whatever," and he was gone, seeking adulation from another.

After a bit I headed to the bathroom and caught a flash of gray hair at the front door out of the corner of my eye. I backed up a step to peer around—and there he was, paying the cover charge. He was alone, and I willed my bladder to relax. I wasn't going to let him out of my sight again.

He spoke to a few men at tables and nodded to a kid on the dance floor, but settled onto a stool by himself. I willed myself to walk over slowly to the stool on his right. He was watching Tony's ass jiggle as his martini was shaken, and I waited until Tony placed the drink down; then I took a deep breath and said, "I'll have another beer, Tony."

Tony cocked his head quizzically, then looked at my eyes and didn't have to ask why I'd moved down the bar. "Sure, Jerry, coming right up."

The object of my fascination turned to me, I think to say good evening, but the words never made it out of his mouth. I was about to make my standard self-deprecating joke, but I took one look at his eyes and was equally tongue-tied.

They were like none I'd ever encountered: large, somewhat rounded at the corners, a bright gray that stopped me cold. They sparkled like highly polished stainless steel, and the thick lashes that encircled them were the same silver-gray as the hair on his head. So was the bushy mustache hanging over his lip, and his ruddy complexion made the intense gray even brighter. And despite the gray, I guessed he was no older than fifty.

He was as surprised as anyone is when he first lays eyes on me, I guess—I'm living proof that they grow 'em bigger out in the Midwest. Indiana-born and raised, I grew up in a farming family and never felt out of place physically until I moved west. I'm six-foot-seven and weigh about three hundred twenty pounds, the last twenty of which is extra weight, gained when I stopped working out, trying to break the jock image I was afraid I'd never shake because of my size and the circumference of my biceps. I have straw-yellow hair, fair skin that reddens instead of tanning, and blue eyes that are considered piercing in their own right, though nothing like the pair staring back at me.

He regained his composure first. "Forgive me, son, I didn't mean to stare, but it's not often you turn around to see a line-backer next to you. I hope you won't take offense."

"None taken," I said, pleased I could speak again. "And I hope you don't consider this a cheap pick-up line, because I don't mean it to be, but I've never seen eyes the color of yours. They're beautiful." I started to blush. I embarrass easily. I tried to cover up by sucking down half my beer.

"I'll take it as a compliment, then," he said with a wink. "Thank you. My name's R.J., and yours is Jerry, right?"

"Right. Jerry Sanders."

"R.J. McIntyre." He offered his hand.

"I saw you here a month ago," I said. "I hoped you'd come back. I wanted to meet you."

He raised one bushy eyebrow. "I don't remember you, and I think I would."

"I sat next to you at the bar, but you were really involved with some guy."

After a beat, he said, "Oh, him. What a waste of time."

"Sorry." I grinned.

"So, Jerry," he said, "I'll be obnoxious. Just how big are you, son?"

"Six-seven, three-twenty." At least he hadn't beat around the bush before he asked. "Does that make some sort of difference to you?"

"No, son, not at all. I'm just curious, and crass enough to ask. But I suppose everyone asks you that."

"Sooner or later. I've got all the comeback lines down pat."

At that, he reached over and patted my forearm, squeezing its muscled firmness gently before reaching back for his drink. I went for more of mine, too, only to find the bottle nearly empty. Tony walked by, and R.J. said, "Another beer for my newest friend, bartender."

Tony smiled. "Sure thing."

"So," R.J. said, "tell me a little about yourself." That was always the next question, after they'd asked about my size. By now, I had an honest, pat answer.

"Midwestern. Farmer. 4-H blue ribbons to prove it. Football and wrestling at Indiana University. Excelled at neither—no killer instinct, my coaches said. Degree in computer science like everybody else in the mid-eighties. Moved to the Silicon Valley just in time for the layoffs to begin. Moved north and managed to get into computer games at just the right time. I make a comfortable living, but don't have many friends.

"And I'm not a top," I finished. "Surprised?"

"Yes, but not disappointed." My heart beat a little faster. "Okay, my turn. California. Common as dirt. No college. Worked for my pop's construction business until he died; that was years ago. Took it over, became very successful, but hated it, so I sold it and live on the dividends. I'm lazy, I guess." He chuckled. "Actually, I raise money for charities, just to keep myself from drying up and blowing away. You gotta do something when you're my age, or your brain just quits."

"You sound like you think you're old."

"I am old."

"Fifty isn't old."

He patted my arm again. "Bless you, son. You sure know how to stroke an old man's ego."

"How old are you?"

"I just celebrated my sixty-second birthday."

"Bullshit."

He reached back and pulled out his wallet with a little sigh, like maybe he too had done this often before, and opened it to the first cellophane window. "Read it and I'll weep for you." Sure enough, the birth date read June first, 1935. I was impressed, and said so.

"Don't be. I've just got good genes. God knows I don't take care of myself like you do." I blushed and he noticed. Slapping his forehead with his hand, he said, "Shit, Jerry, I'm sorry. I just keeping chewing on that foot in my mouth, don't I?"

"It's okay," I said, because I sensed that he was truly contrite.

"It's just that you're so damned built. Good-looking, too." My blush doubled and he chuckled. "So, go ahead, ask me something personal—anything."

I knew just what I wanted to ask. "Is the hair on your body the color of your mustache?"

"Well, why don't you reach over, unbutton my shirt, and find out for yourself?" And he stared into my eyes with those killers of his.

I was flabbergasted. No one had ever been this direct with me, and my cock started to grow in my slacks as I shakily reached out to finger the top button of his cotton shirt. It slipped out of the hole easily, and I ran my hand down to unfasten the next button, and the next. I then used the side of my hand to pull back the edge of the shirt and was rewarded with the gray forest for which I'd hoped. Tony walked by, acted like he was going to say something, then walked on silently.

I sucked in a breath. "Like what you see?" he asked.

"Yes, sir."

"Well, boy," he replied, lowering his voice slightly, "if you've got a place, you could see the whole package."

I was shocked at his candor, but turned on by the direct proposition. I blushed yet again.

R.J. put an arm on my shoulder and kneaded it gently. "Boy, you're just about the best-looking man I've ever seen. Doesn't everyone say that to you?"

"No, they don't.'"

"They should." He stood, left Tony a ten-dollar tip, straightened something that seemed cramped in his pants, and started off through the crowded bar.

He stopped outside. "Where are you parked?"

"Right over there. Do you want to follow me?"

"No, son, I want to ride with you. That way you can't just kick me out the door if you don't like me," he said, laughing.

"Don't worry. I like you. Very much."

R.J. reached up and caught the back of my neck, pulled my face down to his, and kissed me. I could feel the heat in my face as he let me go, and was glad it was dark enough that he couldn't see my now perpetually red face. I couldn't believe how bold he was, kissing me like that out in the open, but I liked it. I knew he simply didn't care who saw.

I opened the door for him, then walked around and got into the Lincoln, one of the few cars large enough for my frame.

My house isn't far from the bar, but the ride was memorable. As soon as I pulled out of the lot, he grabbed my hand and placed it on the crotch of his pants. The bulge beneath the cloth was sizable and rock hard. I kneaded it carefully, gauging its size, then reached down to cup his scrotum and gently squeeze his balls. He sighed and unzipped his pants.

I tried to extract his cock from the folds of cloth.

"Wait," he said. He unbuttoned his slacks, pulling back the edges of the fabric, then reached down into his boxers and pulled out his cock and balls. The car swerved slightly as I looked over in fascination.

R.J. guided my hand to his thick shaft, and I gently pumped him a few times, then kneaded his balls again. I'm especially fond of testicles, and his felt fat, just like the cock above them. I was slightly surprised that he was circumcised, but filed that question away for the future.

"Now, pull on my balls." I complied, and he sighed again.

I pulled into my driveway and had no sooner stopped the car than he was getting out, holding his pants with one hand as he stroked his shaft with the other. I prayed that none of my neighbors were looking out their windows, and moved quickly to open the front door.

He walked right in, then turned to face me as I locked the door. He opened his hand, and his pants fell in a heap at his feet. I stepped forward and pulled the boxers down with a jerk. He kicked off his loafers and stepped out of the heap around his feet. "R.J." I began.

Those beautiful eyes narrowed. "What happened to 'sir'?" There was no menace in his voice.

"I'm sorry, sir."

"Get on your knees." I obeyed. He loosened my tie, slipping it out from around my button-down collar. Then he tied it tightly around his cock and balls. I gasped as his cock grew another inch before my eyes, then looked at him in wonder and lust. "I like that look in your eyes, Jerry. We're going to enjoy this, aren't we?"

"Yes, sir."

He grabbed me gently by the neck and guided my face to his cock. I opened my mouth, saliva collecting in its crevices. In one smooth motion, he buried most of that cock down my throat, backing out gently to let me lube him with spit. Then he plunged roughly down my throat again, and we both moaned in pleasure.

"When I first looked at you, I didn't think I'd have a chance. But when you said that you weren't a top, I knew I was going to have you, boy." I groaned around his shaft, and he continued. "I didn't think you'd unbutton my shirt, but you did. That's when I knew I could probably do whatever I wanted with you. Right?"

I tried to nod, and he backed out so I could get a breath of air. But he plunged back in before I could speak, and I looked up at him as he said, "You don't need to talk, Jerry. I know all about you. I'm gonna work you over good, boy, and we're both gonna enjoy it." A tear slid down my cheek. This was what I so desperately needed and never seemed to find, and I couldn't believe that it was happening to me with this gorgeous man.

He looked down, saw the tear, reached to brush it away, then backed out of my throat. "Stand up." He took me in his arms and I leaned to kiss him. The kiss became passionate, and my breath became ragged as it continued for the next minute.

He broke. "Where's the bedroom?" He stripped off his shirt as he followed me there, then collapsed onto the bed. I turned on the lamp on the dresser so I could get a look at him naked.

He was covered in that beautiful gray hair, and looked as if he had once been muscular. Time and a thin layer of fat, along with all that hair, had softened the outlines of his body. He turned me on naked more than he had clothed, but I found myself constantly drawn back to his eyes.

"Strip for me, boy. Let's see what's under that suit." I pulled frantically at my coat. "Slower." Off came my coat, then, slowly, my shirt, then my loafers. Then I unbuttoned my braces and unhooked my pants, letting them fall as I pulled the braces up over my shoulders. That left only my undershirt and my briefs, which were tented out uncomfortably in front of me.

"That's far enough for now. I want to make you sweat before I peel those briefs off of you." His sexiness made my balls ache.

"Come to me." I walked to the edge of the bed and placed one knee on the mattress, then lowered myself beside him, took him in my arms while he kissed me—for a long time. I was panting again before he let me up for air.

He backed out of my embrace and casually lifted an arm. I attacked the pit without being asked, pleased that he wore no deodorant, and licked and sucked the skin clean, revelling in his musk. He lifted the other arm into the air; I worked my mouth across his hirsute chest, paying attention to both erect nipples before plunging into his other pit, snorting in the thick nest of hair and sweat.

When he was clean, I got up on my knees and licked down his chest, cleaning his navel along the way. My forehead bumped against something and then my lips found the base of his cock.

I made a hard arrow of the tip of my tongue and jiggled it up his shaft, plunging down over him with my mouth when I reached the tip. The wide head bumped against my soft palate and I fought the urge to gag. I forced myself down farther, and the tickle subsided as the shaft penetrated deep into my throat. I held him as long as I dared, then swiftly expelled him, sucking in a deep breath. But his hand found the back of my head and he shoved down, hard. I took all of him again, and we groaned together again as my nose bumped against his soft, fleshy scrotum.

He worked my mouth around his cock, pushing with his hand and urging me on with shallow thrusts from below. I started to sweat. At some point my pelvis began to thrust of its own accord, and soon I felt a knuckle kneading my asshole through my briefs. I backed against it, eager for the pressure. A hand landed on my ass, hard. I groaned louder.

Then R.J. pulled on my balls through the cloth, and groan turned to plaintive moan.

"Like that?" I nodded furiously. "So do I." Still sucking his shaft, I reached around my head to grab his scrotum. His balls had a nice heft, and I pulled them out and away from his cock. I was surprised at how far the flesh stretched, but finally the skin tightened. I pulled my mouth away, then let myself fall on his sword yet again, swallowing hard as my nose touched the tightly stretched skin. I twisted the testicles a quarter turn, and this time the groan from above was half an octave deeper.

"Oh, yeah, Jerry. I like that." His grip on my testicles was merciless, and the bunched cotton cloth was rough against my now-sensitive sac. He released me suddenly.

"Stand up. Take 'em off." I grabbed the hem of my undershirt and pulled it over my head. He gasped when he saw my chest, which I keep hairless despite the fact I'm not working out anymore. It's one of my best features, and he sat up to run a hand over my pecs.

Then I hooked my thumbs in my briefs, turned to face away from him, and bent over as I slid them over my thighs. I wanted him to know my ass was his if he wanted it, and was rewarded with his thumb against my hole.

I also keep the hair around my cock clipped short, which makes my average endowment look just a bit longer. When I turned, he grabbed my cock so hard that I fell to my knees on the bed beside him, and he pumped it several times before letting go.

"Get back on my balls."

I scooped them into my mouth, sucking and chewing for a long time, until precum leaking from his cock ran down the shaft to wet my cheek. He smoothed the fluid into my skin with a finger while a knuckle found my hole. I impaled myself on the folded digit.

"A condom, Jerry. I'm gonna fuck you." I stumbled to the bureau to dig out my stash, chose a black condom, ripped the package open and rolled it down his fat firm cockflesh. Then back to the drawer for lube, which I squeezed over the condom, rubbing until it was slick and shiny. My silk tie would be ruined, but I didn't care.

He stood. "On the bed, on your knees." I crawled up, leaving my ass hanging over the mattress edge. He picked up the lube, went to rummage in the drawer, found a latex glove. He skinned it on over his right hand and squirted a sizable blob of lube into his sheathed palm.

Seconds later, a finger went up my ass with no preamble. "Tight," was all he said, as I sucked in air to quench the fire in my ass. I don't get fucked often, but he calmed me by working the one finger until I was open to it. Then he pulled out, put two fingers together and slowly slid them in.

It felt good this time. I moaned with pleasure, groaned at the shadow of pain. "Tell me," he ordered.

"They feel big. I don't get fucked much, so they're really stretching me out."

"Can you take three, son?"

"Yes, sir." Two were removed, and soon three fingertips were poised at the edge of my butthole.

"Tell me what you want."

"Your fingers in me, sir."

"How many?"

"As many as you want, sir."

"My fist?"

"I've never been fisted, sir. But for you, I'll try anything."

He chuckled. Three fingers pushed inside me to the second knuckle. He stopped briefly, pushed again, and a fourth firm digit bumped against the back of my balls. R.J. rubbed and stretched my hole, and I bucked back to meet them, twisting my pelvis in pure pleasure. My moans mounted in intensity—it was then he slid the fourth finger in.

I was hotter than I'd ever been. I wanted him in me, and was willing to do anything to get him there. I whispered: "Please fuck me, please fuck me, please fuck me, please fuck me," as most of his hand assaulted my ass. He kept lubing me until the viscous goo was trickling down the back of my legs.

"What are you saying, Jerry?"

I gave full voice to my desire. "Fuck me, R.J. Please fuck me, sir. Shove your cock up my ass and fuck me hard."

"Are you hot enough?"

"Yes, sir, yes, sir," I panted, rotating my ass in tight circles around his fingers.

He pulled his fingers out in one smooth motion, peeled off

the glove, rested his slick cock against my butthole and commanded: "Fuck it yourself."

I took him in one hard pelvic thrust. He gasped at the ferocity of my stroke, grabbed my waist tightly with his strong hands, dug his nails into my flesh. The pattern of pain felt good to my pleasure-starved nerve endings. I rocked forward on my knees, then slammed back onto him, setting up a rhythm that he matched quickly. His hands on my waist were merciless, squeezing and pinching, pulling me back onto him again and again. His cock was fully distended, filling me more, far more, than his four fingers had. My asshole was hot and raw from the condom, but I wanted more.

My cock was throbbing and I longed to touch it, but I needed both hands to steady myself. R.J. had taken over: a part of me was shocked by his sudden animal brutality. He grunted with each thrust—"Gnnuhh, gnnuhh, gnnuhh,"— and the sound was hypnotizing. Then I was grunting with him, pleading for his release, and mine.

"Want my load, boy?"

"Oh, yes, sir." He pounded one last massive thrust into me, and didn't pull out, and I could feel his shaft pulsing as he pumped his orgasm into the condom.

It went on for a glorious forever, and then he began to breathe again, a raspy sated sound as he backed out, his cock kissing my ass good-bye with a soft "pop." The empty feeling was horrible.

R.J. walked back to the drawer, returned with one of the large dildos I keep for those lonely nights. It wasn't my biggest, but it wasn't small.

"Up on your knees." I shifted position. "Face me." I did. He lubed the rubber cock. My own cock ached from not being touched.

R.J. handed me the slick cockthing. "Sit on it, then jack off." I grabbed the dildo and positioned it. He untied the tie looped around his softening cock, and peeled off the sticky condom, tied off its end and dropped it to the floor, all the while watching me drop onto the dildo.

Though I was open, I groaned as my ass cheeks brushed the sheet. "Grab your cock."

There was a little lube on my hand from the dildo, and I smeared it around my cockhead. Then he grabbed my cock and scraped excess lube from the fuck off his hand.

"Play with yourself," he ordered, and I began to stroke my aching cock. It felt great. When he leaned over to stare at me intently, I looked into those piercing gray eyes, more blood pumped into my cock. My orgasm welled up in my balls.

I usually close my eyes when I come, but I wasn't about to let go of the sight of him. The first spurt hit his stomach, a good two feet away. "Yeahhhhh, boy, yeah." Stream after stream of semen poured out of me, onto his abdomen, my balls, my sheets, the floor.

At last I stopped. He stepped forward, pulled my head toward his crotch, made me lick my seed out of his stomach hair, then shoved me down farther until I tongued my self off the sheets. The dildo slid out and dropped to the floor.

We fell back on the bed. He kissed me. His cock stiffened against the muscle of my leg, and my cock hardened in response.

He rolled off of me, lay beside, said: "Do you want to come again, son?"

"If you do."

"I probably can't, but I'll gladly do anything to you that you want if it'll make you come like that again."

I chuckled. "I doubt it. It's been a while, so I guess I had it saved up."

"What do you want to do?"

I hesitated. "Just hold me for a while?"

"Happy to, Jerry." He wrapped his hairy arms around me, and we lay back, snuf, and somehow it was morning.

I sat up with a start as I realized the sun was shining through the window. He awoke at my motion. "What time is it?"

"It's seven-thirty. We slept through the night."

"I was comfortable. You?"

"Yeah." I snuggled back into his arms when they were offered. He held me for a minute, and I kissed him, a kiss he returned with gusto, despite our morning breath.

Eventually we broke—nature called—and he headed for the bathroom, then I took my turn. When I walked back into the room, he was partially dressed. I was disappointed. "Leaving?"

"Actually, I thought I'd buy us breakfast."

"Let's shower first." I led him back to the bathroom, opening the door to the shower. Because of my size, I had installed a party-of-four shower stall—more than spacious for the two of us.

I stripped R.J. and we slipped under the hot, cascading water. He pulled me close, kissed me hard as we soaked under the jets, then turned off the water and gave me the soap. Soon his chest was covered in lather, soap bubbles coating his steel-gray hirsuteness, and I was rock hard. I moved to his genitals. He was stiff. He slid the soap out of my hand, turned me around, soaped my back, lathered my chest from behind, massaging my pecs, gently rubbing my balls and my ready cock. When he was done, our soap-slick bodies slid against each other for a few delicious moments; then he turned the water on again and we rinsed off.

"Kneel," he said. "I really like you, Jerry." His cock was fully hard. "I like what we do to each other. Do you?"

"Yes, sir." I looked up at him.

"Good." He guided my lips to his cock, planted his cockhead between them and slid into my throat. My own cock was still hard and ready.

"Play with yourself. I wanna see you come." I grabbed my cock, stroked it fast and hard. "Slow, son, slow," he said.

We settled into a rhythm of sucking and stroking that soon brought us both to the edge. He pushed me off to finish the job himself, pumping his cock until it exploded over my face. Two more strokes, and I splashed my load against the underside of his balls. Jets of water sprayed over us again when he turned the knob, and the feeling against my tender cock head was almost more than I could bear.

R.J. grabbed me by my armpits and hauled me up. He kissed me again, licking a stray strand of his semen off my cheek. I leaned against the tiles and let him soap me up again, then stepped back into the spray to rinse. Then I soaped him again, and he rinsed. Finally, he turned off the water. We could have rinsed forever.

• • •

He decided to cook for me instead, claiming he didn't want to go to all the trouble of dressing when he knew he was going to be fucking me again before long. I didn't argue: my cock grew hard in my sweat pants as I helped out in the kitchen.

He cooked enough for four, but I noticed that he was no slouch in putting away his half. We didn't talk much, but he reached over twice to squeeze my arm while we ate. I was so happy that I couldn't stop grinning, and I finally said, "I guess you think I'm demented, but I've had a really good time, R.J., and I can't wipe this grin off my face." Then I blushed. He smiled.

After loading the dishwasher we moved into the living room, where he settled in one corner of my large sofa and I sat at his feet, my head in his lap.

He sighed softly, then stroked my head. We didn't speak for a long time; he just ran his hand through my hair, and I wrapped my arms around his knee and sat there, content with him, and with myself.

Soon, though, I felt his cock harden along the back of my neck. I turned and opened my willing mouth to take him in, but he suddenly shoved my head away, grabbed me by the hair and dragged me to the bedroom. His sudden savagery excited me. "Up on the bed, on your knees," he commanded, and I knew he was going to claim me with this fuck.

He rolled a condom down his shaft with one hand, smeared lubricant with the other, wiped what was left onto my asshole. He positioned himself, then paused.

"You're mine, now."

"Yes, sir." Tears welled up in my eyes. He buried himself up my ass in one mighty thrust. His balls slapped mine. I screamed with the pleasure of the pain. And I knew—whether we lived together or separately, whether we were exclusive or open, whether it would last forever or not—today I was his, and tomorrow. It was what we both needed.

Tears flowed down my cheeks. It didn't last long—it couldn't. He exploded inside me and I came without touching myself, my prostate and brain both on sensation overload.

My Daddy collapsed onto me. I took his weight easily, lowering us both to the mattress. I rolled over underneath him until we lay belly to belly, chest to chest, muscle to fur, and he covered my mouth with his. Finally we broke for breath.

"I don't know where or how this is going…"

I cut him off. "It doesn't matter. What will happen, will. I want you, and you want me. That's enough for now. Everything else is just…details."

"I thought you were the shy one," he said, his eyes bright.

I looked straight into those steel grays. "Not any more—not with you."

"Damn right," he said, laying his head on my chest.

Stroke the Fire

M. Christian

Lew always knew he'd die someday. Gotta go sometime, sure: Kicked in the head by a horse, catch flying lead over some kind of stupid shit. Snakebite. Damned Indians. Maybe tainted water. Maybe way too much booze after a good haul of pelts. Could even be a fall—at fifty-two his balance and grip weren't what they used to be.

But the one thing he never thought it would be was needing to piss.

All around was white. White, his legs, his coat, his arms, and his gloved hands. White. And all Lew could feel was cold. Damned cold.

Seemed a good idea at the time. It was one of those nights when the west wind came right off the mountain and knocked at his front door, or at least scratched to be let in. He'd been up on old Craggy for more than five years, and the sound of that wind was like a bunkmate. Okay, maybe a bunkmate that snored like a gale, made a horrible mess outside (and never put things back), and would kill you in your sleep if you gave him half a chance. But, still, a regular companion on the mountain.

Going out in the middle of a windstorm, then blizzard, to get wood and stopping in the bracing cold to piss against the side of the cabin seemed like such a safe idea at the time. Christ, he might as well have walked outside naked and shaved.

The steep trail that Lew knew so well, that he could have walked in his sleep, had collapsed just enough to throw him down the hillside.

Now he was surrounded by the white of a snowdrift. His leg felt busted-up, and he was going to freeze to death.

At least, Lew thought, looking down at himself—the only colors in the deathly white of the snow—no one would really know he died taking a piss.

Some consolation.

Lew really didn't want to die. He wasn't old enough yet (his grip was getting bad but not that bad, and he could still plug a stag at one hundred feet with his trusty Remington), he had a few good crotchety years left in him. Hell, he'd only been to Kansas City once. Still hadn't seen Lillie Langtry. God, he'd never even been to the other side of the damned mountain (just never got around to it)—and he would never see Jeff again.

That's what hurt. Damn it, he was looking forward to going down to Stinkhole (Clearwater to those in the "city" limits) and seeing if he'd come through again. Maybe even try and coerce the range hand up to his cabin ("The huntin's damn good" he'd rehearsed to himself). Even thinking about the last time, about his last trip down to Stinkhole, got him going. Christ and fucking shit, Lew thought, kicking out with both legs—and biting his lip at the pain in his right—I can live without seeing Miss Lily, Kansas City wasn't all that fancy the first time, and, damn it, one side of a mountain looks pretty much like the other (don't it?), *but he was gonna miss Jeff!*

Lew was gonna freeze to death and never get his hands on that lanky range hand again.

The real bad part was that he'd fallen sometime after midnight, and dawn was some four or five hours away. If he could last that long, he might get out of this: Wait till the sun came up, get his bearings, try and either make it back up the mountain or limp it down to Mad Jack's. Now the world was nothing but bitter cold white. In a few hours, just a few hours—

Lew checked his pockets. For Christ's sake he was gonna take a piss, not climb the fuckin' mountain. The only thing he found was a cheap little knife in the pocket of his buckskin coat. Aside from that, nothing but white and the cold.

Almost nothing. He also found a hard-on. Lew's cock was iron in his pants, maybe from fear (heard that kinda thing: A boner when they bury you), but more than likely it was thinking about Jeff.

The last time he'd been in Stinkhole was about two months back: He'd come down from his cabin with sixteen hands of fine pelts, a few nuggets of gold he'd managed to scrounge, and a mean itch to scratch. After a quick detour by way of the assayer's office (for the gold) and Long's Whiskey Parlor (to sell Sissy Dan the pelts), Lew had bee-lined for Miss Sally's for a full bottle of her finest redeye (not the cheapest stuff, but not the good stuff either). Lew didn't like to drink himself stupid all that much, but it was just those few months back had been ones of a meaner and bitterer than usual cold up on Craggy, and he had some long, and very cold, nights to thaw out of his bones.

He would have preferred some other kind of way to spend his hard-earned furs and gold, but while he had been a paying customer over at Miss Lavonia's (particularly of Virginia May, who was as tall as he was and could beat him at arm wrestling now and again), his itch wasn't something that her girls could really scratch.

It was sometime after dark when he'd come out of Miss Sally's less drunk than he thought he'd be, sometime after the first bottle had started to taste like old turpentine (knew Sal watered it down some—Lew just hoped it was just with water....) and he wasn't forgetting what he'd come down from Craggy to forget. So, slightly wobbling, Lew stood outside Sal's and looked out on the pitch, sprinkled with lanterns and stars up above, the night of Stinkhole, and thought that he had might as well get Stubborn out of the corral and saddled up for the long trip back up Craggy.

On the way there, though, he got sidetracked: A hole in the "road" (that Clearwater townsfolk called it) filled with mud sucked in his right boot. Just as he was about to kiss the dirt, this tall, thin fella stepped out of the shadows around the city corral and caught him—saving Lew and his town duds from the mud and horseshit. Helping him back up on his slightly unsteady feet, boot sucking and slurping out of the hole, the stranger had leaned back against that fence and appraised Lew while sucking a hot glow from a thin black cigar.

"Thanks, pardner," Lew had said stomping the rest of the mud off on a large rock by one of the corral gates. "Almost got trapped in this-here hell hole of refinement."

"Going back then?"

"Yeah. Sure forget how fast 'civilization' can run through a man."

"Movin' on myself. Come in 'bout ever two months er so fer mail and supplies. A day's 'bout all I can stand." The man's voice had this steel-string twang to it, something Kentucky maybe, or something deeper south. It was a kind of voice Lew liked to hear, a musical kind of voice.

"That way myself. Only come in ta take a bit of the mountain smell off me and put on a little drunk. Man can only get too wild, ya know?" Lew said smiling.

"That I do. That I do. My smell's range, though. Can't see how you can stand to high Jesus the cold up there and those winds...."

In the white, in the now of the cold, cold white, Lew smiled a bit to himself—and tried not to set his dimestore choppers rattling too much—at that. Cold, yeah, Jeff, damned killing cold. Wish I was somewhere warm right now, Jeff, somewhere on the plains with a nice fire crackling....

"Man's got a home, then that's where he sleeps. Can't, myself, see how you can stand the god-derned quiet out there in the flats," Lew had said, listening to the music of the man's voice.

The man shrugged, the tip of his cigar bobbing in the soft night. "That it be. Name's Last. Jeff Last."

Lew wiped the grime off his hands (and hopefully the fool's grin off his face) and offered his own. "Lew. Just Lew around here."

The handshake lasted a bit too long, long enough for the two men to size each other up. Lew in his Stinkhole clothes was a burly barrel of a man, all beard and round blue eyes. He looked fat from aways, but if you'd ever seen him haul cornmeal or lumber you'd know that it was iron, fella, strong, strong iron and not just insulation against Craggy's winds.

Last was long and lanky, and while the light was none too good in that narrow little ways between the public corral and Miller's Fine Feeds, you could tell that he was a beanpole: Six feet easy, in buckskin and serape. In the dark beneath his wide brimmed hat, his shaved face was carved and as Craggy as Lew's mountain home. The handshake had lasted way too long. Now, he thought, how to get this fine feller up the mountain....

"Gotta hit the trail if I'm ta make Ridgewood by dawn," Jeff had said, and Lew's heart had sunk down to his Stinkhole boots.

"Knows how it is—" he had said, starting to turn, maybe extend a hand, and an invitation for another time.

"But you is one fine figure of a man. Might temptin'—"

Lew stared, unsure of how exactly to respond.

"You think the same, Lew of the Mountain?" Jeff had said.

Even in the low light cast from the lanterns of Sal's, Lew could see Jeff's fine figure, out in all its glory there in the "street" of Stinkhole. Lew's breath was stolen by Jeff's cock. Sure, the mountain man had seen a few in his time. Many. Some were as nicely shaped. A few were as tasty-looking. But none were as gigantic. The size made Lew wonder where the man hid the thing. "I think the same, sir. That I do."

"A man after my own, Lew of the Mountain. Care ta share the same with a stranger?"

What with the booze and the excitement (well, mostly the booze), Lew couldn't match the style of Jeff whipping out his beanpole. Clumsily, Lew fumbled with his overalls till he got a cold (shit!) hand around his own iron and managed to haul it out without doing that Jewish-thing to himself on a brass button. Even with the rotgut in his gut, his cock was strong and—Lew was known for being a modest man, but an honest man—his mighty cock. Even in the dim lantern light from Sal's, his was long and strong: Head capped by the smooth cone of his foreskin.

Jeff took a moment to size-up Lew. "Mighty fine, Lew. Mighty fine."

"Could say the same about you, Jeff."

Jeff's doe-skin glove was warm on the skin of Lew's cock. So soft. It felt like pure heat—and not much else. It felt like the glow from a potbelly stove against the chill night air.

In the snow, in his predicament, Lew fumbled through his few—too few—layers to grip his cock. Thinking of Jeff, feeling Jeff again in his recall, made him as iron as that night by the corral. All he wanted, well besides living to see the sunrise over Craggy, was to feel Jeff again, and to have Jeff feel him again....

"Ah'll bet might tasty, too," Jeff had said that night, stroking Lew slow and steady with his soft, soft doe-skin glove. "Wouldn't you say, Lew of the Mountain?"

Lew looked right and left but saw nothing but Stinkhole, dead asleep. "Few have said so, Mr. Late: Those few who have had such a taste."

Not another word: Jeff bent down easy, balancing himself from falling in the mud and shit with another gloved hand, and wrapped soft lips around Lew's cock. The night was cold, and before his lips wrapped, Lew could feel the wave of heat from his mouth, his breath steaming out from him fogged around Lew's hidden head.

Jeff's mouth was like a warm bath and your hand. It was like a fire in the stove and a good pot of coffee. It was like a huge old buck, just *there* on a rise—waiting for you to squeeze off a shot. It was like dawn on old Craggy. It was, well, the only thing you could compare Jeff's mouth on your cock to was the best of everything.

Lew couldn't help but moan at this. He could feel his breath breathing and blowing warm air on the front of his overalls. The heat of him spread out from his cock down into his belly.

Jeff took a deep interest in his cock. He explored Lew with his tongue, pushing his foreskin back gently to tickle the tip, then wash the smeg away with the vigor of Lew attacking a plate of flapjacks in the morning. Lew could feel the flat back of his tongue, the roof of his mouth, the sudden hardness of his teeth.

Cold, cold, cold, Lew...moaned. He remembered it all, hanging onto the fence, opening his eyes and seeing the stars up above, and feeling a freeing breeze whistle by them, tugging at his beard. His hand was around his cock, feeling its heat, its strength. He pulled a bit, and it seemed like this was the one part of his body not freezing, the one part of his body getting hot....

"Yessir," Jeff said, straightening up and wiping his mouth with the back of a doe-skin glove, "mighty tasty. Mighty."

All Lew could do was smile at the man and give a faint nod. This would have been enough for a long time, something that would keep Lew happily jerking off for months on old Craggy, but maybe that night one of those stars was smiling down on him. Jeff smiled at him and pulled something from under his serape.

Lew felt Jeff reach down to his cock and balls (shifting a bit more of Lew's overall's aside), again—stroking him once more with the heaven of the soft glove. Lew looked up the dancing eyes of this handsome stranger and saw them smile at him with an excited glee.

"Let's saddle up this bronco," Jeff said, that *hahahaha* strong in his voice, those eyes, "and see how he rides."

In the snow, Lew had his eyes pressed closed, lost in the memories of that night, that man; his cock iron in his fist. Maybe it was the cold, maybe it was the heat of the memory, maybe it was the life that came into him when he realized that this was probably gonna be it, but whatever the reason, Lew felt like his cock and balls were on fire. As he jerked to the thought of Jeff's eyes, hands, those gloves, he bit his lip and blinked away drops of water.

Jeff neatly lassoed Lew's cock and balls with a neat length of rawhide cord. Though Mountain Lew, bear-skinning Lew, would never have admitted it to none but himself (and then only in passing) the feeling of that cord around his most private of privates was pretty fearful: To have something tight just looped nice and neat around him like that, when all it would probably take would be a harder tug to leave his cock and balls in the mud by the city corral, was something new and more than slightly alarming to him. Pushing himself up and slightly away from Jeff and his little lasso, Lew scooted backward and almost up top of the fence.

The lanky man laughed, the sound of water draining fast from a bucket, "Take it ease there, stud. There ain't nothing here that's gonna hurt ya none. Rest on back and let this old trained cowhand take the reins."

Those laughing eyes and smiling face, maybe just the softness of those gloves and the skill in their strokes—something about Jeff Last made Mountain Man Lew relax and drop himself back down till his boots were once again in the mud. "Just somethin' new, Mister; can't fault a man fer bein' cautious."

Jeff just smiled at the mountain man, and did his magic with the rawhide, roping it around Lew's straining cock and balls like he was going after a prize calf. In a heartbeat, Lew's favorite sausage was trussed like a, well, like the *sausage* it was: Around cock and balls so that Lew felt fit to burst. His cock had been strong and tight before, but now it felt like someone had stuffed even more cock into his cock. Iron before, damned *steel* now.

Despite a sudden urge to keep his manly composure, Lew moaned and jerked his hips forward into the cool night air.

"There, now, that little doggie ain't goin' nowhere now—" Now Jeff's doe-skin gloves were like, well, they might have been like Heaven before, but now they were the kind of pleasure that surely only a devil could deliver. To Lew's straining and hard, hard, absolute hardest cock, Jeff's gentle and sweet ministrations were a real good drunk, and a gleaming lump of gold the size of a good morning dump in your pan.

Lew's cock felt fit to burst, but that damnable cord around him kept it bottled till all Lew could feel was the cum swelling in him behind the cord and the aching, pounding pleasure in his cock. Somewhere along the line, he had closed his eyes, and in an effort to push himself over the edge he opened them again (maybe then he'd break that cord and come!) and found himself staring into the happy eyes of the man called Jeff Last.

"Howdy," Jeff said, smiling even more, before dropping his head down to Lew's fiery cock.

Christ! Lew felt the man's mouth slip over his cock like a hot wet jacket. But this was just a taste for Jeff. He took his mouth away ("Oh, Jesus, man—" Lew mumbled to the chill night), and careful like, real gentle like, peeled back Lew's foreskin and promptly got right back to it.

Lew was gonna explode, it felt so good. Great before, Jeff's mouth was the glory of warm sunlight after a long freezing night; it was a hand of almost all aces; it was two huge lumps of gold in your pan; it was a pair of fine new boots; it was—hell— it was the reason Lew had come out West in the first place, it was a man's doin' for other men with the wilds tossed in!

Don't ask him how, but Lew also knew that Jeff was jerking his own, too, and that added a fire to his own flame: That he had one of those doe-skin gloves working away at his own long tool, pleasuring himself as he sucked away at Lew.

Moaning, Lew tried to keep from jerking back, and pulling his cock from Jeff's mouth. When he came—and Christ did he!—when Jeff carefully untied his cock, it was pails of sticky cum down the back of Mr. Last's throat. It wasn't a normal come, not as Lew had known them to be (a few jerks of the body, that hit of pleasure that was the reason for the trip), this was a jerking and a thrashing of the body, a moan that turned groan halfway outta his chest. It was a rush like falling off a horse, but lots more pleasurable—

Jeff moaned, too, then and there by the fence on that cold night, a little moan but a good one nonetheless. Lew was aware of Jeff's cum like it was some ways down a long trail, and had a sudden mean hunger to taste Jeff's cum, to feel his cock like Jeff had felt his (wonder if I can do that mean rope trick?).

But, leaving poor ol' Lew there by the fence, Jeff had wiped his mouth again with the back of that so-soft doe-skin glove and had simply said, with that smile too wide and gleaming on his face, in those eyes: "See you around, pardner," and walked off into the night.

Just as Lew was about to call after the stranger, to ask when he might be comin' back through Stinkhole, a voice came from down the street, soft but carrying: "Be back through in two months or so, then we can really ride up a storm...."

But now, *now* in the freezing drift, Lew was just a few days away from those two months. A few days away from seeing Mr. Last again and knowing the pleasures of the man's body, his mouth, those hands, that cock. That cock, that mouth, those hands—maybe because of the cold and knowing that this was probably gonna be his last, Lew pumped his flaming cock. All he could see was Jeff and what they were to do, fucking like deers in one of Miss Lavonia's pretty brass beds—Jeff's long tool down his throat, that same tool in his hands while he played Mr. Last like a meaty flute—

His cum came with a wild thrash close to that very one that night near the corral. It leapt from Lew like an angel's ascent, a shuddering quiver that closed his eyes against the deathly white and made him bite his lip.

Later, he tasted the blood and opened his eyes. White, again, but this time stars looked down at Lew of the Mountain and tinkled like Jeff's smile. The night was cold, yes, but it had stopped snowing. No longer wrapped in a blanket of pure cold, Lew reached up and grabbed the branch of a pine that had been overhead the whole time—but trapped by the white. Pulling, and groaning from the pleasures he inflicted on himself and his smashed leg, Lew hauled himself out of the snow.

A brisk night. Dawn was maybe three hours away. More than enough time to make himself a bed of pine needles and get off the freezing ground. Maybe even enough time to make himself a crutch and limp back up to his cabin or down to Mad Jack's. He knew, then and there, that he would see another sunrise on Craggy and, more than anything, live long enough to get his hands on Jeff.

It was damned good to be alive.

Hotter Than Hell

Simon Sheppard

It's back when Buicks had those little chrome-trimmed port-holes. The turquoise-and-white Special DeLuxe is sudsy-wet, steam rising in ripples from its bulbous curves. "Shit, it's hot," mutters the lanky eighteen-year-old. He's got on nothing but Keds and cut-off dungarees. His face and forearms are golden tan, but this early in the summer, his torso and legs still are pale. He draws a hand across his sweaty belly, where a line of blond fur leads down into his shorts.

It's the first time this year he's gone out without underwear, and he's acutely aware of the feeling of his tender dick rubbing up against rough denim. His fingers slip down his hairy belly, down to the base of his peter. "Shit, it's hot." His dickhead's sliding free of foreskin as his dick starts to snake down the leg of his cutoffs.

He opens up the nozzle of the green plastic hose. Cool water pours over his head, down his chest, soaks his denim shorts. His dick is still hard, if anything even harder now, the heft of it clearly outlined by the wet shorts.

He leans up against a soapy fender, presses his crotch

against the warm, wet metal. He starts humping the two-tone Buick. The cheeks of his trim butt clench and unclench as he jams his dick hard against the car. When he shuts his eyes, bright sun filters through his lashes.

The legs of his old jeans are cut off pretty high, close to his crotch, and his wet dick has slipped out past the frayed fabric. He reaches down and gives his swollen dickhead a firm squeeze, rearranges the shorts till most of his dick is lying naked up against the fender. He reaches for the sponge, squeezes a big handful of warm suds down his crotch. Muscles ripple beneath the white flesh of his back as he fucks the fender, head thrown back. In a minute or two, his hot cum jets out, splattering all the way down to a shiny chrome hubcap.

He looks up. His little brother is looking at him, eating a Moon Pie. No telling how long he's been standing there.

"Mama says to come on in," Little Brother says. "Yer lunch is ready."

"My Jesus, what happened to you?" says Mama, careworn as usual. "Go dry off and change before your lunch gets old and wrinkled."

Over peanut butter, banana, and mayonnaise sandwiches, Mama tells them the big news: Cousin Earl is coming to stay with them for a while. The last time they saw Cousin Earl was years ago, before he went off to fight in Korea. Back then, Little Brother had been very small indeed. Big Brother, though, can clearly recall his cousin. Cousin Earl, nine years his senior, had been every inch a man, muscled and deep-voiced, while he was just a gangly boy. He still remembers the way his cousin's good-bye hug felt, firm yet somehow infinitely soft and tender.

But something happened in Korea, Big Brother knows, something that had landed Cousin Earl in a hospital, not for the body, but for the mind. The details, though, remain a mystery.

"...you boys won't mind," Mama is saying. "There's plenty of room on the sofa-bed for you, Little Brother, while Cousin Earl shares the bedroom with Big Brother."

And the notion of sharing his room with a man, a man who's traveled and fought and worn a uniform, the thought of sharing a room with Cousin Earl instead of his pesky little sibling, that thought does not bother Big Brother at all.

When the day arrives, Big Brother walks to the Greyhound stop, down by the filling station. He gets there early, way before the bus is due in.

Toothless Tom is sitting on a crate in front of the filling station, sipping an RC. Toothless Tom is the man who helps out around the filling station. He's old, thirty-five or so, but he's not quite right in the head and he doesn't act much more mature than Little Brother.

"Hey, Big Brother," says Toothless Tom.

"Hey, Tom. Hot enough for you?"

Tom gives a low chuckle. "How hot are you, boy?"

"Oh, hot enough." Big Brother knows what comes next.

Toothless Tom gets up off the crate, unfolds his big husky frame, and shambles into the storage shed behind the filling station. Big Brother follows him. The shed smells of metal and grease.

Tom bolts the door and sits himself on a rickety stool near the workbench in the corner. He takes out his teeth and sets them down on a piece of newspaper on the bench. Big Brother's fly is already open. Toothless Tom takes one last swig of the RC and his mouth, when he puts it around Big Brother's soft prick, feels cool and wet. His tongue, licking and stroking Big Brother's young, sensitive flesh, makes the dick swell up and fill his mouth. The half-wit's greedy, insistent sucking sends shivers of pleasure through the teenager's body. Big Brother shuts his eyes and tries hard to think about

Cassie Renfrew and her enormous titties, but instead his mind homes in on his cousin's imminent arrival.

"Just a second," says Big Brother, backing away so he can unbutton his pants and let them fall to his ankles. Looking down, he sees Toothless Tom stroke his tiny, angry-red dick, which sticks out through the fly of his greasy, dark-green uniform pants. The distant roar of an approaching bus cuts through the humid air. Big Brother plunges his hard-on back into the wet mouth, back between the silky-smooth gums, and pumps until the cocksucker starts to gag, until hot jizz squirts down Toothless Tom's open throat. Without a word, Big Brother wipes off his dick and pulls his pants back up. Toothless Tom's dick is still in his hand, dribbling a rope of cum into a little puddle between his shabby boots.

"Ma's made smothered pork chops. She says that always was a favorite of yours."

Cousin Earl nods in assent. Big Brother expected him to show up in uniform, but when he stepped off the idling Greyhound, he was wearing a tan polo shirt and poplin windbreaker. He's older than Big Brother's memory of him, of course, and a little heavier, but handsome in an unpretentious, masculine way.

When they walk up to the front door, dinner's already on the table. Mama seems bubblingly happy to see Earl again, though for his part, he's a little more reserved. He remains distant over dinner. The conversation moves in fits and starts; the boys have been instructed not to bring up Korea, where, apparently, Something Terrible happened to Cousin Earl.

It's still pretty early when Cousin Earl says, "I'm beat. I think I'll head off to bed."

Big Brother heads up to the bedroom with him, sits cross-legged on the bed while the older man strips down to his underwear. Cousin Earl is hairier than he is, has thick, nicely muscled legs covered with reddish fur. The deep U-neck of his undershirt reveals a tangled patch of chest hair. The bulky outline of his dick is clearly visible through his briefs. Cousin Earl wraps himself in a terry robe and heads off to shower. Big Brother goes over to Little Brother's bed and picks up the tan polo shirt. The dark stains in the underarms are still moist. He buries his face in his cousin's sweat. For a reason he can't quite admit to himself, he inhales the musky-sour odor and holds in the breath. It's almost too hot to sleep.

"Nice car."

"It's the best thing Daddy left us." He thinks, *It's damn near the only thing Daddy left us.*

They're driving to the river over by McCullers' Landing. In the three days since his arrival, Cousin Earl's started to open up a little bit. About how glad he is to be back in the States. About the girlfriend he left behind in Mobile. Playing football in college. About growing up an orphan, being bounced from one foster home to another. But nothing about Korea. And Big Brother hasn't dared to ask.

"Shit, it's hot."

"Sure enough."

In the awkward silences, you can hear the radio talking about Senator McCarthy ferreting out Commies in the State Department. Then an ad for furniture sold to returning vets on easy time payments. Then Eisenhower starts to talk.

Part of the awkwardness, Big Brother knows but can never ever say, comes from knowing how he's lain awake just a few feet away from his sleeping cousin, listening to his steady breaths, watching his moonlit body shift beneath a thin percale sheet. *I ain't a fairy,* Big Brother thinks, *but if I ain't a fairy, then what the hell is going on?*

They park by the roadhouse on the edge of town and walk through the woods to the river. Big Brother, walking behind, can't keep his eyes off his cousin's hairy, freckled legs, shorts revealing the play of muscles, solid calves and thighs. When they get to the river, Cousin Earl right off strips buck naked, T-shirt first, then khaki shorts. It's the first time Big Brother has seen his naked ass, the thick red fur running down the crack, and when Cousin Earl bends over to pick up his shorts, his big hairy balls hang low between his pale upper thighs.

"Well, c'mon then. Git yer clothes off."

Now he's turned around. His dick. His big man-dick.

"Shorts, too. What's the matter, you shy?"

"I'll take 'em off when I'm darn good and ready."

"Only teasin' you. So is it deep enough here to dive in?"

"Plenty deep."

Cousin Earl runs to the riverbank, big dick flopping, and jumps in. Big Brother joins him seconds later, relieved to find that the shock of the cold water shrinks his swelling prick back down.

"Hey, Earl, let's go. Mmff..." Big Brother holds his breath as his head is forced beneath the water. Struggling his way back up, he brushes his arms against his cousin's dick. It's the first time he's ever felt another guy's peter and it's all he can do not to reach for it. He tries to wrestle back, but after a short tussle the older man easily overpowers him, grabs his arms, and pins him against his heaving torso. He can feel Earl's muscular chest and belly up against his back.

"I give, I give."

By and by they get out of the river, return to the grassy bank. Cousin Earl flops himself down on the ground, lies on his back with his arms crossed behind his head and his legs spread wide. As the blazing sun warms and dries him, Big Brother's hefty dick stirs lazily between his legs. He's glad he's kept his own shorts on.

"Hey, Earl," he says at last, "don't you think it's time to be getting back?"

Next day things are tense at the breakfast table. Cousin Earl has just told everybody he won't be going to church with them. He's stopped just short of admitting he's an outright atheist.

Mama is chattering as she serves Little Brother his grits and eggs. "So Earl, I told Freddie Wooten down at the American Legion that of course you'll march with them in tomorrow's parade." Tomorrow is Memorial Day. Cousin Earl says nothing.

Big Brother is short on sleep. The night before, the thought of Cousin Earl's dick rubbing against his arm kept him awake long after the lights were out. When he was finally sure that Earl was asleep, he humped the mattress till he shot his wad, wiping up the sticky mess with a crusted-up old sock he kept beneath the bed. Bleary-eyed, he takes a swallow of coffee and says, "Mama, he don't have to march if he don't want to."

Awkward silence.

"Of course I'll march," says Cousin Earl flatly.

"Of course he'll march," says Little Brother.

All the fat ladies in big hats are fanning themselves incessantly, futilely trying to chase away the heat. Sitting in the stifling closeness of the church he's attended since he was a child, sitting there praying next to his mother, who's taking in washing to keep the little family together, Big Brother is thrown into confusion. He does not *want* to feel this way about his cousin, he does not *want* to be a homo. Waves of sexual guilt overwhelm him. After services, Big Brother waits till his family has left the church and goes up to the Reverend.

"Reverend," he says, real low so the Reverend's wife won't hear, "I got something I got to talk to you about."

"Why surely, son," says the Reverend, with a gracious smile. "What is it?"

"It's important, sir, and it's private."

"Well, perhaps you can meet me at the rectory this afternoon at one." Another gracious smile.

At one o'clock sharp Big Brother is at the door to the rectory. Mama's taken Little Brother to O'Connorsburg to see the new Dean Martin and Jerry Lewis movie, a special treat. Cousin Earl is out somewhere.

The Reverend ushers the boy into his sweltering office and shuts and bolts the door.

"So, son, is something troubling you?"

Big Brother, stumbling over the words, explains about Cousin Earl, about feelings that he hasn't asked for, can't handle. By the time he gets to the part about swimming in the river, there's been a noticeable change in the Reverend's demeanor. His fixed smile has disappeared, and he's moved so close that Big Brother can feel his peppermint-scented breath. A glittering drop of sweat hangs from the tip of his nose.

"So you touched his penis, son?"

"Yes, sir."

"Say it."

"Say what?"

"Say 'I touched his penis.' "

"I touched his penis, sir."

"How did you touch it? Like this?"

Big Brother is frozen. The Reverend's hand has clamped onto his crotch. Sweat pours down the Reverend's face. Big Brother wishes he would take his hand away, wants it with all his heart, but the awful truth is that the Reverend's hand feels pretty good there. When the Reverend unzips his fly and reaches in, he offers no resistance. Big Brother closes his eyes in pleasure.

There's a knock at the door.

"Would you fellas like some nice, cool lemonade?" It's the Reverend's wife.

"No thank you, dear," the Reverend says in a kind of strangled voice.

The Reverend's wife clacks off down the hall. The Reverend has an awful funny look on his face. He hangs on to Big Brother's hard dick a few seconds more, then jerks away like he was hit by an electric shock. "Just go, son," he says, standing up with his back toward Big Brother, "and don't tell anyone about this ever. Not if you want your own feelings to remain a secret. Not if you want your mama not to know. You understand, son?"

"Yes, sir," says Big Brother.

The walk from the rectory takes him through the center of town, past the Chat 'N' Chew and the Will O' the Wisp General Store. Past the road that leads to the colored folks' shacks that stand, like an open secret, out on the edge of town. He knows now that there's no one he can trust with his awful secret, with the ugly, sinful mess his life's become. By the time he reaches the white stucco house, he knows what he has to do.

> *Dear Mama,*
> *I have decided to go away for a while. I do not*
> *know where so please do not try to find me or*
> *nothing. Do not worry, Mama, I can take care of*
> *myself. Tell Cousin Earl good-bye and tell Little*
> *Brother that I will see him soon. Please do not be*
> *angry. I love you, Mama.*
> *Signed,*
> *Your son*

When he finishes the letter, he gets up from the kitchen table and goes to his room. Letter in hand, he opens the door. The shades are down. Cousin Earl is asleep, lying sprawled on his back, a sheet barely covering the lower part of his naked body. Even in the dim light, it's easy to see that Cousin Earl's dick is hard.

Big Brother can scarcely breathe. He stands for a good long time, staring at where Earl's coppery belly hair trails off under the sheet. Gently, he moves his fingertips down to his cousin's armpit, where a flurry of red hair rises from skin shiny with sweat. He strokes the hair, then brings his fingers to his nose, inhaling the deep male musk. Touching the sleeping man's chest, he runs his fingers over a hard pink nipple, down to Earl's belly, to the edge of the sheet. Earl stirs, but remains asleep; his quiet breathing fills the humid room. Slowly, Big Brother moves his hand over the sheet until his palm hovers over the hard dick. He can feel the body heat radiating from the stiff rod. He slowly lowers his hand till it lightly rests upon his cousin's hard-on. Reflexively, Earl arches upward, pushing his meat against Big Brother's hand. The sheet shifts, revealing Earl's swollen dickhead.

With painstaking care, Big Brother lowers the sheet till he can see all of Earl's cock; the large piss-slit, the retracted foreskin, the big pinkish shaft bulging with veins, the luxuriant, bright red bush. Big Brother bends until his face is just inches from the hard penis, till he can inhale the smells of his cousin's sweaty crotch.

Earl's hand descends gently but firmly on the back of Big Brother's head, pushing face against cock. Big Brother's nose is buried in pubic hair. The hand relaxes, allowing him to run his lips up the underside of the shaft, up to the softly throbbing head.

"Why don't you take your clothes off, boy? It's awful hot. It's hot as shit."

Big Brother, naked, positions his head between Earl's thighs, resumes his exploration of the big, meaty cock. When he sticks the tip of his tongue in the glistening piss-slit, Earl bucks his hips and raises his knees. The eighteen-year-old moves his mouth down the dick, down to the hairy, wrinkled ballsac. He tongues his cousin's balls, then licks the sweat-soaked ridge between Earl's legs, moving his tongue until it's up against his cousin's hole. He can feel Cousin Earl open up for him. He swirls his tongue around the earthy-tasting hole, then stiffens his tongue and pushes as far in as he can go and Earl can't stop moaning. Jacking his dick now, Earl screams, "Aww, FUCK!" and comes all over his belly. Big Brother pulls his head from between Earl's thighs, throws himself full length on Cousin Earl's body. His tongue pries apart his cousin's lips. And he humps Earl's hairy belly, slippery with cum and sweat, till with a shudder he shoots, pumping a load of hot cum between their bodies. Kneeling, he rubs his face in the salty stew of their sweat and cum, lapping it hungrily. Then, with a final deep kiss, he curls up in the older man's arms, his face buried in Earl's warm armpit.

He's almost asleep when he hears a noise out in the hallway. Mama and Little Brother are back; he must not have heard the Buick drive up. He's just managed to wipe up and slip into dungarees when his mama calls from downstairs, "How you boys doing? Y'all hungry for supper?"

Big Brother picks up the letter to his mama from where it's fallen to the floor and rips it up into a million pieces.

At the dinner table, Little Brother seems real quiet, real distant. Earl, though, is more animated than Big Brother's ever seen him, which is lucky since he himself, caught up in a muddy swirl of emotions, barely says a word.

"So I figured," says Earl between bites of fried chicken, "I'd head back down to Mobile and ask Muriel if she'll marry me. Golly, you'd like her. She's a real pretty girl."

Little Brother pulls a face.

That evening Big Brother and Cousin Earl go for a ride in the Buick. Sitting there beside his cousin, watching the headlights slice through the night, Big Brother tries to feel guilt, tries to ease it out like his tongue toys with a loose tooth. But all he can feel is happy. "Do you reckon," he says finally, "that what we did was wrong?"

"Big Brother," says Earl, his voice strangely gentle, "after all the things I've seen, I've clean given up on trying to figure out sin."

Cousin Earl has been driving down the dirt road to the river. He pulls off to the side of the road, kills the lights. "You don't have to do nothing more with me. Not ever," he says.

"But I want to," says Big Brother real quietly, laying his hand on his cousin's muscular thigh. Both their dicks are already hard. Earl reaches over to unbutton Big Brother's fly, bends to take his cousin's dick in his mouth.

"Damn, that feels good," says Big Brother, and it's true; he never felt anything so good in his entire life. Earl takes his dick deep down in his throat, backs off, using his tongue to caress dickflesh, then plunges all the way back down, swallowing the shaft.

"Let's get out of the car." The scent of night-blooming jasmine hangs heavy in the air. Big Brother leans against the car door, dungarees down around his ankles, while the older man takes him in his mouth again. Big Brother feels Earl's hands on his butt, spreading his asscheeks apart. When he feels fingers on his hole, he freezes up for a minute before he decides that it's all right and relaxes into the heat of his feelings. Earl takes a second to spit in his hand and then eases a finger up inside his cousin. Big Brother is surprised by how good it feels, how much he wants Earl inside him.

"I got some hair tonic in the glove compartment," he says. He reaches in the open window, gets out the bottle of Wildroot Cream Oil and hands it to his cousin, who's buck naked now, hairy body gleaming in the watery moonlight.

Earl gets his big dick all slicked up with hair tonic and gives it a few hard squeezes till it's standing straight up against his belly. "Turn around and bend over," he says, and Big Brother leans on over, onto the still-warm hood of the car. He feels Earl's oily thumb massaging the tight ring of his asshole. "I'm just gonna open you up real gentle," Earl says, pushing in a couple fingers, rotating them until the muscles give way. Big Brother moans. He wants to be fucked. He wants to be fucked real bad.

When Earl slips the head of his dick inside, it hardly hurts Big Brother at all. And when Earl sinks the length of his shaft all the way in, waves of pleasure wash over Big Brother. Crickets cry loud through the sultry night.

"You all the way inside me?"

"Sure am, boy."

Big Brother reaches back to check that it's true. Cousin Earl's big, furry bush is smack up against his butt. He pulls his hand back to his face, sniffing in the mix of hair tonic and his own ass juices.

Earl is banging away now, and every time he slams into Big Brother's ass, the teenager's sweat-soaked torso slides across the Buick's well-waxed hood. Earl grabs hold of Big Brother's hips and pumps harder.

Just when Big Brother is wondering whether he can take much more of this, Cousin Earl starts bucking real fast, yells "Aww, JESUS!" and shoots his hot load deep into his young cousin's ass.

When he gets up off the car hood, Big Brother feels weak in the knees. He leans up against the car door and Earl is immediately down on his knees, taking Big Brother's half-hard cock in his mouth, sucking it expertly till it expands down his throat, till it explodes with a rush of cum down his throat, cum as sweet as pecan pie.

When they walk in the front door, Mama is waiting there, still wearing the flowered apron she wears to do the dishes, grief and anger on her face. She's been crying. "Little Brother has told me what you two have been up to," Mama says. "How could you, Earl? How could you do that to my boy?"

Big Brother drags himself awake after a night of fitful sleep. He's been dreaming of someone—a senator, a preacher— yelling at him and grabbing at him. He slugs the man, but just before the man disappears, he turns into Cousin Earl, who smiles and takes him up in his big, strong arms.

Big Brother looks around the familiar room. Suddenly he jerks himself fully awake. The bed next to him is empty. All Cousin Earl's things are gone.

It's only when he makes his bed that he discovers a letter slipped under his pillow.

Dear Big Brother,

Your mama don't know that I'm writing you this. I am real sorry that I got you in trouble. Do not blame your brother for spying on us yesterday afternoon, nor for telling your mama. Whatever happened is all my fault, and I know that going away for a while is the best thing I can do. Maybe your mama is right and you should go talk to the Reverend about changing your ways. I do not know.

I do know that being this way is not easy. I want to tell you about what happened in Korea, but you must not tell nobody else. When I was there, I fell in love with another soldier. We loved each other very much. For months, we'd sneak around so we could spend time together. We planned to get through the war and then spend the rest of our lives together when we got

*back home. That's how much we loved each other. I
don't expect you to understand.*

*Then one day he was killed in battle. I watched
him die. I never felt so helpless in my life. I could not
tell anyone what I was going through for fear of
getting kicked out of the service. I had to go through
losing him alone by myself, and it made me go a little
crazy. That is what happened and why I was shipped
back to a hospital in the States.*

*Big Brother, you are a wonderful guy and I hate to
leave you at a time like this but your mama and I
talked and I think for now my going away will be
better for all concerned. Do not worry about your
mama, she loves you very much. And do not worry
about me. I will be okay.*

*I truly believe that someday soon I will see you
again. Until then, take good care of yourself.*

Love,
Earl

At the bottom of the letter, *Love* has been crossed out and
then written in again, this time in big, defiant letters.

That afternoon, the family goes to the Memorial Day parade
at McCullers' Landing. Down Main Street they go, the aged
veterans of the Great War, the maimed middle-aged men who
fought in World War II, the young vets just back from Korea.
All the men whom the world has left damaged. Big Brother
doesn't feel much like cheering.

He wanders off, down to the riverbank. Thinking of his
cousin, he strips down and lies on the grassy bank. He grabs
his balls in one hand and peels back his foreskin with the
other. Spitting in his palm, he gets the shaft wet and slippery,
uses his other hand to play with his warm hole. "Earl," he

says out loud, "Earl, Earl, Earl." And spurts hot cum high up in the air, up toward the heat of an unminding sky.

Big Brother spends the rest of the humid afternoon down by the river, till sunset, till darkness falls on Memorial Day. As he heads off toward home, a few raindrops fall, then many more, until the darkness is split by sheets of lightning and howls of thunder. Big Brother, soaked through and through, can see his way back home in sudden flashes of an unnatural clarity. The heat is broken, if only for a while.

Heat Wave

Kevin Killian

Carey heard a chuckle, and turned around on Sixty-eighth Street. The man was gone, the place where he'd been now an empty space filled with sunlit air. Some kind of optical illusion, perhaps? Like the silhouettes they showed you in the service: are you looking at two vases or a woman's head? Carey could have sworn he'd seen a man, sandy or auburn hair, slinking behind him, then again maybe it was just his hangover. "Next I'll be seeing little green men from Mars."

The sun was high, and the top of his head felt warm. He stood and watched with quiet eyes down the warm pavement that lay behind him. All was quiet as in a dream landscape. Silver sunlight and the black patches of adjacent alleys—nothing else could he see. Then from out of the silence, very close by, there came once more a low, throaty chuckle, louder and closer than before. There could no longer be a doubt. Someone was on his trail, was closing in upon him minute by minute. Carey stood like a man paralyzed, still staring at the ground that he had traversed. Then suddenly he saw him. Maybe fifty feet down the street, a man, studying a shop window with minimum interest. A young man with red hair, a shock of it standing on top of his head like a rooster's red comb. Idly the man turned from the window display and looked inquiringly at Carey, who averted his head.

Carey stepped into a restaurant he'd never been to. Just to see if he'd be followed. The maître d' was stern and authoritative. "Table for one?" he asked, holding a pink finger up in the air to summon a waiter.

"I'm not really hungry," Carey thought, but he sat down at a booth, feeling the tight friction of the leather seat against his thighs like a warning or a caress. A slight breeze waved a plummy perfume from a large bouquet of red roses standing at the center of the table. He'd been seated at the last booth from one to the men's room, by no means a choice placement. Bearing a fly-specked menu, the waiter approached. The wallpaper was flocked with water spots that streaked through a design of mallard ducks rising up out of a reed-strewn horizon. Carey read from the menu, "Victoria's Canadian Tea Shop."

"Thanks, that'll be all," he told the waiter, handing back the menu. "I'll just have a bowl of soup."

"No soup today," replied the waiter, without emotion. "Too late, mister."

Carey took back the menu as expected. "Ain't that the story of my life."

Then the front door opened and in walked a man, a man with bright red hair the color of fire. Carey opened the menu and covered his face with it. Prices and entrees swam before his eyes.

"Mister, what you like?"

"I'll have the Salisbury steak," he said quickly. "Maybe a couple of vegetables. I don't know, go away and let me think about the vegetables."

But the waiter wouldn't leave. Steadfastly, he stood there with his palm out like maybe he was expecting a tip.

"People steal our menus," the waiter observed, with a vast shrug. "I don't know why."

With a guilty start Carey passed the menu to the waiter, who nodded imperturbably, and added:

"Irving Berlin used to eat here and write his tunes on our menus. The owner's got a couple of them framed in there—" pointing to the men's room, which more and more seemed to be the heart of the restaurant. "Some men like a tea room, it brings something out in them. Maybe you agree, mister?"

Carey jumped up. "I'll take a gander," he said brightly, slipping into the alcove. "Irving Berlin…'White Christmas,' right?"

"Right, mister."

Carey could see the red-haired man approaching the maître d' with a question in his eyes. He saw the man take a photograph out of a card-case and display it. Lingering no longer, he pushed open the heavy door to the men's room and hurried in. He tried to lock the door from within. But the catch was broken, and dangled loosely from the clasp.

The restroom was fairly large, about thirty feet long and ten feet wide. An elderly gent stood whistling at a sink, patting his face with some kind of green unguent: liquid hand soap. He stopped whistling when Carey barreled in.

"Look like you just saw a ghost," said the old man.

"The prices scared me," Carey said. "The prices on the menu."

"Wait till you hit my age, sonny boy," said the geezer to Carey. "Nothing scares a man of eighty but a flu bug or a warm pussy." The old man chuckled and turned the tap with a great flourish. Cascades of faintly red water steamed out of the tap and soaked the old man's green, slimy hands.

Four urinals lined the wall to their right, one a little shorter to accommodate child patrons. On the left a row of stalls stretched to the far wall, in which was set a window—one window, too small to climb through, covered with a fine metal mesh. Street noise. Irving Berlin's lyrics to "Heat Wave" hung, framed, next to this window. Very nice. Very nice decorative bullshit. One of the doors to the toilets was ajar, and Carey slipped inside it.

"Yessirree," called the old man. "When you hit eighty, you're not scared of the Devil himself."

"I bet," Carey called, over the partitions. Then, breathless, he examined his surroundings. One door, two marble walls that stopped a foot from the floor, a toilet built into the far wall with a flush handle. The walls were covered from top to bottom with messages from other men. Graffiti, that lined the gray marble from top to bottom. Just the kind of reading Carey preferred in lighter moments.

In the stall, Carey sat down on the cracked black wooden seat and put his head in his hands. He needed pictures, though, pictures more vivid than the graffiti. Lifting a hip, Carey reached back and took his wallet from the back pocket of his slacks. He'd had this wallet since the service, and it looked it. "I'll buy you a new one," his wife had said.

"You buy too much," Carey had said.

The money he opened to now had come to him from his wife. All in all, there must have been sixty or seventy dollars in the wallet. "I don't want you arrested as a vagrant," she said.

Fuck *vagrancy*, Carey thought, in the toilet stall. From an inner compartment of the scuffed brown wallet he pulled out a fistful of mementos and pictures. This was his past: somehow it felt correct to bring it out now, here, amid the pungent scents of Lysol and men's piss. This handful of memories and impressions. A subway token clinked on the damp tile floor— Carey let it lay where it fell.

"Yessir," called out the old man, "when you get to be my age, every day you wake up to some new terrible thing."

Carey shuffled the stack of cards and papers from hand to hand, while listening with one ear to the sound of the tap water and the old man whistling Irving Berlin's "White Christmas."

"So long, sonny boy," called the old man, finally finished cleaning his old palsied hands. Carey heard the restroom door swish open and shut. Then, in the sudden gray silence, he pulled out a card—"any card," as the jokers in the bars tell you to—and turned it over from back to front. It was a picture of himself at eighteen. He looked frank, confident, alert. Now he was thirty-two. Carey took a deep swallow and waves of feeling washed over him in deep, regressive movement.

He was sitting there, his cock draped across his palm neither soft nor stiff, with its usual dead weight and perplexity, when he saw the hole in the wall. When he noticed it wink at him.

His eyes widened forcibly, as though he'd been given a jolt of electricity or shock treatment. Again he saw the wall blink, or appear to blink, its gray solid surface part and join again. There *was* a hole in the wall, and someone was standing in its light, in the next stall.

The wall that separated the two stalls was a thick slab of Italian marble, and in its center a hole had been drilled in the ancient, sexual past; through this hole now a finger poked, nail upward, and then twisted to measure the dimensions of the space it was in. Three-inch circle? Something like that. Carey gazed steadily at the moving, questing finger, thinking to himself, "It's the red-headed guy."

The finger continued to probe, leaving fingerprints all over that portion of the inner wall it touched, greasy finger-prints, as if left from liquid hand soap or semen. In his fantasy that finger wanted to stretch to an unimaginable length to touch the very tip of his penis, which he held firm in his own right hand. He looked down at himself, and his cock slid forward in his lap, gaining on him. He felt his balls tingle, and grow warm.

The finger withdrew and Carey next saw an eye staring at him, a placid green eye that blinked once or twice but otherwise made no signal. Carey smiled at the eye politely.

The eye closed, then withdrew. In a moment Carey heard the sharp sound of a zipper descending, then the soft ribald fold of cloth. He began to tremble in his loneliness and his longing, waiting for what he knew must come. Next an enormous cock, bigger than his own, appeared through the hole, inch by inch, to come to rest, ringed in a nest of soft, crisp, orange pubic hair, like a birthday corsage for a little girl, a toy. Finger, eye, cock: finally Carey put together the various parts of the body that had been shown him, figured they were all one male. This sum of addition made Carey swoon; if this wasn't the man who'd followed him into the restaurant, Carey would eat his hat. In sexual life, he'd always had a weakness for redheads. Why not go for it? *Here I thought I was being followed. Hell! I was being cruised.*

A strip of ripped toilet paper, ringed with gray moisture, floated to the wet floor. Carey read the words. *Touch it.* Then they dissolved.

He raised his left hand shakily, to the bobbing cock, felt its satiny heat with two fingers. In response it lifted its weight to meet his tentative touch. The ringing in his ears vanished, his headache with it. The cock shot forward; Carey put his mouth to its head and kissed it. Inside his mouth the cock had little volume of its own, but a great suggestion of propulsion and questioning. Carey's nose hit the marble wall, which deflected it..."I'll make it easy for you," said the man in a low throaty whisper. Bent in two, Carey sat back onto the toilet seat sideways as, from under the marble partition, two bare knees came forward, followed by long white thighs, then the whole crotch was squatting directly into his face. An athletic guy, obviously, confident, bouncing on his heels with his pants and underwear drawn down to his ankles. I could pick his pockets in twenty seconds, Carey thought obliquely, as he leaned down to the floor to suck Red's dick. Down so low his face felt damp and clammy, and the muscles in the left side of his face started to harden and contract, as he pressed his mouth over the large head of Red's expansive cock. "Red" spoke the familiar words of praise and contempt.

"That's good, Carey," he said. *How'd he know my name?* "That's as good as a woman any old day, I guess."

Athletic guy—mysteriously knowing guy—and a guy who really knew not only what he wanted but how to get it out of Carey. *How'd he know my name?* All in all Carey had to hand it to him, but now wasn't the time or place. The thick stern hardness in his mouth was smooth to his tongue, to his throat, filled him to the tonsils. He was breathing through his nose like a drowning man.

Carey reached up through Red's legs and his hands passed through the light growth of hair on the thighs, till he felt the creamy weight of the ass in his hands, then the delicate filigree of the balls. Red was practically sitting on the floor he was so excited. "Is your dick hard?"

"A little," Carey replied, and the sound of his own voice unnerved him. Again the hardness in his mouth throbbed, as though he was hitting some kind of nerve. "Mount me," the voice said. Obediently Carey let Red slip out of his mouth, which instantly felt hollow. "Slide under," Red commanded, and Carey, oblivious to the piss spilled on the tile, slid his crotch into the crack of the freckled butt, which glistened from exertion and summer heat, his smooth cheeks pulled neatly open with most of his fingers and from sheer will. A pale hand, coated in some shiny invisible glop, guided A to B. From there nature took its course. Carey grabbed Red's waist with both hands; inside, Red's asshole was sweeter and warmer than Carey would have thought possible. From every surface it sank around the column of Carey's dick, and together, through some unspoken physical signal, the two men began to heave slightly, in and out, in a 3-D tangle of limbs and swollen distended muscle. Carey's lungs started to expand at approximately the same rate as his cock. "Don't cream in me," Red pleaded.

"Maybe I will," grunted Carey.

"Don't come in my fucking ass," Red begged, with a long gasp between each syllable. "Don't shoot no big wad up my hungry hot hole."

"And maybe I won't," Carey said.

After a while, Red rose, adjusted his clothing and left. Carey lay back against the stubby toilet and panted. The cards and photos he'd taken from his wallet were spread on the wet tile exactly as they had fallen. His hands were grimy, thick with sweat and shit, urine and cum.

Outside, from the dusty corridor, he heard a pleasant chuckle. *"We're having a heat wave,"* sang a whiny tenor. *"A tropical heat wave."* Only other thing Carey heard was running water, the white sound of water through underground pipes.

See Dick Deconstruct
Ian Philips

I'm thinking of an image. It's from one of those stories where Our Father throws Lucifer out of the house for good. I can't remember which.

Maybe *Faust*.

Maybe *Paradise Lost*. It doesn't matter. All I remember really is the image.

It's of the future Satan sitting among us and forever looking back towards the one place he would never be able to return. Which leads to more stories. Ones where, to soften the pain of remembrance, The Fallen One tries to stick it to The Man by sticking it to one of The Man's favorites.

Think Job. Think Jesus.

In a way, this is one of those stories.

Sort of.

I have no idea what The Man or any other god thinks about my little boy. But I do know that before we met he was fast becoming a darling of the Académe. Not just any old university—the Académe, site of all discourse and inquiry located in that great metanarrative in the sky.

I'd seen his name several times before he told it to me that night. He'd been a contributor to various anthologies. Ones with glossy covers in garish colors drawn on a computer. Covers that promise a mondo-pomo-homo-a-go-go world within. Then you turn the page. Instead it is only a book filled with straggling bands of menacing, jibbering words from the clans Tion or Ize. Words which must wander those pages forever at war—sometimes even with their own in the same sentence. Leaving behind a field of white, strewn with participles dangling, dying.

To be honest, I don't know if it was just dumb luck or synchronicity that led me to answer his personal. And, after what I did to him our first night, he's the one who'll want to dig up Jung and ask him whom or what to thank. I merely made the most of a moment.

His personal? Something about a Queer, White Dork, this weight and that height, goatee and glasses. Has a hard spot for hairy, horny daddies. Grooves on the transgressive in theory and praxis. Then the standard blah blah blah.

I had no plans for what we'd do if things clicked. Not even after I recognized QWD's name. My inspiration came only after he offered me a cigarette.

I smiled and shook my head. His brand, not his offer, had surprised me. American Spirit. This boy had spent a lot of his time and someone's money redecorating his mind in early 1970s French cultural critique. I'd expected Gitanes. Or maybe, in the down-and-dirty spirit of Genet, that he'd have rolled his own. But no, he smoked American Spirit—filtered. He'd been out here on our brittle bit of the Rim of Fire longer than I'd thought.

He lit up. A real feat since we were sitting outside this cafe on Market Street. That shouldn't mean anything to you unless you've been to San Francisco in the summer. It was late afternoon when we put our first pints on the table. And a late summer afternoon in San Francisco means that the fog flying in over Twin Peaks uses Market Street as its landing strip.

So as gust after gust touched down, he lit up. On the third try. And, by then, he was curled so tightly around the cigarette he looked like a fetus hugging its heart.

He sucked a few times on the burning paper and then spoke. I had the masculine signifiers he wanted—bulk, a beard—or so he said. But, he added, I was smaller than the men he'd been with before. And I thought, yes, I am small; beware the small.

I know. I know. You probably don't give a shit what we said or what I look like. You only want me to describe my dick and what it did. I won't. Call me a tease, but we both know one man's dick is another man's dink is another man's dong. Besides, I'd rather give your puny little imagination a workout. So maybe I have one. Maybe I don't.

The boy and I kept talking. Through several more beers, cigarettes, a course of spring rolls and pad Thai, then along the streets and up the stairs to my apartment and down the hall to my bedroom.

We stopped beside my bed. I put one of my short, thick fingers to his lips. I stepped back. "Strip."

He beamed. Quickly, he gripped the bottom of his terry-cloth shirt of many colors and yanked it over his head and down his arms. His nipples stood out on the pale skin. Two dark dots. Alternating patches of muscle and bone. All strung together by a few hairs running from his breastbone to the rim of his shorts. He knelt and unlaced his Airwalks. They'd been the color of wet sand, but in the unsteady light of the room's candles I could barely see the whites of their laces or his socks. He put them all against the wall and returned to the spot beside my bed. He unbuttoned his shorts, let them drop, stepped out of one leg and, with his foot in the other, kicked them over towards his shoes. I could forgive this smiling eagerness to please as a bit of nervous excess, but that kick smacked to me of precociousness. My suspicion was confirmed when he tried to lock eyes with me as he tugged his white cotton briefs down over his budding cock and then his thighs. He had to look down once he got to his knees. As soon as his underwear was at his ankles, he raised his back so I could get a good view of his dick. It was long and fat like an animal's snout. It flopped against his balls while he shook one, then another, foot free.

It'll do, I thought.

I looked up and met his eyes. "It's interesting how it's often the choices made with the least thought that carry the most damning consequences." He blinked. "Like your high kick. Very precious. I don't like precious." His eyes widened. "Maybe I should just send you home...." He blurted out something. The beginning of a plea. I jerked my right index finger to my lips. He swallowed a paragraph of yet-to-be-spoken words.

"What—no one's ever spoken to you in the conditional? I said 'maybe.' I said 'should.' You'll stay as long as I want you to stay. And that might even be the whole night if—if you obey my one rule: you may speak, but each sentence may have only three words; and each word may have only one syllable. Otherwise, you can jabber away at the cab driver on your way home. Agreed?" He nodded. "Are you sure you don't need me to diaper that mouth with a gag?" He shook his head so hard his balls swung from thigh to thigh.

Always the student, I thought, craving tests. Good, we'll begin with the hardest. So I decided to take a few long minutes and bind him tight with the one thing I knew he feared most—silence.

It began when my face stiffened into a stare. He smiled nervously for the first few seconds. I think it was a minute before I even blinked. By then, his lips had filled in the gash of teeth.

We listened to our breathing. To the sputtering of the candles. Finally, I turned and walked out of the room. I left him alone in the squirming shadows. It would be three, maybe five, minutes more before I'd return with a wad of pink fabric tucked in my right fist.

I tossed it towards his feet. The wad fluttered up into the air and blossomed into a pair of pink silk panties, a size five women's, a snug fit even with his narrow hips. The one-petaled flower fell fast to the ground. "Put them on."

He crouched to pick them up. He fumbled trying to get the crotch going the right direction. He stepped out of one leg and turned the material around the pole of his other. The panties slipped up his calves and over his knees. Then, he had to tug slowly up along his slim thighs, over the ass I'd yet to see, and around his resistant cock. The waistband snapped at his hips and his dick was plastered against the right side of his pelvis. He looked up. Either the material chafed or he was pantomiming defiance. I didn't care.

"Take off your glasses."

He chirped. Something about no longer being able to see. "What's to see?"

I walked up to him, pulling a strip of leather out of my back pocket. I let it hang out of my right hand, though I doubt he could see this. I got behind him and lifted it above my head, then over his. I tied it around his eyes. I stepped back in front of him. As I pressed my hands close to his eyes to adjust the blindfold, I could smell his face. It was bitter with smoke and fear. I lingered long enough for his cold skin to feel the warmth from my breath.

I moved away. "You've talked a lot today. Most of it, I enjoyed. In fact, by dinner, I felt like I was back in school. Shooting the shit at three in the morning with a paper due at ten." I paused to cross the room and return with my butterfly knife.

"I have just one question. It's about what makes a man. You seem to know. Well, you did in that article for *Homosex(e)*." He started as he realized how naked he'd become. "What was your thesis for that one? Something about 'penetration being a mode of production in the manufacturing of the masculine'?" I stopped to let his own stilted words limp over to him.

"I'm sorry. Here I am contextualizing my question and I haven't even asked it. Let me try this again. First, I'll introduce some givens, then the question." I opened my left hand. "This is a dick," I said while I pushed my palm flat against the pink panties and then his prick until each were mashed against the wall of pelvic bone. I waited for his dick to stiffen and push back. Hand and cock then began a little dance until the hand had shuffled the tip of the dickhead up and under the strangling elastic waistband. Below it, a swelling pink stem was pointing towards the ceiling.

"Then," I said as I plucked the head, nearly in full purple bloom, "to use your own terms," and I pulled flower, stalk, and the taut rim of the panty out to me as far as I could—I almost lifted him up off his feet—"there's what you called the concretized phallus." And now my right hand and its knife reached into the gap between his dick and his belly.

I turned the knife on its side and stroked the dull edge of the cold blade up the shaft, prickling with hairs and goosebumps. "Actually, anything with a point'll do." My left hand slowly let go so that only the knife held his cock and the overextended waistband in place. "So here's my question. If I took this," and I flicked my left index finger at his dickhead, as if it were a marble and this were a game. I paused to feel it thud against the warming metal. "If I took this and left you with this," I pushed the concretized phallus against the cock that was trapped on the other side by my finger, "would you still be a man?"

I waited.

The muscles of his stomach flinched, shaking the skin that rippled the air that stirred the hairs on my arm holding the knife. I hoped that this was his answer. I waited. It was.

I almost smiled. I was beginning to enjoy our date. For now I could spend the rest of it teaching him the deeper meaning of his wordless response.

I pulled the knife out in one stroke. The panties snapped his prick back in place. He gasped. He was stung but uncut. I grabbed both his hands and pulled them towards me and the bed as I jumped up onto it. I rolled off the other side still holding him. I let go and he lay across it. I took his left hand and tied it to the left post of the black metal headboard. I moved around the bed knotting and cinching his three remaining limbs to the three remaining corners. Then I stood. Breathing deeply. I'd worked fast and was winded. I'm sure he could hear my snorts over the thudding of his own heart.

For the first time, I saw his pink ass. I jerked the waistband down and under the curves of his butt. The smooth, round, white cheeks plumped like breasts lifted by an underwire bra. I cupped them with both my palms. They grew warm. Pap. Pap. Pap. Three swift slaps to warm them more. I allowed a few moments of silence. Enough time for his ears to stop ringing. So he'd be able to hear this. I yanked the tail of my leather belt out of its buckle so hard that it creaked. Next belt and buckle slithered into my hand. The treated and tanned skin groaned as I bent it, then snapped it taut.

"You cocky little fucker. Answer me." The dead animal's hide slapped across the hide of my little live one. The echo of the clack somersaulted around the room. The candles wavered. But he said nothing. This boy who, in print, had never made his point in under fifteen thousand words, said nothing. I was growing quite excited as I realized there might be a spark of brilliance in him after all.

"Or maybe you can't." I began to punctuate each sentence with the end of my belt. "Not because you're too dumb." *Thwack.* "Not because you're too smart." *Thwack.* "But because you're one of those pitiable scholars who can't speak without citing someone else." *Thwack.* "Must explicate." *Thwack.* "Must legitimate." *Thwack.* "Must use the f-word." *Thwack.* "Foucault." *Thwack.* "Foucault, Foucault, Foucault." *Thwack, thwack, thwack.*

His ass was pink again. Almost roseate. I took my left hand and let my fingers survey those patches that even in this dim dark shone. "Such a hot ass," I said. I lowered my head towards it. My tongue slipped and slid over the nearly hairless skin as if it were ice. Ice that seemed cold and smooth, but my tongue grew warm against it, felt its throb. "Such a hot ass," I said again, and left the room.

The kitchen isn't far from the bedroom. A few feet. He must have heard me open the mouth of the freezer. Heard it sing its one long, cold note. Heard the spine of the ice tray crack in my hands. "Miss me?" I think he moaned some answer. "Miss this?" I dragged my tongue back along the trail left by my belt. I'm certain he was groaning when I took my tongue and pried at his crack, digging deepest near his hole. He tried to push his ass closer to my face. So trusting for one I'd thought so critical.

I lifted my head. Now, before my saliva could dry, I pressed down the melting cube. His butt muscles clenched. I retraced where the tongue, first of my belt and then of myself, had been. His whole body tensed as I pushed the cube down between his cheeks. "Such a hot ass," I whispered. I nudged the ice over his hole. It was sweating its own lube. I took my thumb and ground it into his asshole. He rolled his head over the pillow, biting at it. "Go ahead. You still have your dick. Be a man and scream." He tried to kick me off. Maybe he yelped. I dug at the decomposing ice cube with my fingernail. It plopped out. I slid it down towards his balls, leaving it to melt.

He began to twist against his ropes. All this show to shake off a shrinking chip of ice. I grabbed the scruff of his neck. Then I gave him a swift, sharp blow with the belt. He was still.

"You lied to me." I struck him again. "I've read everything you've been able to get published so far. You posited yourself over and over as a master theorist. Acted like you could demystify any obfuscation thrown your way. Like you were going to deconstruct the cosmos. Down." *Thwack.* "And down." *Thwack.* "And down." *Thwack.* "Until your praxis led to your dick. But why'd you stop there, boy." *Thwack.* "What's so fucking special about your dick?" *Thwack.* "Is it magical?" *Thwack.* "Is that where you keep your male essence?" *Thwack.* "Your fucking trans-historical male essence?" *Thwack.* My left hand pulled at his hair and shook his head while my right hand flung the belt over my back. "You fucking hypocrite." *Thwack.* "You're nothing but a fucking," *thwack,* "closeted," *thwack,* "essentialist." Mid-stroke I stopped.

The harder I had hit, the higher his ass had leapt. On the last stroke, it jumped up to meet the belt. "No," I said out loud. I wasn't going to let him take control of the scene. This was about my revenge. Not his pleasure. Not tonight. Not on our first date.

I climbed onto the bed. I sat on his butt. Even through my jeans, I could feel the warmth of his skin. I sat there a moment, like a hen on her almost-hatched egg. I sat there a little longer. Soon, I thought with instinctual certainty, soon.

I leaned over his back until I was crouched over him, my belly pushing his head deeper into the pillow. I untied the left hand, then the right. I crawled off him and the bed. I untied the left leg, then right. With both hands, I dug for the waistband that had now burrowed under the cheeks of his ass. I took the elastic and scraped it up along the skin. Before I let go, I gave a final yank and, snap, his panties were pulled up.

He began to mutter, reciting a rosary of "no's." He must have thought I'd untied him to send him home.

I tugged the ropes and the boy over to the chair and down across my legs until I felt the smooth fabric and the stiff cock slide across my right leg. I stopped when I had his dick bent over my knee just so. As if it had been scaling the outer wall of my leg and was now stuck, unable to heave the balls over.

Keeping the ropes in my left hand, my right hand was left alone to tear down his panties for the last time. I could feel the faint pulsing of his cock. It wouldn't be much longer before he wet himself. A few good slaps. So I decided to take my time. I ground my palm into the small of his back. Then I turned it on its side and started to push at that firm pink border wall. It gave a bit. A budge more. Then it recoiled, scooting my hand back to where it began.

Once more. This time I rolled my hand back onto its palm and let it curl into a fist. I plowed against the panty waist. My knuckles, like the broad lip of a shovel, tried to lift it. Instead, they pushed under the rim and over the warm earth of his ass, until all momentum was lost and my hand flattened again, this time over that long fissure venting heat from its deep hole.

It was a pleasant moment. Unexpected. I dragged my hand out to try yet again. I placed my knuckles half on skin, half on silk. The boy squirmed a bit. I felt his cock flatten against my leg. He was growing impatient, insecure. Good. I would go even slower now.

I took my knuckles and rubbed at the edge of his right hip. Several tries and I got the rim to fold over on itself. I moved my hand towards the left hip. I did the same there. Soon I had the elastic turned in and out all along the edge of his butt. Now I would knead and roll and knead and roll the panties down as if I were making a pie crust. By the time I had them tightly under the ledge of his ass, I'd left his skin stinging, throbbing even, where the elastic, like a crude lawnmower, had torn out some of the few black hairs. And, though I was pleased, I could feel that my little man's interest had waned.

"Don't fall asleep on me, boy." I slapped his cold butt hard enough that my baby had to fill his lungs with air. "Do I bore you? Afraid you'll drift off before your queer elder passes the staff along to you?" I felt his body hesitate. He actually thought of answering me. "Oh, is that it?" I yanked the ropes and his wrists to the floor. I let my voice drift back in time and up an octave. "Fuck me, daddy, sir." Possessed, I began to bounce him against my knee and whack out a beat while I said, "Yes, sir. Yes, sir. Fill me full."

I stopped. His skin shook. His cock quivered. I leaned towards his left ear and whispered hoarsely, "I will, young man, but when I'm good and ready. Do I make myself clear?"

I tugged the ropes again. His dick slid over my leg until his balls were flat against the side of it. "Huh?" I let go and he slunk back. I pulled again. "Well?" Then several more times until I knew these slow kisses between his silk and my denim must have been burning his dick. I could feel it swelling. I let him slide back and forth over my leg several more times as I kept shouting, "Do I?" The last time I didn't let go of the ropes. His cock and balls could barely teeter on the edge of my quite warm thigh.

"Now, you're going to tell me the truth. Aren't you, my queercore kid?" I slapped his ass twice. My palm stung. "You're going to tell me just how much of a lying essentialist hypocrite you are. Aren't you?" And I began to whack at the fleshy underbellies of his cheeks. Soft fat, some muscle. I kept whacking all the while I kept shouting. "Aren't you a liar? Aren't you? Aren't you a fucking closeted essentialist? Queer theorist, your ass. You never read Judith Butler. Did you? Did you? No, you hunched under your covers with a flashlight reading Judy Grahn and diddling yourself. Didn't you? Huh? Didn't you!"

By hitting the undersides of his butt cheeks, I'd been lifting his ass with each swat, forcing him to rub his cock over and over against the hard muscle and bone in my leg, making his own body first slap his balls and then mash them against the side of my thigh, so hard and so fast that the silk and denim were close to sparking. Even if I'd wanted to stop beating on his beet-red butt, it wouldn't have mattered now. He would've kept on humping my leg like the precocious panty-wearing dog he was.

Now, for every word I would speak, I batted at him with whatever strength was left in my nearly numb hand. "I know you read Mark Thompson's *Gay Sprit* over and over and over…" A yes spilled out of his mouth. "And over and over and over…" Another yes. "Until you were weeping and clapping for fairies."

YES! He bucked forward and then rocked back on the fulcrum of my leg. It shook wildly, then he did. And did. And did. He was spewing a loud stream of yes's now.

I waited. He moaned, a low sound, while rolling from side to side. I let go of the ropes and let my left hand fumble about until it found my knife again. I passed it over to my aching right hand. In a series of jerky, sawing strokes, I cut up the left side of his panties. When I reached the waist, they sprang apart. Now I leaned forward and cut open the right side. I put the knife down and steadied the boy's butt in my hand. With my left, I reached under his panting chest and pushed him up. Next, I grabbed the soaked front of his panties and pulled. My right hand felt the back end come slithering from both sides into his crack and up the crevice towards his balls. I watched his face contort as the fabric brushed up and up his still-too-tender shaft.

I shoved his left shoulder gently. He dropped slowly to his knees, dragging his drooling dick along the denim, leaving behind a silvery streak like a snail's trail.

Once he landed on his knees, the real dumbshow began—
he was bobbing up and down like a puppet with a broken
string. One awkward attempt after the other to balance the
weight of his body on his calves without letting them actually
touch his butt. For a minute, it was amusing. Certainly more
arousing than his striptease. But he kept on squirming and I
grew bored. I bent sideways and fumbled along the floor. I
was looking for the other thing I'd brought back with me
from the kitchen. My hand patted the rug until I saw it glint in
the candlelight. It was one of those tiny spoons used for cracking the boiled shell of an egg and scooping out its jiggling
white insides.

I opened my left hand and dug around in the pink wad
with the spoon. I slid it under a shimmering blob of cum.
"Open wide." I turned towards him. Even with the blindfold,
I could sense his blank stare. "Your mouth, brainiac." He hesitated, then dropped his jaw. "Here comes a little spoon for
my little man. Filled with man essence. Your man essence. Eat
up." I rested the spoon's cold underbelly on his lower lip.
Instinct and that even crueler master, desire, made him do the
rest.

"That's it. Eat up all the sacred man essence. We wouldn't
want your sex to grow up without a gender, would we? No, we
want your sex to have a gender," I said as I wrapped my hand
around his plump cock and squeezed. "A manly gender."

I scooped out an even larger dollop. And, while he sucked
down that spoonful, I smiled to myself. I was humming by the
time I made him lick the still-sticky insides of his panties. And
it wasn't because I knew my little man was ready to be fucked.
It wasn't even because I knew, from that night on, I could have
this little man as long as I wanted him. It was simply because
nothing soothes the forever-broken like breaking another.

The First Branding Journal
Cornelius Conboy

Sunday, May 21

In three weeks I will brand my number one boy. A month ago he asked me if I would mark him permanently, and after much thought and negotiation we arrived at the branding. It will be an "11" on his butt. Eleven is our number; I was born on one, he was born on one, we met on one. On 11/11, that is to say November 11, eleven years ago, we snuck into St. Patrick's Cathedral in New York City and, before they had a chance to throw us out, we married each other.

Since that time we have explored and expanded our limits. His request for a permanent external mark is an outward manifestation of the commitment, love and trust that we have for each other. I can hardly wait.

Wednesday, May 24

In three days I will be attending a workshop on branding being held in a de-commissioned army barracks (God, I love San Francisco). A friend sent an in-depth magazine article that has proved invaluable. Online, I have discussed a New Yorker's experience being branded six years ago. Others have offered their experiences, good and bad, with the subject. I am not ready to administer the kiss of fire today but I know that I soon will be.

Friday, May 26

The anticipation of the branding is making the boy insatiable. Last night's sex was transcendent, the kind of over-the-top power exchange we fantasize about often and achieve too rarely. I have a new element of play with him. Once his hungry ass has been opened up, after he allows my hands full play inside him, I press my fingers against the inside wall of his butt and trace the brand inside him.

When the moment comes for the red-hot iron on his quivering flesh he will feel it this deep, he will know that my energy will be on him, will go through him to his center and will transform him forever.

He asked that the first thing he feels on his flesh after the iron is my cum.

Saturday, June 2

Last night I realized that, although I am left-handed, the boy has a right-handed butt. While I was inside him tracing out the 11 from within, I got a sudden charge by the thought of having my right hand inside him while applying the iron with my left on the outside. He may end up breaking my wrist, but it is too hot a scene not to pursue.

Saturday, June 10

Tomorrow night we do it. This week has been the most mentally intense period I can remember. One month of foreplay is nearing fruition and it has already exceeded my wildest fantasy. I stopped drinking for the week prior to the branding, he has fasted for the last three days. The sacrament we are about to carry out is not being taken lightly, nor is the potential risk. The branding iron is completed.

I will do the brand in two strikes. The interlude between strikes will fuel his desire and send our endorphins into overdrive. Eleven guests have been invited. At least two are skilled with a whip. The boy's backside will be red hot before a torch ever gets near metal.

Tuesday, June 13

It is done. The night went so far beyond my wildest fantasies that I don't know where to begin. Saturday afternoon the first of our guests from New York arrived. Uzi is an old friend, a filmmaker whose work I have long admired, and I was honored that he could share the ceremony with us. My boy was beyond feeling by this time, he drifted almost in a trance through the day's routine. Finally eleven P.M. came. I look at the assembled guests. Each brings a distinct energy.

At this point my boy needs to be alone, and I take him into a back room and hold him. Our eyes and spirits lock together in anticipation and terror of what is before us. He strips down to his boots and I lock the jewelled collar around his neck, noticing how the large ruby burns with an inner fire, knowing that he will soon burn from an outer one.

I go to see how things are progressing and find the entire party preparing the dungeon. The sling is hung as I instructed, the flogging post is cleared and there is much debate over the height for the stocks. The bottoms are different heights and each has their own preference. I move through the room, picking up the floggers and the cats, laying them out near the whipping post, arranging the candles, double-checking that all restraints are where they need to be and in good condition.

At last I am satisfied that we can begin. I go into the back where my boy is waiting. He shakes as if his spirit is breaking free of the body; he knows that the journey we are embarking on will take us where few have gone, will test us physically and emotionally, will sear through us in ways we have no way of knowing. We lock eyes and souls. We are ready.

Earlier in the day my boy presented me with a wrapped box. I open it to discover a leather hat, its brim as polished as mirror. I put it on and feel a power surge through me. I lead him outside to where the guests are sitting. I thank our friends for coming tonight to help with our ritual, to bear witness to our love, trust and devotion. I look into my boy's eyes and tell him that soon he will be wearing my mark, our mark, that he will have it on him forever just as I am with him forever, just as we have always been and always will be together forever. He speaks softly. He tells me that he is more scared than he has ever been, but with the love and energy and help of our friends he knows that it's going to be great. We laugh and embrace.

I lead him to the flogging post. Slowly, deliberately, I fasten restraints around his wrists and around the pillar. Not too tight, but they will hold him well. I buckle other restraints around his ankles and connect them with chain. I make sure that he has enough room to keep his balance, and know that the pillar will support him no matter what. Finally I bring out the blindfold. Black leather slips smoothly over his head. Softly I whisper in his ear. "Boy, are you ready?" He nods and we begin.

Slowly I lift the flogger over his head, its leather tails cascade down over his shoulders and lower back. I caress his body with my whip, let him get the feel of each pointed strip of leather on his body. Gradually I settle into a rhythm, slowly and gently I increase the force, bringing my arm down over my head and hearing the cadence of each successive strike on his body. The cat dances up and down his back, from shoulders to butt, paying special attention to the right cheek, where our mark will soon be placed. The rhythm increases steadily.

The force behind each stroke grows in intensity. I shift speed and my flogger becomes an extension of my arm. With each blow, I transfer energy to the boy. We dance like that and I lose track of the time, I see welts raise up on his body and bring him down slowly, as I had taken him up.

I pick up a new whip, an innocuous-looking instrument to the unknowing, a simple group of a dozen rawhide strips woven together at one end to form a handle. Much lighter than my favorite cat—but this one holds a surprise. At the end of each strip is fastened a sharp metal spike about three-quarters of an inch long that comes to a splendid point. In the wrong hands, this little baby could do serious damage. In mine it takes him to the next level of ecstasy. The boy's backside glows red. He has stopped screaming and now emits only the occasional "Thank you, sir," his voice coming from far away.

Then it is another's turn. Steve is a major Daddy who is well known for his skill with the whip, and I turn the boy over to him. I watch nervously as he uses a leather slapper to supply delirious sensations, and the boy is off again. Though I trust Steve, it is difficult for me to watch as he takes the boy into unknown realms. Their dance together thrills me and I remember that when playing with friends you should always share your toys. With permission, Leather Daddy moves on to my flogger. I am surprised to see it in someone else's arm. His style is different from mine, side strokes prevail compared to my overhead motions. Daddy Steve is exhorting the boy: "Show us how tough you are, show me how much you can take, so that when that red-hot metal comes down on you, you can take it. Show me how strong you are!" To his sublime credit, the boy answers from another plane: "It is not tough, sir, it is want."

I direct Steve away and proceed back into our special communion. The boy has just experienced the flogging of his lifetime and I know it is time to let him down. Pressing my body against his, I slowly undo his wrist restraints and hold him as he collapses against the whipping post. I remove the chains around his ankles and we breathe together. I will not let him come too far down for there is still much to do. I lift him up and lean him against another pillar.

I turn on the torch. The boy is turned around with his back to the pillar, his wrists locked with handcuffs. Again the chains surround his ankles, fastening him securely as I heat the iron. The hissing sound of fire fills the room and a blue light gives out heat freely. The iron takes on a glow of its own, pure heat shines in the darkened room. Slowly I remove the branding iron from the heat and bring it towards my boy, immobile, powerless to resist that which he so wants. I comb his pubic hair with the glowing wand, the smell of burning hair fills the room. Never touching steel to flesh, I stroke his pubes, singeing the curly mass above his dick into a burnt tangle. I hear his breathing coming shorter now; his dick stands rigid out from his body. The hair is gone.

Now he is led to the sling. I watch as he is strapped into place and compose myself for the ultimate focus of the evening. At the table, I handle everything that I will need: the torch has proven its efficacy, the iron is resting. Rubber gloves are in place next to a new jar of Crisco. We are ready. The boy is surrounded by our guests. His butt faces me hungrily and I caress it. I lube up my hands, first pressing one then the other against his waiting hole. Slowly I let him pull me inside, first one finger, then two and three. My hands are alive unto themselves as I work them in and out, back and forth, my thumbs pressing above his balls from the outside as my fingers work the internal muscles they knew so well. He rocks slowly in the sling as with each caress I am pulled further inside him, now four fingers, now six. With parts of both hands inside, I stretch him wide.

Deep inside I see him red and throbbing as I relentlessly stroke his sphincter, urging it to open up and accept me. With four fingers from each hand inside I rotate slowly, rocking the hole back and forth, readying it for the final thrust that takes me totally inside. His sphincter hugs my wrist and I hold it in place, feeling his pulse surround me, feeling the connection of our two bodies. His heartbeat pounds against my arm in a steady rhythm and my wrist responds in kind. I open my fingers and explore the boy's depths. Lightly I brush against the top and bottom of his insides. The left cheek is thoroughly massaged and I move my hand into position on the right.

I can see through his flesh, I can see a straight line from the inked 11 on his outside to where my hand now rests inside. My fingers trace the 11 on him inside and they go through to the surface where it will be marked in fire. I nod to a slave who ignites the torch. He holds the iron over its heat and soon the familiar glow appears. The steel tool stirs from within and comes alive. Our guests gather closer and I remind them to hold down the boy. Eighteen hands are on his body as our eyes meet. "We're going to go there now, boy," I say. I take the iron from our slave. Holding it over the torch, knowing that it is full of its own fire, I move it deliberately to the inked guide.

I didn't hear him scream until later when I watched the video. What I remember is the sudden bucking up, the involuntary reaction when flesh met red-hot metal. The first strike slid for an instant until I exerted more pressure and held it on him, letting my arm and the iron follow the movement of his body. I removed the iron and dropped back, little expecting how drained I would be. I saw the mark, the "1" clearly burnt into his body. There was also a shadow strike, much lighter, but there nonetheless. Our friends had indeed held him but it was a loving laying on of hands—not the immobilizing grip called for.

The iron is repositioned at the torch and I am overcome with the beauty of the brand. This time I make sure he is held securely. I look over at the boy, who is in trance state. His glazed eyes bespeak a bliss unseen before. He now knows what awaits him and desire fills the space. Again the steel glows red, again I take it in my hand and calmly make the second strike. Securely held down, his only movement is a clenching of the teeth, the handle of my flogger held in his mouth for this eventuality. It is done.

I pull myself up, using the chains that hold the harness for support. I walk around to where the boy rocks gently, a drained look of pure ecstasy on his face. I lower myself into his chest and we cling in an embrace of souls. Our bodies have exploded. Like Daedalus and Icarus, we have flown close to the sun. Its energy does not destroy us as we soar through it, rather it caresses us with warmth and light and lets us go, every molecule in our body shattered and drifting back down to the plane of existence we know as reality. I can feel us intermingling on the way down yet somehow we reassemble intact. Physical bodies are altered and psyches are forever changed. At last I am aware of my breath.

The boy is lowered out of the sling. He stands, shakily, his feet connecting with the earth and grounding him. We touch and remain that way as the guests release their energy. Is my boy sucking on Sur's huge black dick? Do I fist one of the boys? It is a blur. I know that when at last I ejaculate it is directly on the brand. Over the next few days I come on it eleven times.

How many of us passed out in my bed later? When I woke there were five. The rest of the weekend blurs: some friends went out, some home. Some returned later, needing to be with others who had shared the experiences. At one point Uzi came by and we watched the video. Eighty minutes of unedited footage, footage I knew had been shot but had been totally unaware of. When we get to the actual branding I lose it. Lying on our bed with my boy's body against me, I know what is coming yet at the first strike I break down and sob uncontrollably. Hearing him scream, seeing him buck, is more than I can handle. I watch as it continues and only regain my composure later, seeing the bliss in his face, matched only by the ecstasy in my own.

The next week in summary

The other boys behaved well, checking in several times a day, stopping by after work. They and I made sure mine spent the next week with his naked butt in the air sipping martinis, eating bon-bons and watching TV. Some boys will do anything to get a week off from work.

Friday, June 22

After ten days, I picked up the flogger again. It was all I could do to remain in control, to only work his upper back and left ass cheek. I had to move around to his front and whip his tits, knowing that the brand is not yet ready for heavy play, as much as both of us want it to be. There will be time for flogging soon enough.

Wednesday, July 12, Final Entry

A month has gone by. My "11" has become a raised mark of pride for the boy. Its flesh responds as sensitively as his nipples and offers all of their possibilities.

Yellow
Kirk Read

Mama died peaceful. She didn't want us wailing and squeezing her hands as she made her exit, and she knew the only way she'd win was to beat our planes. The neighbors had called us all, seven kids, and said "Come now, 'cause she's close." We'd obliged, hopping into bereavement-discounted aisle seats to accompany her to the next world. But, as usual, Mama got her way.

By the time I got there, she'd been gathered up into a neat pile of bones and taken away for cremation. She wasted no time, even in death. Slow was never Mama's way.

I arrived after midnight. Mama had died that morning, and everyone else was sound asleep or staying at a motel. From the cars out front, I figured that my brothers Dennis and Troy were home, and my Aunt Ruth was in the guest house. She was always in the guest house. Dennis and Troy, no doubt, were passed out in their childhood beds. They drank hard, and they drank for hard sleep. The boys had all left home. My four sisters lived nearby with their families. Mama had always talked about getting us all out of the house so she could have some peace, but none of our childhood rooms had been redecorated.

So I was alone in the house with nothing but the smell of my Mama and the sight of hallways stacked so high with boxes that you could barely pass without elbowing the packed-up remains of one ancestor or another.

I'd known for years I'd be responsible for all this splendor, the scattered belongings of my parents. Mama always told me that as the baby, I was bound to turn out right. I stopped in front of the hallway mirror and looked at myself. I saw the baby Mama had loved hardest. The crushed beer cans in the background confirmed that my brothers were home. They lined the mantle in the living room with the precision only drunks can muster.

Six—no, eight—cans stood proudly under the portrait of my grandfather. Between the third and fourth cans was the urn Mama had rescued from the fire that took up our first house. It had held many Entsmingers, plus one beloved neighbor, and was about to be filled again.

I turned back to the mirror. I was an orphan now—a dazed, blush-stained orphan. I walked into the bathroom and stared into the full-length mirror opposite the sink. I turned the water to hot, stripped off my clothes, and stood, mesmerized by my reflection.

A few days earlier, I'd asked a barber to buzz my reddish brown hair "so I could see skin on the sides." My green eyes, changeable as a mood ring, were muddy, and missed the shield of my unruly bowl cut. I wondered when my cheeks would grow out of their perpetual blush. At that moment, I felt eleven years old. I figured I might as well look it.

I reached onto the counter for what appeared to be the only razor in the house. My brothers, too shiftless to replace or purchase razors, shared until they bled. I lathered my body, armpits to ankles, with the shaving cream Mama had stopped using on her legs six months ago. Slowly, with insistent strokes, I removed every offending trace of adulthood. Hair by hair, I scraped away the years. I was thorough. I knew I'd need to remove every follicle, from the knuckles of my fingers to the swollen joints of my toes.

I ran my fingers over the tiny boy mound of my groin, now cool and hairless. I rubbed circles over the skin and traced a path to the inside of my asscheeks, which were damp and scraped clean. I was again the rosy-cheeked boy who stuffed stolen grocery store candy into the side pockets of Mama's purse.

I opened the cabinet and pulled out one of the diapers we'd put on Daddy when he was getting ready to leave us. Having changed Daddy a thousand times, Mama wouldn't let a diaper touch her hips.

"Just pile towels under me," she said. "That's why God made washing machines."

I pulled the adhesive strips into a tight fit around my waist. I ran my fingertips from the prominent bones in my ribcage down to the place where my hipbones gave way to flesh so tender it tickled when anyone touched it. At five-six, I was still the runt of the family.

I turned out the light. The plastic sounded like a distant fire as I walked into the hallway. I reached into the blackness and pulled down the steps to the attic.

I'd been up there so many times I trusted the dark. I felt my way through instinct and memory to the dim corner under the skylight. Hanging on a piece of fish line was the mobile I'd had over my crib. I turned on the bulb. Amazingly, it still worked, and dozens of yellow pinpoints of light filled the attic. It's a wonder every child in my family wasn't epileptic.

Beneath the mobile stood our family crib, the post-womb home for all of Mama's brood. I'd spent several years climbing out of it, and now I was climbing back in. I was a late walker and talker. Mama always used to point to the places on the crib where I'd gnawed on the wood, saying "You always did like that crib. It kept the boys from throwing you around."

I lay on my back, mesmerized by the lights. The oak crib was huge, more like a puppy cage, with one hinged side that could be lowered to the floor.

I cry until Dennis gets there. Sometimes, when he passes out, the only thing that works is dragging my silver rattle along the side of the crib, like an inmate in some deep county jail. He reaches into the crib, cupping the back of my two-year-old head, holding my skull with his hand, callused at sixteen by chopping firewood. His sandy knuckles rub at the blond wisps on my skull. He hoists me to eye level and pulls me to his chest. I pull the hair sprouting on his chest and bite his collar with the beginnings of teeth. He feeds me two of his fingers. No matter how hard I bite, he never flinches or jerks them away. He stares placidly into my face and rubs his fingertips across my gums. That's when I stop crying.

I reached into the corner for that silver rattle, found it at my feet, and raked it along the slatted sides of the crib. I started on the right, then dragged it over every standing piece of wood, until I was in a frenzy. Soon I was shifting the rattle from hand to hand and hammering the metal into the corners. My brothers always said I was "strong as hell for such a little mutt." I figure it was either from fighting my brothers off or demanding that they pay attention to me. I knew that if Dennis was still breathing, somewhere in this house, he'd be joining me tonight under the yellow lights. I mumbled his name, whispered it, gurgled it up to a scream, until suddenly the rattle flew from my hand. It hit the floor, bounced down the steps to the bedroom-lined hallway below.

I heard footsteps, then the muffled sound of a beer can being crushed. With each creak of the attic steps, I tensed, my skin slick with sweat; I shivered so violently I was almost paralyzed. When I saw the top of his dirty blond head rise over the steps, my skin flooded with goosebumps. I soaked my diaper. My screaming turned into a soft whimper, and a warm sheet of urine trickled over my quivering buns.

Dennis stood over the crib, a cigarette in his right hand, the crushed can in his left. He dropped the can and kicked it into the darkness of the attic. I'd always been able to smell Dennis before I saw him. Mama always said he smelled like a billy goat, but I swapped our pillowcases to smell him until I was eleven, when he moved out for good.

He dropped the expired Winston to the floor, twisted the ball of his bare foot to crush it, and unlatched the hinged side of the crib. He reached down with both hands and gripped my hips, pulling me to him. My butt slid along the sweaty vinyl that lined my childhood bed. My ass was now balanced on the edge of the cushion, my ankles resting in the grooves of the flattened, hinged door.

Neither of us said a word. Two long fingers brushed my cheek, stroked my lips, and wormed gently into my mouth. I closed my lips around his tightly bent fingers and tasted nicotine and gasoline. His other hand reached for my hair, which he was used to tugging. Instead, he rubbed my head like a dog he was about to reward with a biscuit. He fixed his foggy green eyes on my face and matching eyes. Then he winked at me as he undid the snaps of his overalls. They slid to the floor; he stood naked and half hard. I sucked a third finger into my mouth and traced his fingernails, bitten to the quick, with my tongue.

Dennis brushed the palm of his hand from the top of my chest down to the top of my diaper, then sank to his knees to lick my belly. He knew, from years of tormenting me, where I was ticklish, and dragged his tongue, carpet-like from cigarettes, over the skin barely beneath my bellybutton. I bucked, giggled, and kicked. I slapped the side of his head hard enough to make him look up and grin.

He stopped.

He pulled his fingers from my mouth, replaced them with his tongue, heavy with beer and smoke. He cradled my head now with both hands and pulled me to a sitting position. His knuckles, more callused than the last time he held me, moved to my shoulders, then to my hips. He tugged gently at the diaper's adhesive bonds. The jagged skin of his palms brushed against the head of my dick, now poking out the top of the diaper. He pulled down the front and laid it flat against the bedding. His mouth moved over my cock, still warm with piss. He licked me clean, tracing his tongue up over my silky belly, then back down to my cock and around my ballsac, which was bunched up from the chill of the shave. He stretched his lips over his teeth and pulled on my balls. He sucked them so far from my body I thought he was going to swallow them.

I took a deep breath and he let go, wrapping his hand around my sac, which was now stretched thin. He licked precum from my dickhead, catching a few stray drops which had rolled into my belly button. He took my cock deeply into his mouth, his nose rubbing against my pubic bone.

His fingers, still wet with my spit, pushed at my hole. I moaned softly, then felt his middle finger sinking into me. After years of yelling at him for biting his nails, I was now relieved by his habit. He dropped a long stream of spit and worked in his second finger.

With the other hand on the back of my head, Dennis pulled my face to his now throbbing cock. I'd always dreamed about what it would look like hard. As he stood there, hands on his belly, his cock pointed due north. It was so hard it twitched every few seconds. Like mine.

I closed my eyes, opened my mouth, and saw blotches of yellow light through my eyelids. Dennis filled my mouth, shoved so far into my throat that his balls pushed against the tiny cleft in my chin. The two fingers in my ass became three as he again dribbled spit onto my crack, then smeared it over my sphincter.

He was cut, like the rest of us, with the impossibly long, skinny dick God sometimes gives tall boys. He dragged his fingers across my head as his cock picked up speed in my mouth and his fingers plunged deeper into my ass. His cock-head curved gracefully down my throat, then withdrew to the edge of my gums. I was trying like hell to keep up with his thrusts. Drool was running out of the sides of my mouth, and with each thrust, I gripped the sheet beneath us.

Dennis sensed my mouth was tiring, my jaws were numb, and sank his cock into my throat in one long, slow push. His hand still behind my head, he pulled out and lowered me to the floor. He placed my ankles over the top of the crib, so that I lay back staring into the torrent of spinning yellow light.

Dennis cupped his hand over my mouth, and I filled his palm with spit. He coated his cock with it. He leaned back on the balls of his feet and pulled his fingers from my ass. The sudden void made me shiver. With my propped feet, I lifted my ass from the diaper. Dennis clamped his hands around my hips and worked himself in.

Several handsfull of spit later, we were belly to belly, his cock deep into my hole, and I ached for the relief of an upstroke.

My eyes rolled back. I was mumbling gibberish, the long forgotten language of my infancy. Dennis tightened his grip on my hips, pulling my ass into the air to match his rhythm. Each stroke was heaven until that last excruciating inch. After fifteen minutes of steady pounding, that last inch wasn't any easier. Finally, I bit my tongue. I tasted bittersweet blood on the roof of my mouth.

I clutched the sides of the crib with both hands to steady myself: Dennis had forgotten all about tenderness now and was slamming my ass with the fervor of a careless schoolboy. I took shallow breaths and squeezed my ass muscles as hard as I could around his cock. He gritted his teeth, closed his eyes, and growled like I'd bitten him. His body shook and in wild, angry bursts, he filled my ass. I couldn't tell when he stopped coming, because his pelvis kept slamming into me in wild, involuntary bursts.

He knelt in front of me for what seemed forever, then pulled out slowly, as if removing a Band-Aid. He stood just as slowly, and without saying a word pulled up his overalls, snapped them on, and knelt down again. His cum was dribbling out of my ass, onto the diaper.

Dennis tugged the front of the soaked diaper to my belly, wrapped the wings around my hips, and resealed the adhesive. He covered me with a blanket draped over the side of the crib. He let the blanket waft down over my body as if I were asleep and he didn't want to wake me. He lifted the crib's open side and closed its latch.

He bent down, ran his fingers across my close-shorn scalp, and pressed his lips to my forehead. He retreated to his bedroom. My breathing slowed and deepened, and the spinning yellow lights lulled me to sleep.

About the Authors

DIMITRI APESSOS, a freelance writer, keeps his stuff in New York but lives on Amtrak, in an attempt to confuse evil spirits. It is not working. He is writing three novels, all of them queer replicas of the work of James Joyce, though he has yet to read *Finnegan's Wake*. Dimitri lives vicariously through his e-mail address, TilApplesGrow@yahoo.com.

PANSY BRADSHAW is co-author of the best-selling *Betty & Pansy's Severe Queer Review of San Francisco* (now in its fifth edition) and was a contributing editor to Scott O'Hara's *Steam (A Literary Queer's Guide to Sex and Controversy)*. Born to poor white trash more than half a century ago, he was wrapped in swaddling clothes and laid in a manger…the rest is history. He now lives in rural Montana, where he writes, teaches and nannies, and is at the center of an active queer community.

KEN BUTLER grew up in the Bible Belt but managed never to feel guilty about being queer, perhaps because he figured out early that many of those farmers and miners liked getting their cocks sucked by another guy. He has a degree in music and works in theatre administration. He's been happily ensconced in an intergenerational relationship of very long standing.

JUSTIN CHIN is the author of two books, *Bite Hard* and *Mongrel*. His poetry and prose have appeared in several magazines, including ZYZZYVA and *The Harrington Gay Men's Fiction Quarterly,* and several anthologies, including *A Day For A Lay, The World In Us* and *Male Lust*. He lives in San Francisco.

M. CHRISTIAN has been called "one of the finest living writers of erotica" by Pat Califia and "today's premiere erotic shape-shifter" by Carol Queen. The author of more than one hundred published short stories, his work can be found in previous volumes of *Best Gay Erotica, Best American Erotica, The Mammoth Books of Erotica* and many other books and magazines. He's the editor of several anthologies, including *The Burning Pen, Guilty Pleasures,* and *Rough Stuff* (with Simon Sheppard). A collection of his short stories, *Dirty Words,* is forthcoming from Alyson Books. He thinks WAY too much about sex.

CORNELIUS CONBOY, SF Leather Daddy XIII, has been called a natural-born sadist. He has written for *Oblivion* and *Drummer* magazines, and spoke on "family values" at San Francisco's 1996 Pride celebration. Prior to his relocation to Los Angeles he was a sought-after emcee within the San Francisco leather community. He celebrates change, growth and the spiritually transformative nature of radical sexplay whenever he can.

JORGE IGNACIO CORTIÑAS' fiction has been awarded first prize in the 1998 *Bay Guardian* Fiction Contest, and the 1999 James Assatly Memorial Prize. His plays include *Maleta Mulata* (Campo Santo Theatre Company, San Francisco) and *Odiseo, could you stop for some bread and eggs on your way home?* (INTAR, New York). His most recent play, *Sleepwalkers*, recently completed a two month run at the Area Stage in Miami. It was awarded a Carbonell Award by the South Florida Critics Circle in the category of Best New Work.

JAMESON CURRIER is the author of a collection of short stories, *Dancing on the Moon,* a documentary film, *Living Proof,* and a novel, *Where The Rainbow Ends,* which was awarded a fiction grant from the Arch and Bruce Brown Foundation and received a 1999 Lambda Literary Award nomination. His short fiction has been anthologized in *Men on Men 5, Man of My Dreams, All The Ways Home, Men Seeking Men, The Mammoth Book of Gay Erotica, Best American Gay Fiction 3,* and several editions of *Best Gay Erotica.*

GRIGORAKIS DASKALOGRIGORAKIS was born in Crete, grew up in the Rocky Mountains, lived a while in Manhattan and now lives in Los Angeles, where he sees a lot of movies.

JACK FRITSCHER is a San Francisco humanist writer/photographer/videographer who in 1967 introduced emerging gay culture into the new American Popular Culture Association. With a doctorate in American Literature and Criticism from Loyola University, Chicago, he was founding San Francisco editor-in-chief of *Drummer* magazine. *Some Dance to Remember,* his epic novel of gay history in San Francisco (1970-1982), will be released as an Alyson Classics Edition in 2002. His nonfiction titles include his memoir of his scandalous lover, *Mapplethorpe: Assault with a Deadly Camera,* as well as *Popular Witchcraft: Straight from the Witch's Mouth,* which in 1972 was the first book to address gay wicca. Not a prisoner of gender, he is also the author of the humanist novel about young lesbians in the 1950s South, *The Geography of Women: A Romantic Comedy.*

KEVIN KILLIAN is a poet, novelist, critic and playwright. His books include *Bedrooms Have Windows, Shy, Little Men,* and *Argento Series.* With Lewis Ellingham he has written *Poet Be Like God: Jack Spicer and the San Francisco Renaissance* (Wesleyan, 1998), the first biography of the important U.S. poet. "Heat Wave" became a chapter in a novel, *Arctic Summer* (New York: Hard Candy, 1997). Kevin lives in San Francisco.

MICHAEL LASSELL is a poet, writer and editor and the author of five books, the most recent a collection of short stories titled *Certain Ecstasies* (Painted Leaf Press). His poems, stories, and essays have been included in scores of anthologies and textbooks, including *High Risk, New York Sex,* and *The Mammoth Book of Gay Erotica,* and translated into French, German, Dutch, Spanish and Catalan. He is the editor of *Men Seeking Men: Adventures in the Personals* (Painted Leaf) and five additional books of poems and essays, including *Two Hearts Desire: Gay Couples on Their Love* (with Lawrence Schimel) and, with Elena Georgiou, *The World In Us: Lesbian and Gay Poetry of the Next Wave* (St. Martin's Press, 2000).

AL LUJAN is a San Francisco-based visual artist, filmmaker, performer, writer, lover, bastard, liar and backup singer/mudslinger for the all-girl post-punk ranchera band "Las Cucas." His writing has appeared in numerous anthologies, most recently *Virgins, Guerillas and Locas* edited by Jaime Cortez (Cleis Press), *Too Sexy* edited by Antonio Cuevas (North Atlantic Press), *Besame Mucho* edited by Jaime Manrique (Painted Leaf); and *Best American Erotica* edited by Susie Bright (Simon & Schuster). His first film, *S&M in the Hood* was picked up for distribution by Frameline. He recently received the Nuevo Potrero grant to complete his upcoming film *Corn in the Front Yard.* He also has performed at Highways, the late Josie's Cabaret, Somar, Theatre Rhinoceros, BRAVA, Glaxa, Build, Intersection for the Arts and the Mission Cultural Center. He founded Latin Hustle, a queer Latino comedy troupe, in 1997 with Lito Sandoval and Jaime Cortez, which received a San Francisco Arts Commission Cultural Equity grant to mount its first show Full Frontal Nudity, at Theatre Rhinoceros.

SCOTT O'HARA remains rentable at your local video store in about two dozen skinflicks; he also founded and for three years edited *Steam (A Literary Queer's Guide to Sex and Controversy)* and edited the anthology *Stallions and Other Studs.* His erotic fiction was published in 1996 by Masquerade/Badboy Books in *Do-It-Yourself Piston Polishing (For Non-Mechanics);* essays and memoirs appeared in *Autopornography: A Life in the Fast Lane* (Harrington Park Press, 1997) and *Rarely Pure & Never Simple* (Harrington Park Press, 1999). He died in 1998.

IAN PHILIPS is an unassuming abomination who lives in San Francisco. This story along with other pieces of literate filth he's penned appear in a first collection of short stories titled *See Dick Deconstruct: Literotica for the Queer in the Head,* due in the fall of 2000. He can be reached at iphilips@aol.com.

ANDY QUAN's first piece of published smut was "Six Positions," written in London, England. It appeared in *Quickies and Best Gay Erotica 1999.* New erotica has since appeared in *Quickies 2, Best Gay Erotica 2000* and *Carnal Nation: Writing Sex in New Canadian Fiction* (Arsenal Pulp Press). Less spicy writing credits include *Gay Fiction at the Millennium* (Alyson) and *Take Out: Queer Writing from Asian Pacific America* (Temple University). He is the co-editor of *Swallowing Clouds, an Anthology of Chinese Canadian Poetry* (Arsenal Pulp Press). Currently working as the international policy officer for the Australian Federation of AIDS Organisations, Quan was born in Canada of Cantonese origins. He is a singer-songwriter, poet and voyager, currently landed in Sydney.

CAROL QUEEN has a doctorate in sexology, which she uses to impart more realistic detail to her smut. She is the author of *The Leather Daddy and the Femme* (from which "Ganged" is excerpted), *Real Live Nude Girl: Chronicles of Sex-Positive Culture, Exhibitionism for the Shy,* and co-editor of *Best Bisexual Erotica, PoMoSexuals, Switch Hitters,* and *Sex Spoken Here.* She lives in San Francisco (where else?); come visit at www.carolqueen.com.

KIRK READ grew up in Virginia, where he was the editor at *Our Own Community Press* in Virginia. His writing has appeared in over seventy-five LGBT publications around the world, including *Philadelphia Gay News, Washington Blade, Frontiers, QSF,* and *Lambda Book Report.* His work appeared in the anthology *A Day for a Lay: A Century of Gay Poetry* and can be seen at www.temenos.net/kirkread. As a volunteer, he is on the organizing collective of the Gay Men's Health Summit, helps with a weekly homeless feeding in the Castro, and is an intake counselor at the St. James Infirmary, a free health care clinic for sex workers. He can be reached at KirkRead@aol.com

PAUL REED is the author of more than a dozen books, including the novels *Facing It* and *Longing* and the memoirs *Q Journal* and *Savage Gardens.* His work has appeared in *The Advocate, The San Francisco Chronicle, Honcho* and *Drummer,* and his short fiction has been anthologized many times, including in the *Best American Erotica 1995* and in *Noirotica 2,* where "We Own the Night" first appeared. He lives in San Francisco and is working on a novel.

MATTHEW RETTENMUND, a magazine editor living in Manhattan, is author of the novels *Boy Culture* and *Blind Items: A Love Story*, plus the nonfiction books *Totally Awesome 80s* and *Encyclopedia Madonnica*.

MICHAEL ROWE, born in Ottawa, Canada and raised in Beirut, Havana and Geneva, is an award-winning journalist and essayist, author of the critically-acclaimed *Writing Below the Belt*, and co-editor of two Lambda Literary Award-nominated anthologies, *Sons of Darkness* and *Brothers of the Night*. His journalism has appeared in *The National Post, The Globe & Mail, The Harvard Gay & Lesbian Review, The Body Politic* and *Torso*, among others, and he was founding senior writer for *FAB National*, where he was a finalist in 1997 for a Canadian National Magazine Award. Some of his essays and journalism are collected in *Looking for Brothers* (Mosaic Press, 1999). He can be reached at Mwriter35@aol.com.

D. TRAVERS SCOTT is the author of *Execution, Texas: 1987*, editor of *Strategic Sex: Why They Won't Keep It in the Bedroom*, and had a blast as guest judge for *Best Gay Erotica 2000*. Trav currently lives in Seattle.

LAWRENCE SCHIMEL is a full-time author and anthologist, who's published over forty books, including *Switch Hitters: Lesbians Write Gay Male Erotica and Gay Men Write Lesbian Erotica* (with Carol Queen; Cleis Press), *The Mammoth Book of Gay Erotica, The Drag Queen of Elfland, Boy Meets Boy, Food for Life and Other Dish* (Cleis Press), and *PoMoSexuals: Challenging Assumptions About Gender and Sexuality* (with Carol Queen; Cleis Press), which won a Lambda Literary Award.

SIMON SHEPPARD is the co-editor, with M. Christian, of *Rough Stuff: Tales of Gay Men, Sex and Power*. His work appears in dozens of anthologies, including four editions of *Best Gay Erotica* and two of *Best American Erotica*. His collection *Hotter Than Hell & Other Stories* will be published by Alyson Books in 2001. And his column, "Sex Talk" appears in queer publications and on Websites nationwide. He just loves writing about dick.

DON SHEWEY has published three books about theatre and written articles for the *New York Times, Village Voice, Esquire, Rolling Stone* and other publications. His essays have been reprinted in such anthologies as *Contemporary Shakespeare Criticism* and *The Mammoth Book of Gay Erotica.* He grew up in a trailer park on a dirt road in Waco, Texas and now lives in midtown Manhattan.

JOHN TUNUI is a co-founder of Tatau, a writing group of Polynesians in San Francisco, and a member of UTOPIA (www.polyutopia.com), which is a social group for Queer Polynesians from around California. He lives with the love of his life, Kiwi, in the Castro.

EMANUEL XAVIER got his start in *Best Gay Erotica 1997.* He is now author of the poetry collection, *Pier Queen,* and the Lambda Literary Award-nominated novel, *Christ-Like,* featuring the character of Mikey X, who first made his debut in the short story, "Motherfuckers." Winner of the Marsha A. Gomez Cultural Heritage Award, his work has also been published *in Men on Men 7, James White Review, Virgins, Guerillas and Locas,* and *Urban Latino Magazine.*

About the Editor

RICHARD LABONTÉ has worked with A Different Light Bookstore since its founding in 1979 in the Silverlake neighborhood of Los Angeles. He is general manager of its stores in New York, West Hollywood and San Francisco, where he lives with his plant-growing picture-painting dog-walking lamp-building partner Asa Liles, and Asa's dog Percy. Both are very protective of him, fending off the world so he has plenty of time to read—and not just erotica. He writes on gay books for the *Feminist Bookstore News,* has a regular column for *Q San Francisco,* and is an occasional contributor to *The Lambda Book Report.* He also writes about gay books and bookstores for PlanetOut, adlbooks.com, and contentville.com. He can be reached at tattyhill@hotmail.com.